The Young Wives

Ginny was elated and devastated in turns. The arrangements had gone like clockwork. Sheila's dress was beautiful, so was Rosaleen's. She had a great liking for Fergus. But all the same she wished he wasn't a soldier. Wasn't taking her only child far away. And so soon. Their flight was at six o'clock. By the time the nuptial mass was over, the photographs taken and all the kissing, hugging and congratulations finished, there'd be little time left for much of a wedding. It wasn't how she would have wanted it. But not by look or word did she let it be known that she harboured such sad thoughts. For when all was said and done it was Sheila's and Fergus's day. And wasn't it on their own they'd long to be?

Elaine Crowley lives in Port Talbot with her husband. She has six children. *Dreams of Other Days, The Ways of Women, A Family Cursed* and *Wayward Angel* are all available in Orion Paperback.

By Elaine Crowley

Dreams of Other Days
Man Made to Measure
Waves Upon the Shore
The Petunia Coloured Coat
The Ways of Women
A Family Cursed
Wayward Angel
The Young Wives

THE
YOUNG WIVES

Elaine Crowley

ORION

An Orion paperback

First published in Great Britain in 2001
by Orion
This paperback edition published in 2002
by Orion Books Ltd,
Orion House, 5 Upper St Martin's Lane,
London WC2H 9EA

A CIP catalogue record for this book is available
from the British Library.

Typeset by Deltatype Ltd, Birkenhead, Merseyside

Printed and bound in Great Britain by
Clays Ltd, St Ives plc

Chapter One

Sheila Brophy sat watching her mother feeding the white satin brocade under the foot of the sewing machine. A sheet was spread on the floor in front of the machine on to which long lengths of bridal material going through the machine would land.

Sheila loved being in the room when her mother was sewing. The stuff had a gorgeous smell. The machine had a garland of flowers painted on its front. Sheila often tried copying them on to paper with her crayons but they never looked right. She also liked the sewing room because while her mother was using the machine they had great chats. But only when the work was simple like sewing straight seams. Now her mother was making the skirt, long straight seams, so Sheila could chat and ask questions. 'You'll make my wedding dress, won't you, Mammy?'

Without raising her head her mother replied, 'Of course I will, love. Didn't I make your First Communion one and wasn't it the most beautiful dress in the chapel? Everyone stopped to admire it. It'll be the same with your wedding dress.'

'Yeah, but . . .'

'But what?'

'I'd like a pink or a lemon dress for my wedding. I don't think white is a nice colour. It's all right for knickers and vests and petticoats. Will you be long? I'm freezing, so I am.'

'Another half an hour. Your father'll be back from the pub about then and you know what he's like when he's drunk. All over me with a fag hanging out of his mouth and an inch of ash on it, not minding where it falls. Drop

1

that on the dress and it'd be destroyed. And don't worry about your wedding dress. You're only eight. By the time you get married white might be a nicer colour.'

'When he comes in sure you won't fight with him?'

'I never fight with him.'

'You do sometimes shout at him.'

'That's not fighting. And I only shout when he starts blathering about the Rebellion and his time in the IRA.' She talked without altering the rhythm of the treadle. 'Telling how he only took to drink after his hero, Michael Collins, was killed. Michael Collins was the hero of hundreds and thousands; they didn't all take to drink.'

'Who was Michael Collins? And why did my daddy take to drink?'

'Ask your father about Collins, he'll be only too delighted to tell you. And as for the drink, I really don't know. Some men and women can take it or leave it. Your father's not one of the lucky ones.' She sighed as she stitched the last couple of inches, clipped the thread and the material fell in a silky heap on the sheet.

'Why does he drink?'

'God alone knows. I suppose it's a kind of flaw in a person's constitution. To tell you the truth I don't really know.' She went to the front of the machine and picked up the material from the sheet, folded and laid it on her cutting table. While doing it she told Sheila how every Catholic took the Pledge when they made their confirmation. 'It's a promise never to let drink pass your lips. Not everyone keeps it. Your father's one that broke his Pledge.'

'Would that be a mortal sin?'

'Ah, no, love, I think it would be only a venial one.'

'Then Daddy won't go to hell?'

'I'm sure he won't. He's harmless in drink. All he wants to do is fall asleep. He's a good man but he'd be better if he left the gargle alone. And I'd be in pocket. If it wasn't for my dressmaking you wouldn't be in the Loretto Convent, nor Lily Comerford's dancing school. He earns

2

good money in the Corporation and then there's his pension.' Mrs Brophy was now wiping the machine's surface and told Sheila to bring the brush so she could sweep up the threads.

When Sheila came back she asked her mother what a pension was. And she explained it was money paid every week to old people, widows and soldiers who were wounded in the war or had been years and years in the army.

'But me daddy isn't any of them things and he wasn't in a war.'

'The Rebellion was a war, not a long one but a war all the same. Later on, when we had our own government, men who'd fought in the Rebellion got pensions and good jobs. That's how your father got his.'

'Where did he work before he was a soldier?'

'You have me moidered with your questions. He didn't work, he was in a seminary going to be a priest.'

'A priest!' Sheila exclaimed. 'I'm glad he left that place. He couldn't have been my daddy if he was a priest.'

'He could not. Now you go into the kitchen and build up the fire, there's a good girl.'

'No, I don't want to. I want to keep on talking.'

'Well, I don't,' said Mrs Brophy. 'I'm going to tack the yoke and it's a tricky job, so do as you're told.'

Sheila's pretty face looked angry and she stared defiantly at her mother who stared her out. 'It's not fair, so it's not,' Sheila said, pouting her beautiful mouth, but she went to the kitchen, put coal on the fire and blew with the bellows until new flames licked the coals. Then she sat in the rocking chair with the *Evening Herald* and read the Mutt and Jeff comic strip.

In a little while her mother came into the kitchen. 'Thank God I got the yoke together,' and glancing at the clock she said, 'Look at the hour of the night and him not in.'

'He said he'd get me fish and chips from Burgess's.'

3

'And carry them home inside his overcoat. They'll be in mush and his coat destroyed with grease.'

'Sh, I think that's Daddy now. I heard the key in the lock.' Sheila ran into the small passage to greet her father. They came into the room. Mr Brophy's trilby was pushed to the back of his head, a hand on Sheila's shoulder, the other one clutching the parcel of fish and chips to his stomach.

His wife lit the gas under the kettle and said over her shoulder, 'A nice hour of the night to come home.'

'Ginny, darlin', sure it wasn't my fault, the chipper was packed. Look at your mammy, Sheila, isn't she the beautiful woman. The black curly hair of her and the dark eyes dancing out of her head. Amn't I the lucky man to have two beauties, for you're the image of her.'

'Will you stop blathering and give me the fish and chips.'

He fumbled with the buttons on his overcoat. The greasy parcel smelling of the most tasty fish and chips in Dublin fell to the floor.

Mrs Brophy wet the tea and told Sheila to pick up the parcel and bring it to her. 'And you,' she told her husband, 'take off that coat and jacket. I told you, didn't I, the chips would be bet into each other.'

'They'll still taste gorgeous, Mammy.'

Her mother shared out the food, poured the tea, and she and Sheila sat to the table and ate the fish and chips off the white, vinegar-soaked paper with their fingers. Mr Brophy was sitting in an armchair still wearing his hat.

'Are you going to have some?' his wife asked.

'I won't, they mightn't agree with me at this hour of the night.'

'Suit yourself. I expect your belly's full enough.'

'Comfortable, you might say. Aren't you up very late? You'll be jaded in the morning.'

'It's Saturday tomorrow, Daddy.'

'So it is, I forgot.' He yawned twice, then fell asleep.

'Look at him, the poor unfortunate. God's curse on the same drink and them that make and sell it. And you pray every night to Our Lady that you'll never marry a drunkard. Finish your tea and then go to bed. You won't do well in the Feis tomorrow if you're jaded.' She kissed and hugged Sheila, and Sheila gently kissed her father's cheek before she left the room.

Ginny began to tidy the kitchen. She washed the delft, emptied the teapot, wiped the oilcloth covering on the table. Screwed up the fish and chip papers tightly and put them in the fire, and placed the guard in front of it. Then she took off her husband's hat, loosened his collar and tie. 'My poor fella,' she said and smoothed his hair and kissed his cheek. From the rocking chair she took a big crocheted shawl of many colours and put it over him, and left the light on in the kitchen, knowing that after an hour or two he would wake and not be able to find his way in the dark.

She went to bed. She prayed to the Sacred Heart. Beneath the statue the little red shaded lamp cast a ruby glow. Ginny prayed for God to spare her until Sheila was reared and that her husband would turn over a new leaf. She prayed for her dead parents and relations, for friends who were sick, those with troubled minds, and lastly for herself that she might have a happy and not sudden death. Before she fell asleep she thought about the dancing competition tomorrow.

Sheila was a great little dancer. Already she had won two silver cups and had ten medals. She might win another tomorrow either for the hornpipe or slip jig. Sheila looked gorgeous in her dancing costume: the saffron kilt, black short jacket, white blouse with a flounce on it. The saffron fringed shawl fastened with a Tara brooch gave it the finishing touch.

There was a lot of envy and begrudgement among some of the mothers. Leppin' if their children didn't win. Sheila was tall for her age, and many a one said she lied about it and entered with children younger than her so she had the

5

advantage. To herself, Ginny said, God help their senses getting their hair in a knot about a dancing competition. I love to see her win, but when she doesn't I take it in good part. She does as well. If she sulked and carried on I'd have her out of the dancing in a minute. There'll be times in her life when to be disappointed, even angry, will be justified. But only over important things. And children's dancing competitions aren't that important.

On Saturday morning Sheila woke and looked at her dancing costume hanging on the wardrobe door and on a chair her black patent hornpipe shoes with their big silver buckles on the front of each shoe and beside them the soft leather brown pumps she would wear to dance the slip jig. On the back of the chair hung a pair of hand-knitted lace-patterned snowy white socks.

She wanted to jump out of bed and put the clothes on. Then she thought of her hair being done – her mother combing her long, thick, black, curly hair into ringlets – and wished her hair was straight. If it were she'd have it wrapped in rags the night before and no pulling and tugging. Sometimes she'd get in a temper, stamp her feet and cry and shout that she didn't want ringlets. And her mother would tell her that nearly every girl in the competition wore them except for a few whose mothers were copying American fashions and having the girls' hair bobbed and worn with a fringe. And a right show they were.

Her mother came into the room and told her to get up, her breakfast was almost ready. 'Afterwards you'll have to get the bread for me and then we'll go to Camden Street for the messages.'

'Is my daddy up yet?'

'Are you losing your senses? When on a Saturday does he stir before eleven or twelve? Come on now, hurry up. You won't feel the time flying before we have to go to the Feis.'

On Saturdays and Sundays they had a cooked breakfast, during the week porridge and fried bread or toast. Sheila ate a rasher, two Hafner's pork sausages, two rings of black pudding, one of white pudding and an egg. When she had eaten everything else she sucked every bit of fat from the bacon rind. 'I'm glad you don't cut the rind off, Mammy, only nick it in places. I love sucking it.'

'Who cuts it off?'

'Teresa Donnelly's mammy. D'ye remember, I had my tea there once and it was rashers and eggs and no rinds on the rashers.'

'I never heard of anyone doing that. Another American fad, I suppose. Finish that tea and get washed and dressed, and go for the bread.'

Sheila and her family lived in the Iveagh Buildings: apartments built by Guinness. The flats were in a compound with high iron gates. Some were one-bedroomed and some, like Sheila's, had two bedrooms, a bathroom, a kitchen-cum-living room and a parlour. Her mother said that it was great place to live. Five minutes from the centre of the city, less than that to Stephen's Green and Grafton Street. The same distance to Sheila's convent and less to Lord Edward Street where Mr Brophy worked.

But her mother had told Sheila as a secret that she was saving up for a purchase house. 'This place is grand, I've nothing against it really. But wouldn't it be great to have your own garden.'

'There's the park round the corner,' Sheila said.

'The park's not the same as your own garden. And there's always oul fellas out of the Iveagh lodging house stretched on the benches and in the alcoves, sleeping and snoring and full of Red Biddy. You're not to go in there on your own.'

'I don't want to move away. I love it here.'

'Don't worry, love, it'll take me years to get a deposit

saved. Maybe so long that you'll be married and living somewhere else.'

'I want to get married,' said Sheila, thinking of a long veil and wedding dress, 'but I'll never move away from you. I want to live beside you.'

'So you will. I tell you what, we'll buy two houses next door to each other, how's that?'

Sheila clapped her hands and said, 'That's great. I never want to leave you and Daddy.'

On her way to the baker's Sheila stopped to talk to other little girls from the flats. She was the only girl from the Buildings who went to a private school. Her friends didn't mind that but other girls called her names. 'Stuck up, who does she think she is? She's no better than us.'

Sometimes a couple of them would try to pick a fight. But Sheila was tough and would stand her ground, daring them to touch her. Then walk away chanting, 'Sticks and stones may break my bones but names will never hurt me.'

The only time she avoided the bullies was when the Poppies were being worn. The majority of the men in their families had been in the British army. They celebrated the Armistice and their children, though few if any had ever seen the sky over England, went round the Buildings in gangs shouting 'Up the Poppies'. In other streets, where there were as many families with allegiance to the Free State, one lot shouted 'Up the Poppies' and the other half responded with their war cry of 'Up the Lilies', the lilies being the emblem of the Easter Rising. There was seldom anything to it but the shouting of the slogans. And the next day it was all forgotten until the following year.

Sheila's father had explained to her that because he hadn't been a British soldier on Poppy Day she was to come straight home from school into the house. 'Not that I think for a minute one of the children would hurt a hair of your head. All the same, it's better to be sure than sorry. D'ye see, there's a gang of them and only one of you.'

Sheila wanted him to tell her more about the Lilies and the Poppies. He promised that he would when she was older.

After chatting to her friends she left the compound, walked to the end of Bride Street and into Johnson, Mooneys and O'Brien on the corner of Kevin Street. Though it was only twenty minutes since she had had her breakfast the smell of the newly baked loaves and turnovers made her feel hungry.

The woman serving knew her. Asked how her mammy was and about the Feis, while she wrapped white tissue paper around the two crusty loaves. 'Don't you be picking that bread on the way home.'

'I won't,' Sheila said. 'I have to do another message for my mammy. Can I leave the bread till I come back? I wish the bread was white like it used to be. It's grey because of the war, isn't it?'

'The same feckin war and that oul Antichrist Hitler. All the lovely young fellas getting killed. And poor unfortunate people in England being blown to bits. Not to mention our own in Dublin, them poor people on the North Strand blown to smithereens. But sure it was in forty-one, you wouldn't remember it. And we're giving out about the dark bread and the half-ounce tea ration. And shaggin' robbers selling it on the Black Market for a pound a pound. I'm telling you if Ireland lay the other side of England, Hitler would have invaded us already.'

Sheila thought how her father always praised Hitler and that a nun in school had a map on the wall and when the Germans were winning, pinned flags on the map to show how well they were doing. She nearly told Maggie but, remembering her husband was a soldier in the British army, didn't. Instead she asked her again if she could leave the loaves.

'You can,' said Maggie, 'so long as you're not telling me lies about the message for your mammy.'

'As true as God I'm not,' said Sheila, smiling at the

woman and thinking at the same time, that's a venial sin I'll have to tell in confession. Then off she went across the road to look in at the rag pickers. The rag store had a long open front. There were two women climbing through the raised pile of rags, picking and sorting, throwing anything wearable into one of three crates along the wall, into the second one was thrown torn woollen clothing and the third crate received rags. The wearable items were sold on to second-hand clothes dealers who in turn sold them to the poor; torn woollens were bought by the makers of 'shoddy' who processed them into an inferior type of woollen cloth; the rags were used to manufacture paper.

Sheila had a vague idea of all this. One of the rag pickers lived in the Buildings and sometimes came to chat with her mother after she had washed and changed. Many a time Sheila had heard the woman say, 'I wouldn't darken your door, ma'am, coming straight from that kip. The filth of the city, that's what we handle. Never knowing who'd worn the things, what complaint they were dying from. The bad disease, consumption, the smallpox. That's bad enough but the stinking bandages, lint, cotton wool saturated in blood and pus. It's a sin against God for that carry-on to be allowed.'

In the course of these conversations between the rag picker and her mother Sheila learnt about the second-hand clothes. Shoddy, the real rags, going to paper mills and how the stinking acrid smoke which made her eyes water and her throat sore came from the burning of the soiled dressings.

The rag store was forbidden her along with St Patrick's Park. She sidled into the store and watched the women working. Her mother's friend was singing 'South of the Border' as she picked and threw. The acrid smoke irritated Sheila's throat and she coughed. The two women looked round and her mother's friend ploughed her way through the rags. 'How many times have I heard your mammy threaten to cut the legs off you if you set foot in here?'

Sheila looked contrite and hung her head. 'And you can stop looking sorry for yourself. You're a bold child and disobeying your mammy is a sin. You've made your Communion; you should know all about sin.'

Sheila began to cry. 'Ah, come on now, love, sure I'm only telling you for your own good. Go on home. Here take this.' She took a penny from her overall pocket. 'Buy a Fizz Bag, it'll clear your throat.'

Sheila managed a few more tears and sniffs before taking the money, then said, 'You won't tell me mammy, sure you won't?'

'I should but I won't, that's if you promise not to do it again.'

'As true as God,' Sheila promised and ran out of the rag store. Next door to it was a huckster's shop. It sold coal by the stone, paraffin oil, sticks, bread, stale cakes, babies' soothers, potatoes and cabbages, on Fridays and Wednesdays fish that wasn't very fresh and Fizz Bags.

Sheila bought one for a ha'penny, stuck the liquorice tube in her mouth and took a long suck of sherbet. Then went on her way past the police station, which had once been the Archbishop of Dublin's palace. She paused to look up the narrow street a little further along and gaze at the beautiful house which faced down the street and wondered, as she did many times, who lived in it and how they must be very rich. As she turned into Patrick's Street she heard the Angelus bell and knew it was twelve o'clock. The bell was being rung in Francis Street where she had been christened and made her First Communion. She thought about confession and how she had two venial sins on her soul and by going to the park would commit another one. Venial sins she knew weren't too bad. A good Act of Contrition would make her soul spotlessly white and she could receive Communion in the morning.

But at the park gates she hesitated. She could see the men sleeping on the benches and the pigeons waddling about searching for worms or crumbs. She loved pigeons.

11

Their mauve and silvery coloured feathers. If only she could catch one, she thought, and bring it home, get a cage for it, wouldn't that be grand. There were purple and yellow flowers, small ones in the flowerbeds. She didn't know what they were called. She only knew the names of wallflowers, roses and tulips, the flowers girls brought to school for the altars.

At the right-hand side of the park St Patrick's Cathedral's grey stone spire pointed to the sky. Once she had stood in the porch, the doors were open. She could see into the church and didn't like what she saw: all the raggedy flags and you could smell the cold. She wasn't sorry it was a Protestant church. She was glad that bad king had robbed it from the Catholics. And she wasn't sorry that because she was a Catholic she'd go to hell if ever she went into it. What Catholic would want to when their own chapels were gorgeous: all the lighted candles shimmering, the lovely statues and the holy pictures? She decided not to commit the third venial sin and, feeling very holy, ran all the way to the bakery, collected the bread and went home.

'I thought you were baking the loaves it took you so long. What kept you?'

'The shop was packed,' Sheila lied.

'Wash your face before we go out. You've been sucking sherbet. Where did you get the money?'

'I found a ha'penny in the gutter.'

Chapter Two

'Isn't the weather grand, thanks be to God,' passing women said to Ginny as she and Sheila set out for Camden Street.

'Your man has tea in today. And the price is still the same,' another woman told Ginny.

Ginny agreed that the weather was grand, hoped it would hold and thanked the woman who had told her about the tea. There were no tenement houses in Wexford or Camden Street, though families lived over the shops. Neither were there rag stores, beautiful houses, chapels nor churches. Only shops, crowded shops, butchers, fancy bakeries, greengrocers, provision shops, pork butchers, public houses, drapers and shoe shops. And by the kerb old prams, from which women, wearing black shawls, whose faces were rosy or weather-beaten, sold fruit, flowers and fish. They called out their wares and prices, cajoling the passing women to buy from them: 'Jap' oranges, lovely bananas, Kerr Pinks the flouriest potatoes going. Are you buying, ma'am? If you're not, stop mauling the fruit.' Ginny knew most of the dealers – many of them lived in the Buildings. She knew who was honest and those who would put a mouldy orange at the bottom of the brown paper bag.

Sheila breathed in the myriad smells, all pleasant except those coming out of the public houses. The sweet smell of fruit, of pungent cheese which made her feel hungry imagining the hard red cheese on a cut of buttered bread. Not much scent from the spring flowers except the bronze and red velvety wallflowers. And overpowering all other smells the aroma of sweet biscuits, chocolate and all other delicious things being baked in Jacobs, whose factory was at the corner of the street.

Nearly everyone was in good humour, laughing and joking with the butchers as they haggled over the price of a sirloin, a piece of corned beef, silverside, tail-end or brisket. While waiting to be served the women gossiped with each other. They carried marketing bags, the majority of which were made from black American oilcloth, and clutched purses in their hands.

As Sheila and her mother went from shop to shop she became fidgety, tugged at her mother's coat and asked when were they going home.

'When I'm ready,' was her mother's reply. If Sheila persisted nagging she would be warned to behave herself, if she still persisted she was slapped and ordered to wait outside. She was delighted. She loved the street, the noise, the horses and carts driving by. Sometimes the horses raised their tails and expelled balls of manure without pausing in their trot. She would walk a way up the street, stopping now and then to look in a toyshop window. Occasionally she'd walk as far as the beginning of Camden Street to look at the stills on display outside the De Luxe picture house.

She loved going to the pictures, especially cowboy and Indian ones. She'd cry when a child was stolen by the Indians. But the end was always a happy one. She used to think that the film stars lived at the back of the cinema and wonder why she never saw them in the street until her father explained what films were.

Before very long her mother would catch up with her, as she did on this Saturday. 'I got everything except the ribbons for your hair.' Sheila grimaced as she thought of her ordeal when the ringlets were made. In a drapery her mother bought several yards of wide green ribbon and then they went home. 'Daddy's gone out,' she said when they went into the house.

'Doesn't he always,' her mother retorted as she unpacked her messages.

'I wish he'd come to the Feis, so I do.'

'He never will, love. Few men do. I wouldn't fight with him over that. I wouldn't want him to anyway.'

'But why?'

'Well, for one thing he'd be half cut and for another it's not a place for men.'

'Why isn't it?'

'Don't be moidering me – it just isn't. Go and give yourself a good wash, scrub your knees. You don't want people seeing dirty knees under your lovely kilt.'

The Feis was being held in a hall the other side of the

Liffey. There were all sorts of Feis: ones for poetry, music, dancing and Irish speaking. When she was in the primary school Sheila had been entered in one for Irish. Her mother and father were thrilled and convinced she would win first prize. 'I can see you getting a silver Fainne and before you know it the gold one,' her father encouraged. Ginny made her a turquoise panne velvet dress with a hand-crocheted ecru collar.

Being the best in the class at Irish, Sheila had no worries about the competition. But once she was on the stage with other competitors, judges and the sea of faces looking up at her she lost her nerve, couldn't answer some questions and answered others wrongly. She cried all the way home on the bus.

But she was never nervous when dancing. Holding her mother's hand, they walked down Winetavern Street across its bridge and up the side of the quay. Her mother pointed and said, 'That's the Four Courts. There was trouble there during the Civil War. Your father will tell you all about it one day,' as they passed a large imposing building. Sheila was only half listening. It was just recently that she had been up the quays and there was much to occupy her mind. The Liffey, how it smelled differently when the tide was in or out, the seagulls screaming and swooping, the barges laden with barrels of porter. Sometimes there were swans. Lots of antique shops. Often there were dolls in the windows, beautiful old-fashioned dolls. She wanted to stop and look at them, but there was no time, her mother always told her.

They arrived at the turn into a street where the Father Mathew Hall was. Before turning into it her mother pointed to the facing bridge. 'That, so they say, was the first bridge in Dublin. Not like it is now, but the first all the same. It's just as well we came early; look at the crowd already.' Then Sheila's mother went to a table in the porch where a woman was checking in the competitors. Sheila's name was found on the list and a tick put beside it.

'Isn't it a grand day, thank God.' Ginny agreed that it was. The woman said how lovely Sheila looked and wished her great success.

'Into the lavatory, now, have a good pee and afterwards I'll tidy your hair. Mild and all as the wind was, it tossed your hair.' Sheila made a face. 'That'll do, off you go.' Ginny said a silent prayer that if Sheila danced well she would win a medal.

There were many girls and some boys wearing the same costume as Sheila's. Others wore the costume that Ginny thought was the loveliest of all: girls from another less well-known school of dancing than Sheila's and not as good, some believed. The tunic was knee-length, made from cream-coloured bawneen, heavily embroidered with Celtic designs in vivid colours.

The fiddlers tuned up; the competitors lined up. The youngest children aged five and six danced first. Some were excellent, their carriages perfect, only ringlets bounced and feet and legs moved.

Ginny's pride and delight surged through her as Sheila's group came on to the stage. She stood motionless, her face expressionless, waiting for the music. She danced the hornpipe with verve, the metal taps on the soles of her shoes beating a staccato rhythm. Clamorous applause clapped the dancers off the stage. Another group of hornpipers took their place.

A woman sitting next to Ginny whose daughter was a couple of years older than Sheila and was in the same dancing school whispered, 'I'd say your Sheila will get the gold medal.'

Ginny hoped she would. But you never could tell. To the woman she said, 'I hope so, though in the long run it depends on the adjudicators.'

Later Sheila danced the slip jig. It was the dance Ginny admired most of all and watching it she thought, as she always did at such a time, how if there were such a thing as fairies it was how they would have danced: lightly and silently.

Sheila won the first prize, a gold medal and the second, a silver medal for the slip jig. Ginny kissed and hugged her, so did her teacher and friends. Ginny saw the begrudging glances and heads together whispering.

'Wasn't I right?' asked the woman who had forecast the result.

'Indeed you were but look behind you.' Ginny nodded towards the envious. 'Next time I'll stitch her birth certificate on her coatee.'

'Pay no attention. Jealousy is what ails them.'

Ginny smiled. 'I was joking about the certificate. They don't take a feather out of me.'

'The evenings are lengthening, thank God,' Ginny said as they waited opposite the quays for a bus to take them into town, from where they would catch another to take them to Christ Church, from where the Buildings were but a short distance.

'Will me daddy be in?' Sheila asked as they approached home.

'He might and he mightn't.'

'The lights are on, Mammy, look at the lights. He's in. I knew he'd wait.'

He hadn't, as Ginny knew he wouldn't.

Sheila went into every room hoping to find him. After the search she came into the kitchen, threw herself into the rocking chair, and cried with rage and disappointment. 'I hate him. I hate him, so I do,' she screamed in between her crying.

Ginny said nothing, knowing that Sheila's anger would soon subside. Gradually the crying stopped, she wiped her eyes, and said sorrowfully, 'It's only that I wanted to show him my medals. And for him to tell me I was a great girl.'

And Ginny thought, you bloody louser, I'll give you the length and breadth of my tongue when she's in bed.

17

'Maybe he forgot, Mammy. Maybe he thought the Feis was tomorrow.'

'Maybe,' Ginny agreed.

''Cos, he'd never do it on purpose, sure he wouldn't?'

'Never,' said her mother. 'Never on purpose. Wash your face with cold water, it'll soothe your eyes. And then we'll have a cup of tea and the cream buns I bought this morning.'

'That child,' said Sheila's father, looking after her as she left the room, 'is growing in leaps and bound.'

'That child, as you call her, is becoming a handful,' Ginny said.

'I wouldn't say that. Apart from her shooting up I see no difference in her.'

'How would you and you never in the house for five minutes.'

'Sure don't I have to go to work?'

'It's not work I'm referring to and well you know it.'

'What ails her, then?' asked Mr Brophy in a concerned voice.

'Her age, going on twelve. Beginning to smell herself. She hates school and is fed up with the dancing. Wants more of a say in what she wears. Give her stew for her dinner and she wants a fry. Give her a fry and it's bacon and cabbage she's looking for. Any excuse to be contrary. I was the same myself, only my mother, Lord have mercy on her, wasn't the eejit I am. Look crooked at her and she'd rosen your jaw. Refuse your meal and she'd say, "Turn your arse to it then." You ate what you were given or went hungry. She'll grow out of it. Being an only child makes it harder for her. A brother or sister to ballyrag me to would have been great. Someone else to tell how much she hates me, how she'll never treat her children the way I do. Someone else to fight with, to vent her spleen on. But God only blessed us with the one child so there you are.'

'But hasn't she plenty of friends, Ginny?'

'Not so many nowadays. The young wans in the Buildings are counting the months until they can leave school, they're out in the evenings tricking with the young fellas while Sheila's going boss-eyed doing her homework.'

'Better that than leaving school at fourteen for Jacobs or a sewing factory. You wouldn't wish that on Sheila?'

'You know bloody well I wouldn't. Amn't I the one who sent her to the convent and pays her fees?'

Sheila's father made no reply. For a few minutes he concentrated on eating his dinner before asking Ginny for another cup of tea. After pouring it she said, 'I was thinking you could take her for a ramble across town of a Sunday. Maybe go to the pictures. Or into one of the ice-cream parlours in O'Connell Street. All sorts of American concoctions. Sheila's mad about the Knickerbocker Glory. When we're in town we always go into the Palm Grove.'

Mr Brophy lit a cigarette and smoked half of it before saying, 'That's a grand idea. The only thing is I'm in the habit of having a lie-down on Sunday after the dinner . . .'

'Having a lie-down during the Holy Hour when the pubs shut, then up like a shot for opening times. I know all about your habits. Now is the time to start changing them.'

'Easier said than done – old habits die hard. Couldn't she join the Fianna. She'd have the company, Irish music and dancing, the culture of her country and learn the history of her country. And that's not all. They go rambling and hiking. She'd get plenty of fresh air.'

'Sheila's joining no Fianna. Sheila's not having Republican views drummed into her brain.' Ginny's voice rose and she continued, 'Irish dancing, music and the language she has in abundance.' Bloody drunken oul eejit. Any excuse not to interfere with his drinking. God, she thought, I'd love to split him. Fire a cup or the sugar bowl at him, the oul divil. She said a silent prayer not to let her temper get the better of her. Filled a glass with water and sipped it until her composure returned. Then began to talk, to play

19

her cards right. 'Maybe you're right about the Fianna, sure what do I know about them. Only I think she'd learn more from you. Head of knowledge, that's you. Kings and queens, risings, hangings, them pictures in the art gallery, sure you know all about them day and date.'

Mr Brophy smiled and said, 'Well, if I say it myself I know the city inside out. I know the history of my country. And it's the truth I'd tell the child. None of the putting in and leaving out what doesn't suit the government and historians nowadays. And what's more, I'll be talking from experience.'

'So you'll do it, then?' asked Ginny.

'I will but not for the time being. The weather's still very changeable. By the time it warms up I'll have adjusted my habits and be ready for the excursions.'

And so, for the time being, Ginny settled for that.

Eventually Sheila's father conceded that taking her into town on Sundays was a good idea. Before doing so he made lists of the places he wanted her to see. Lists of the heroes who had died for Ireland. Telling himself that by the time he had finished with Sheila she would be well informed about the history of her country.

When he told her of his decision Ginny praised him sky high and thought, God look down on him, he's an oul eejit. I knew from the word go he wouldn't refuse. But I'll let him think that it wasn't an easy decision to make. Now all I have to do is break the news to Sheila.

She reacted as Ginny had expected. 'I won't go. You can't make me. Not with him.'

'Your poor father, sure I thought you loved him.'

'So I do. Better than you. He's not always giving out to me. But that doesn't mean I'm going into town with him on a Sunday to be left outside public houses between here and O'Connell Street with a bottle of red lemonade while he's inside drinking.'

'Deed you will not. Your father's a decent man. He'd

never plank you outside a pub door. In any case he couldn't. The pubs will be shut for the Holy Hour.'

'I'm sure he knows plenty of pubs that don't shut. I'm not going and that's all there is to it.'

Ginny decided to leave the matter alone for a few days and then did a bit of coaxing. Told Sheila how much her father loved her. How sad, sad and hurt, he'd be if she turned down his offer. Her tactics worked. After a lot of grumbling about all the other things she could do on a Sunday afternoon, Sheila agreed to the outings.

'We'll take our time. Ramble into town slowly,' Mr Brophy told Sheila as they left the house on the first of their outings. 'The General Post Office will be our first stop.'

Hand in hand they walked through Upper Kevin Street, Cuffe Street and turned on to Stephen's Green, continued down Grafton Street, past the Bank of Ireland and Trinity College, down Westmoreland Street, crossed O'Connell Bridge and arrived at the GPO. It was open for the sale of stamps.

Mr Brophy took off his hat as a mark of respect for the place he was in and moved with Sheila to a space where there weren't many people. 'This is where it all happened. Many of us were no more than seventeen. Children. Though years ago at seventeen you wouldn't be thought of as a child no more than poor children are today. Out into the factories, or labouring at fourteen. Their heads stuffed with Religious Knowledge and Irish. God look down on them. It's a hard road they have in front of them. It wasn't what we fought for. Our independence from England, that's what we were fighting for, and a decent life for the people.'

Chapter Three

'In here it was that I started my fighting. The fighting was ferocious. There we were, a handful of fellas taking on the British army. And we kept them at bay for a week, even though they brought a gunboat up the Liffey and shelled us. We surrendered to stop more killing.'

'What were you doing, Daddy?'

'The same as the others, firing my rifle.'

'Did you kill anyone?'

'Maybe I did, I'm not sure.'

'Would that have been a sin?'

'Not according to the Catholic religion. Just war, self-defence and the execution of a criminal aren't sins. And if ever there was a just war that was one. The joy and pride we felt when Padraig Pearse pinned up the Proclamation of Independence and our own flag was flying over the Post Office.'

'What happened when you gave up?'

'That was a shame and disgrace. Our own people mocked us as we marched through the streets.'

'Why? Didn't they hate the English?'

'Not the majority. They had their reasons. Some had sons, brothers, husbands fighting in France with the British army. British soldiers were stationed throughout Ireland. Decent skins on the whole. They spent their money here, made work for the Irish.'

Sheila was getting bored, tired and thirsty. She began fidgeting, shifting from one foot to another, pulling on her father's hand.

'Ah, love,' he said, 'I've been moidering you and you only a little child. There's years ahead for me to tell more. We'll go up to that ice-cream parlour, rest our legs and fill our bellies. What d'ye say to that, eh?'

For the next two years, if the weather was fine, the Sunday

walks and talks continued. Sheila now knew that Patrick Pearse, his brother and other leaders of the Rebellion had been executed in Kilmainham gaol. James Connolly, a prominent figure in the Rising, wounded during it, unable to walk, had been propped on a chair in Kilmainham's yard and shot.

And on one of their rambles her father told her about 'The Troubles'. 'D'ye see,' he said, 'we were determined to get our independence. It started in 1919 and a ferocious war it was. Michael Collins was the leader then. Black and Tans were sent from England, ex-soldiers and officers, called Auxiliaries, supposedly to take on the role of police. No restraint on them. They murdered and pillaged. Collins's men were well able for them. And whereas the British soldiers were liked, the Black and Tans were loathed. Even the English papers spoke out against them.'

She knew the name of the beautiful house that looked on to Kevin Street. It was Marsh's Library, the first library in Ireland.

She had been to Saint Werburgh's Church where the rebel Lord Edward Fitzgerald was entombed after his arrest and death from the wound he suffered being captured. To Thomas Street where outside St Catherine's Church Robert Emmet, another Republican, was hanged, drawn and quartered. To St Michan's Church where the Brothers Shears' bodies lay in a state of preservation which according to nuns in school had not decomposed because they were innocent of the crimes for which they were executed. Her father told her that might not be strictly true. The extraordinary dry air in the vaults of St Michan's made decomposition less likely.

In Glasnevin cemetery she visited graves of other Republican martyrs and went with her father to Bodenstown where Wolfe Tone – a Protestant, as was Robert Emmet, and Lord Edward Fitzgerald but also great Irish patriots – was buried.

And during the summer holidays, when she was nearing

the age of fourteen, her father took her to West Cork, to Michael Collins's birthplace and the spot where he was assassinated.

In the years she had wandered the city with her father she came to know every street and the majority of lanes and alleys on the Southside, and had a good knowledge of the Northside. She adored it all; the Georgian squares, some with immaculately maintained houses, others lined with tenements where women sat bare-breasted suckling their babies and hordes of ragged barefoot children cried and laughed, swung from lamp posts and shouted obscenities at passers-by. Their idle fathers congregated at the street corners, sucking the last drag from a Woodbine butt. Some were consumptive, coughed and hawked globs of yellow, greenish phlegm on to the pavements: men who could never work again and men who might never find work again.

The poor streets and the prosperous streets lay cheek by jowl, as did Grafton Street with its splendid shops: genuine antiques; paintings on display in art shop windows; out-of-season fruits imported or hot house grown; shops which sold exquisite baby clothes; others which sold only sweets and chocolates of the finest quality; and Bewleys from which the aroma of coffee being ground overlaid every other smell. There were flower sellers at several corners of lanes and alleys – flowers bought only by those with money to spare. And music floated on the air: a woman harpist whose husband carried the harp from one place to another; a tenor voice singing a Moore's melody.

Then there was Brown Thomas, the queen of shops. On rare occasions Sheila went there with her mother. They never bought anything, just wandered around looking at shoes, handbags, scarves, jewellery, umbrellas that her mother said cost more than her father's wages. After viewing the ground floor they climbed the wide staircase to the floor above where the clothes were sold. Ginny studied them to see what was fashionable; what, if anything, she could copy – a neckline, a collar, a skirt cut on the bias – and incorporate into a garment she was making. Sheila followed her around. Neither one touched anything, aware they were being watched by assistants ready to pounce if they did. During one of the visits to Brown Thomas Sheila thought how she would love to work there when she left school.

Of one thing she was certain: never would she leave Dublin, convinced that nowhere in the world could she be happy away from her city. On Sunday morning the bells woke her. From the chapels in Francis Street, Whitefriars Street and Clarendon Street they reminded people it was time to set out for mass. Later in the day the bells of the two Protestant cathedrals, as near to the Buildings as were the Catholic chapels, sent out their joyful peals. 'Jesus, Mary and Joseph, them bloody bells are killing me,' Ginny would say, clutching her head, looking for a seidlitz powder and if there wasn't one sending Sheila to the huckster's shop that sold the blue paper packets of seidlitz powder.

'D'ye blame me,' Ginny would say when the sick headache subsided, 'wanting to get out of here? Them bells will be the cause of killing me. And don't you be rolling your eyes to heaven,' she'd shout at her husband getting ready to go to the public house. 'The drink has numbed your senses. How could anything annoy you except not having the price of a pint? But just you wait. One day we'll be out of here and with God's holy help the pub will be miles away.'

'Ah, now, Ginny, don't be like that,' he'd say, approaching her with arms open wide. 'Sure you know how much I love you.'

'Go on, off with you and I hope you get arrested for being drunk and disorderly.'

And when he'd left she'd say to Sheila, 'I might as well talk to the wall.'

Sheila no longer worried about her mother shouting at

her father. They loved each other, of that she was sure. Her poor father had a weakness for the drink. So had lots of her friends' fathers. He couldn't help it. Nor could her mother help shouting at him. They understood each other. All the same she would never marry a man with the weakness. As her mother said, it was a sin to waste money that should have been for the family. And for another thing Sheila hated the smell of drink. She always turned her face away when her father kissed her.

When she was almost fourteen, Sheila announced that she wanted her hair cut.

'What about your ringlets?' asked Ginny.

'I'm giving up the dancing.'

'Ah, come on now, love, you can't do that. You're a champion. With the war being over the troupe will be going abroad, England, America, you'd love that.'

'I would not. I want my hair cut and no more dancing classes.'

'Have it your way, then,' said Ginny and thought, it's her age, they get all sorts of vagaries once they begin to smell themselves. The moods'll pass and she'll be herself again most of the time.

But most of the time Sheila wasn't herself. She hated school where she was studying for her Intermediate Certificate. The green uniform made her look sallow, she believed. Her periods hadn't started and she was the only flat-chested girl in her class. She had overheard two girls talking about her one day. One said, 'All the same, isn't Sheila Brophy lucky.'

'How d'ye say that,' asked the other?

'She's lovely and slim, she can wear anything.'

And the bitchy one retorted, 'Anything except a bra.'

Sheila was mortified, locked herself in the lavatory and cried bitterly until a nun came and pounded on the door. Sheila's explanation was that she had been sick. The nun told her to splash her eyes with cold water and then come back to her classroom.

She hated herself and her flat chest. Maybe if she had breasts a fella would look at her. Chase her like they did other girls, feck her beret or scarf, make her struggle to get them back. On the way home from school walking through the Green it happened all the time to her friends. She was fed up with everything, especially the Sunday afternoon outings with her father.

And then one day her breasts began to grow. Maybe I'm only imagining it, she thought. She wasn't. Her periods started; her breasts grew bigger. And her mother bought her two brassieres. In no time she needed a bigger size. With a bust she could flaunt, her short hair curling on her forehead and cheeks, and top marks for most of her school work, she felt on top of the world and decided she no longer wanted to ramble with her father on Sunday afternoons. But she wasn't sure how she could break the habit. Letting on to be not well would work now and again. Now and again wasn't good enough. She couldn't ask for advice from her mother who had initiated the outings and was still in favour of them.

On her next outing with her father, while they were having coffee in a café he was explaining that wearing poppies was to remember the dead: 'All the millions killed in the First World War. During some of the worst battles the cornfields round about were ablaze with poppies. Poems and songs were written about them, many by fellas out there fighting. So when the war was won the poppy was picked as an emblem to be worn every year on Armistice Day. Now it'll be worn as well to honour the dead from the last war. Hundreds and thousands of Irishmen fought in both of them.'

Sheila had picked up this information already so hadn't bothered listening. Having hit on an idea how to avoid the Sunday outings, her mind was occupied with how she would put her plan into action. While her father talked on and on the solution came to her. But she would wait until they got home before mentioning it.

'There y'are,' Ginny greeted them. 'Take off your coats and sit over to the table.' It was laid, a platter of cold boiled bacon, beetroot, a bottle of brown sauce and a home-made apple cake.

Mr Brophy took off his coat and sat down. 'Well, did you enjoy the ramble?' asked Ginny as she wet the tea.

'We had a grand time, didn't we, Sheila?'

She didn't answer him and her mother said, 'Take off your coat and sit down. What are you crying for?'

'I don't want my tea. I never did my exercise. I'll have to do it now or Sister Mary Rose will kill me.'

'And why didn't you?'

'I did some of it; there's an awful lot now that I'm working for my Inter Cert. I'll have to stop going out on Sundays.' The volume of her crying increased. 'And I'll hate that, Daddy, because we have grand times.'

Ginny smelled a rat but said nothing.

Mr Brophy, not overfamiliar with Sheila's wiles, called her to him and put an arm round her. 'Don't cry, child. We've had grand times but sure your school work has to come first. We'll have our outings again in the holidays.'

'I'm really sorry, honest to God I am, Daddy.'

'There, there,' he comforted her.

'Take your coat off,' her mother ordered, 'and sit to the table. Your brain won't work on an empty stomach.'

For several Sunday afternoons Sheila stayed in and studied until her father resumed his habit of lying down during the Holy Hour. No sooner was he asleep than she was out of the door and called for a friend. They walked up and down Grafton Street, strolled through Stephen's Green and sometimes got off with fellas of their own age.

Her mother told her after the first outing, 'I had you weighed up all along – you're a conniving little knat.'

'I got fed up listening to me da. He never stopped

talking from the minute we left the house. Patrick Pearse and Robert Emmet. I wanted to scream, so I did.'

'There's no real harm done and you didn't hurt his feelings. I'm glad about that. A little lie is often kinder than the truth.'

Barring accidents, it was a foregone conclusion that Sheila would do well in her exams, Sister Mary Rose told Ginny. 'She's a born scholar. Would she never stay on for the Leaving Cert.?'

'I doubt it. Her heart is set on working in Brown Thomas.'

'A grand position that. But if she got the Leaving there could be university or teacher's training.'

'Maybe she'll change her mind,' said Ginny.

'At her age they often do,' the nun agreed.

When Mr Brophy heard what the nun had had to say he kissed Sheila. 'Sure didn't I know you always had it in you. With the head on you you'd walk the Leaving. Go to university and be a lady doctor. Wouldn't I be the proud man the day your degree was conferred. I'd see you all right. I'd take the Pledge and this time keep it. With the drink finished the fees would be no bother.' After the speech he went to the pub.

'Live horse and get grass,' Ginny said contemptuously. 'Imagine depending on him. He's full of good intentions but intentions won't pay your way. The Inter will do you fine. Walk into any job in the city. Office work, shops like Switzer's and Brown Thomas.'

Sheila put her arms round her mother and kissed her.

Ginny said, 'God help him; if he wasn't a perpetual drunkard he'd spend his last penny on the pair of us. But when drink takes hold the money for it comes first. Remember that if you ever think of falling for a fella with the weakness, God forbidding all harm.'

And Sheila thought, I love the two of them. Me fiery

tempered ma, just like me. And me da, an oul slob, kind and harmless. But you couldn't depend on him. Me ma's a saint to have put up with him. I wouldn't. If I married a fella and he took to the drink I'd fire him out. Please God I won't. I'll have learnt my lesson. I'm not that much like my mother. I couldn't love a man always smelling of drink and looking like an eejit.

She got honours in her Intermediate Certificate. Before going on a week's holiday with her mother to Bray she applied for a job in Brown Thomas, convinced that if she got one she would be the happiest girl in Dublin.

'Don't be disappointed if there isn't an answer when we get home. This time of the year Brown Thomas will be swamped with job applications.'

'I expect you're right, Ma,' said Sheila, sucking an ice-cream wafer. 'All the same, I hope they don't keep me hanging around too long.'

A few days after coming back from the holiday the letter came. Ginny brought it to Sheila who was having a lie-in. 'Here it is,' she said, handing the envelope to her.

'D'ye think it's good news, Ma?' Sheila asked and sat up in the bed.

'Open it and see.'

'I can't – I'm in bits.'

'Yes you can. If you're old enough to leave school and apply for a job you're old enough to open the letter.'

Sheila did. Her mother watched her face as she read it. The disappointment on it, her eyes filling with tears.

'Don't tell me they turned you down. The bloody cheek of them. It's the Buildings. It's not a good address. Here, give it to me.'

Sheila handed the letter over. Ginny read it. 'For all your schooling you're a feckin eejit. They're asking you for an interview. That means they're interested in you. Didn't the nun who prepared you for looking for jobs say how employers went about taking people on?'

'Maybe she did. I don't remember. What'll I have to do?'

'Look your best, answer questions, I imagine.'

'What kind of questions?'

'That I couldn't tell. They know you passed the Intermediate so it won't be sums or spelling. More likely to make sure you speak well and have a pleasant manner. You'll walk it.'

Chapter Four

Sheila got the job. She was thrilled. So was her mother. 'That'll be one in the eye for the begrudgers,' she said, hugging Sheila.

Her father was also pleased, but still regretting that she hadn't done the other two years in school and tried for university. 'You know I'd have seen you all right.' Behind his back her mother winked.

Sheila thanked and humoured him. 'I know you would, da, but honest to God, I couldn't stand the sight of blood and the smell of ether would turn my stomach. And Brown Thomas is grand. I love it. It's like Aladdin's cave: silks, satins and jewellery, china, crystal. The eyes are dazzled out of my head. And the scents! Every department you go to has its own gorgeous smell. Especially the cosmetic and perfume counter. I'm hoping that once I've done my training I'll be on that counter.'

After her training period she was indeed on the cosmetic counter, she and an older assistant. A nice girl called Rosaleen showed her the ropes. For a long time she thought Brown Thomas was heaven, Brown Thomas and working. Ginny was generous with pocket money. Now she was allowed to go dancing and to the roller-skating rink in Duke Street. There for many nights she stayed in Mug's Alley, learning how to balance and watching the experienced skaters dancing in pairs. Dancing military two-steps and waltzing. When she was confident enough she ventured onto the rink and skated round and round it, now and then practising how to stop, now and then falling down. She, like the majority, hired their skates at the entrance. But several people had their own attached to lovely white boots. The professional girl skater wore them. Sheila watched every move of hers, admired her short flared skirt, her long tanned legs, the tan applied with Miner's leg make-up. The skirt was always white and with it the girl wore different brightly coloured tops.

She got to know boys and girls in the rink. And boys began to partner her and eventually ask her to dance. Ginny encouraged Sheila's skating. The rink closed earlier than the dance halls, there wasn't a bar and it was unlikely that drunken men would attempt skating. She took Sheila to Elvery's in O'Connell Street and bought her skating boots, and made her short flared skirts. By the end of three months Sheila was waltzing and two-stepping; dating some of her partners; going to the pictures with them and afterwards having gorgeous concoctions of ice cream, fresh fruit topped with double cream.

Sheila fancied none of the boys who took her out. She liked tall men and none of them was. Many had pimples, their hair flattened with Brylcreem and some had dirty nails. She went to the rink less and less. She had many casual girlfriends but no one special. Rosaleen, the girl she worked with in Brown Thomas, suggested she should go dancing.

'On my own?' asked Sheila.

'I'll go with you.'

'But what about Brian?' I thought you were doing a serious line with him.'

'I am, but next weekend he's going down the country to see his parents.'

'I wouldn't mind. Where will we go?'

32

'The Olympic, it's smashing.'

'It's not far from the Buildings. OK, I'll give it a try.'

Rosaleen met her outside the ballroom. 'It's gorgeous,' Sheila said after they had left their coats in the cloakroom and checked their hair and faces in the big mirror, where many more girls were doing the same thing. Some of them Sheila recognised, girls from the Buildings, from school, others that she knew to see.

She and Rosaleen joined the group of girls standing at one end of the ballroom, facing the men who stood at the other end and who would, when the band played, come and choose a partner.

'I only ever come here with Brian,' Rosaleen said. 'I used to hate this part of it – waiting to be chosen. And hated it even more when I was and the fella was a sight.'

'Why didn't you refuse him?'

'You're not supposed to. Well, if he was legless I suppose you could. But you can be put out for refusing, so I'm told, though I've never seen it happen.'

'Put out or not, I'm not dancing with someone I don't want to,' said Sheila.

And in all the times she went dancing, Sheila stuck to her word. If she didn't like the look of whoever asked her up she made an excuse. She had hurt her ankle, had a headache, was going home in a minute. There was never a scene, even though in a few minutes she might waltz past the one she had rejected. It never seemed to bother any of them. They went to their second, third or last choice and were eventually accepted. Sheila had no qualms of conscience, thinking that it was no worse for the men than the girls, who stood like heifers on show waiting to be chosen.

Not that she ever waited long. She was pretty, vivacious and her mother made her glamorous dresses. Sometimes Rosaleen and Brian came to the ballroom. Not that it mattered whether they did or not. For now Sheila had many acquaintances there.

When she came home after a dance her mother would quiz her about whom she had met. 'Well, did you enjoy yourself?' she'd ask while making sandwiches and pouring tea for Sheila.

'Yeah, I had a great time. Up for every dance.'

'Did you come on your own?'

Sometimes the answer was 'yes', sometimes 'no'. If it was 'no', Ginny would want to know all about who had left her home. Usually Sheila would tell her. But if she was in bad humour she'd pretend to be more tired than she was and go to bed. Where she would lie thinking how going to dances wasn't as exciting as it once was. Nothing was exciting any more. Even Brown Thomas was beginning to get on her nerves. Dancing attendance on oul wans buying make-up and perfumes. Taking ages to decide. And sometimes not even bothering to say 'thank you'.

And as for the fellas she danced with, she had never fancied one of them. Though now and then she made dates. Went to the pictures with them, and practised her kissing on them, stroked their necks and fondled their ear lobes. They were either too hot or too holy. The holy ones probably saying prayers to keep their chastity; the fast ones she stopped in their tracks. In the bed she'd say to herself there must be some gorgeous fellas somewhere.

Though maybe they've all gone to England. Work was so scarce that the mail boat was packed day and night, taking the Irish to look for work in England. That was how the saying 'see you on the boat' came about. She would soon be eighteen and was getting nowhere. Rosaleen was giving up work after she married. God only knew who would replace her. Several of the girls she had been in school with were going steady; girls from the Buildings were getting engaged, some of them younger than her. They didn't believe in long engagements like the girls she'd gone to school with who waited years to save a deposit for a house. Girls from the Buildings put their trust in God, married young and lived with their mothers or mothers-in-law.

She was fed up. There was nothing to look forward to. The way things were going she could finish up an old maid. She needed to change her life. Maybe take the boat. Be a nurse. The paper was always full of ads for nurses in England. But she'd hate to leave her mother and father. It might be terrible lonely in England. She could do a commercial course in Greggs on the Green. They had evening classes. Then she'd get a job in an office. 'Doing what?' she'd ask herself and reply, 'Banging away on a typewriter and taking dictation from some baldy oul solicitor. Stuck in an office that was up over a shop. The only decent offices were in the Civil Service and she'd die rather than be a civil servant. You'd see them pouring out of the government buildings on their bikes. She'd definitely finish up an old maid if she were a civil servant, God forbidding all harm. Anyway, she'd decide nothing in a hurry. For all she knew, tomorrow or the next day she could click with a smashing bloke. She'd give it another six months and then think about England and nursing.

A week after her eighteenth birthday, while she was in Bewleys eating her lunch of sausage and chips, a man came to her table. 'You're not keeping the other seat, are you?'

'No,' she said. 'You're lucky it's slacked off a bit. Ten minutes ago the place was packed.'

He put down his tray of bacon, egg, sausage, chips and coffee. Unloaded the tray, took it back to the rack. Sheila watched him. Admired how tall he was, his carriage and jet-black curly hair. When he came back and sat down she said, 'I've been coming in here for two years, I've never seen you before.'

'I'm away a lot.'

Oh, you're a picture, she thought watching him cut a rasher, dip it in the egg and fill his mouth. His teeth were white and perfect, and she thought of all the fellas with bad or false teeth she had danced with, kissed. And, what was so unusual, his face and hands were brown as berries.

Where would he have got the sun? she asked herself. 'Are you working in England?'

'I'm a soldier.'

'In our army?'

He laughed and said, 'No, I'm a soldier of the Queen. I wanted to see the world. Not much chance of that in the Free State army. You're a Dubliner?'

'So are you. Where are you from?'

'Heytesbury Street.'

'I live in the Iveagh Buildings, your street's only up the road from them.'

'Neighbours, eh.'

She looked at the clock on the wall. In ten minutes she'd have to go back to work. Oh, God, she thought, it's not fair. I've never seen a fella like him before. And I'll probably never see him again. What'll I do? Talk, anyway. 'How are you so brown?' she asked. 'It's a gorgeous tan.'

'I was in Egypt for a few years.'

'Egypt!' she exclaimed. 'I saw a film about it. All the sand and the camels and Cairo and the Pyramids and a place called – what was it? Let me think – Alex something.'

'Alexandria.'

'That's it, Alexandria.'

'Well, I saw the camels and the sand, but not much else.'

'How is that?'

'There's a war going on out there. The Egyptians, like everyone else, wanted us out of their country. You haven't eaten much of your food.'

How could she tell him she was so enthralled by him she wouldn't have been able to swallow. So she lied.

'I never eat much at this hour of the day.' The clock on the wall said five to two. She stood up. 'I'll have to go back to work.'

'Where d'ye work?'

'Across the road in Brown Thomas.'

'Not worth me walking you there, then.'

Her heart sank. She'd never see him again. She'd fallen in love with him and she'd never see him again.

He stood up as she inched her way out of the narrow place in which the table stood. 'I'll be hanging around town for the rest of the day. Maybe I could meet you when you finish work. We could have a drink if you like.'

'That'd be great, just after six.'

'Fine, I'll see you then.'

When there was a lull in customers she told Rosaleen, 'You want to see him. He's gorgeous. He's meeting me from work. He's home on leave from the British army.'

'I wonder what your father'll make of that,' Rosaleen said.

Sheila was more concerned about going into a public house than what her father would think of her being with a British soldier. We don't even know each other's names she thought as she combed her hair and put on lipstick before leaving work. He was waiting for her and took her round the corner into Duke Street and Davy Byrnes.

She had never been in a public house and had never, except at Christmas, drunk alcohol. And then only one glass of sherry.

'What'll you have?' he asked when she was seated.

'Lemonade, please.'

'You sure?'

She said she was and watched him at the bar. He was wearing cavalry twill trousers and a light-brown tweed sports coat. She thought, I'll never see him after this. I expect he'll walk me back to the Buildings. It'll still be light. Now I'll never know what his kiss would be like.

But she did. He made a date for the following night, for all the nights and the weekend of his remaining leave. They went to cafés, cinemas and always a public house. But he never drank more than two pints of Guinness.

Never got like her da. And after all, he was on leave and that was like being on a holiday.

And how he could kiss! Like on the pictures: no fumbling, no bumping noses. The kissing thrilled her, sent sensations she had never experienced before, gorgeous tingling feelings from her toes to her head but they were stronger round her breasts and her belly.

The first time she stroked his neck and caressed his ear lobe he took hold of her hand and removed it. 'Cut that out,' he said.

'Didn't you like it?'

'I liked it all right. Where did you learn that?'

'A girl in work had an American magazine. All about necking. Fellas were supposed to like it.'

'Fellas do like it. They get worked up. Want more touching and stroking.'

'On their necks and ears?'

He laughed. 'All sorts of places.' He kissed her gently – held her away and said, 'Sheila, you haven't been around much, have you?'

'You've an awful cheek. I've had loads of fellas,' she said indignantly. 'I think we'd better go home.'

On the walk home he told her that on his last leave his father had died. Sheila said she was sorry for his loss. 'What ailed him?' she asked as they neared the Buildings.

'Old age, I suppose.'

'And your mother, is she alive?'

'No, she died a while back, Lord have mercy on them both.'

'So who lives with you?'

'I'm all on my ownio. We didn't own the house. My father was reared in it but his eldest brother inherited it. He rented it to us. Now it belongs to his son. He'll sell it but not for a while. It needs doing up. I can stay in it for six months at least.'

'Then what'll you do?' Sheila asked.

'I'm a soldier. I have a roof over my head. I won't come

to Dublin so often, I suppose. I'd find it hard doing bed and breakfast.'

Sheila's heart sank. When the six months was up she might never see him again. Then she consoled herself. Six months was a long time. Time enough for two more leaves.

Chapter Five

His name was Fergus Brady. He had one brother. Sean was in the IRA and had been interned on the Curragh many times. Fergus told Sheila how often during the Thirties and Forties Sean had been 'lifted'. 'Police cars outside the door, my mother crying as Sean was taken out. The neighbours behind the curtains gawking.'

'Were you in the army then?' Sheila asked.

'Still in school slogging for my Leaving Cert. I wanted to go to university. Be an engineer. But I failed the Cert. I joined up then – 1944.'

'What did your mother and father think about that?'

'Me ma was broken-hearted.'

'Because you were joining the British army?'

'No, because I was leaving home. Sean had cleared off to America, now I was clearing off. The war was still on. A year to go. I was there for the end of it. So there was I, fighting my way up to Germany: Sean God knows where in America. We never heard from him. It was the death of my mother, Lord have mercy on her. She had a stroke just before VE Day and died.'

They were, as usual, in a public house when this conversation took place, Sheila still on lemonade and Fergus stretching the two pints until closing time. There were only two more days left before he went back to England. He promised he would write and be home again in three months. Sheila was besotted by him. She couldn't believe her luck. She was sure he would tell her that he loved her before he returned to England.

Rosaleen threw cold water on her hopes. 'He's gorgeous-looking I have to admit, but he's a soldier. Here today and gone tomorrow. I only hope to God you won't do anything foolish,' she said on the day before Fergus's leave finished.

'What d'ye mean, do anything foolish?'

'Like letting him take advantage of you. It does happen.'

Into Sheila's mind flashed an image of Rosaleen's fiancé, Brian: lank ginger hair and eyebrows; 'awfully nice'; a right-looking eejit. She couldn't imagine him attempting to take advantage of Rosaleen. Not until after the nuptial mass, papal blessing and all the rest, and then it wouldn't be a sin.

But as the thought registered in Sheila's mind she recognised it as being uncharitable. Rosaleen was her friend and her Brian was a nice bloke. They were good practising Catholics, and good practising Catholics remembered their vows of chastity. Rosaleen was concerned for her, was giving her good advice. So she would put her mind at rest. 'You needn't worry. Fergus wouldn't take advantage of me. It's the other way about.'

Rosaleen looked astonished. 'What do you mean, it's the other way about?'

Sheila told her about the neck and ear stroking, and how Fergus had responded. 'We kiss that's all. But such kisses! I go weak at the knees, honest to God. I think I'm a very passionate person.'

'I suppose that's more of your American magazine stuff.'

'Yeah,' admitted Sheila. 'We'd better shut up, there's a customer heading this way. I'll tell you more about it when we're slack.'

It was almost closing time before they had another chance to talk. 'Maybe Fergus is respecting me because he's not interested in me. He's never once mentioned love.

He's going back tomorrow. I won't see him again for three months. He says he'll write. But maybe he won't. I'll die, so I will, if it was only a flash in the pan.'

'Well, with you being so passionate, thank your lucky stars he didn't take advantage of you. He must be a decent fellow. Have you told your mother about him?'

'Not yet.'

'Where does she think you go every night?'

'Dancing, the pictures, out with you.'

'She's not suspicious?'

'Not a bit.'

But Ginny was suspicious. Sheila came in every night glowing. She's met a fella, Ginny thought, and she's in love. But no amount of clever questions elicited information from Sheila. That is, until the night Fergus kissed her goodbye. The minute she came in the door Ginny knew she was downhearted. Her face had a forlorn look about it. Dejectedly she took off her coat and threw it on a chair. 'The kettle's boiling. I'll wet the tea.'

'I don't want any.'

'What ails you, are you not well?'

Sheila put her head in her hands and sobbed. Ginny held her and didn't ask questions.

'I really love him. He's gorgeous. And now he's gone and I'll never see him any more.'

'Who's gone, love? Tell me all about it.'

Sheila did. His name, how they had met. That he was in the British army. How he was older than her. That he lived in Heytsbury Street. How gorgeous-looking he was. How much she loved him and would die if he didn't write to her.

Ginny held Sheila's head against her breast. 'My poor little child. It breaks my heart to see you grieving. But sure don't give up hope so soon. What makes you think he won't write? Isn't he as likely to as not?'

'Because he never said anything about us being serious. He never said he loved me.'

41

'Now listen to me,' Ginny said, 'few fellas, sincere ones anyway, would say they loved you after only knowing you ten days. A chancer would hoping to take advantage of a lovely innocent girl like you.'

'But I loved him from the minute I laid eyes on him.'

'I know, I know. Women are like that. Our heart does the ruling. And many a time it's the ruination of us. This Fergus fella is older than you for a start. Very sensible, probably a decent man who wouldn't want to raise your hopes until he was sure.'

Sheila's sobs were subsiding. Ginny stood up from where she had been kneeling by the chair, stroked Sheila's hair and said that now she would make tea. While she was doing so Sheila, through whose body a sob now and then hiccuped, said, 'He could be a married man for all I know.'

'Hardly, if he's been seeing you all this time. Where was it you said he lived?'

Sheila told her and Ginny said, 'I know a lot of people in that street. What's his surname?'

'Brady, Fergus Brady.'

'I'll go to mass in St Kevin's in the morning. Meet a few of my cronies who live in his street and we'll know whether he's married or single.' She put a small table in front of the fireplace, brought the rocking chair close to it, then fetched the tea things and bread and butter for Sheila. 'If he is married, which I doubt, then put him out of your mind. Don't even open a letter from him. D'ye hear me?'

Sheila nodded her head, then said, 'Suppose he is single and does write and we get serious, what about me da?'

'What about your da?'

'You know, with Fergus being in the British army?'

'If the fella's right for you your father wouldn't care if he was in the Foreign Legion.'

'But me da was in the IRA and he's always on about us having the Six Counties back.'

'I know and he's right about that. They're ours. But that's got nothing to do with British soldiers. I'm sure he's told you on the rambles that it was only the few who felt enmity towards the soldiers. Didn't hundreds of them marry Irish women and settle here? And seldom did anyone look crooked at them. If this Fergus loves you and your father takes a liking to him his uniform won't matter.'

'Well,' said Ginny when Sheila came home from work the next evening, 'your man's not married. His mother and father are dead and his brother who was in the IRA went to America and hasn't been heard of since.'

'He told me that. What else was said about him?'

'He comes from a decent family. His father was a gentleman. Only died recently. Catholics, decent respectable people like ourselves, so there.'

Sheila was thrilled when Fergus's first letter came but disappointed after reading it. He wrote of how much he had enjoyed her company, the best leave he had ever spent in Dublin, and he was counting the weeks until the next one. He described where he was stationed in Wiltshire: the beautiful rolling countryside, the Beacons, hills not big enough to be classed as mountains, easy to climb over them and down to villages where there were public houses that must have been there for hundreds of years. He described the enormous kiwi carved into the chalky hill by New Zealand soldiers stationed there during the First World War: 'You could see it from miles away.' The garrison church was a posh red-brick affair and the Catholic chapel small and looked as if it had been slung up: corrugated roof. But inside it was pleasant, everything a chapel should be, and the priest great: not a pulpit thumper; Irish but not a bog trotter. 'He's attached to the Paras. You'd like him.'

He described Salisbury, the nearest big town, how beautiful it was and the Cathedral breathtaking. There was a clock in it, going, keeping the proper time, one of the first clocks ever made, hundreds of years old. On Saturdays there was a market held in the town square, all sorts of stalls. The butchers wore flat straw hats and you'd see old men wearing embroidered smocks. Shepherds, he believed they were. And lots of antique furniture, as good as you'd see in Wines of Grafton Street any day of the week. 'Shops that you would love around the square selling expensive ladies clothes. It's a grand place altogether. Old-fashioned public houses, not like in Dublin named for the owner. Fantastic names: the Haunch of Venison, Rose and Crown, those sort of names. And there's the new NAAFI club: game rooms, great grub. You'd love this place.'

He signed off with 'See you soon, Fergus'.

Ginny watched Sheila's face as she read the letter and could tell that whatever he had written hadn't pleased her. 'There y'are, didn't I tell you not to give up hope?'

'I might as well have for what's in it.' She handed the letter to her mother. 'Read it,' she said.

Ginny did and handed it back. 'He has a lovely hand, like copperplate. And I don't see anything wrong with what he wrote. And furthermore, look how he finishes off.'

She gave back the letter and Sheila glanced at it again. 'Oh, that,' she said, throwing it on to the table. 'You'd love it. Isn't that grand. But not a word about me did you notice. I think it's a pen friend that fella's looking for. Throw it in the fire. I'll never answer it.'

Ginny picked up the letter, crumpled it and threw it into the empty fireplace. For the time being she'd be wasting her time talking to Sheila. Leave her to come out of her humour, then see how the wind blew. 'There's a few things I forgot to get. I won't be long,' said Ginny, throwing a cardigan over her shoulders and, taking her purse from the dresser drawer, went out.

She bought the evening paper from the boy at the corner, walked to the end of Kevin Street to kill time and thought about the letter, thanking God for it being a letter that anyone could have written to anyone. To a man or a woman. A nice friendly letter. Of course, had it been of another sort Sheila wouldn't have let her read it. Thank

God it wasn't. It was unfortunate that Sheila had taken up with a British soldier. If anything came of it he was bound to take her away from Dublin. And that would break my heart, she said to herself. She remembered how Sheila had said long ago that when she married she wanted to live next door to her. Wouldn't that have been grand. Or even the next street, anywhere in Dublin. But married to a fella in the British army, God only knew where she would finish up.

The letter had been taken out of the fireplace. Sheila's humour had improved.

'Your father's gone to a union meeting so we'll have our dinner and I'll warm his when he comes in.' While they ate Sheila didn't mention Fergus nor the letter and neither did Ginny.

The next week two more letters came from Fergus. Again there was nothing intimate in them and Ginny was given them to read. Three arrived during the following week, but these Sheila kept to herself, and thereafter never less than two letters a week from Fergus dropped on to the mat.

'How is he?' Ginny would ask occasionally and Sheila would reply that he was great.

There was no need for her mother to ask how she was. Her face glowed with happiness, she sang as she went about the house and went out only with Ginny and sometimes Rosaleen.

Every minute of the day Fergus was in her mind, even though he still hadn't said he loved her. But his letters talked about how much he had enjoyed her company and how he was longing to see her again. He wrote that he couldn't get her out of his mind. Asked her to send him a photograph. He wanted to see her face again, her smile, her eyes.

Ginny went to Mass every morning and prayed that Sheila's love for this stranger would be reciprocated. She also said a special prayer to Our Lady that he should be worthy of her child's love. And she asked the Blessed Virgin to reconcile her if the time came when Fergus would marry and take her beloved daughter away.

Mr Brophy wasn't told of Sheila's romance until the week before Fergus was coming to Dublin on leave. He was being asked to the house. 'Sheila's been writing to a fella in the British army. He's Irish. She met him in Bewleys a couple of months ago. He's from Heytesbury Street. Brady's his name, Fergus Brady.'

'Brady, is that so. I knew a lot of Bradys years ago when I was in the Movement. One of them was with me in the GPO. Lord have mercy on him, he was a nice young man. This fella could well be a relation of his.'

'You could be right there,' said Ginny.

'Heytesbury Street, wasn't that what you said?'

'I did.'

'D'ye know, Ginny, I think that's where Peader Brady came from. But sure it's a long time ago. I might be mistaken. Your man in the army, what is he?'

'A sergeant, so I believe, and he's stationed in Wiltshire and that Sheila's serious about him. Apart from that I'm as wise as yourself.'

'She might get over it. She's very young. I hope she does for it would break my heart if he took her away from us.'

'There's not much we could do about it if he did. But I know only too well what you mean.'

Seeing the sad expression on his wife's face he tried to cheer her up. 'Still and all, England's not that far away; we could go over.' And then the optimism left him and he said, close to tears, 'For all that their empire's crumbling, there's still plenty of foreign places left with their stamp on it. He could be sent to any of them and our little girl with him.'

And then it was Ginny's turn to be the consoler: 'We're meeting trouble halfway. She could take a dislike to him like that,' she said, snapping her ⸻ wait and see. And if the worst co⸻ he's never sent foreign. Think of the ⸻ have in England.' She reached for his han⸻ continued, 'And sure, when all's said and d⸻ have each other?'

'Please God, we will that,' he said.

'Wasn't it a great coincidence, Ma, that my holidays is the same time as Fergus's leave.'

'Couldn't have worked out better,' Ginny said.

'We'll go up the mountains, out to Bray, see all the latest pictures, maybe go to a play if he likes plays. I think I'm dreaming and that any minute I'll wake up. You know about me bringing him home – well, I don't want to do that on his first night.'

'Whenever you like, so long as you give me a bit of notice. I'll get in a dozen of stout. That'll put a stop to your father's gallop to the pub. I'll buy a big piece of silverside. Fergus won't have had corned beef over there. Corned beef and a salad. I'll make apple cakes, a lemon meringue pie and buy a brack. D'ye think that's suitable?'

'Gorgeous except for the brack. I hate currant bread.'

'Too bad,' replied Ginny. 'Me and your father love any sort of a fruit loaf.'

He was every bit as handsome as she remembered, Sheila thought, as she met him at the corner of Grafton Street. They embraced and he kissed her cheek, then took her arm and asked if she'd like to go for a meal.

'I've just finished my dinner, but if you're hungry let's go to a café.'

'I'm not. I've been eating on and off since I got in this morning. There's nothing like Irish grub. There's a great cocktail lounge, the Four Provinces, it's . . .'

'In the dance hall?'

... ame that's all. It's just across the road.' He ... to a building at the top of South King's Street. 'You're a terrible one for the pubs.'

'Eh, come on, I am not and this isn't a pub. Wait'll you see it.' He took her arm and crossed the narrow street. The cocktail lounge was upstairs.

Sheila was very impressed with the snazzy decor and no smell of porter. 'It's lovely,' she said, sitting down and looking around. 'There's a good few women here. There was in Davy Byrnes as well. Women, except for very old ones, wouldn't be seen dead in a public house where I live. You'd get your name up. The old women sit in the snug, a little room all to theirselves. When you come to the house tomorrow night, don't mention that I was in here. My ma would be raging.'

Fergus smiled at her, she blushed and thought how she adored him. Wanted to be on her own with him. A private place where he would take her in his arms and kiss her. 'I won't mention anything about your drinking.'

'My drinking!'

'I'm codding you. What'll you have?'

'Lemonade?'

'Be daring – try a cocktail.'

'Maybe next time. Maybe when we're out for the day. By the time I'd get home my breath wouldn't smell.'

Fergus had a pint of Guinness. Sheila was thrilled with lemonade on ice and a slice of lemon fixed on the rim of the glass. There was a bowl of mixed nuts on the table, which she helped herself to while listening to Fergus making plans for the next ten days. She agreed to all of them.

'Another lemonade?' he asked as he finished his pint and stood up.

'You must have been choking with the thirst,' she said staring at the drained glass. 'Are we going or what?'

'D'ye not want another drink?' asked Fergus.

'I haven't finished this one yet. I'll leave it if you want to go.'

'I'll have another first. You're sure you won't try something else?'

'I'm sure.'

She watched him go to the bar and thought, much as I love him, I'm not sitting here for the rest of the night. 'I don't know how you can drink that stuff. The smell of it makes me want to be sick,' she said when he came from the bar.

'It's good for you. Builds you up.'

'You should see what it's done for my father. It's built up his belly all right and the rest of him looks like a skeleton. D'ye drink every night in England?'

'Give over, Sheila, amn't I on my holliers? This one only and then we'll go. And I'll buy a packet of Sen-Sens.'

'Why?'

'So that the smell of my breath won't make you sick when I kiss you goodnight.'

'Oh, you,' she said and blushed at the thought of being in his arms, his lips on hers. And she wouldn't stroke his neck or fiddle with his ear.

It was a lovely evening and Fergus suggested they take a bus to Dun Laoghaire. 'Watch the mail boat going out.'

'I thought after spending the night on it you'd have seen enough of it, let's go up the Park instead.' They walked to the quays and took a bus to the Phoenix Park. They sat upstairs where they could smoke. She was new to smoking. Fergus had introduced her to cigarettes on his last leave. While he was away she hadn't smoked. She couldn't in work and her mother would have given out yards if she had lit up at home. So inhaling the first cigarette for a long time, she coughed and spluttered. Fergus thumped her back, then kept an arm round her. She leaned into him. She loved the smell of him and was glad it was to the park she was going. There they could find private places to lie on the grass and, as the saying

49

went, have a 'good court'. She knew from girls in the Buildings and dance halls that a 'good court' had been many a one's downfall. If you gave in to the heat of the moment you could finish up with a baby and a fella who didn't want to marry you. It was up to the girl, according to everyone.

Her mother had warned her when she first started going out with blokes that you shouldn't lead them on. Stroking their necks and ears was probably leading them on. She wouldn't do it again. Kissing and cuddling was as far as she would let it go and courting in the park would be bliss instead of huddled in a shop or tenement doorway.

If the romance lasted – and she prayed it would – maybe the next time he was on leave her mother would leave them alone in the parlour. That'd be grand. For the next leave would be when the weather was drawing in, cold and damp outside. I'm counting my chickens before they're hatched. He still hasn't mentioned a word about love, or going seriously. There may not be another leave for me. I'll die if I never see him again, she thought, as the bus passed Church Street. She pointed out the hall where she used to dance at the Feis.

'I suppose you've got medals down to there,' Fergus said, pointing to the end of his stomach.

'I have,' Sheila said and added, 'You haven't forgotten your Dublin sayings. And along with medals down to there I have cups as well. I'm a great dancer.'

'I'm not that bad myself. I'll try you out during the week. We'll go to the Olympic,' he said as they sat on the grass in the Hollow.

Chapter Six

Fergus was coming to the house at seven o'clock. During the afternoon Sheila helped her mother to prepare the meal, after complaining that she knew nothing about cooking. "Deed you do. Sure you were always under my feet when I was at the stove. And making tarts from the leftover pastry. Anyway, I only want the egg whites whipped for the meringue.'

'I hate doing that. They never get stiff enough for your liking.'

'They will this time. I read a tip in my magazine. You whip them in a draught. Get air into them.' With a loud sigh of exasperation Sheila took the egg whites on a shallow enamel plate to the back door, opened it a little and began whipping. 'God, you were right,' she said when the eggs started to peak. 'But I'll tell you one thing, whoever I marry'll do without lemon meringue pie. My arm is paralysed. I hope me da won't go to the pub tonight. It'd be grand for him and Fergus to have a chat.'

'There's enough stout in so he shouldn't, but don't bank on it. Men like your father believe stout doesn't taste the same in the house. It'll all depend on him taking a liking to your man.'

'You mean,' said Sheila, 'that he mightn't warm to him because he's in the British army.'

'Sometimes I think you're losing your mind since you met this fella. You asked me that before and I gave you the answer. Your father will be weighing him up to see what sort of a man he is. If he'd make you a good husband. I wish to God my father had weighed him up.'

'You don't really mean that, Ma?'

'I do sometimes. I hate drink. I hate your father's eejity look when he comes back from the pub. And I bitterly resent the waste of money. But for that, again he's not the worst in the world. He's a quiet man, not violent. I've

51

never felt the weight of his hand and neither have you. So I've that to be grateful for. There's women all over the city of Dublin bet black and blue, their unfortunate children kicked and beaten by drunken fathers.'

'Why don't the women leave their husbands?'

'And go where? Live on what? Anyway, let's stop blathering. You lay the table and then you'll have oceans of time to doll yourself up.'

She bathed, perfumed and powdered, wore a red full-skirted dress and black patent stilettos. She had washed her hair earlier in the day and it framed her face with lustrous black curls. Her brassiere was a Maidenform, which did justice to her breasts. Gazing at herself in the mirror, she hugged herself and thought, surely tonight he'll say something, let me know I'm special, not just a date for his leave.

Then she realised that tonight there'd be no place for a 'court', just a quick kiss in the hall, her mother and father in the kitchen, the door ajar. But she consoled herself that there was more than a week left. A week in which they'd go to beautiful places, up the mountains, to Pine Forest, to beaches where there were sand dunes. Places where they would be alone. Where he might tell her he loved her. Even was very fond of her. Talk about his next leave and what they would do then. It'll be six months, then, since we first met. Surely to God he'll have something to say one way or the other by then. Unless there was someone else. He wasn't married but what was to stop him being engaged to someone over there. One of the girls in the army. He'd mentioned girls in a letter. Told how he and his mates played badminton with them. She had worked herself into the depths of despair.

She heard her father come home from work then him going into the bathroom. Despite her misery she smiled and thought how unusual it was for him to wash when he came home from work. All he ever did was give his hands a quick wash at the kitchen sink. Poor Da, wanting to make a good impression. Thinking that this must be serious, otherwise her mother wouldn't have asked him to the house.

She heard the knock on the front door and her heart raced. It was him. Well, she'd be very cool with him. The cheek of him, using her as a companion during his leave. Tonight she'd make an excuse about tomorrow. She wouldn't be able to see him. Why drag it out? The sooner it finished the sooner she'd get over it.

'Sheila,' her mother called. 'Fergus is here. Hurry up and come out.' She took a few deep breaths, had a last look in the mirror and went out. The sight of him sent her fears flying. He was the most gorgeous man in the world. No film star could hold candlelight to him. I love, I love, I love him. I'd die for him, she said to herself.

'Will you look what he brought,' said Ginny, showing her two bouquets of flowers. 'In all my life no one has ever bought me flowers. These are yours.' And she passed the red roses to Sheila. 'Say thanks or at least hello. Give him a kiss, it's the least you can do.' Sheila thanked him and kissed his cheek. They looked into each other's eyes. His beautiful brown eyes. She could have eaten him and all her doubts were gone for ever she told herself.

Her father joined them, newly shaved and in his best suit. Ginny, behind Fergus's back and out of her husband's vision, made a moue. Sheila, knowing every expression on her mother's face, could interpret what, without speaking, Ginny wanted to convey: 'Will you look at the get-up of him. Anyone would think it was the Pope himself or the Taoiseach paying us a visit.'

The introductions were made. 'Brady,' said Mr Brophy. 'There might be nothing in it for it's a common enough name in Dublin, but sure the question's worth asking. The world's a small place and Dublin smaller still. Years ago I knew a fella called Brady. And the wife tells me you're from Heytesbury Street. So was he. We fought side by side in the Post Office. Lord have mercy on him, he was shot.

He was a grand young man. The heart of a lion. Poor Peader Brady, I can see him still.'

'He was my father's brother. Killed before I was born.'

'Well, well,' said Mr Brophy, 'didn't I say it's a small world.'

'Me and my brother grew up hearing all about Uncle Peader and his stand for Ireland. I often think it was what influenced Sean into joining the IRA.'

'Is that so, is he still in the Movement?'

'No one knows where he is. Rumour had it he was involved in the bombings in London and Birmingham. Every so often the squad cars would be up the street and Sean be lifted. Nothing was ever proved and after one of his releases he did a runner. Probably to America. No one's heard tale nor tidings of him since.'

Ginny, serving the meal, said, 'Isn't Ireland the strange country all the same. Families with sons in the British army and sons in the IRA. It's a wonder they let you join, Fergus.'

'You don't have to tell the gospel truth about everything. And during wartime they don't probe so much. In the Twenties and Thirties they did. You'd have to have a reference from a Protestant clergyman in those days.'

The men drank stout with their food. Mr Brophy asked Fergus about the army. Where he'd served during the war. How long he had signed on for.

'The full whack, twenty-two years. But I could come out after twelve; smaller pension, though.'

Sheila was delighted with how things were going until after the pudding was served and her father suggested that he and Fergus went to the pub.

'That'll break up the evening,' said Ginny. 'There's still half a dozen of stout left. That should be plenty.'

'Don't you know very well, Ginny, it would. But sure drinking in the house is never the same. We'll be gone no time, sure we won't, Fergus.'

Sheila willed him to refuse her father but he said nothing

and out the two of them went.

'I expected that might happen. Your father wouldn't get his health if he missed one night in the pub.'

'I'm choked,' said Sheila. 'If I wasn't so furious I'd be breaking my heart crying. I can't believe he'd do that to me. That's me finished with him. I'm going to bed.'

'Ah, don't, love. It was your father's fault not his.'

'He didn't have a gun to his head.'

'It wouldn't have been polite to refuse.'

'Polite! Was it polite to walk out on me? Answer me that.'

'That's how men are, Sheila. You should know that by now.'

'That's how my father is. I don't want a fella the same. So I'm going to bed. Tell him what you like. I've a headache. I got sick. And tell him I won't meet him tomorrow.' She flounced out of the room. Ginny washed the delft and thought what a pity it was that the night was spoiled. She had taken to Fergus and so had Jemmy. She knew Sheila was mad about him and, though she couldn't be positive about it, he appeared to feel the same about her. Please God, she prayed silently, let them not stay long. If they come back soon I could coax Sheila to come out of the bedroom. As she washed, rinsed and dried, she kept an eye on the clock. Eight o'clock they'd gone out. Surely to God they wouldn't stay until closing time.

She listened at Sheila's door but heard no sound. Had she been crying she'd have gone in to comfort her. But maybe she was asleep. She wouldn't disturb her. She'd tell the lie that she wasn't well, but mention nothing about Sheila not seeing him the next day. In the morning she might change her mind.

As the time went on she revised her opinion of Fergus. Good-looking, charming and generous he might be, the flowers wouldn't have been cheap, but she now suspected he had a liking for the drink. It would be better for Sheila to finish with him. She'd have no trouble finding another fella. An Irishman who didn't drink. They'd marry and settle in Dublin.

Fergus and Jemmy came back at a quarter to eleven, by which time Ginny was in bed. She had been afraid to stay up for fear her temper got the better of her. Not that the loss of her temper would have bothered Jemmy. In the early days of their marriage she had rowed, screamed, threatened to leave him. Goaded him to the extent where a less gentle person might have given her a black eye or split her lip. He grinned his eejity grin, collapsed in a chair and was asleep in a minute. But losing her temper in front of Fergus was another thing. He was a guest in her house, if only for a short time. He was also a stranger and his going to the pub was none of her business. And for all she knew he and Sheila might patch things up. Might marry. She hoped not. But you never could tell and she didn't want to make an enemy of a future son-in-law.

She could hear them in the kitchen. Jemmy called hers and Sheila's names. Then there was silence and soon afterwards the sound of the front door closing. 'Feck you anyway, Jem Brophy. You can sleep in the chair and perish to death. I'm not getting out of bed to loosen your tie, stroke your baldy head and throw a cover over you.' She said her prayers and an extra one for Sheila's happiness.

Chapter Seven

Ginny brought Sheila a cup of tea to her bedroom. 'You've slept your senses away, it's eleven o'clock.' She saw from the state of her eyes that she had been crying but made no comment.

'Did you tell him what I told you to?' asked Sheila, hoisting herself up in the bed.

'I didn't. To tell you the truth, I couldn't face the pair of them with the state I was in, so I went to bed.'

'Did you hear them come in?'

'I did. Drink the tea before it goes cold.'

'What time was it?'

'Nearly eleven I'd say.'

'Oh, Ma, what'll I do? He'll be standing at the top of Grafton Street waiting for me. We were going to have a grand time. Go to Howth for the afternoon and tonight we were going to a dance. I've been awake for hours thinking about him. I could kill my father.'

'But sure you know what he's like. And if you asked him today why he went and invited Fergus, he'd say, "Sure wasn't I only making a friendly gesture to a stranger in the house."'

'He was in my eye. He wanted to go to the pub, that's all. Would you say Fergus has a liking for the drink, Ma?'

'How could I say that? I've only met him the once.'

'What'll I do? I'm mad about him. I'm sorry in one way that he'll be standing like an eejit waiting for me and for that again I think it serves him right.'

'I think you should get up, have a bath, dress and put on your make-up. Then I'll fry you a rasher and egg. You'll feel better.'

'I'll never feel better again. I wouldn't care if I died this minute.'

'You'd be better off dying nice and clean. I'd be ashamed of my life letting one of Fanagan's men coffin you and you looking the way you are.'

'It's no good trying to make me laugh. My heart's broken, so it is. I suppose if I had a quick wash and threw something on I might still catch him in Grafton Street. He's bound to wait for a while. What d'ye think, Ma?'

'You'll do what you want to. I'll advise you neither one way nor the other. But hurry up and decide. I want to go out after dinner.'

'Where are you going?'

'To see Mrs McClusky in the hospice, she's on her last. Come with me. The walk'll do you good.'

'The hospice! That's all I need to cheer me up. Everyone in it dying. It's even written up over the gates. "Our Lady's Hospice for the Dying". I went there when my grannie was dying. And the way she was breathing frightened the life out of me. I had nightmares for weeks.'

'Please yourself,' replied Ginny. 'I'll fry the rasher and egg, if you don't want it turn your arse to it.'

Sheila stayed in bed. The smell of the bacon frying made her realise how hungry she was. But she'd starve rather than go into the kitchen. Her mother might talk her into going to see Mrs McClusky. That was all she needed now, a visit to the dying. She heard her mother go out and in a little while fell asleep, and was woken by a knocking on the door. For a while she ignored it. But whoever was knocking was persistent and continued banging the knocker. She put on a dressing gown and, without bothering to look in the mirror, went to the door and opened it. When she saw Fergus her first thought was of what a sight she must look.

'Can I come in?' he asked when she hadn't uttered a word.

'I suppose so.' She stood back to let him pass. He waited in the hall while she shut the door. 'Go into the kitchen,' she said, 'put the kettle on. I won't be a minute.' In the bathroom she splashed cold water on her puffy eyes, cleaned her teeth and brushed her hair. She also drank a glass of water and took a couple of deep breaths before going to the kitchen.

'I waited for more than an hour,' Fergus said. 'Where's the tea?'

'Beside the teapot.'

'I had to come and see you to apologise about last night.'

'Why?' And she thought, you're not going to get round me.

'I shouldn't have gone with your father. I shouldn't have stayed so long. I didn't get drunk, honest to God.

58

There was more talk than drink.' He made tea and poured two cups. 'I relived the Rebellion and Peader's part in it.'

'Don't blame my father. You went of your own free will. And when you've finished your tea you can go. I never want to see you again.' A lump was growing in her throat, in a minute she'd be crying. Only she wouldn't let it happen. She wouldn't give him that satisfaction. She had remained standing.

Fergus came towards her with a cup of tea. 'Drink it,' he said, 'it'll buck you up.'

'I don't want tea. I only want you gone. D'ye hear me. I hate you.' Her voice rose. 'I hate you, hate you.' Then the tears had their way and fell from her eyes.

Fergus put the cup down and took her in his arms. She struggled to get free but he held her tightly. 'Listen,' he said. 'I love you. I think I did from the minute I met you in Bewleys.'

She was aware of his body next to her, his smell, and the words he had spoken sang joyously in her head. But I'm no fool, she said to herself. Fell in love with me at first sight! There's no green in my eye. Fell in love the minute he saw me indeed. Then isn't it the queer thing that it's taken him three months to mention it.

'You probably don't believe me but it's true. You're probably thinking I took long enough to mention it. So I did. I was afraid you'd think I was chancing my arm. A chancer with only one thing in mind.'

She had stopped struggling and crying. She leant closer to him.

He continued talking: 'Another thing that made me cautious was being so much older than you. I was afraid that if I spoke too soon you'd have laughed and said I was an oul fella.'

'Thanks very much for having such a great opinion of me. And in any case if what you're saying is true about love, what was to stop you putting it in your letters?'

'I wanted to say it to you. I have now. I love you. I've

never been in love before. After all the standing in Grafton Street my legs are jaded. Can we sit down, d'ye think?'

For the first time since yesterday she laughed. 'There's a sofa in the parlour, we'll sit in there, it's also my mother's sewing room.' She closed the venetian blinds, then taking his hand led him to the sofa. 'Say you weren't codding me, Fergus.'

'I wasn't codding you.' He drew her to him and kissed her gently, then long and passionately. 'I love you. I want to marry you. On my next leave we'll get engaged and marry the next time I come home. That's if you'll have me.'

'Oh, I will, I will. I loved you too the minute I set eyes on you. I'd marry you tomorrow. Of course we couldn't but we'll be engaged from this minute. We could go down town now and buy the ring.'

'We could if I had enough money. But we'll have a ringless engagement until my next leave and then you'll have a daddy of a ring.'

'I don't care if I never had one.'

They were kissing again passionately, when her mother's key was heard in the door. 'Me ma,' said Sheila smoothing her hair and calling to her mother, 'I'm in here, Ma.'

Ginny came in. 'I didn't expect to see you here, Fergus.' She looked surprised, angry. 'And why aren't you dressed?' she asked Sheila. 'Go and put something on.'

'I wasn't expecting anyone to call. Fergus caught me on the hop.'

'I didn't know you'd be out, Mrs Brophy. I came to apologise to both of you about last night.'

'Didn't I tell you to get dressed, Sheila?'

'All right, all right, don't get your hair in a knot.'

'Last night wasn't all your fault. If I seemed a bit short when I came in I'm sorry. But it was a shock finding you here, and Sheila not dressed and the blinds closed. I only hope no one saw you come in. Everyone in the Buildings knows everyone's business. I'd have been seen going out.

You'd have been seen coming in. The closed blinds would have drawn attention, and two and two put together.' She raised the blinds and told Fergus to come into the kitchen. 'Sit down,' she said. 'Will you have a cup of tea?'

He thanked her but refused. 'Can I stay for a minute? I want to fix up about tonight.'

'Stay as long as you like.'

Sheila came in having dressed.

'Would you like to come to a dance tonight?' Fergus asked her. The band in the Olympic is supposed to be great.'

'Can you jive?'

'Wait'll you see me.'

'Then I'll come.'

They arranged a time to meet and he left.

'I like him,' Ginny said. 'And it was the decent thing to do, coming to apologise. Keep him away from your father in future.'

Sheila wanted to tell her mother that Fergus had asked to marry her but didn't knowing that her mother would say, 'Well, he may be a decent fella but you've known him no time. Ten days on his last leave and a couple on this one. Hold your horses for the time being.'

He could jive and so could she. Other dancers cleared a space for them in which to perform and clapped when they finished the dance. Girls looked enviously at Sheila's full-skirted emerald-green dress and her handsome partner. The men's eyes were fixed on Sheila's gyrating body, her long thighs and glimpse of black panties when Fergus swung her round and her skirt flared in a high arc.

For the remainder of his leave they went to beaches, the mountains, into the countryside, places where they found privacy for their courting. Consumed by passionate desire, Sheila could have been putty in Fergus's hands. But he controlled the situation, disengaging, lighting cigarettes for both of them and laughingly saying, 'A good, chaste

61

Catholic girl and that's what you'll be when I take you to the altar.'

'Oh, you,' she'd say, punching him playfully. But she was pleased nevertheless. He respected her. She liked that. And supposing he'd taken advantage of her and she'd got pregnant, her mother would have been leppin'.

A visit to a public house was always part of their outings. Sheila had succumbed and drank gin and it, gin and orange, and tried several cocktails. Never more than one drink. She didn't like the taste of alcohol, but realised more and more that Fergus did. She no longer commented on how much he consumed. After all, he was on his holidays and she believed that if after they were married he still drank she would be able to cure him.

Once he had gone back to England she broke the news of the engagement to her parents. Her father said he was pleased. 'Fergus is a grand man. He couldn't be anything else coming from the Bradys. My only regret is that he'll take you away from us.'

Ginny said little. 'I hope you'll be happy,' was all, in a voice that conveyed she wasn't happy.

It was Christmas when Fergus came on his next leave. The ring set with three small diamonds was bought and an engagement party arranged for St Stephen's Day, and the date of the wedding announced, March the following year.

Ginny watched like a hawk how much Fergus drank, not only the amount but the variety. She talked about it to Sheila, advising her to think carefully before getting married. 'An engagement can be broken; a marriage is a different kettle of fish.'

Sheila was furious. 'D'ye know what, Ma, you're an oul killjoy. It was a party. Everyone drinks at a party for God's sake. You don't want me to marry him. You want to keep me tied to you. Well, I'm marrying him and that's it, and what's more the minute he finds us a place I'm gone.'

'Suit yourself,' said Ginny. 'But remember this, you make your bed and you lie on it.'

They made it up the next day. Sheila apologised. 'I'm sorry, Ma, for taking the head off you. I know Fergus likes a drink. But once we're married I'll sort him out.'

'I thought the same myself,' said Ginny. 'It seldom works. But if you're willing to risk it that's your business.'

Chapter Eight

'You didn't give me a lot of notice,' Ginny said in January. 'There's your dress and the bridesmaid's for me to make, arrange for the chapel and the wedding breakfast.'

'I suppose I didn't, but we'll fit it all in. Thank God we're not a long-tailed family, neither is Fergus.'

'Thank God again. We can have the breakfast at home. Listen, now when was your last period?'

'Ma!' Sheila exclaimed. 'What d'ye want to know that for? You're not suggesting . . .'

'No, I'm not. But you don't want to be having it on the day you marry. So work out the dates and pick one when you won't be unwell. Then I can book the chapel.'

'What difference would it make if I was having my period?'

'Ah, now, love, I know you're an innocent girl but you must have picked something up here and there. Like what happens on your first night. You can't sleep with your husband if you're bleeding.'

'I never gave it a thought. I suppose you're right, though.'

'Of course I am. And apart from that, imagine if you flooded standing at the altar and stained your dress.'

Now a letter came from Fergus every day. Declarations of love, his impatience while he waited for her to be his wife. Had she made up her mind as to where they'd spend their honeymoon? He also wrote that he would look for a flat while they waited for married quarters to be allocated. Sheila tied the letters in bundles of six with blue ribbon and kept them in a decorative deep box.

The wedding date was set. Rosaleen came to be measured for her dress. She, Ginny and Sheila discussed what colour Rosaleen would wear. Finally Rosaleen said she would like pale-pink. 'Are you sure?' asked Ginny. 'Only Sheila wants pink or lemon for her wedding dress. You can't wear the same colour as the bride and imagine pink and lemon!'

'Ma, are you losing your mind or what? I never mentioned pink or lemon.'

'You did so and very definite you were about it. You didn't think white was a nice colour.'

'I still don't, I'm having cream. But where did you get the idea I wanted pink or lemon?'

'I'm having you on. You did say it but you were only eight then. It seems like yesterday. Ah, love, I hope you'll be very happy. He's a decent fella but why did he have to be a soldier? As your father said, he'll take you away from us. Pay no attention to me, I'm an oul fool.'

She blew her nose and dabbed her eyes. 'Now Rosaleen have a look at this pattern book and give me an idea how you'd like the dress to be.'

Sheila's dress was cream heavy satin, a fitted bodice, a sweetheart neckline and full skirt. The cuffs, neckline and bodice were decorated with tiny imitation pearls. The headdress also had pearls and she wore a long veil. Rosaleen's dress, while not being identical, was similar. Sheila's bouquet was roses, the same colour as Rosaleen's dress, and Rosaleen's flowers matched the cream of Sheila's gown.

The wedding was in Whitefriars Street chapel at three o'clock in the afternoon. Sheila's distant relations, a few men who had known Fergus since their schooldays and whom, when he was in Dublin he had a drink with.

Rosaleen's parents and a couple of girls from Brown Thomas. But the majority in the church were friends and neighbours. Girls Sheila had grown up with in the Buildings, their mothers and fathers, some young men who were courting the girls.

All the women had borrowed or bought new rig-outs for the wedding. Brightly coloured hats trimmed with feathers and flowers adorned their heads. Blue, pink, lilac, green and mauve costumes were worn, some home-made, others bought. Debts incurred for the style. But as the saying was, 'there's no pockets in a shroud' and they had splashed out for the wedding.

The men wore their best Sunday suits. A few had bought new shirts, had haircuts and shoes newly heeled. Sheila's father, Jemmy, had fortified himself with a couple of whiskeys for his walk down the aisle to give Sheila away.

It wasn't a custom in the city to walk to your wedding, so two cars had been booked even though the church was only round the corner. Flower dealers from the Buildings had given armfuls of blossoms to lay on the back window of the bridal car. Miss Clements, the organist in White-friars Street, was giving her services and wouldn't hear tell of taking a penny.

Ginny was elated and devastated in turns. The arrangements had gone like clockwork. Sheila's dress was beautiful, so was Rosaleen's. She had a great liking for Fergus. But all the same she wished he wasn't a soldier. Wasn't taking her only child far away. And so soon. Their flight was at six o'clock. By the time the nuptial mass was over, the photographs taken and all the kissing, hugging and congratulations finished, there'd be little time left for much of a wedding. It wasn't how she would have wanted it. But not by look or word did she let it be known that she harboured such sad thoughts. For when all was said and done it was Sheila's and Fergus's day. And wasn't it on their own they'd long to be?

There was a Roscrea ham with a golden bread-crumbed crust, a turkey, a joint of corned beef, salads and hot, floury potatoes; cakes and pastries galore, gallons of stout, whiskey, sherry, cream soda and red lemonade for the non-drinkers, and pot after pot of tea was made. After the meal and toasts the three-tier wedding cake was cut. Slices passed round. Other portions would be cut the following day and sent to those who couldn't come to the wedding. Unmarried girls would put the slice of wrapped cake under their pillows when they slept and hope to dream of the men they might find and marry.

The time flew. Jemmy falteringly made a short speech. Fergus thanked Jemmy and Ginny for giving him Sheila. Toasts were raised and then the wedding breakfast devoured. Ginny laughed and joked, and watched the clock. In no time the taxi would arrive for the airport from where Sheila and Fergus would fly to London, spend their first night there and travel to Salisbury the next day to honeymoon. No one at the wedding breakfast had ever flown and they marvelled at Sheila's courage.

'We're going to miss the best part,' Sheila said as the time for her to leave approached. 'I'd have loved the hooley.'

The women laughed. One said, "Deed you won't. It's your first night and if your man's as good as he looks it's not hooleys you'll be thinking about. Sure you can have a hooley any day of the week. But your first night you'll remember till the day you die. Isn't that a fact, Maggie?' Maggie assured her it was.

When the meal was finished one of the guests played an accordion. He was an old man and played old songs: 'The Rose of Tralee', 'Danny Boy', 'Love's Old Sweet Song'. The guests sang along, though the young men nudged each other and whispered, 'Bloody oul come all yes' and one shouted, 'Eh, Mick, how about something with a bit of jizz.' Ginny looked daggers at the young man. But the accordionist said, 'Certainly, son,' and played 'The Kerry

66

Dances'. Feet tapped, chairs were pushed back and old and young danced. It was music to dance to, to listen to. A lovely song recalling dancing to pipers and fiddlers at a crossroad down the country. A song about youth. A song about times long gone and with it lost youth. A very Irish song. It wrenched Ginny's heart and she went to the bedroom to cry, forgetting that Sheila was there changing into her going away outfit.

'Ma, what ails you? God, you look terrible.'

Ginny let the tears she had kept back fall. 'That bloody oul song. Everything ails me. But don't mind me. I'm sorry. I was holding my own till Mick played "The Kerry Dances". It was played at my wedding and that only seems like yesterday. You were only a light in your father's eye then and now I'm losing you.'

'Ah, for God's sake, Ma, give over. I'm only going to England. I'll be back in no time.' She put her arms round Ginny. 'You'll never lose me. Now stop crying or you'll start me off. I love you.'

Ginny laughed. 'I'm an oul eejit. And I'm delighted for you.' She wiped her eyes and blew her nose. 'Finish what you're doing. I'll go back inside. God bless and spare you. And have a lovely time on your honeymoon.'

The taxi arrived. Sheila was hugged and kissed. Jemmy was well cut already and kept hold of her for a long time until Ginny, appearing composed, told him to let go of Sheila and have a lie-down. They were showered with confetti. It covered their shoulders, Fergus's hair and lay in the brim of Sheila's blue hat, which matched her going-away costume. 'Don't throw that stuff on the floor,' the taxi driver said when Sheila took off her hat.

Fergus lowered the window and tipped out the confetti. 'Are you not putting it back on?'

'I am not, it's an awful-looking thing. Throw it out the window. Me ma talked me into getting it. I'll never put it on my head again.'

'Eh, Mrs, the wife's mad about hats, throw it over here,' the taxi driver said. Fergus did, then kissed Sheila. The driver, who had at first seemed surly, began to talk and never stopped until they arrived at the airport. Fergus winked at Sheila.

While waiting to board he said, 'It's only in Dublin you get taxi drivers like him. Talk, talk, talk. Some are great gas. Before you reach your destination you know their life history. And more often than not you've told them yours. Are you frightened about the flying?'

'A bit,' Sheila admitted.

'I'll hold you tight and we'll be in London before you know it.'

'It'll be too late to see much of it I suppose.'

'We could take a little walk. Though you might be jaded and want to go to bed, that's what I was hoping.'

She nudged him in the ribs with her elbow. 'The woman beside us is giving us quare looks,' she whispered.

'Will I explain that we're just married?'

'I'll kill you if you do.'

'Jaysus!' exclaimed Fergus, after seeing their accommodation. 'I thought we'd have had a jacks and a bath. Hang on a minute, I'll look for them,' he said leaving the room.

'Don't get short taken during the night, the jacks is miles down the corridor,' he informed her when he came back. 'I think we should cancel the walk. Come and lie down, Mrs Brady.' He took her in his arms and kissed her. 'My little wife. God, I love you,' he said manoeuvring her towards the bed. 'Will we get undressed and stay?'

'In one way I want to, only I'm starving. I want a cup of tea and a sandwich, maybe.' She sat up, then bent and kissed him. 'Come on, we won't stay long.'

'Our wedding night and all you can think of is food,' Fergus said, pretending to be annoyed.

'If I don't eat I'll be awake all night.'

'I want you awake all night.'

'If you don't get up I'll go down on my own.'

'OK, OK, Mrs Brady, you're the boss.'

In the bar they had a pot of tea, sandwiches and Fergus two whiskeys. 'Right so are you ready?' Fergus asked when the food and drink were finished.

'Isn't it funny,' said Sheila after they had made love for the second time, 'if we'd done this last night it'd have been a mortal sin and now . . .'

Fergus silenced her with a kiss. He was an experienced lover. Not that Sheila was aware of that. All she was conscious of was delirious pleasure. In the short intervals when they were not making love she wondered if it was the same for all couples. She didn't think so. Her mother and father would never have loved as she and Fergus did. No married couple that she knew could have experienced what she and Fergus had. Happiness would be written all over their faces. She was surprised and disappointed next morning when she looked in the mirror. Her face wasn't radiant, it looked tired and drawn.

By the time they arrived in Salisbury she was rested and radiant, having slept for most of the journey with her head on Fergus's shoulder. He had told her that the hotel they were to stay in was one of the best in the town. 'It's old, has beamed ceilings.' Then as the train approached Salisbury Station he asked Sheila had she ever heard of Constable.

'D'ye mean a policeman?'

'No, an artist.'

She shook her head. 'I should with all the time I spent in Art Galleries.'

'I didn't know you were interested in art.'

'I'm not. My father was and dragged me with him.'

'Anyway, what I was going to say is that Constable painted a famous picture of Salisbury Cathedral and it's believed that he painted it from our hotel.'

Sheila was more interested in the hotel than Constable

69

and said, 'If it's very old maybe we'll have a four-poster bed and a fire, wouldn't that be very romantic.'

'If you didn't think of all the people who had died in a bed that old.'

'Oh, you,' she said, pretending exasperation. 'You've no soul.'

The beds were twin and there wasn't an open fire. So Sheila and Fergus slept in one bed and she tossed the other one. 'Why are you doing that?' he asked.

'Why d'ye think – so the maid won't know we only used the one.'

He laughed and took her in his arms. 'I could eat you,' he said and kissed her.

She pushed him away. 'And I could eat my breakfast. Get dressed.'

They explored the city, had lunch, went to an afternoon film performance, had dinner in the Haunch of Venison, returned to the hotel. Fergus had two whiskeys and they went to bed early, made love several times before sleeping and again in the morning when they woke.

'I wish', said Sheila, lying with her head on his chest, 'that we could live like this for ever.'

'There's nothing to stop us,' Fergus said and kissed the top of her head. 'We'll love each other for ever and ever.'

He hired a car and they explored the county. He took her to the village where he hoped to rent a flat and to the garrison where eventually they would live in married quarters. She admired the rolling fields, the hills, while at the same time realising that it would be a lonely place in which to live. She told her thoughts to Fergus. He didn't disagree but assured her that she'd soon make friends, he would be home every day for his dinner. They'd go to Salisbury every week, there was a cinema, the mess, a club for the women, a dramatic society. 'Grand entertainment. And don't forget the nights.'

Chapter Nine

He took her to London to catch her plane. She clung to him, crying, telling him she'd die without him. He consoled her by promising that he'd chase up the flat. 'You'll be back within the month. The time will fly.'

Her mother had a small party for her homecoming. Everyone had questions to ask about London, the flying and Salisbury. They offered consolation for her being parted from her husband so soon and said they'd offer their prayers that she and Fergus would soon be together again.

She wallowed in their warmth until she went to her empty bed, where she cried for the loss of Fergus. Ginny heard her but didn't go in. It wasn't a little child or a lovelorn girl crying. What comfort could she offer?

The month didn't fly. She counted the days, the minutes, while waiting for word from Fergus that the flat was theirs. She was moody and silent in the house. Ginny knew what ailed her and also knew that no word of hers would console Sheila. Then, three days before the end of the month, the long awaited news arrived. 'Ma Ma,' she shouted, 'we've got the flat. Isn't that marvellous. I'm over the moon.' She began to cry. 'Don't mind me, they're tears of joy. Oh, Ma, I'm so happy.'

'So am I love,' said Ginny taking Sheila in her arms, holding back her tears of sorrow that her only child would soon leave home for ever.

'When will you be going over?'

'This minute if I could. Next week I've the wedding presents to pack and send. Next Friday at the latest.'

During the following week she missed her period but didn't tell Ginny. She'd worry and in any case it might be a false alarm. Though as her periods had never been irregular she didn't think so and several times, passing the

Baby Carriage Shop, she'd point out to Ginny a picture of Gene Tierney advertising a Dunkley perambulator, pretending it was the film star she was admiring.

When word got around the Buildings that she was going to live in England for the foreseeable future, girls she'd gone to primary school with, most of them now working in factories, flocked to the house to wish her well. Some brought small gifts – keepsakes, they said. Others gave her prayer leaflets for her to read daily for any special intention. Ginny was run off her feet making cups of tea and buttering slices of soda bread for the visitors.

Rosaleen made Sheila promise to write and gave her two Irish linen tea towels with Dublin scenes on them. And in Brown Thomas a collection was made for a going-away present. With the money Rosaleen bought two etchings – one of O'Connell Bridge and the other a view of Trinity College, Dublin. At the presentation she said, 'You're to look at these every single day so you won't forget us.'

'As if I ever could,' Sheila, wiping her tears, replied.

She shed many tears in the last few days. So many that Ginny held hers back and scolded Sheila. 'It's only to England you're going, not the ends of the earth. And me and your father'll be over a couple of times a year, and you and Fergus will come home from time to time. So stop bawling like a jackass.'

Her mother and father saw her off at Harcourt Street Station, from where she would travel to Rosslare, take the night boat to Fishguard and a train from there to Salisbury, where Fergus would meet her.

'I wish you'd gone on an aeroplane. You'd have been to London in an hour.'

'I told you, Ma, I'd be afraid of my life flying on my own. And I've got a bunk and the sea's going to be calm. Honest to God I'll be grand.' She hugged and kissed them both, and promised to write the minute she arrived. She stayed by the open window waving to them until they were out of sight, then found a carriage, went in and sat down.

Facing her was an old woman with a pleasant face who yawned and said, 'I'm jaded. I haven't closed my eyes for two nights. I was up in Belfast. My sister, Lord have mercy on her, died. And talk about a wake! I never saw the likes of it. Of course she had a big family and they gave her a grand send off. All the same I'm glad to be going home.'

'Have you far to go?' asked Sheila.

'Rosslare Strand, and yourself?'

'The harbour.'

'You're going over?'

'I am,' replied Sheila.

The old woman yawned again. 'I'll close my eyes,' she said. 'If I drop off you'll give me a shake when we get to the Strand.'

'I will of course.' She seems nice enough but all the same she could keep blathering for the next couple of hours, Sheila thought, and I'm not in the humour. All I want to do is think of Fergus. I can't wait to see him. God, I love him, I'm mad about him. I still can't believe the miracle that happened. There I was, nearly giving up hope of finding someone to love me. Thinking about going to England being a nurse and I walk into Bewleys and there he was. It was a miracle. Imagine if I'd decided to go into Roberts instead. It was meant to be – that's what me ma would say. 'God had a hand in it as He has in everything,' that's what she'd say as well.

At Rosslare Strand she woke the old woman and helped her on to the platform. 'God Bless you, child, and have a safe journey, and may wherever you're going be the place you want to be.'

'It is. It is,' said Sheila, 'oh, it certainly is.'

They bade each other goodbye and Sheila got back into the train for the ten minutes it would take to arrive at the harbour. On board she bought a cup of tea and ate the sandwiches she had brought with her. And all the while her thoughts were of Fergus and their reunion. When the boat sailed she went to her bunk and didn't wake until it docked at Fishguard.

Leaning out of the window as the train drew into Salisbury Station she saw him. Her heart leapt with joy. Fergus, her gorgeous man, her husband.

Sheila took an immediate dislike to the flat, which was drab and not very clean, and a greater dislike to the cranky landlady who lived on the premises. She rowed with her during the week when she was pegging clothes on the line. The landlady said it wasn't allowed. She was in bad humour anyway. Fergus couldn't make the village for his dinner. She was alone from eight in the morning until six in the evening. So she told the landlady no agreement had been signed and she'd hang out clothes whenever she liked.

But the quarrel upset her. So far she had only spoken to the old woman and to shop assistants. Asking for what she wanted to buy, please and thank you. She longed for the sound of an Irish voice, an Irish face. She longed to be back in Dublin instead of sitting on a sunken sofa staring at *The Monarch of the Glen*, which hung above the fireplace. But as it neared six o'clock her spirits rose. Soon Fergus would be home. So long as she had him she could put up with anything.

One day she made a meat pie. In school she had learnt how to make pastry and as she rubbed fat into the flour she remembered her mother making meat pies, how before she put on the top crust a cup or eggcup was placed in the centre of the pie dish, so she put in an eggcup.

Fergus sniffed when he came home. 'A queer smell, what is it?'

'That's the thanks I get and me after making you a delicious meat pie. I paid a fortune for sirloin steak into the bargain to be sure the meat wouldn't be tough. Take off your tunic and sit down.'

He kissed her and said the smell must be coming from

74

outside. She had taken great pains laying the table, using her wedding present cutlery and a cloth with matching napkins.

'Jesus Christ Almighty, what sort of a pie is that, Sheila?'

She was looking at the blue gravy and melted egg cup with lumps of sirloin steak adhering to it. 'Oh, my God, what happened? I did it the same as my mother did. I even remembered the eggcup.'

'I don't suppose your ma used a plastic eggcup.'

'How do I know what kind she used? How was I supposed to know it would melt? And you can stop laughing. It's not funny.' He couldn't stop laughing. Sheila flounced out, went to the bedroom and threw herself on the bed.

It wasn't long before Fergus followed her. 'I'm sorry,' he said and kissed her. She pretended reluctance but not for long. After they'd made love Fergus told her he would do the dishes, throw out the pie and then they'd go to the village and have fish and chips. 'Do yourself up,' he said, 'we'll call in the pub. A few of the blokes'll be there. I want to show you off.'

When she missed her second period she told Fergus. He was delighted and then concerned. 'You'll have to see the MO.'

'The who?'

'The medical officer, the doctor.'

Fergus treated her like a piece of fragile china, not allowing her to lift anything heavy, bringing her breakfast before he went to work: golden toast, segments of oranges and apples, propping her up on pillows. She felt like a princess. But only for a while. His fussing irritated her. 'For God's sake,' she said one day, 'I'm only having a baby, you're worse than my mother. And in any case when you're at work don't I have to lug home potatoes and my messages.' He looked like a little boy who had been slapped. 'Oh, love, I'm sorry and you're so good to me. I know I'm cranky but that's nothing to do with having a baby. It's living here, this flat, the oul landlady and I'm lonely. I miss Dublin. I go all day without talking to anyone. I swear to God I'll lose my voice.'

He kissed her. 'I didn't want to raise your hopes but having a baby will get us the quarters sooner than we thought.'

'Just as well, your woman warned me the other day that children are not allowed in the flat. Bloody oul bitch. And every Sunday she's off to her church.'

Her pregnancy was confirmed. She sent the news to her mother, who answered the letter by return post and promised that she'd come over when, please God, the baby was born. And that she wasn't to be flying in the face of God buying prams, cots or clothes before the child arrived.

Their quarters were allocated. Sheila was disappointed with how they were furnished. But they were big enough, two bedrooms, a living room, kitchen and downstairs bathroom. And she'd buy bright curtains and put out some of her wedding presents. 'Not holy pictures of the Sacred Heart in gores of blood,' she said aloud and continued voicing her thoughts. 'Sure that'd be as bad as *The Monarch of the Glen*.' The houses were surrounded by green fields. On some, sheep grazed – a novelty for Sheila. She was familiar with live cows on their way to the slaughterhouse in Dublin. She had seldom seen sheep. Another novelty was a view from the back bedroom of huge standing stones in a circle. Fergus told her it was Stonehenge, and that it was thousands and thousands of years old.

Her days were no longer lonely. On either side of her lived two friendly women, Babs and Dora, women in their thirties who had married during the war. Babs was a Cockney and Dora from Liverpool.

The day after she moved into her quarters the two women came to her door, bringing a plate of scones and a home-made pasty. They welcomed her to the road and offered to help in any way they could. From then on they would go to each other's house to drink coffee and gossip.

Sheila described Dublin to them and what her mother and father did for a living. Where she had worked and how she had met Fergus. Babs talked about her childhood in Bermondsey, her father who was a docker and her mother who had been killed when the docks were bombed. When she was eighteen Babs had joined the Land Army. She'd worked on a farm in Suffolk. At a dance in Long Melford she met her husband. They were married before D Day and she had died a thousand deaths until the war finished.

Dora's story was similar. She had met her husband in the camp where both were stationed. She was a private in the ATS and he a corporal with the REME. Babs's husband was also a corporal in an infantry regiment. Babs and Dora each had two children.

Sheila was fond of both women. They assured her that the hospital in which she would give birth was great. No shortage of staff so you were danced attendance on. The nurses were young, not like the crabby old things you'd come across in civilian hospitals. There were plenty of gorgeous fellas about, young doctors. And you could tell them and the nurses had a thing going.

They swapped magazines, gave Sheila tips on cooking and promised that when the baby was born they'd help all they could. They visited usually in the mornings, occasionally in the afternoons, but never once the men were home in the evening. If Babs's and Dora's husbands drank it was at home. There was a mess for junior NCOs, a dismal kip was how Fergus described it when Sheila commented on Dick and Charlie not going out in the evenings. 'If I was a corporal neither would I,' he had said. And Sheila wished he were a junior NCO, or that Dick and Charlie could use the sergeants' mess. Then she, Babs and Dora could put in the evenings. Talking and listening and laughing would distract her mind from thoughts of how often Fergus drank, how she missed Dublin: the liveliness of it; the streets and buildings she loved; the Liffey, but most of all the people and the laughter.

Her morning sickness passed, she felt well and was contented until one evening Fergus said he had to go to a mess meeting. 'It's official so I have to go but I'll be home early.' He went at half-seven and didn't come back until midnight. Sheila stayed up worrying at first, then getting angry. Angrier still when he arrived looking like her father: the same foolish smile. She wanted to rant and rave, scream, throw something at him, run home to her mother. Thinking of the baby, she worried that working herself up wouldn't be good for it. So without uttering a word she went to bed.

He was contrite the next morning, explained how he'd met someone he hadn't seen for years. They got talking and the time flew. 'A one-off, Sheil, honest to God.' She didn't answer him but after he'd gone to work she cried and told herself she'd married a man who liked his drink. But she'd cure him or die in the attempt.

At one of her later appointments at the clinic the doctor asked if there were twins in her family. 'Not as far as I know,' she replied.

'Well, Mrs Brady, there may very well be in the future. I can hear two heartbeats. Next month we'll do an X-ray and confirm it one way or another.'

'You mean', she asked, 'I'm going to have twins?'

'I'd take a bet on it,' the doctor said and smiled at her.

And twins she had, identical girls who, though born several weeks prematurely, had good birth weights. Fine healthy babies who only needed a very short time in incubators. She was in hospital for ten days and Fergus visited her every night. Her mother, he told her, was leppin' at not being allowed to visit her and her grand-children, and was cursing the army inside out. 'Wait'll you see the things she's bought for you and the girls. The spare bed is piled up with baby clothes, and there's a cot and pram.'

'I wanted to choose the pram myself. But that's me Ma all over.'

'You won't be disappointed, it's a great-looking yoke.'

She wasn't. 'Ma!' she exclaimed, 'how did you know that was the pram I wanted?'

'Wasn't I sick and tired every time we passed the Baby Carriage Shop being made to look at Gene Tierney's picture advertising a Dunkley pram? I had my suspicions then that you might be in the way.'

Ginny stayed for six weeks, not letting Sheila do anything except look after the twins. Arranging two pillows on her lap, laying the babies on them their heads facing inwards and lifted by Sheila to her breasts, their lips fastened on like limpets. They were baptised in the small corrugated Catholic church, christened Deirdre and Niamh.

During Ginny's stay Fergus was a model husband, only drinking an occasional glass of the Jameson's Ginny had brought over. Surrounded by her husband, mother, the babies and kind neighbours, Sheila was contented. But after her mother went home Fergus attended mess meetings or the pub in the village. She ranted and raved, cajoled and pleaded.

He made promises never to touch a drop again – promises he didn't keep. Madly in love with him, desirous of him always, Sheila forgave again and again. During the next five years they moved three times. One garrison the same as the next: miles from the nearest town; an unreliable bus service. But all basic requirements provided by the army: Churches, libraries, medical rooms, a NAAFI and in some camps a short street with small shops, newsagents, wool shop, cafés selling chips with everything. In one such street even a tattooing parlour. Every year, Ginny and sometimes Mr Brophy came for a week. Ginny never failed to say 'I wouldn't live here if you paid me. The house is grand and I know you're not in want. A week in the summer's one thing. Like a holiday. But to live here for more than that would send me mad. Nothing to see but fields. I have to hand it to you. I'd have run out of it long ago. Still, you're young and have your children and love your husband. At your age maybe I could have put up with it. All the same I wish Fergus wasn't in the army.'

On days when she was depressed Sheila would long for the buzz of Dublin and, when Fergus got drunk, consider going back there. But all it needed to change her mind was a sober Fergus making love to her.

When the twins were three and a half Fergus went to the School of Artillery to do a long gunnery course. It lasted eighteen months. If he passed he would be promoted to warrant officer as an assistant instructor of gunnery. He came home every weekend and was always sober during his stay. Sheila didn't quiz him as to whether or not he drank during the week. Nothing should spoil her weekend of bliss. Nothing did, except the twins waking during their lovemaking, and then only for a moment or two.

Fergus passed the course and was posted to Germany. Sheila would join him when married quarters were available. From other wives she had heard that Germany was a great posting. The overseas allowances were smashing, cigarettes and booze duty free. She was delighted at the prospect of travel, seeing new countries, different people. Even so she dreaded the separation while waiting for quarters. And without Fergus beside her in bed she wouldn't sleep. She slept always in his arms, safe and secure as when she was a child sleeping with her mother.

She confided her fears to Nin and Vida, her present neighbours. Nerves, they said it was. The first posting abroad always hit you like that. 'And don't you worry about hospital, love. God forbid you should get taken bad, you've got me and Vida,' Nin assured Sheila. 'We'd mind the twins, wouldn't we, Vi?'

'Course we would, kid,' Vida replied. 'And haven't you got a mam that would come over? What's worrying you is being without your old man. First week's the worst. But think on, chuck. Think about when you get to Germany. It'll be like your first night all over again. No kidding.'

When Sheila's mother heard about the posting she offered to come immediately. 'I'll be worried sick, thinking of you and the girls stuck in the back of beyond. I've half a mind to come straight away. Only I know you and your contrary ways. So I'll wait to hear from you.'

Sheila wrote and told her mother not to come. 'I'd love to see you. But you could arrive just as quarters were allocated. In any case postings will always be part of my life while we're in the army and I'll have to get used to them. What you can do is offer up a novena for us to get quarters sooner than later. I know you'll worry, but I'm OK really. You met my neighbours. They're grand. God forbidding all harm, if me or the girls were seriously ill you'd be one of the first to know.'

For comfort she had the girls to sleep one each side of her in the double bed. They knew that one day a letter would come from Fergus telling them he had accommodation. And there would be another letter with the date of their going to Germany. Every morning when they woke they wondered whether this was the morning the letters would come. From the window they watched for the postman. Scarcely had an envelope hit the floor when Sheila was there to pick it up.

Eventually the letters arrived. They cheered and laughed and danced round the kitchen, hands joined as if they were playing 'Ring 'a Roses' singing, 'We're going to Germany. We're going to Germany. Daddy'll come to meet us. Daddy'll come to meet us.'

Babs and Dora had helped her when she moved from her first quarters, minding the girls while she scoured the already immaculate house for the 'handing over'. So had other neighbours in future moves: minding the children, helping with the cleaning and always serving breakfast or lunch, depending on what time you were leaving the house.

Sheila had also taken her turn helping whoever was marching out. Now she was the one needing assistance. It was given generously by her present neighbours, Vida and Nin. When it was time to leave they kissed each other and the children. The same farewells she had bidden Babs and Dora, the same promises to keep in touch. The promises were seldom kept.

Chapter Ten

In November 1961 Sheila boarded a train at Liverpool Street, which would take her to Harwich from where she would sail to the Hook of Holland. From there another would take her to Germany and her adored Fergus. She sailed overnight and after disembarking and showing her passport, on which the twins were included, went to the regimental transport office. There she received instructions as to which train she would board and the coach in which she would travel. Three other women received the same instructions.

Their names were Lizzie, Beth and Yvette. They were unknown to each other but the four, including Sheila, were bound for Soltau in northern Germany, to be united with their husbands serving in BAOR. Lizzie had three children, Paula who was six, Susan five and Tom nearly two. Beth and Yvette didn't have children. Sheila's twins, Deirdre and Niamh, were five years old.

The women travelled in the same coach but in separate carriages. The carriages were pleasantly warm and roomy. Lunch and dinner would be served there, and coffee mid-morning and in the afternoon. From time to time they walked up and down the train corridor, sometimes to use the lavatory, sometimes to stretch their legs, and hoped that during their walks they might meet one of their fellow travellers. The coach in which they were travelling had white stickers pasted on the carriage windows. Soltau, they read. The women were familiar with the name. Their husbands had written several times that Soltau was where they would meet them.

Surreptitiously from their carriages they observed each other as they walked the corridors. Lizzie admired Sheila's black curls, her jaunty walk and skilfully applied make-up. Beth's light-brown bouffant hairstyle was collapsing. She wore no make-up. But once, as she passed, Tom was standing on the seat, secured by his mother's hold on his jumper, his lips pressing against the glass, saliva dribbling down the pane. Beth smiled and waved at him, and Lizzie thought she had a pleasant face.

Lizzie was already exhausted and uncomfortable. While Bob was away she had put on weight and had been persuaded by advertisements in her women's magazine to buy a Sarongster. The all-elastic corset promised a miraculous transformation of the figure. Lizzie chose a pale-blue one. It did flatten her belly but pushed the surplus flesh up past her midriff. The bulge was obvious beneath her maroon hand-knitted jumper and the Sarongster had a suffocating effect on her. 'For two pins I'd go to the lav and take it off. Let my belly escape, only my stockings would fall down.' She spoke her thoughts aloud. The children, absorbed by the picture and colouring books she had brought to keep them occupied, paid no attention. In any case they were used to hearing their mother talk to herself aloud. Her hair was also worrying her. It was thick, wiry and red. Two nights before leaving her previous quarters a friend had persuaded her to have a home perm. She did, but the result wasn't anything like the picture on the box of lotions and curlers. Her friend massaged Vita Point into the hair. 'Look at it now. That's better, isn't it?

And the night before you leave I'll set it again. You'll look gorgeous,' she said.

On the day she left for Germany it did seem to have improved, if only slightly. 'Tonight on the boat, smother it in Vita Point and set it again,' her friend had advised. So she did and it looked passable. But as they disembarked it rained. She didn't have an umbrella and in any case couldn't have carried it. One arm was filled with Thomas and Paula had hold of her hand. She thanked God that porters had seen to their luggage: all the towelling napkins for Tom, the zinc and castor oil ointment, spare knickers for the girls in case of an accident packed in a holdall and two big suitcases. The rain driven under the platform roof had saturated her hair, she saw after boarding the train and looking in the carriage mirror. A rusty red-haired Zulu, that's what I resemble, she thought.

She was exhausted from all the cleaning she had done to prepare the quarters for handing over, or as the official title had it, 'marching out'. The wives 'marched out' and the husbands in their new stations 'marched in' and took over the new quarters they had been allocated. Jammy buggers, Lizzie thought, nothing to it. Only signing that everything on the inventory was there. Not an ordeal such as the wives went through. She had never known an army wife who didn't dread 'marching out'. For weeks beforehand you were a nervous wreck. No matter how clean your quarters were you felt they weren't clean enough. Scrubbing, polishing, dusting the bed springs, scouring the window frames with a toothbrush and Vim. Peering anxiously at mattresses, pillows and cushions, seeing nonexistent stains of dribble, pee or, worst of all, blood.

The arrival of the quartermaster and his minions, puffed up with importance. Carrying their inventory and clipboards with blank sheets on which to itemise losses of War Department property; breakages of crockery above your allowance. Clinking cup against cup to detect cracks. Holding blankets up to the light to look for moth holes.

Bent double over beds inspecting the mattresses. Was it any wonder, she asked herself, that a ghosted article about an army wife had her waking in the middle of the night, haemorrhaging, and her first thought was: 'Oh, my God, the mattress will be destroyed.'

She had tried explaining to Bob how terrible it was to live in a house where nothing, not even the light bulbs, belonged to you, the anxiety women suffered.

'But love,' he'd said, 'there's nothing to worry about. If you lose or break something, even soil a bed, you only have to pay barrack damages. And as for not having your own furniture and things, that wouldn't work. It would cost the army millions to shift it round the world.'

'It's easy for you to talk. You don't have to do the handing over. You don't have to trudge to the stores to change burnt-out bulbs and clothes lines with more knots than rope. And no matter how clean you leave the quarters word goes round the camp that they were in a terrible state. Ask any of the women how they feel about not owning anything. How they feel about handing over. It's like having your knickers inspected.' Feeling less tired, she smiled as she remembered him laughing at her and saying, 'Liz, you don't half exaggerate. Inspecting your knickers, now I've heard everything.'

She relaxed, lit a cigarette and when she finished smoking stood up and looked in the carriage mirror, grinning at her reflection, her resilience rising. Sitting down again she lit another cigarette and thought how in a few hours she'd be seeing her beloved Bob. He'd hug and kiss her and the children. And later on hold her in her arms. They'd make love and her red wire-wool hair and her belly wouldn't matter one bit. Neither would any of the inconveniences of army life.

She had only one regret about the posting to Germany. It was for five years and she would sorely miss her mum and dad who at least once a month visited, or she went to see them. They were lonely when her two brothers emigrated to Australia. They wrote coaxing their parents to follow them out on the concession fare for close relatives. It would mean their father leaving Filton, where he was an aircraft fitter, and Mum leaving her job as a district nurse. But there were thousands of opportunities for skilled people in Australia.

Lizzie recalled that the idea was toyed with. No one was keen on leaving Bristol, she least of all. Bristol was her city. She knew it inside out. From the time she was six or seven her father had taken her most weekends to the city, to the zoo, for walks on the Downs, to Blaize and Berkeley Castles. In streets off Park Street to visit the Georgian and Tudor houses: not stately homes but big town houses once owned by wealthy merchants who made their fortunes from sugar plantations in the West Indies worked by the slaves the merchants owned.

She loved her fiery father. The gentlest of men except when he talked about the injustices to which poor unfortunate people had been subjected, white and black. Passing the mansions facing the Downs he would get red in the face and say, 'Thieving bastards the English were and still are, though their days are numbered.' On a trip down the river he showed her a fig tree growing out of the quay's wall. He pointed it out, saying, 'Imagine that, a cargo of figs for the gentry brought by the English from some country they'd overrun. A fig must have fallen, wedged in a crevice of the quay wall and seeded itself.'

As the train speeded on its way to Germany she recalled other places she and her father had visited. A museum with showcases of clothes worn by wealthy women in the eighteenth century. Hand-stitched gowns in oyster-coloured satin, lacy fans and satin slippers. She stayed so long in front of the showcases, marvelling at the exquisite clothes and accessories, that her father became impatient. 'That's enough, come round the corner and I'll show you what the husbands and fathers of those women were really like.' Around the corner were other showcases displaying man traps. 'Don't know what they are, eh?' Take the leg off you, part of it, anyway. Set for men not animals, though they did that, too. Poachers were the justification. But the majority were poor men wanting to snare a rabbit, a bird to feed their starving families. And the same land they were on had belonged to them in the past. Bastards! Robbers! They did it all over the world. And there's little or no recognition of the slaves they brought to Bristol two hundred years ago. There's a statue in a graveyard. It's of a black slave all dickeyed out in his flunky's gear. Eight or nine at the time he died. A mascot or pet monkey that's how he'd have been thought of. A little child. And his master, an insensitive, arrogant hypocrite, had a verse inscribed on his gravestone. I can't remember all of it but the gist was that he was a lucky boy to have been brought to England, converted to Christianity and so was assured of a place in heaven. Poor little sod, torn away from his family, sold by an African chief. Oh, yes there were money-grabbing Africans too. Sold to a slave trader and on to his charitable Christian master. I wanted to vomit when I read the verse.

'But the descendants of those slaves will come into their own one day. Maybe it'll take a long time. Seven hundred years it took for Ireland to get its freedom and then it wasn't all of it. Six of our counties robbed from us. My father and his drummed it into me how Ireland had never given up the fight and never would. And how the English had robbed and plundered every country on the face of the earth.'

She had asked him, 'Dad, if you hate the English so much why don't you go back to Ireland?'

I'll never forget his face, she thought. The look of astonishment on it. 'Hate the English? Me hate the English! I was born here. I got a good education and a great trade. I don't hate the blokes I work with, the men I drink with, the neighbours, the shopkeepers on the Gloucester Road. It's not them I'm on about. They didn't fare much better than the Irish Scotch or slaves years ago. It's the aristocracy, jumped-up gentry, land agents, land grabbers and robbers, English officials. It's them I hate.'

Lizzie had thrown her arms round his neck, kissed him and said she loved him.

After marrying Lizzie had never lived too far from Bristol. She and Bob were lucky that most of their postings were in or around Wiltshire. Now she faced the prospect of five years stationed in Germany. No more weekends nipping back to her lovely city. But she knew that with Bob no matter where in the world she was stationed she would be happy and content.

The children were still sleeping and she was sleepy. She folded her coat to make a pillow, lay down and positioned her legs in front of Tom so he couldn't fall off the seat.

In between dozing she recalled her meeting with Bob. At the time she was seventeen and a shop assistant. A shop that sold materials. She wasn't interested in the work but neither had she any ambition to find a different job. She loved clothes, make-up, going on dates, smooching in the back row of the cinema and dances. But always after a few dates she would pack the latest bloke in.

Her home life was happy. Her mother and father doted on her. They were still toying with the idea of going to Australia. She remembered how sometimes she thought that emigrating might be exciting. That she might meet in Australia a smashing-looking bloke. But her interest in the move never lasted for long.

Then she met Bob at a dance. She recognised him immediately, he had been friendly with her brothers. They were at the same school. She had always fancied him though she was only eleven and he fifteen.

Watching him in the ballroom she saw that he had hardly changed. He had always been tall and his hair curly. It was him all right. The MC announced an excuse me quickstep. Bob asked a girl up. They went twice round the floor. Her heart was racing, her face scorching and her legs shaky as she walked into the dancers and tapped him on the shoulder. His partner glared at her before letting go of him. He took her in his arms and they danced. He made small talk. 'Great band. The floor's good. Do you come here often?'

She knew he didn't recognise her. Last time he had seen her she was gawky, fat and had red pigtails. Now she wore make-up, her hair was short and she was dolled up to the nines. She wondered if she should introduce herself. Decided she would. For when the quickstep ended he might not ask for another dance and she couldn't cut in a second time.

'Lizzie, Lizzie Banister! I don't believe it. The last time I saw you were only that size,' he said taking his hand from her shoulder and indicating how small she had been. He was gorgeous. He had a gorgeous smell, not aftershave, nothing like that, his own gorgeous smell. She didn't remember him smelling like that when he used to come to her house before his family moved to another part of Bristol. When the music stopped he took her to the bar and they drank orange juice talking between sips about her brothers and how her parents were thinking of going to Australia, if she was happy to go with them.

'And will you?' he asked.

She shrugged and replied, 'It all depends,' on you, she was thinking as she spoke. He said he'd like to see her parents again. 'I'm sure you'd be welcome. I'll ask them. Ring me during the week.' She wrote the shop's telephone number on a page he tore from a notebook. She wondered as he took her home if he would kiss her. He did, but only on the cheek. Even so she knew that she had fallen in love with him. When they were parting she reminded him about telephoning.

He came to the house during the week, and the next week, and the next one, by which time they were kissing passionately. She promised she would wait for him while he was doing his National Service. It was to begin the following month.

'But you're too old. Eighteen I thought was when you were called up for National Service.'

'Yeah, you're right. That's the usual age. I went to college, Bolton, so my call-up was deferred. But I didn't get a degree. I lived it up while I was there. That's my excuse, anyway. The truth is I didn't have what it took.'

Her mother and father treated him like a son, and all talk of emigrating finished. She stretched and yawned and said aloud, 'And that's how it all started.'

Sheila read the twins a story but refused to read a second one. Instead she painted her nails and thought about Fergus.

They had been married for six years, had furious rows, kissed and made up. If the twins, as they grew older, weren't about they'd make love whether they happened to be on boats, trains, the floor, in the bath, on the dining-room table. Only once she had refused him. They were walking home from a summer ball. It was almost morning. They had danced all night, eaten delicious food, had oysters and champagne cocktails. She wore a short evening dress of lime-green organza over a grey silk bodice and underskirt. Languorously, still tipsy, arms around each other they took a short cut through a little copse. Fergus stopped walking, turned her to him and kissed and caressed her. The organza and silk rustled as he raised her skirt. Still kissing, they lowered themselves on to the short, velvety grass and then, as he was about to enter her, Sheila had a vision of St Patrick, his foot crushing the life out of a snake. 'Jesus, Mary and Joseph!' she exclaimed, taking her lips from Fergus's mouth. 'Thank God I remembered in the nick of time. I'm in England not Ireland.'

Fergus, left high and dry, was irate. 'For Christ's sake, Sheila, what ails you?'

She was up off the grass rearranging her clothes. 'The

snakes,' she said. 'There's snakes in England. Wouldn't I have looked great going to the hospital with a snake bite in my arse.'

'What are you laughing at, Mammy?' the twins asked in unison.

'Nothing, darlings, just remembering something funny.'

'Tell us.'

'I will when you're big girls, read your comics.'

She knew there was a fourth woman in the coach, also travelling to Soltau. A waiter who had brought lunch told her. So far there had been no sign of her. Then, as she was thinking this, Yvette came along the corridor.

The train was travelling very fast, rocking from side to side, so that Yvette had to walk slowly. Outside Sheila's carriage she paused and steadied herself with a hand on each side of the corridor. She glanced quickly in, then away again. It gave Sheila time to have a good look and, she thought, God, she's gorgeous. I wonder if that titian hair is her own colour? Probably, it's the same colour as her eyes and she didn't buy her suit in C&A. Having worked at Dublin's Brown Thomas, Sheila knew clothes. Every day she studied and admired outfits she could never afford. The cloth, the cut, the accessories to complement them. How, she wondered, could this woman whose husband must be the same rank, earning the same money as Fergus, afford such clothes.

For a brief moment she wondered if her husband was an officer. But no, she told herself, if he were the woman would be travelling first class. She watched for her return but was either distracted by the twins or the woman was returning to her carriage further down the train. She hadn't seen her make the initial trip.

Lizzie also saw the beautiful woman. Her spirits sank as she noted the sleek head and perfectly arranged chignon. She felt a wreck again.

Beth too, caught a look at the beautiful, elegant woman.

91

Admired her, wondered if she was going to join her husband. She supposed so. Maybe they would become friends. Her bouffant hair had drooped. Before they arrived at their destination she would backcomb it, tease it into some sort of shape. Not that Bill would pay much attention to her hairstyle. Like herself, he would be so overcome with joy at them being reunited as not to notice anything but her presence. She'd had a letter from him a couple of days ago. He had taken over the new quarters and wrote that they were smashing. But she'd wait and see. Bill wasn't the best judge of what was a nice house. So long as it had the basic requirements that was OK by him.

Chapter Eleven

It was beginning to snow. Sheila watched the flakes float down, those that settled on the glass melting instantly. She admired the Dutch houses, their beautifully curtained windows and the plethora of plants on the indoor windowsills.

'Arnhem', she read, as the train passed through a station. Arnhem, she thought, it must be the same one. Where Terry was killed. Many and many a time she'd heard her mother tell the story of what had happened to Terry. 'A lovely young fella, he was a messenger boy for Pierce Redmond, on a three-wheel bike with a big basket in the front.' Sheila could in her mind hear her mother's voice as clear as if she were sitting with her in the carriage. 'When he first got the job he was that small his feet barely reached the pedals. Sometimes if he was going up a slope you'd see him cycling standing on the pedals. But then he got a good stretch and could manage the oul bike.

'I used to deal in Pierce's shop and of a Friday Terry would bring the order. You wouldn't remember him. He joined up as soon as the war broke out, you were only three then. He doted on you. Forever hooshing you up in the air and never came empty-handed, always a bar of chocolate for you. He'd tell me you reminded him of his little sister who was killed by a bus. They were an unfortunate family. His poor father was hanging alive in consumption.

'Anyway, Terry joined the British army. His mother encouraged him. All belonging to her had been soldiers. She'd talk the head offa you about the Great War and the Boer War, and which of her brothers, uncles or cousins were in them. And she'd had a brother who'd been an India man. He died out there.

'You should have seen the change in Terry when he came on leave. He'd filled out, was earning treble what Pierce paid him and looked better than at any other time in his life. He'd always drop in to see us and bring something for you. He loved the army. It was a great life, he said and it was the first time he ever had a bed to himself.

'Then I heard from his mother that he was in the Parachute Regiment. He'd have to do a course and at the end be entitled to wear a red beret and a parachute badge on the sleeve of his tunic. When he got his red Beret you'd think it was the Irish Sweepstake he'd won. His mother was delirious with joy. But the poor child didn't wear his beret for long. Him and hundreds more jumped from the sky and landed in the fires of hell.'

Her mother's voice faded and Sheila recalled her irritation when she was growing up at having to listen to Ginny's stories, and how many a night since she married, when Fergus was in a pub or the mess, she'd have given anything for her company and storytelling.

Poor Terry, she thought, floating down from the sky like a snowflake and like a snowflake on the window pane he too was obliterated. She made the sign of the cross and said a prayer for his soul to rest in peace. Then she hugged herself as she anticipated her reunion with Fergus, her adored and adoring husband, even if he did drink too much. It had been a lousy nine months' separation, missing his arms holding her, his kisses and loving.

The twins fell asleep. Sheila stretched out on her seat with a coat for a pillow. Soon the warm carriage, the comfortable seat and the rocking of the train lulled her to sleep and she dreamt of Dublin. She was back in her beautiful Dirty Dublin. She was home. She was happy. A whimpering twin woke her. 'Shh,' said Sheila, 'it's all right. Go back to sleep.' The whimpering stopped and she closed her eyes, trying to re-enter the dream but it eluded her.

She felt miserable and talked to herself. 'I'll never get used to being away from it. At the back of my mind it's always there. Why couldn't Fergus have been anything but a soldier? A bus driver, a carpenter, a clerk in the Corporation like my father. I'd have loved him just the same. If we lived in Ireland even his drinking wouldn't bother me so much. Years and years of army camps, army quarters and I'll lose my mind. But as me ma says, "You make your bed and you lie on it." I suppose that's right. It's always been that way for women of her age. On the other hand times are changing. Maybe younger women won't lie on the bed for ever.'

The train stopped while German customs officers came aboard to inspect passports.

Later dinner was served. After it, Sheila's mood lifted. 'Only another hour,' she told the twins, 'and we'll be there and Daddy will be waiting for us. I bet he'll have bought you lovely presents.' The girls clapped their hands and whooped with joy. The three of them talked and laughed until Niamh complained that it was dark. 'So it is,' Sheila agreed. 'I'll fix it.' She switched on the lights and pulled down the blinds. 'Now, isn't that grand and cosy?'

Beth wasn't fashion conscious. She bought from chain stores and catalogues, wore a lot of pink and blue, pretty clothes, blouses with frilly necklines more suitable for an older woman. While she was doing her housework she wore enveloping aprons, coarse, heavy ones for washing clothes and cleaning grates. But always before Bill came home she tidied her hair, dabbed a powder puff over her face and put on a frilly pinnie when serving his meal. Her mother had always done the same.

Beth was born and reared in a small Midlands town about twenty miles from Birmingham. She was born when her parents were in their forties, by which time her two older sisters were married and living in America. Her father was retired and her mother had never worked.

Although her parents had promised her a bicycle if she passed the Eleven Plus and she had worked very hard, she failed the exam. The bicycle was her consolation prize. Bill also failed and they both went to the secondary modern school.

They had always known each other. Their families went to the same Baptist chapel, the children to Sunday School and to social gatherings arranged by the chapel. In their new school they became firm friends and, before they left, childhood sweethearts. Bill got an apprenticeship as a motor mechanic and Beth went to a secretarial college.

Then Bill joined the army, where he was found to have an above average IQ. He was earmarked for promotion. Made up to bombardier and eventually sent on a long gunnery staff course to Larkhill. The course lasted eighteen months. He came third in the final exam and was promoted to warrant officer. In the meantime Beth qualified as a shorthand-typist with typing speeds of 50–60 words a minute. She had no difficulty finding a job. With her salary and the huge increase in Bill's they married and he applied for married quarters.

Their families crowded the railway station to send them on their honeymoon to the Isle of Man. Before the wedding they had decided not to have children for the time being. 'We need to get a few bob together love,' Bill told her. The decision not to have children was his. He was posted to Brecon, Beth got a job with a local solicitor and lived with her parents while waiting for married quarters. It was six months before they were allocated. She liked the little Welsh market town. Bill left early in the morning and didn't come home until evening. So she got a job as secretary to the NAAFI manager.

Everywhere she went there were babies and pregnant women. She became broody. They'd been married for eighteen months when she broached the subject of starting a family.

'But we agreed, love.'

'I know we did, but now all I can think of is a baby. Our baby.'

'I wasn't going to tell you this, so far it's only a rumour – I may get a posting to Germany. If a rumour's all it is then we'll try for a baby. But if the posting comes off we'll have a rethink. From Germany we could see a lot of Europe and it mightn't be wise hauling a young baby around. But if I do go to BAOR we'll be there for five years. Bags of time for having children.'

She was thrilled when the posting came through. 'We can start now. Oh, Bill, just think, this time next year we'll have our own baby.'

'Hang about, Beth. In the first place I'll be leaving you on your own maybe for months. We might have to wait six or nine months for quarters. And didn't I say how we could do a bit of travelling in Germany? Not a good idea that, with a baby.'

'I wouldn't mind. Nowadays people travel everywhere with babies.'

'No, it's not on. I want you to enjoy yourself over there.'

She was angry now and shouted, 'No, it's not for my sake – it's the bank book you're thinking of. Each time we put money in there's a gloating look in your eye and I'm getting older.'

'Say what you like, it's only you I'm thinking of. And come off it about your age, you're only twenty-five.'

The following week he came home one night looking down in the mouth. 'Are you not well? You look terrible,' Beth said. 'Maybe you're coming down with flu.'

He undid his gaiters and boots before answering, 'I wish it was only flu.'

She made tea for both of them. Lit two cigarettes and placed one between his lips. 'Drink some of the tea, then tell me.'

'The posting to Germany was a rumour – or rather, as far as I'm concerned. Chalky White's got it.'

'But that's not fair – he's just come back from Singapore.'

Bill shrugged. 'You don't argue with the army. Just soldier on.'

For his sake Beth was disappointed but silently she rejoiced. Now there was no reason why they shouldn't start a family. They made love frequently. Each month she was convinced her period wouldn't start. Each month it did.

'It's early days,' Bill consoled her and a neighbour she had confided in told her they were probably trying too hard.

'What you should do is go home to your mam for a couple of weeks. Sometimes a separation works wonders.'

After six months, and still not pregnant, she went to the doctor. He was an elderly Welshman with whom she had recently registered. 'You didn't choose an army doctor. Any particular reason?'

'They're all so young,' she told him. 'I'd feel embarrassed.'

He listened to her tale of woe, smiled and assured her that six months was a very short time to be trying for a baby. 'I have patients who've waited several years before conceiving. Not many, I grant you. Usually it's the other way about, but it does happen.'

'There must be something wrong with my insides, Doctor.'

'I doubt it.'

'But with each month that passes I'm getting older.'

'Twenty-five's an optimum age to conceive. What makes you think otherwise?'

'I read it in my magazine that the older you are the less likely to conceive.'

'You misread that – or the journalist hadn't done her homework. It's when you're thirty-five things start to slow down.'

'Aren't there any tests I could have?'

'Lots of tests but strictly speaking you wouldn't qualify. At least a year, preferably two, is the required time before you'd be tested.'

She started to cry. 'Please,' she pleaded. 'My husband could be sent abroad. I might not see him for a long time. It wasn't really my idea that I shouldn't have a baby. I could pay to see a specialist. Please.'

'Don't cry,' he told her. 'Let me have a look at you, go there behind the screen and take off your skirt.' She looked healthy. But without an examination you never could tell. There could be a heart problem and nature in her great wisdom had decided against this girl reproducing. Of course, nature slipped up sometimes. All the pregnant women he'd seen before miracle streptomycin and antibiotics. Women with TB, leaky heart valves, damaged kidneys. Women who needed babies like holes in their heads. Women who inevitably miscarried or died giving birth. He took her blood pressure, sounded her heart and lungs, palpated her belly for signs of cysts or fibroids. It was as he had thought. She was a healthy young woman.

He left her to get dressed and debated in his mind what to do. Then decided he would explain the situation: husband in the army; possible separation for a year; the woman's desperation for a child. Roper was a compassionate man. He'd see her.

The tests began the following month. In the same month Chalky White was killed in a helicopter crash in Germany and Bill took his place on the gunnery team and was allocated the quarters when Chalky's wife had to move out. He left England in November. Beth would join him when she handed over her quarters in Brecon. Her medical records would be sent on.

Yvette also stared through the window at the snow that didn't settle. Dreading being reunited with Victor: a man she loathed; a man who bought her expensive clothes; a man who only on rare occasions let her mix with her neighbours. The majority were women who dressed within their means, bought their clothes in chain stores, while she, at Victor's insistence, dressed like a model. Her appearance and Victor's ban on her being friendly towards her neighbours alienated the other wives.

When it was a mess function, which they were obliged to attend, he contrived to be late so that the tables were filled. Another would be found for them, fitted in at the back of the room where there was little or no contact with other guests.

The train sped on and her thoughts with it. Why was he so secretive? What did he fear that she would tell the other women? There was nothing to tell. She knew nothing about him except his brutality: punching her on parts of her body where the bruises wouldn't show; more often than not committing buggery on her but who could she tell that to? Her mind was permanently filled with thoughts of being without him. A fatal car accident. An accident with the gun, a premature, when the shell exploded before leaving the barrel, she tried to block from her mind – for such a catastrophe would kill many other men.

She prayed for a solution as to how she could leave him. Find somewhere to live after the army evicted her. Find work to support her. But when she contemplated the obstacles she was overwhelmed with doubt and confusion. If he injured her seriously it might be possible. If sodomy were a reason for a divorce, if he was unfaithful, or she was. She was sunk in a morass, pinned down, imprisoned, in fear of being homeless, not able to find work, for she had no skills. She had left school without finishing her education.

She let her thoughts take her back to happier, carefree days. To 1950 when she was fifteen, in grammar school. In a green gymslip, cream shirt and matching green blazer, popular with teachers and pupils. She and her parents still proud that she had passed the Eleven Plus. She wore her glorious auburn hair in two long plaits, was happy with her parents, adored her easygoing mother.

Her father was irritable and moody. Mam said it was because he'd been gassed in the First World War. He never looked healthy but kept down his job in local government. He was very involved in his church. A sidesman, in charge of the building fund, always at Father Deegan's beck and call. He neither smoked nor drank and, though not popular with the men in his office or in general, was respected and regarded as 'a big Catholic', a term used by the Welsh for people like him. He was proud of Yvette but never demonstrative. He had never been, so she didn't miss it.

Her mother was warm and affectionate, hugged and kissed her, made sacrifices to buy her an occasional dress and shoes for weekends.

Yvette had no fault to find with her life – except for Sean. He was a sixth former, tall and blond, popular with boys and girls alike. She thought of him as a god and had done so since she was thirteen, although she believed he wasn't aware of her existence. She seldom saw him after school. He wasn't a Catholic and church was the only place where on Sundays they would have seen each other. She consoled herself that in any case she wouldn't see much more of him. He was being coached for the

Oxbridge entrance exam and interview. Everyone said he would walk it. Then, she knew, he'd walk out of her life for ever.

The town in which she lived was small, many of the inhabitants were Catholics, descendants of Irish people who'd come to escape the famine in Ireland during the 1840s. It was fronted by an enormous, safe, sandy beach. In between the beach and a range of Welsh hills the little town huddled: rows and rows of small terraced houses where the women waged a constant battle against the polluting dirt blown by the wind from the smoke stacks of iron and copper works, and would be added to by the new steel works being completed. Windows were cleaned weekly, the front doorstep scrubbed daily, the garden path and outside pavements swilled and brushed with buckets of soapy water.

From the works men had brought home iron posts, some as high as twenty feet. One was fixed into a patch of earth outside the back door, the other at the end of the garden. Sometimes the poles were made more secure with a covering of cement. Agile men shinned up, attached pulleys, threaded ropes through, descended and repeated the process at hand height. On washday the bedclothes and other clothing was pegged 'tidy' to the line and hoisted almost as high as the roof, where they flapped and danced in the wind, where passing women could see and comment on the standard of the wash. Favourably or, on those not snowy white, contemptuously: 'Look at the grain on that. Ashamed to peg it out I'd be.' The descendants of the Irish immigrants, wanting to escape their initial labelling of 'Dirty Irish', worked hard at washing.

The town didn't offer much in the way of recreation: a few small cinemas, a main and smaller library, church halls for dances and socials. But religious needs were well catered for. Several Anglican churches, one Catholic and many different branches of nonconformist chapels. There had been, until recently, a synagogue.

In the summer, if the weather was reasonable, the beach drew the crowds of young and old. There were sand dunes where courting couples found privacy, older people shelter from the wind. Young boys made dens and defended them. On the flat of the beach games of cricket, football and rounders were played. The girls positioned themselves where they could watch.

That was when Sean and Yvette had their first contact. She was propped on an elbow, ostensibly watching the football match, but had eyes only for him. She had borrowed a swimsuit, a turquoise, skirted one. Sean's body, from many games played on the sand, had a golden tan. She was dazzled by its beauty, longed to touch it, ached for him to glance in her direction. Then the ancient football with many knots in its laces flew through the air and hit her in the face. She fell back on to the sand. For a minute she thought she had been blinded. She rubbed her eyes, getting sand into them. They stung and watered.

'Sorry about that. It was an accident,' Sean said, kneeling beside her.

Chapter Twelve

From then on Sean acknowledged Yvette in school and in the Italian café where many of the pupils went after school. Sometimes he walked her part of the way home. He asked her to go with him to the pictures. That wasn't possible, she explained. Her father didn't allow her to go out in the evenings.

He sat the Cambridge entrance examination and later went for interview. School broke up for the Christmas holidays. This gave Yvette the opportunity to meet him in the café when she went shopping for her mother. He bought her coffee and cakes, and introduced her to smoking. He was pessimistic about his acceptance at Cambridge. But Yvette knew he lived in hope. He would know before Christmas. She prayed he would get in, but knew immediately she saw his face that he hadn't. He was pale and drawn. She thought he had been crying, but put on a show of bravado. There were other universities he could go to.

He pleaded with her to go out with him and she agreed, telling her parents she was going to confession. Permission to go to confession would never be refused. They walked along the river bank, he held her close for a long time and told her he loved her.

Knowing she couldn't use the confession excuse more than once a week, Yvette told her mother about Sean. How she loved him, how upset he was that he failed to get into Cambridge. 'Mam, I have to see him. I have to. I'm afraid he might do something terrible. Help me, Mam, please.'

'But love, what'll we tell Dad?'

'You could say I was babysitting for Mrs O'Dwyer. Her mother's in hospital, she broke her hip yesterday.'

'I suppose so. But you couldn't stay out late. The hospital visiting finishes early. And supposing your father bumped into O'Dwyer?'

'Mam, how could he? O'Dwyer works afternoons, then goes to the pub. How could Dad ever see him? Please, Mam, just until Sean gets over his disappointment, please.'

'Let me think about it, love,' her mother said. 'But tell me this, the weather's very cold. Where could the pair of you go?'

'Just walking, up town, down the beach. Just talking and walking.'

Her mother thought about it and agreed. 'But not a minute later than half past seven, promise me that?'

They walked and talked, and Sean took her into doorways in buildings by the river that she had never known existed, where they embraced and kissed . . . and gradually became more intimate. Desire engulfed her. For many nights with tremendous effort Sean restrained himself. Then, one night, he didn't and Yvette didn't attempt to restrain him, so carried away was she on the pleasure of his foreplay, and stood on trembling legs facilitating him to enter her. It hurt and she cried, and was disappointed, having believed what was happening would suddenly become magical. More so than what had gone before.

He cried with her. Apologised for hurting her. Telling her how he had never done it before. 'Maybe I didn't do it right. I love you. I would never want to hurt you. I don't suppose you'll come out with me any more.'

She reached and kissed his lips. 'Oh, love, of course I will. And the pain is gone, only a little bit sore. I'll come whenever I can and definitely tomorrow night. Dad won't mind me babysitting two nights in a row.'

Her father told her she was a good girl, doing a neighbour a charitable turn. 'That's what's wrong with the world, not enough charity in it. You can oblige Mrs O'Dwyer any time you like. How is her mother?'

Yvette's face was scarlet with the shame of her deceit. 'She's doing fine. Had the operation. She's eighty-three.'

'A dangerous age for major surgery. I'll ask Father Deegan to say a prayer for her.'

Yvette's mother said, 'Mrs O'Dwyer was telling me she's making a great recovery. Her heart's strong and she never smoked a day in her life, which will stand to her. She won't be out for a while yet. Go to the annexe to build up her strength.'

'Remember that, Yvette,' her father said. 'Never put a cigarette in your mouth. And you carry on with the baby minding.'

She met Sean every night until the one before Christmas Eve. He gave her a bottle of lavender water, told her he'd have to spend Christmas and Boxing Day at home, they always did. But he'd see her after the holidays.

They had made love every night. It didn't hurt any more but she still found the lead up to intercourse the most pleasurable.

After Christmas she went to the café. He wasn't there. She went in on three other days. A mate of Sean's gave her a letter. 'It came to our house. It's Sean's writing and the postmark's London.'

She knew as she tore open the letter that it was bad news. He had written:

My Love,
   I've packed in school. I couldn't face going back. All the false sympathy. I know it's foolish but I had my heart set on Cambridge. I'm going to join the army. I'd ask you to marry me but what would we live on and where would we live? I'll do well in the army, I can feel it in my bones. I might even get a commission.
   I'll write to you every day and as soon as I'm settled we'll think about getting married. That's if you'll have me. I love you so much. I want you for my wife. I want you to be the last thing I see before I go to sleep and the first thing I see when I open my eyes.
   I want to see your glorious hair spread on the pillow. I want to see your body. I want you to sleep in my arms, feel your sweet breath on my cheek. I want you always and for ever.

Tears poured down her face.

Sean's mate, embarrassed by her crying, went and got a handful of paper serviettes. 'Dry your eyes. Everyone's looking at you. They'll think your mam or dad's dead. Would you like a coffee?'

She shook her head, sniffed, dried her eyes and blew her nose. 'I'm sorry,' she said.

'Oh, that's OK. Have a fag.' He gave her a Player's Weight. 'So where is he, what's he done?'

'Joined the army.'

'The bloody fool. The bloody army. He could have gone to any university. His National Service would have been deferred, maybe finished altogether by the time he graduated. Where is he now?'

'There's no address. He'll send it next time.'

Next time was the following week. The address was a barracks in Aldershot where Sean was doing his basic training. Then there would be another course before he went to Korea. He apologised for not writing sooner. His arm had been swollen and sore from the injections and his right hand nearly paralysed from all the bulling. He explained: 'That's polishing buttons and boots.'

He didn't write every day but several times a week. Yvette went back to school. None of her friends knew that she had been going out with Sean so she was saved the questioning. His mate, who knew they'd been seeing each other, continued to bring her letters. He told her Sean's mother and father were frantic with worry. But as he was over eighteen the police weren't interested.

The waiter brought her dinner of overcooked beef and soggy Brussels sprouts, and told her they would arrive in Soltau in an hour. She put Sean back in the special part of her mind where she stored her sad and happy memories.

The train arrived on time. Beth, Sheila and Lizzie lowered the windows and leant out. Yvette didn't. It was snowing. The husbands were waiting.

Sheila called loudly, 'Fergus, Fergus, here, I'm here.'

She lifted a twin in each arm. 'Look, look, there's your daddy over there.'

Fergus lifted down his twin daughters, then Sheila, they kissed and hugged. Bob helped Lizzie and his children down. They kissed and embraced again and again, crying and laughing at the same time. Wrapped in Bill's arms, Beth's tears of joy ran down her face unchecked. The last one to get out was Yvette. Over the donkey-brown suit she wore a three-quarter-length ocelot coat. Victor held her close and kissed her passionately.

While the four women's luggage was being unloaded introductions were made.

'Well, I am surprised', said Fergus, 'that you travelled all that way in the same coach and didn't get acquainted. Especially that Sheila didn't. Not a bit like her.'

'Never mind,' said Victor. 'They've five years to get to know each other.'

'We better get a move on. You'll freeze standing here. The wind's from the Steppes,' Lizzie's husband advised.

Parked in the station's concourse were three army staff cars and a new green Citroën.

'I haven't seen that before,' said Fergus, as the car carrying Yvette and Victor drove away.

'It's gorgeous. What's it called?' Sheila asked.

'A Citroën, a French yoke. Two bloody cars they have now.'

'Is he rich?' Sheila asked Fergus as they set out for the camp in a staff car.

'Golden balls? Oh aye, he's rich.'

'How?'

'A legacy according to him. I think it's the Black Market, coffee, tea, sugar, fags, petrol coupons. The Germans pay over the odds. Did you see her coat? That cost a bob or two.'

'What's he like to get on with?'

'Don't know, really. He's in an infantry regiment.

Something peculiar about him. Uses our mess more than his own.'

Victor told Yvette how beautiful she was. 'I saw Fergus giving you the eye, but you're mine, never forget that. I'd kill you, you know that.'

'Yes,' replied Yvette. 'I know that but I've never looked at another man. I love only you,' she lied.

'Keep it that way. The day after tomorrow Charley's wife has invited you and the others to a coffee morning so you can get to know each other.'

'Who is Charley?'

'The gunners' senior warrant officer. Nothing to do with me.'

'Then why am I invited?'

'A friendly gesture. We're living on the same block as the others. You can go. But keep your distance. No making bosom pals. You know the drill.'

Once, a long time ago, Yvette had been a Catholic. When she married Victor he had forbidden her to go to church. But she still prayed. Now, as they sped along the autobahn, she prayed silently: 'Holy Mary, Mother of God, deliver me from this devil. Show me a way of escape.'

Army quarters in England were pre-war, small rooms, small windows, poky and dismal, the floor covering top-quality linoleum in a drab shade of brown. Porcelain sinks, wooden draining boards, inadequate electric fires mounted on bedroom walls. Serge curtains, dark-green or airforce-blue. All quarters' furniture identical.

Bicycles were the popular means of transport between work, home and the mess. Childless women rode bicycles. Those with children pushed prams or go-karts and walked sometimes miles to the nearest village or NAAFI. Most camps were situated near a bus stop where buses, according to the timetable, came every hour. But unlike Mussolini's trains they seldom ran to time.

Soldiers and their wives didn't have high expectations and generally were content with their lot, so they were expecting similar houses to those they had left in England. Only Bill had written that the German quarters were super and Beth hadn't believed him.

Lizzie, Beth and Sheila were momentarily struck dumb when they saw the attractive block of four modern houses. Each one was fronted by a grass plot, red-brick steps led up to the front door, which was stained to look like oak and had brass fittings. There were also glass panels inset in the door, above which was an attractive white bowl light fixture.

Their husbands opened the doors. A waft of warm air enveloped them as they entered the houses. Lizzie cried with delight as she went from room to room. Bob following her carrying the sleeping Tom, Susan and Paula, opening drawers and cupboard doors.

'Oh, Bob, it's beautiful. I've never seen such a kitchen except in magazines, everything fitted and a fridge. I've always wanted a fridge and see the size of it. It's as big as me. Cupboards and counters the whole way round and central heating. Oh, Bob, it's fabulous but where's the cooker?'

'Here,' he said, going to a white enamelled box-like fixture and lifting its cover.

Lizzie gasped, 'An electric cooker. I've never cooked on one. It's fabulous. I'll never say a bad word about the army again.' She put her arms round him and said, 'I love you.'

Susan and Paula were exploring the living room emitting squeals of joy. 'Better see what they're up to.' Bob carried the still sleeping Tom into the combined living and dining room where Susan and Paula were using the three-seater sofa as a trampoline.

With Bob being either on practice camp for weeks at a time and then in BAOR for months, Lizzie did the correcting and chastising. Now, exhausted from the journey and delighted amazement having seen her new home, she wasn't up to tackling the children. So Bob took over. 'Eh, you two, stop that at once,' he roared. The girls were terrified. They'd never heard their father roar before. In fact, they'd seldom heard his voice. They collapsed in crumpled heaps.

Lizzie came to their rescue. 'Anyone would think you were dealing with rookies on the square. They're not used to bawling and yelling. Are the beds made?'

'Yeah, I did them this afternoon.'

'Then lay Tom on the sofa and warm some milk. I'll take the girls up. One night without a bath won't kill them, nor sleeping in their vests and knickers. Up you get, come on. Daddy'll bring you hot milk.'

She shepherded the sleepy little girls up the stairs and into an amazing white bathroom with shower, mixer taps and a continental lavatory. First time she'd used one had been on the train. Paula had cried when her poo didn't go down into the bowl. Lizzie didn't think much of the design. Too easy, she thought, for curious two or three-year-olds to do a bit of finger painting.

They were in bed asleep before Bob brought up the milk. 'What'll I do with Tom?' he asked.

'Bring him up, and a jug of milk and my baby bag. I'll have to change him.'

'It's a pity to disturb him.'

'He'll get a sore bum if I don't. There's a sterilised bottle in the bag. You'll boil the milk?'

'Of course I will.'

'Then bring him and the things up, wash your hands, put the milk from the jug into the bottle. If you stick it in his mouth before I undo his nappy he won't waken. Oh, and put the lights out, I don't want to go downstairs again, do you?'

Naked in their bed, he whispered as if someone might overhear them, 'You've been taking the pill?'

110

'Yes,' she lied, 'for a whole month. You have to take it for that long before it'll work.'

'If you knew how I missed this. Every night and when I'd waken in the morning.'

She wound her legs tighter round him, forgot they were having intercourse without contraception and gave herself up to the moment.

Chapter Thirteen

Beth and Sheila were as impressed and delighted with their quarters as Lizzie. They inspected the bedrooms, liked the white furniture, the tallboy on which the mirror folded down.

Sheila regretted that the floors weren't carpeted. 'Spoil the ship for a ha'p'orth of tar. Still, the oilcloth's a lovely shade of green. You can see your face in it. But it'll take some elbow grease,' she said to Fergus.

She wanted to tear off her clothes and tumble with him on to the bed. He was, she thought, as she often did and had as when she saw him tonight on the Soltau platform, the most handsome man she had ever seen. She felt like strangling the twins who wanted to explore the attic which Fergus had mentioned, explaining that when you pulled down the trapdoor there was a ladder fixed to it, which could be brought down and then climbed. And great cellars, four of them where they could play. 'Can we see them, please, Daddy, can we now?'

Sheila gave a definite 'no' for an answer They then demanded tea and toast, chanting together they were starving. 'Milk and biscuits,' Sheila said, 'or nothing.' Niamh and Deirdre knew their mother well and the voice she used when no meant no. 'And no bath tonight – it's too late. Sleep in your vest and knickers. I'm too tired to unpack,' she said while herding them up the stairs. 'Now say your prayers before Daddy brings up the milk and biscuits.'

'What about our story?' Niamh asked.

'Not tonight, pet – I'll tell you two tomorrow.'

'God bless Mammy and Daddy, Grannie, Grand-dad and all my friends and relations, and make me a good girl. Matthew, Mark, Luke and John, God bless the bed that I lie on. If I should die before I wake I pray to God my soul to take.'

Their eyelids were drooping, the long black lashes touching their flushed cheeks. Sheila went to each bed and kissed their cheeks. Then the good Catholic girl who never missed Mass, went to confession and received Communion, and never forgot to take her birth pill, put out the light and tiptoed from the room.

Fergus lay waiting for her. Tantalisingly she undressed, imitating stripteases she had seen in films, swirling garments round her head before flinging them to the four corners of the room. In her black lace brassiere and matching panties she put one leg up on a chair. Black suspenders bit into her plump white thighs. She fumbled with the fastening, delaying releasing the button from its loop. First the front one then the back one. The elastic released, snapped back to just below the edge of her panties. Mesmerised, Fergus watched as slowly she eased a sheer nylon stocking down her leg, rolled it and threw it at him. He pressed it to his lips. She repeated the routine on the other leg, turned her back, removed her bra, threw it down and, bare-breasted, turned again to face Fergus. She left her panties on. Fergus liked to remove those.

They were making love for the second time, she astride him, when the door opened and one of the twins came into the room. Sheila thanked God she hadn't left the light on. It was difficult to tell one twin from the other, even their voices were identical, their crying and sobbing, too.

This child was sobbing. 'I'm frightened, Mammy, I don't know where I am.'

112

'Which of you is it?' Sheila asked, getting off Fergus and slipping on a housecoat. 'Don't cry, love, Mammy's here.'

'I'm Deirdre.'

'Don't cry, you'll waken Niamh. Get into the bed. I'll bring you a drink of water.' In the doorway she collided with Niamh, also sobbing that she didn't know where she was. 'Get in beside Deirdre, pet.'

Fergus moved to the edge of the bed. Sheila gave each child a beaker of water and got into bed. Fergus's exasperation and frustration subsided.

'Drink your water. You're safe now. Mammy and Daddy are here. I'll put my arm round you.'

Sheila said the same comforting words and the four of them fell asleep with arms round each other.

Beth and Bill showered separately. He put on his blue and white striped army issue pyjamas. Beth's attempt at seductive nightwear was a pair of lace-trimmed baby doll pyjamas. But their lovemaking was intense and passionate. Afterwards they sat up, each lit a cigarette and they talked.

'The hospital in Brecon is forwarding my records. So far the tests have been OK. He told me that sometimes no reason shows up for not conceiving. He also told me that providing our tests are fine this separation might be a good thing.' Beth felt the tingle in her belly and his erection when he took her in his arms, held her and kissed her.

Yvette's and Victor's house was the last one on the block. A wide expanse of grass swept round its corner. Across the road, well-distanced from path and grass, were other houses.

Victor switched on the light above the door before opening it. 'You go in,' he said. 'I'll bring the cases, then garage the car.'

She went into the red-tiled hall, savouring the warmth that enveloped her. She was eager to explore the house but desisted. Victor would want to do that with her. He rarely allowed her to make decisions. It would be all right to go into the kitchen, he'd expect that. Expect the kettle to be on, a tray laid for coffee. The kitchen was a dream. Long and narrow. Superbly fitted. Straight out of a magazine. How, she thought, if they were a normal couple, she'd enjoy cooking delicious meals for Victor. She opened drawers and cupboards. Shelves of thick white crockery, a teaset, dinner service, eggcups, cereal bowls. In another cupboard mixing bowls, soufflé dishes, a nest of ramekins, flour dredger, everything white except the earthenware mixing bowls.

She heard his footsteps, closed the cupboard, took off the ocelot coat and hung it over a chair. He was such a perfectionist. 'Slut,' he'd have called her had she laid the coat down carelessly. He came in. 'I waited for you to show me round. If the kitchen's anything to go by the rest must be wonderful.' The kitchen's like a bloody operating theatre, clinical, cold. But I'll soon alter that. 'You must be tired and chilled. I'm making coffee, it won't be a minute.'

'I don't want coffee. I want to go to bed. I want you to come to bed.'

'But please, please can I see the other rooms?'

'There's only one – the latest combined living and dining room. Three-piece suite, dining-room suite, one coffee table, one bookcase.'

'When our packing cases arrive I'll make it lovely.'

'Bring that coat upstairs. It cost a fortune.'

'Yes, of course.'

Why did I come? Why didn't I stay in England? And a voice in her head replied, 'The army would have evicted you. Your allowance would have been stopped. You've no friends, no family. No one except him. You had to come.' She draped the coat over her arm, stroked the fur for comfort.

He stood in the doorway. 'I'm waiting,' he said.

She picked up her handbag. Once she reached the hall

he switched off the light. 'I'll want the small case. My dressing gown, nightdress and toilet things are in it.'

'You won't need them. I've bought you presents.'

He led the way upstairs and into the master bedroom. She hung the fur coat in the fitted wardrobe and marvelled at the sight of one wall wardrobed from floor to ceiling. Victor took off his tunic, undid his collar and tie. She noticed he had put on weight. The beginnings of a double chin, a belly. 'Let down your hair,' he said.

She took out the hairpins, laid them on the bed and shook out her hair.

'You look like a little girl.'

From the chest of drawers he took a tissue-wrapped bundle and gave it to her. 'Open it,' he urged.

The garments were the colour of blood, brilliant against the white wrapping. Crotchless knickers, a laced-up-the-back corselette.

'Put them on,' he commanded.

'I don't like the knickers,' she protested.

'They're for my enjoyment not yours – put them on.'

He undressed and came naked to lace her into the basque. She could feel his erection. 'Are you back on the pill?'

'No,' she said.

He punched her between the shoulder blades. 'Why not?'

'The doctor said my blood pressure is still unstable. He prescribed a diaphragm.'

'Have you put it in?'

'It's downstairs in one of the suitcases.'

He punched her again in the same spot. He never hit her where it would show above her clothes. 'Get into the bed.' He pulled back the bedclothes.

She watched. His penis was flaccid. Please God, she prayed, don't let it rise again. Let him be too tired.

'Roll over.' She did and he lay on her. The laced stays pinched her waist. The wire cups dug into her breasts. 'No

115

more fucking kids,' he said softly. 'We don't want any more do we, cherie?' Then his erect penis forced its way into her anus.

She lay in great pain, crying silently. She heard him leave the room. The lavatory flushing and then the sound of a door closing. She waited, watching the digits on the clock move the seconds and minutes, little flashing lights like those on an aeroplane high in the sky, and imagined she was up there, safe in the sky flying far far away.

In a single bed in another room Victor thought of his trip to Hamburg the previous week and the sex toys he had bought. The cuffs for ankles and wrists, the straps and buckles. He had noted the space between his house and the ones across the road. She'd have to scream like a hyena to be heard. But before he tried out the toys he'd have to keep tabs on Bill and his wife. What time did they go to bed? What time did the light go off? Perhaps they read for hours. He couldn't imagine them humping for long. Among the toys there was a gag.

Not until Yvette heard his snoring did she creep downstairs to get milk and the small dressing case that had painkillers, Vaseline and soothing ointment among its contents.

He woke her next morning. 'I brought you tea and toast.' He put the tray on the bedside locker. 'The keys for the Citroën,' he said, 'are there too.'

'I couldn't drive that. I'd be terrified.'

'You're a great driver. Just go easy on the accelerator. I want you to drive to Charley's in it. No lifts for anyone. And wear your green outfit.'

'I don't know where Charley's house is.'

'His wife is calling to pick the wives up. Just follow her. Don't let your tea go cold.' He kissed her cheek. 'See you tonight.'

While she soaked her bruised, aching body in the bath she thought of the ordeals in front of her. A car she wasn't

116

used to and the coffee morning. She feared that more than driving a high-powered car for the first time. Meeting strangers, alienating them, as she always did. In their chain store or catalogue outfits they'd smile, shake hands and their eyes would scrutinise the Jaeger suit, matching three-quarter-length coat, her pure silk blouse and supple shoes. He bought her expensive clothes, clothes he knew the men he soldiered with could never afford to buy for their wives. Yvette believed the clothes could have been forgiven by the women. But not the aloofness Victor forced her to cultivate. The ban on casual dropping in on neighbours, or they on her. Here in Germany as in other stations, neighbours would take the place of families. To compensate for being separated from close relatives women bonded; looked after children if their mothers were sick or hospitalised, helped each other in every way. Yvette envied them their closeness. Knew she was thought to be stand-offish. After five years of marriage she had never fathomed his reason for not allowing her to mix freely.

Once in the beginning she had demanded to know why she had to keep her distance from her neighbours. 'Because I tell you to,' he'd replied.

'It's so difficult. After a few rebuffs most of the women think I'm odd, snobbish, but there are others who persist in wanting to be friends.' She tried explaining further, hoping to make him understand.

That was the first time he beat her severely. She prayed every night that he'd have a fatal accident. She was tempted to throw out the shocking underwear. But fear made her resist the temptation.

By ten o'clock she had washed and dried the crockery, made up, was dressed and brought out the car from the garage, her hands trembling, her legs almost paralysed for fear she press too hard on the accelerator. She manoeuvred it carefully, stopping outside her house, hoping it was pointing in the right direction.

A battered station wagon drove up, parked behind her

and its horn sounded. Charley's wife, Yvette guessed. She was a thick-set woman, wearing ski pants, a pink anorak and matching woolly hat.

Yvette got out of the car and introduced herself. 'I'm Emily,' the older woman said and shook the proffered hand. 'The car's terrific – Charley told me about it.'

Sheila, Beth, Liz and the children were on their doorsteps. 'Come on, girls, don't stand about, it's freezing. Pile in. Keep the introductions till later.' Deirdre and Niamh asked, 'Mammy, can we go in the lovely shiny car?' Sheila looked questioningly at Yvette.

'I'd be afraid for them,' said Yvette. 'It'll be my first time to drive it. I wouldn't risk your precious children.'

'That's OK.' Sheila smiled, though her eyes were like gimlets, pricing every stitch Yvette wore. There must be big money in the Black Market.

Emily settled the women in her car and told Yvette to follow her. 'Don't forget you'll be driving on the right-hand side of the road.'

'Fine.'

Emily started her car and cautiously Yvette followed. Niamh and Deirdre waved to her from the back window.

Emily's house was big and detached. A smell of coffee and recent baking pervaded it. A young girl took the women's and children's coats.

'This is Gisela, I don't know what I'd do without her. In here, make yourselves comfortable. Can he walk?' Emily asked Lizzie, nodding at Tom.

'This long time.'

'Put him down, then, you look tired. In a minute Giselle will take the children in the other room. There's a few toys in there and cushions and low tables. But we won't rush them out yet a while. After the introductions.'

They introduced themselves. 'Did you like the quarters?' The women enthused about them. Beth and Lizzie were shy.

Sheila never, anywhere. 'I couldn't believe my eyes. And

isn't the central heating great and all the cupboards. I'm going to like BAOR.'

Beth said how marvellous the houses were compared with quarters in England. Lizzie and Yvette agreed.

Giselle asked the children their names, admired them and marvelled at the identical twins. They quickly became friendly and she took them to the other room. Emily assured anxious mothers there was nothing dangerous or breakable in there.

Gradually they relaxed. Emily served good coffee, filtered. She said she preferred it to the other coffee-making methods. 'And God knows I've tried them all. And it's more economical if you only want one cup. The NAAFI sells packs of individual filters.'

'Sounds great but I think I'll stick to my jar of Nescafé,' Lizzie said.

The scones were delicious. The women complimented her on them. 'A "Women's Institute" recipe. I'll give you it. What do you think of the fireplace?'

Sheila admired the wooden kerb and mantelpiece stained to look like mahogany and said, 'It's smashing. The one fault with the house was no fireplace.'

'Central heating's grand but you can't group chairs round a radiator. That's why I had the fireplace and electric fire. I love direct heat on my legs and feet. Tell Fergus to ask the carpenter Dieter, a German, a great worker who doesn't charge much. You can even pay him in fags.'

To make some contribution to the conversation Yvette said she'd like an electric fire and an imitation fireplace. Emily as the hostess felt obliged to bring her into the conversation.

'Was this your first time to drive a Citroën?' she asked.

'Yes,' Yvette said but added, 'I've been driving for years, we've always had a car.'

'I know Victor has a Consul. I love the colour. So now you're a two-car family.'

Was it a criticism? Yvette wondered.

Emily continued, 'Our station wagon's two years old. Though from its appearance you'd think it was ten. Charley doesn't care. He says he's not spending his time off washing and polishing a car.'

From the other room there came loud screaming. 'Tom,' said Lizzie. 'Oh, God, I hope he hasn't hurt himself.' She jumped up, her face ashen.

Gisela brought him into the room. Not a tear in his eyes. His face red and angry. 'He wanted the last biscuit – so did his sister. She got it.'

'Just like my Tim,' said Emily and told Giselle to let Tom sit with his mother for a while. And to make another pot of coffee.

'You have a little boy too?' Yvette spoke for the second time since arriving.

'He's a big boy now, fifteen, away at boarding school. I've a daughter sixteen, she's also away at school. The army has two boarding schools, Tim and Sarah are at Wilhelmshaven. We see them often.'

'Where's that?' asked Sheila.

'In Germany. They could have gone to England. The army would help with the fees. But I couldn't part with them for three months at a time.' From the imitation mantelpiece she took two photographs and passed them round. 'Tim and Sarah.' The wives gave deserved praise for the children were attractive.

'I'm sure all your husbands will soon buy cars. Then you'll be OK,' Emily said.

'I'll learn to drive,' Sheila declared.

'Probably.' Emily sounded doubtful. 'Not many other ranks' wives do.'

'Why not?'

'I'm not sure. Charley's not keen on me driving. Afraid, so he says, I'll go on the autobahn. Terrible accident rate.'

'Yvette's driving a Citroën, for God's sake. I don't

120

suppose she'll just patrol round the camp. Will you, Yvette?'

Yvette, not knowing what she'd be allowed to do, told some of the truth. 'It all depends on Victor, Sheila. Tonight he might forbid me ever to touch the car again!'

'Well, girls,' Emily said, 'it was lovely meeting you. We'll be seeing a lot of each other.' She stood up. The women took the hint. Gisella brought in the children, sorted out who owned which coat.

'Before you go I've a bit of advice. It gets bitterly cold here and in a week or two we'll have snow. Lasts for weeks, sometimes months. So you'll have to dress the children as the Germans do. Anoraks, *Strumpfhosen* and thick fleece-lined trousers. They're essential. Buy them in the Karstadt. You'll be going to Celle, lovely town. The Karstadt's there. You'll need sledges too.'

'Sledges, you're joking,' said Sheila.

'I'm not, but they can wait for a week or two.'

Sheila had talked, listened and weighed up the other women. How would they get on? she asked herself. Would she make a best friend of one of them? And if so, which one? Continuing to smile and chat, she studied each of the wives. Emily was out for a start. She had given them a great welcome, was good with the children. But she was bossy, an organiser, an army wife. Wives of senior warrant officers often were. No, she and Emily wouldn't be close friends.

And Yvette? Not her either. You'd always feel at a disadvantage in Yvette's company. Her withdrawn manner and appearance. I'd love her coming into my kitchen in the morning! Done up to the nines and me looking like a streel.

Beth seemed harmless enough. Gentle, softly spoken, already she had mentioned her husband's name several times. 'Bill says, Bill believes', that sort of thing as if she hadn't a thought of her own. Lizzie, fat Lizzie with her wild hair, no do up. I think she'll be the one. I warm to her. It's early days but all the same she's the one I'd like for a friend. She has enough to say without being pushy. And she's got children. We could babysit for each other. Anyway, I'll wait and see. We're here for five years; no need to rush into something I might regret. That can happen when you move to a new camp. Make a friend in haste and repent at leisure.

'Before we leave,' said Lizzie, 'how about arranging another coffee morning?'

Sheila let go of her summing up the women and said, 'I'll give the first one, you've got a young baby.'

'Don't count me in, I'm involved in so many things, but I'll come when I can,' Emily promised.

Sheila and Lizzie were arranging a coffee morning for the following week.

Sheila repeated she'd give the first. 'You've more to do than me with the baby.'

Beth didn't remind them that she, like Yvette, had less to do than they did and Yvette said nothing.

'Look,' said Sheila. 'We're living next door to each other, we'll probably be having coffee with each other every morning. But let's agree on next Thursday for the official one.'

They agreed, then thanked Emily for a lovely time. She drove them home with Yvette following.

Chapter Fourteen

Lizzie postponed telling Bob that she wasn't on the pill, deciding instead she'd pretend her period had started. But overcome with desire when she saw him undressing, thought to hell with it, I'll take another chance. After they'd made love twice and as he was about to fall asleep she shook him and whispered, 'Wake up, I've something to tell you.' When he didn't respond she poked him in the ribs. Startled, he shot up in bed. 'Christ Almighty, what was that for?'

'I told you a lie last night. I'm not on the pill.'

'You what?'

'I'm not on the pill.'

He switched on the bedside lamp. She thought how Tom was the image of him. Tom when he was furious. 'Jesus, and we've done it three times.'

'Four,' she corrected. 'There was this morning but you were half asleep.'

He lit a cigarette and inhaled to the pit of his stomach, it seemed, then exhaled through his nostrils. He reminded her of a bull, a red-faced angry bull. 'You wrote and said it was all fixed. Why didn't you tell me – even last night I could have got condoms. I could have pulled out.'

'That's how I got pregnant the first time. In Mum's parlour. You said it would be all right and I let you. The next thing we were putting in the banns.'

'OK, but now we've three kids. Why didn't you refuse me last night?'

'I can just imagine your reaction. Nine months without it and I refuse you. You'd have gone berserk. In any case I'd gone without it for nine months too, love. I'm sorry, but after all I am a Catholic.'

'Some Catholic.' He lit another cigarette. 'You don't go to Mass regularly.'

'I go sometimes. In any case that doesn't mean I don't believe in hell. And it's only since I got married, often I'm too tired and when I was having the children too sick. So that's not a mortal sin. Contraception is. The Pope says so.'

'What do you think French letters are – banana balloons, pulling out, that diaphragm thing you had. Where's that?'

'I threw it out. I could never get the hang of it. It kept jumping off that plastic stick. I'm sorry, love. I couldn't help not going on the pill.' She began to cry. 'We can use the rhythm method.'

He couldn't bear to see her cry. He put out the cigarette and took her in his arms. 'You got Paula on the rhythm method. Forgot to take your temperature or some bloody thing.'

'I know, I know, it's all my fault. But it isn't only because I'm a Catholic. It was something I heard on *Woman's Hour*. This man, Arthur Street, I think, was talking about the pill. You know who I mean, he has a funny accent, very broad, Somerset, I think. He knows a lot about animals, maybe he's a farmer. Anyway, the interviewer asked his opinion of the pill and he said after seeing what hormones do to cows he'd never let his wife or daughter take it.'

'What are hormones?'

'I haven't a clue except they're in the pill and someone else on the programme said the side effects of it won't be known for the next fifty years, until women taking it now have died and what they died of is known. So between roasting in hell and getting something terrible wrong with me I was petrified.'

'Oh, lovely Lizzie, you're a fool of a woman. Doctors and scientists know what they're doing.'

'It's easy for you to say that, you wouldn't be the one taking it nor going to hell.'

'According to your Catholic religion because I'm a Protestant I'll go to hell anyway. Don't cry now. Maybe we'll be lucky. Maybe we'll get away with it this time and if we don't so we'll have another baby, a brother for Tom. But we won't risk it again tonight. Stop crying. I'll make you a cup of tea and from now on I'm in charge of contraception.'

There was a note pinned on a cupboard in Yvette's kitchen. 'Forgot to tell you, Wednesday's half-day here. In the army, I mean – football, hockey etc. The older men are not expected take part except as referees, linesmen etc. Voluntary. I never volunteer for anything. I'll have something to eat in the mess and then go to Hamburg. Want to get some photographic equipment. Don't wait up, I'll be late back.'

She changed into slacks and a sweater, did her hair and lay on the bed thinking. His darkroom was already set up before she arrived. She would never be allowed to see inside it. Victor had forbidden her, his reason being that there were dangerous chemicals in the room. She knew there were pictures of her being developed. Pictures of her naked, lying on the bed, standing, sitting. In the beginning she didn't object, her body was beautiful. She wasn't a prude. But later on he made her pose in other positions. One with her legs open showing her private parts, holding her breasts pushed upwards by her hands. When she refused he beat her. She wondered if the crotchless knickers were for more photographs.

Emily had mentioned how dangerous the autobahns were, maybe he'd have a fatal accident. How else would she get away from him? She'd have to leave the quarters. But the army would try to get her a council flat or house and she'd have a widow's pension. Though having no children she might be expected to work. There again the army might help. And at least she'd have a shelter.

She went downstairs, made coffee and a sandwich, and continued thinking about her plight. If only she had a friend. Someone to talk to, to advise her. She thought about the women who'd been at the coffee morning, wondering which one she could confide in. Emily, she supposed. She was older, had a sympathetic manner and probably knew more about what she could expect in benefits if she were widowed while Victor was in the services. But how could she ask such questions? Emily would think her mercenary. To be worried about an accident was one thing – that wasn't abnormal – but to couple her worries with questions about housing and pensions would seem callous and calculating. And in any case Emily didn't belong to Victor's regiment.

125

And it wouldn't be fair to inflict her troubles on Lizzie. Lizzie had three small children.

Beth, well, she like herself had said little during the coffee morning. So it was difficult to form an impression.

Sheila, on the other hand, was talkative and lively. Good company, seemingly well up in the ways of the world. But she sensed hostility in Sheila's eyes when they looked at her.

'Stuck-up bitch. Not a word to throw to a dog. And did you see how quick she was with her excuse not to take Niamh and Deirdre in her car. Afraid to endanger them my eye,' Sheila proclaimed as she served coffee to Beth and Lizzie.

'She didn't have much to say,' Beth admitted.

Lizzie offered an excuse for Yvette. 'Maybe she's shy, but isn't she beautiful, and her clothes!'

'What I want to know is how she can afford them?' asked Sheila and offered her cigarettes around. 'And they've two cars, a brand-new Citroën and the Consul. Something fishy there.'

'Maybe it's true about him inheriting money,' suggested Lizzie.

'Maybe,' conceded Sheila. 'Listen, is it agreed about Celle on Friday? Take the kids.'

'I'd be all for it – but Tom's the drawback, he'd miss his nap, be cranky and most of the time I'd have to carry him.'

Sheila suggested taking the pushchair.

'It won't fold down, something wrong with it. I can't see the conductor taking it on the bus.'

'I'd love to go to Celle. But I don't have to buy clothes for children. So I'll have Tom.'

'Oh, Beth, that would be smashing but I couldn't let you, thanks all the same.'

'I'd love to Lizzie, honestly. I'll babysit in your house, then Tom can nap in his cot.'

'That's a great idea,' said Sheila. 'I couldn't imagine her

nibs offering her services and she can go to Celle any time she likes.'

'What excuse did she give for not coming this morning?' asked Beth.

'She had to go somewhere.'

Yvette wasn't going to Celle. She intended driving round the local countryside, knowing that concentrating on driving the new car in an unfamiliar area would block out other unpleasant thoughts. Victor hadn't come back from Hamburg. She had slept fitfully and when she did, woke several times during the night wondering where he was. That he might be with another woman was of no interest to her. That he might be dead her permanent hope. She imagined the overwhelming sense of relief. To be free of him. Free of the humiliations to which he subjected her, the terrible tragedy he had brought into her life. For although the death of little Sean had been deemed accidental she knew instinctively that Victor had been involved.

Once during the night she had brought her dressing case to the bed, emptied out the contents, listening all the time for the sound of a car, and with trembling fingers peeled back the layer of material which covered the bottom of the case and lifted out a photograph of a little boy. Her son Sean. The photograph had been taken on his sixth birthday not long before he and Victor had gone for a weekend to Amsterdam. I let him go. He adored Victor who showered him with expensive gifts. Who never scolded or smacked him, she mused, staring at the photograph.

She had no qualms about letting him go to Amsterdam. They were flying there. Sean was excited about going up in an aeroplane. For the rest of her life she would blame herself for not stopping him. She could hear his voice asking, 'Can Mama come too?' And Victor's reply. 'It's a boys thing. Girls would spoil it. Your mother would want to go shopping. Dresses and that sort of thing. There'd be no time for boat trips on the canals. I'll hire bicycles for us. Everyone rides bicycles in Holland. And there'll be other little boys to play with. My friend, the one we'll stay with, has two sons. His wife is going to visit her mother so we'll be all boys together. You can race up and down the stairs, throw your clothes on the floor. Eat what you like and stay up late. And if the weather is fine we'll camp out one night. Pretend we're soldiers. You'll like that, won't you?'

'I'll love it, I'll love it,' Sean had said and raced round the room.

Oh, God, why didn't I insist on going? Yvette thought. But Sean was so excited, so happy and it was only for a long weekend. I had no reason to be anxious, Victor was a model stepfather, always indulging Sean, photographing him, the camera always at the ready, especially as he grew older.

Sometimes I was jealous, thinking he loved Victor better than me. And always wondering how a man so brutal towards me could be so gentle with my son. Tears ran down her face as she looked at her son's picture. The only picture of him she had. After the accident Victor burnt every other photograph. Sean as a toddler, naked on a rug, in his bath, naked on a beach.

The day she was expecting them back the telegram arrived telling her there had been an accident. Victor would be home the following day. So she knew it was Sean who was injured. She wanted to fly to Amsterdam.

Afraid to approach Victor's CO for advice, she went to the police. A friendly sergeant looked perplexed when she told him why she had come and showed him the telegram. 'What's the problem? If you've got a passport you just go.'

'But I don't know where in Amsterdam my husband is.'

'I couldn't help you there. I doubt if Interpol would get involved. Your best bet is to see your husband's commanding officer, but as the telegram says he'll be home tomorrow there's not much point. Sorry, love.'

She didn't dare approach Victor's CO. He had warned her never to do such a thing, threatened her with terrible consequences. 'You go through special channels in the army. And you never ever approach a senior officer.'

So she went back to her quarters, trying to convince herself the accident was a minor one. A broken bone, just a simple fracture . . .

But it wasn't. Sean, her adored son, was dead. Suffocated.

Victor seemed for once in her knowing him to have lost his composure. 'It was an accident. We were camping. The boys in one tent, me and their father in another.' As he told her he chain smoked and poured a second glass of whisky. 'In the morning we found him dead. The police thought he'd suffocated, that there'd been horseplay between the boys. But we won't know for definite until after the PM.'

She listened as if in a trance. This wasn't real. It couldn't be. Any minute now the door would open and he would charge in, throw his arms round her and babble excitedly about what he'd seen and done.

Victor was solicitous. He gave her brandy and sweet tea, suggested calling the MO who'd prescribe a sedative.

When the reality had sunk in she asked questions: 'Where was he? When would he be brought home?' She wanted to see him, to touch and hold him.

Victor lied. 'In the hospital's mortuary chapel. I saw him. He looked as if he was sleeping. The doctor said he wouldn't have suffered.'

'I want to go to him. Now, tonight. We'll fly or go from Harwich. I have to go.'

'No,' he said, using the tone that would brook no argument. Sean was in a refrigerated drawer in the morgue. There was slight bruising on his throat, on parts of his body. He was naked in his icy drawer, she would go hysterical, create a scene.

'Then I'll go alone,' she said, her voice rising. 'He's my son. I have to go.'

He resorted to violence. She bent over gasping for breath. On her bent back he rained blows until she lay prostrate on the floor.

Stroking the photograph, she talked aloud: 'I wonder what really happened to you, my darling. You'd be eleven now.' The other little boys couldn't remember. They were five and six years old. She saw them in their father's house when she attended the inquest. By which time Sean had already been buried.

It was Victor's colonel who suggested she should go to the inquest. Victor had forbidden her but the CO didn't think it wise that she should be left alone in England.

The PM confirmed death by suffocation and the coroner's verdict was accidental death. 'Young boys tussling and struggling. Playing roughly. Perhaps Sean had been the baddy. He had to be restrained. Overpowered. A game that went horribly wrong.'

Before the inquest his body was flown home and buried in Victor's family grave in the north of England.

Kissing the photograph and putting it back in its hiding place, she remembered her futile objections to where Sean was being buried and Victor's honeyed tones: 'But darling, we could be posted anywhere in the world, several times before I finish in the army. Buried in the family grave, every time we come on leave we'll visit the relatives and Sean's grave.'

They had never visited his relatives. Her first sight of them was at the funeral. They sympathised, spoke words but she was still in shock and couldn't now remember what they looked like or what they had said. She and Victor went from the cemetery straight home. Perhaps his family had asked them back to their house, she couldn't recall having been invited. It was only a few months since they had been in the new posting. It was unlikely they'd be posted elsewhere for at least a year or more.

For however short or long it was she could visit Sean's grave, tend it, put flowers on it.

It was an old graveyard. Trees grew there, birds nested and wild flowers grew in profusion. The headstones were simple, the inscriptions weather worn. It was beautiful in contrast to where he was buried: an enormous place on the edge of an industrial city. Smoke from the mills and heavy industry even on a fine day darkened the sky. Trees were stunted, no birds nested there, no wild flowers grew. Sean wouldn't like it.

She secured the covering in the dressing case, put back the toiletries and slept for a couple of hours.

Sheila and Lizzie were charmed with Celle, by the medieval buildings and the modern ones built in the same style and from the same materials. Everywhere was so clean, the coffee and cakes delicious, the Karstadt enormous: clothes, food, drapery, table linen, china, toys. Lizzie was amazed at how cheap everything was until Sheila contradicted her. 'Cheap! How can you say that!'

'Sheila, look at that dress, it's only twenty-five shillings.'

'You bloody-looking eejit. Twenty-five marks not shillings. The mark's worth about one and eight pence to the shilling so the frock isn't cheap at all. Don't forget when you go shopping it's roughly twelve marks to the pound.'

They bought the warm clothes for the children and had no trouble making themselves understood, for most of the shop assistants spoke English.

'I know Hitler was an Antichrist but I think Germany's fabulous,' Sheila said as they approached the Christmas counter, where they bought new tree decorations, Advent calendars and wreaths. Again congratulating themselves on living in Germany, where spirits bought in the NAAFI cost seven and six a bottle, cars were hundreds of pounds cheaper and, providing you had owned them for a year, you could sell them in England at a great profit.

Laden with their purchases, they went to a café before

going to catch their bus. Sheila thought the women were frumpy in their felt hats and flat-fur-collared coats, and watched them eat enormous portions of gateaux and sponges piled with cream. 'Very sensibly dressed, you might say, but no style, even the youngish ones. Haven't the kids been great?'

'I'm only hoping Tom's been as good for Beth. Wasn't it nice of her to mind him?'

'She's a good sort. Not like our other neighbour. God, she's got everything, smashing figure, gorgeous clothes, gorgeous hair, he's attractive and on top of all that a Citroën.'

'But she hasn't got a child.'

'I bet that's from choice.'

'Maybe,' said Lizzie.

While the women were in Celle, Yvette drove round the camp. There was a speed limit of 10 mph. It was excellent practice for her. Then she drove through the camp gates. From a map she had discovered where the village of Bergen-Belsen was and the railway sidings. She drove there first, saw closed trucks on the sidings and thought of the Jews, gypsies and others Hitler considered subhuman. She imagined the women, children and elderly people hungry, cold and tired after travelling for days in the trucks. She knew from all she had read that the concentration camp at Belsen was not one used for extermination. Even so, thousands had died there from starvation and disease, Anne Frank among them, it was believed.

It was the first camp to have been liberated by the British. While she was still at school she had gone to see a film about it. She went with her mother. It was unbeliev-able that the pyjama-clad skeletal figures were human beings. Even more incredible were the open pits with hundreds of naked dead bodies piled in them. Her mother had cried throughout the film and was still crying when they arrived home.

My poor, kind-hearted mam; she cried in the same way when she found out I was pregnant.

'Oh, Cariad,' she sobbed using a Welsh term of endearment. 'What'll we do? What will your father say? Did it happen with the boy you went walking out with?'

I couldn't talk, only nod my head.

'I never saw him. Didn't even know his name. Have you told him?'

'I can't,' I sobbed.

'Doesn't he love you? Won't he marry you?'

'He's dead, Mam. He was killed in Korea.'

Then I told her about Sean and Cambridge, how he left school, went away and joined the army. 'I only found out today. A mate of his from school told me he'd been killed.'

'The poor boy, Lord have mercy on him. It's a wonder I never heard about him.'

'Word only came through yesterday, in any case he was from Margam and a Protestant. I expect it'll be in Thursday's *Guardian*. What am I going to do, Mam? I loved him so much. Oh, Mam, I wish I was dead.'

My lovely, kind mam. She held me close, comforted me. 'It'll be all right. I'll make it all right. Say nothing to no one. Tonight when your father's gone to bed we'll talk about it. I'll have given it a lot of thought by then.'

She had and outlined her plan. 'Your father needs to know nothing about it. He's a good man, but hard, unforgiving. He loves you in his own way but he'd never forgive you. The shame would kill him. And in my own way I love him, feel sorry for him. I couldn't go against him. So you'll go to London to Mags in Paddington. You'll go to school for another couple of weeks and let it be known you're thinking of leaving. Going in for nursing in London. I'll write tomorrow and tell her all. You'll be all right with her and your child as well, for the time being that's as far ahead as we'll plan.'

And in a few weeks I went to Paddington, believing my broken heart would never mend.

Yvette turned the car round and drove to the concentration camp. It was sixteen years since it had been liberated. She didn't know what to expect. Certainly not the immaculate landscaped park, beautifully tended grass, slight rises and hollows. Hard to believe it had been a leprous huddle of huts, open graves of hundreds of dead bodies. Here and there, laid on the grass were the slabs of stone which read 'three thousand buried here, two thousand buried here'. The numbers varied but were always in the thousands.

In the centre of the camp there was a tall monument commemorating the dead. There were no names. She prayed for them, for her little son, her wonderful mam and Aunt Mags.

Driving back to her home, she remembered the tall house in Paddington. The coming and going of the B&B guests, the majority Welsh, in London for a rugby match, a day's shopping. Mags kept her out of the way if among the Welsh guests any were from her home town. 'No good, love, filling their mouths. Let your father believe it's nursing you are. Not much nature in that man. Trying to make his bed in heaven collecting pennies for the priest. I'm sure God has a different set of values.'

As broken hearts do, hers healed. She was young, in the loving atmosphere of her Aunt Mags. There were always people coming and going, and her mam occasionally.

'Your father prays for you, has Masses said for your success nursing but would have preferred you to be a teacher. But he doesn't want you to write. He'll never forgive you for leaving home without consulting him.'

Chapter Fifteen

In no time Lizzie and Sheila became friends and if Bill was on duty and Fergus gone to the mess, Sheila would go to Lizzie's and they'd spend the evening talking about everything under the sun. Sheila went back at short intervals to check on the twins.

Lizzie told Sheila about Bristol and Sheila told Lizzie about Dublin. They discovered they had a lot in common. Both were Catholics and Lizzie's father second-generation Irish. Before much time had elapsed each knew how the other had met her husband and they would talk for hours about the meetings, their weddings and the births of their children.

On the subject of husbands. 'For me it was love at first sight,' Sheila said one evening.

'The same for me,' said Lizzie. 'Weren't we lucky.'

Before replying Sheila thought, you more than me, Bob's on duty. Fergus is knocking back pints. 'We were very lucky, but sometimes I think I'd have been luckier still if Fergus wasn't in the army. It's not my cup of tea.'

'Not much you can do about it now. Nice houses, good money, great security.'

'I know all that but I'd still rather be a civilian. Live in a city. You lived in a city. D'ye never miss Bristol?'

'Not a lot. But then again we were always stationed on the Plain. Bristol was never far away.'

One night when the two husbands were on duty Lizzie told Sheila that she wasn't on the pill.

'You're out of your mind. Is it because you're a Catholic?'

'In a way, other things too.'

'What other things?'

'It's supposed to be dangerous.'

'That's rubbish. That's the Catholic Church trying to

135

frighten women. I suppose you wouldn't want to tell it in confession.'

'Terrified.'

'You don't have to tell it.'

'But then I'd be committing a sacrilege.'

'I don't care. I'm on the pill and that's my business. I don't believe God expects a women to have a child every year. That's what'll happen to you. By the time you're thirty you'll have eight kids.'

'I know. I don't want eight kids. I know I'd love every one of them but sometimes I find three hard to manage. I'll think about the pill.'

The three men had ordered their duty free cars. Bill was having a Consul, monzo red, Fergus an Opel, silver grey and Bob a Ford Prefect. When the cars arrived they'd take their wives shopping in Bergen, which was nearer than Celle. There Lizzie and Sheila would buy the sledges.

They bought the majority of their wants in the NAAFI, which was in the Roundhouse, an enormous building that had once been a German officers mess. Besides the NAAFI there were shops run by the YMCA, a book and gift shop, also a café. A group of officers wives operated a bring and buy. There was another enormous room, round like the building. Dances were held there and on Friday nights Bingo with snowballs sometimes reaching hundreds of pounds. A German bath house was converted and consecrated as a Catholic church. Teachers came from England to teach in the primary school.

Every Saturday night there was a dance with buffet provided in the sergeants mess. There were, though, no adolescents to babysit, they were away at boarding school, but the wives quickly got a babysitting rota organised.

Sheila still considered Emily a bossy boots but also recognised that her intentions were of the best. The more she got to know Beth the more she grew to like her. Beth would never be the life and soul of the party but she was sweet-natured, always willing to help out. The fly in the ointment was Yvette. Sheila judged her to be a cold creature. She had little to do with the wives, was done up from morning to night, never a hair astray. 'I'd like to put a stick of dynamite up her arse, make her react like a human being,' Sheila said one day to Lizzie.

'She doesn't interfere with us, she's nice to the kids. Forget about her, Sheil.'

'You're right, I should. Maybe I'm a bit jealous, you know, all the gorgeous clothes, a smashing-looking husband and two cars.'

'It's not jealousy. Not you. I think it's because you haven't managed to get round her. Beth thinks the world of you and Emily admires you. Thinks you're a great character. But it's your Irish charm that's the gift. I watch you sometimes when we're shopping. How easy you find it to talk to strangers and how they respond. But it doesn't work with Yvette. Not so far, anyway.'

'You're telling me! You could be right, though. It's not that I want to be her bosom pal.' Sheila shrugged. 'Far from it. But here we are, four young women stuck in this place for five years, three of us get along great and she's like a spectre at a feast. Let's forget about her. When are you going to the MO about the pill?'

'Soon.'

'You're an eejit.'

'We take precautions.'

'Well, that's something. But whatever precautions you take except the rhythm method you're committing a sin. So why not go to hell for something that's almost one hundred per cent safe?'

'Don't be doing an Emily. I'll go when I'm ready, OK?'

'OK,' Sheila said and changed the subject. Lizzie was placid and easygoing, listened to what you had to say. But she made her own decisions.

Most Saturday nights they went to the mess with their husbands.

Lizzie's hair had grown longer and the frizzy perm calmer. She could now have it rollered, backcombed and lacquered into a bouffant style. She, Beth and Sheila wore full-skirted dresses, made to puff out by layers of stiff petticoats, and stiletto-heeled shoes. They drank more on Saturday nights than they ever had in their lives: Bloody Marys, Blue Niles, Pimm's and John Collins. All pleasant-tasting drinks, the liquor disguised. Curries or cold buffets were served for supper. Those who could bop did and others who couldn't sat the fast ones out, then smooched to romantic slow rhythms. The sergeant in charge of the sewage plant never tired of telling how on Sundays you couldn't see the sewage for the condoms.

In between dances, party games were organised, couples dancing with balloons between their bellies. If the balloon burst or dropped the couple were eliminated. There were knobbly knees competitions and 'flap the kipper'. From a newspaper, giant-sized kippers were cut out, placed on the floor and the contestants lined up holding folded newspapers. On a given signal they flapped their papers to race the kipper past a finishing line at the end of the room. Laughter and squeals of delight ricocheted off the walls. Spectators gathered cheering on the contestants and clapped when the winners were given their prizes of a bottle, chocolates or scent.

Sheila, three-parts cut as the majority were, always said the same thing every time the game was played: 'Flap the fuckin' kipper, kids in Ireland wouldn't play that.' Beth thought it was a bit of fun and several times Bill got his kipper over the line first.

The week before Christmas it snowed and, as Emily had forecast, it was gorgeous snow that settled, transforming the landscape. It lay inches thick on the open space facing the quarters and there, after school, Niamh, Deirdre, Paula and Susan made giant snowballs and snowmen. Sheila and

Lizzie took the girls to school on their sledges. Tom sat in the special seat for toddlers. Never before in Lizzie's, Sheila's or Beth's lives had they had such an affluent Christmas, or gone to so many functions and parties, smoked or drunk so much, had such prettily decorated trees or so many presents beneath them. Germany, they agreed, was a fabulous posting.

Sheila gave a party on Boxing Day to which Beth, Lizzie, Yvette and their husbands came. Charley and Emily brought their son and daughter, home for the holidays. Other men from the gunnery staff and their wives were also invited.

Yvette had redeemed herself somewhat in Sheila's opinion by giving the children presents on Christmas morning. She had also introduced their mothers to the cranberry bushes growing on the grassy patch near their house and told them that next year in the autumn they could pick the berries and make sauce to go with their turkeys. Sheila said she had never heard of cranberries and asked how Yvette knew about them.

'I read about them. Americans always serve them with turkey.'

'We'll give them a try if God spares us,' Sheila said.

'Don't you love Germany, darling?' Fergus asked, grabbing hold of Sheila in the kitchen as she checked that the vol-au-vent cases weren't burning. 'Only one thing could make it more perfect,' he added.

'Men!' she exclaimed and pushed him away. 'D'ye never think of anything else?'

'Seldom,' Fergus replied.

The living room was packed, chairs brought in, seats and arms of the sofa and easy chairs occupied. The men stood. The radiogram was stacked with LPs, favourites from the Fifties included Chuck Berry, skiffle groups, Lonnie Donegan. 'Our music,' Sheila said to Fergus. 'God, couldn't we bop. I bet we still could.'

'Not in here, you couldn't. Not unless we threw everyone out.'

'Aye,' she agreed. 'Then there'd be no one to show off to.'

'That's what you loved.'

'Of course I did. Tantalising glimpses of my drawers. Were you mad jealous?'

'I'll always be mad jealous of you.'

Victor danced with other wives, smiling, flirting. Yvette danced with other men. But her demeanour and her fabulous dress discouraged them from flirting. Her dress was white, a Twenties shimmy, waistless, short, silk with sequins from her chest to above her knees.

'That cost a fortune,' Sheila whispered to Lizzie, as she watched Yvette and Fergus move on the thronged floor. Pat Boone crooned 'Thee I love'.

'Can you see where his hand is?'

'On her back, her waist, you know.'

'He's legless, tell me if his hand touches her any lower and I'll leave him legless for life.'

With any of the other women Fergus's hand would minutes ago have found her bum, but liberties with Yvette were verboten. Move your hand a fraction of an inch from her waist and she made an excuse to leave the floor. And somewhere not far away stood Victor. 'Your dress is gorgeous. Can you do the Charleston?' Fergus asked.

'The Charleston, what's that?'

'A dance from the Twenties. Your dress, it's what the flappers wore when they did the Charleston. You know. The one with knees bent and your hands changing from knee to knee.'

'Oh yes, I've seen it on the pictures. I never knew what it was called. I couldn't do that. I can't really dance – only this sort of shuffling and a slow waltz.'

The record stopped. Yvette and Fergus made their way to where Victor was. Fergus asked, 'Are you OK for a drink, Vic?'

'Fine,' Victor said, holding up a tumbler.

'So what were you and him talking about?' He always quizzed her after she'd danced with another man.

'My dress. He told me it's for dancing the Charleston in. I didn't know that.'

'How would you? If I didn't choose your clothes you'd still be wearing your Paddington things. A tatty dressing gown!'

She remembered the first time she had seen him. He had arrived late. All the guests were in bed. She had hung the 'No Vacancies' sign on the door and was getting ready to go upstairs when the doorbell rang. It often rang late at night and after a short while stopped. But not this night. It rang continuously. She wasn't sure what to do. Mags would have known but Mags wasn't well.

Sean woke and began to cry. She went to him, comforted him and he went back to sleep. The bell still shrilled. She decided to go down, thinking it might be the police. Her hair was loose about her shoulders. The light was on in the hall. She went to the window and pointed to the sign. The man ignored her and continued to ring. Eventually she opened the door. There was a reinforced chain so she wasn't unduly frightened. 'Please stop ringing, you'll wake the house. We're full.'

He took his finger off the bell. 'Fetch Mrs Graham, I've stayed here many times. Tell her it's Victor Smithers. She always finds me somewhere to sleep. You can shut the door. I'll wait, but fetch her now.'

He didn't look threatening, well-dressed and he spoke nicely. She had thought him ugly but revised her opinion when he smiled. 'Mags – Mrs Graham – isn't well. I don't like to disturb her.'

'In that case let me in. She knows me well. You won't get into trouble. I've stayed here before. The room at the top of the house. We have an arrangement, me and Mrs Graham.'

141

She knew there was such a room. Knew that Mags favoured certain people. 'I've never seen you before.'

'I haven't been for a while. Three years, I think.'

She hadn't been with Mags that long. She decided to let him in.

'I know it's late. The train from Dover broke down,' he said and followed her to the little counter-cum-desk.

She apologised for being barefoot, not dressed.

'It's your hair I'm looking at – it's beautiful.' He gave her the information she required. Victor Smithers and the address of an army barracks in Wiltshire.

'Oh, you're a soldier, then.'

'For my sins. I've been to France for a few days taking photographs. It's my hobby.'

He was tall, wiry looking, he smiled a lot, but now she noticed the smile didn't reach his eyes. 'How long will you be staying?'

'I'll sort that out with Mrs Graham tomorrow. I haven't seen you here before.'

'Mags – Mrs Graham – is my aunt.'

'There used to be a porter – old. He knew me well.'

'That would have been Tom. He died last year. I should ask for your identification but Mags will see to that. I'll go back to bed but would you like a cup of tea and a sandwich?'

'A cup of tea would be fine. You never get a decent one in France.'

'While you're drinking it I'll see to your bed, switch on the fire.'

She made the tea, went up to do the room. Sean cried out, calling 'Mammy'. She gave him his dummy. He quietened and she went down again to collect the used crockery and tell Victor the room was ready.

'I thought I heard a child cry.'

'That was my son.'

'So you're married?'

'I was,' she lied. 'He was a soldier, killed in Korea.'

'I'm sorry.'

She removed the crockery, put the lights out. 'I'll see you in the morning.'

They bade each other goodnight.

Emily's daughter and son came to Sheila's party.

Sarah talked about the changing fashions in England. 'Everything's going to be shorter, hair and dresses, straighter as well, according to the fashion magazine one of the girls had sent from England. Still, I suppose it'll be years before it catches on here. This place is the back of beyond. When and where's the next party?'

'*Silvester*, New Year's Eve. Yvette and Victor are giving it,' her mother replied.

'I suppose if it's anything like her clothes it'll be caviar not lump roe and buckets of champagne. She's OK but he gives me the creeps.'

'That's enough,' her mother remonstrated. 'Remember it's supposed to be the season of goodwill.'

To change the conversation Sheila said, 'Listen, kid, when you go back to school, send me a loan of the fashion magazine. I'm dying to see what's the latest. As they say in Ireland you might as well be dead as out of fashion.'

Chapter Sixteen

Although Yvette's house was only a stone's throw away, over their party dresses Lizzie, Beth and Sheila put on warm coats as it was freezing outside. The path had been cleared but everywhere else the crisp snow lay inches thick. Everyone had had a couple of their favourite tipples before setting out and they were in great humour, the women keyed up with curiosity as to what sort of a party Yvette and Victor would throw.

Earlier in the day they had seen how the house was

decorated. Expensive fairy lights strung round the door and windows, and on the door one of the biggest Christmas wreaths the wives had ever seen: red, green and silver was the colour scheme. It was festooned with generously berried holly sprays, bells, a variety of ornaments, and wide satin ribbons, green and red, trailed from it.

The hall door was ajar. Even so Fergus rang the bell. 'Come in, come in,' Victor said, coming into the hall. 'I'd left the door open so you could.' On the coconut mat inset in a depression behind the door the guests wiped their feet.

Sheila pinched Lizzie's arm. 'For God's sake will you look at the floor,' she whispered. The red tiles, which even with electric polishers showed every footprint, making it impossible to keep a shining surface on, had been changed. The kitchen's floor surface that, in the few weeks they'd been in Germany, caused Sheila and Beth great frustration, had been overlaid with Marley-patterned tiles matching those in the hall. They weren't fanatically house-proud but hated how, despite their scrubbing with bleach, Vim and all sorts of powders and liquid cleaners, their kitchen floors had yellowed. Lizzie, not as fussy about the colour of a kitchen floor, couldn't understand why they fussed so much. Nevertheless she was greatly impressed when she saw the floors at Victor's.

Yvette came and took the women's coats while Victor showed them round the alterations he had made to the house. The kitchen had been transformed. Shelves had been built wherever there was wall space. Beautifully decorated plates adorned them. From cup hooks hung brightly glazed mugs. The kitchen walls had been emulsioned in a a pale shade of lemon, the saucepan rack emptied of its aluminium ware and replaced by Le Creuset pots. The army issue austere white light shades, like those in public libraries, hospitals and schoolrooms, had been replaced with china globes, which cast a pleasanter light.

The young wives ooh'd and ah'd in admiration while at the same time Sheila's dislike of Yvette increased.

'Well, what do you think of it?' asked Victor.

Fergus replied, 'I didn't think it was allowed. I didn't think you could paint or alter your quarters!'

'I don't give a toss. In any case I'm improving the place, not damaging it, Fergus.'

'Oh, I couldn't agree more, Vic. Only you know what a stickler the army is for uniformity. All quarters are identical, furniture, bedding, maybe a different coloured carpet or curtains. And all walls the same shade of emulsion. At least for non-commissioned ranks. What an officer's place is like, that I don't know.'

'You ain't seen nothing yet. Come through to the living room.'

They were struck speechless. An army room wallpapered! Thick, embossed, expensive paper expertly hung.

Sheila could have cried with vexation. 'The conniving bitch never mentioned it. She'd been to Lizzie's and Beth's for coffee and not a word said,' she whispered to Fergus. Her enjoyment was ruined. And there she'd been thinking what a great splash she had made for Christmas.

Not only was Yvette's tree magnificent, the balloons twice the size of hers, but the table! So much food, such a variety. A huge salmon in aspic, a golden-crusted ham, a turkey, salads and side dishes, and a plugged-in hostess trolley on which a fragrant curry stayed warm. Jesus Christ Almighty! Where did they get the money? Yvette was a smug, self-satisfied bitch. Handing round drinks. Her tits practically spilling over another of her gorgeous dresses.

Sheila's night was spoiled. She was going to have one drink and then have a dizzy spell, palpitations, something, anything to get out of here. And wait until she got Fergus home. As for Beth and Lizzie, all they ever did was backbite Yvette. And look at them now. Like a pair of gobshites admiring everything.

'A drink, Sheila. It's my special punch.'

Victor took a glass and ladled in the punch. Waterford, she recognised the tumbler, bowl and ladle. A fortune. He must be counterfeiting.

There was a record of the Everly Brothers playing. The punch was delicious, cloves, cinnamon, the liqueur she didn't recognise. She sipped it. The tension flowed out of her. Victor refilled her glass. Everyone was talking, laughing, sipping punch. Everyone except Yvette. Before the guests arrived she had seen Victor pour something into the punch.

Sheila forgot her fit of pique and with it her palpitations, and dizziness. She was floating in Fergus's arms. Inching closer to him with every step they danced. Her black curly hair had grown longer. She leant her head back and it hung over a bare shoulder, everything was coming up roses, she inhaled Fergus's alcohol and tobacco breath, and was overcome by a longing to taste his mouth. Swallow his saliva as they did when making love.

Victor watched, so did Yvette. He had forbidden her to drink the punch. She suspected him of having laced it with an aphrodisiac. Now she was sure as she watched Fergus and Sheila. He had rucked Sheila's petticoats and dress up so high her black lace panties were showing and Fergus's hand groping. Everyone else was dancing, no one else noticed.

Victor left the room, came back with his cine camera and began filming the dancers. Fergus's hand was well entrenched between Sheila's legs. The record changed, 'La Compasita' took its place. Fergus bent Sheila back. Her hair touched the floor. She made no move to rise but was pulling Fergus down towards her. The other dancers were kissing, but only Fergus and Sheila were abandoning themselves. The cine camera continued whirring. Oh, my God, Yvette thought, they're going to do it. Fergus and Sheila are going to have sex on the floor in front of everyone and Victor will film them. Tomorrow they'll die of shame. I must stop them, create a diversion. But he'll

146

know. He'll kill me. No one else has noticed. What'll I do? Knock something breakable over. Stop the music and let him kill me. What do I have to live for anyway?

Then there was a banging on the front door, loud and urgent, a voice shouting, 'Come quick. Something terrible's happened.'

Emily opened the door. Victor turned off the cine camera.

Lizzie's schoolgirl babysitter Jane had Tom in a blanket. He had been crying, now he smiled when his mother appeared.

'It wasn't my fault. I didn't do anything,' the babysitter sobbed.

'Hush now, Jane, you'll only frighten the child,' Emily said, bringing the girl in. The men and women crowded the kitchen and hall. Jane's shouting had sobered them quickly.

Lizzie took Tom from the babysitter. 'What happened? Did you let him fall, did he swallow something?'

'No, no, it was worse than that. But it wasn't my fault. He woke up crying. I brought him a fresh bottle. He kept calling for you. He wouldn't take the bottle, just kept drawing his knees up. So I thought he had pains in his stomach and I knew you were trying to train him. So I took off his nappy and I nearly died. Something was hanging out of his bottom. It must be his intestines.'

Lizzie screamed, 'Oh, Tom, my lovely baby. Oh, what'll I do. Emily, Emily, tell me what to do.' Tears were streaming down her face.

Bob put an arm round her. 'He looks fine, love. Calm down.'

'Calm down. Just like a man! For all you know he could be dying.'

'He's not dying, look at him, Lizzie. Let's go back to your house. We can do nothing standing in Yvette's hall,' Emily said.

Victor suggested going for the doctor.

Emily said she'd have a look at Tom and if it seemed serious she'd ask him to fetch the doctor.

Lizzie was still crying, Tom smiling, now and then grunting.

Emily took Tom from his mother and carried him into the living room where she opened the blanket.

Lizzie screamed, 'Oh, God, it is his intestines.'

Sheila and Beth hovered behind the sofa. The intestine wriggled another inch down Tom's leg.

'I guessed as much,' said Emily. 'I'd say it's nearly all out. Timmy had one in Egypt. Stop crying, Lizzie. It's only a worm. A long roundworm. Though the first time you see one it does give you a terrible fright. They can be ten to twelve inches long.'

'You're not just saying that to comfort me?' asked Lizzie who'd calmed down a little.

'I'm not. If I had any serious doubts I'd get the doctor. But for your own peace of mind get some tweezers and a jam jar. I'll pop the worm in the jar and you take it to the MO tomorrow.'

Tom squirmed and the remainder of the worm emerged.

'Now, darling, isn't that better out than in,' Emily cooed.

A happier Lizzie took Tom upstairs to wash his bottom. Beth put the blanket in the dirty linen basket.

Sheila put the kettle on and Victor arrived to ask about the baby, bringing with him generous helpings of the buffet.

'Where would he have got it from?' asked a more relaxed Lizzie.

'Dogs, usually.'

'But Emily, we haven't got a dog.'

'I expect they come into the garden to poo.'

'In this weather?'

'In all weathers. Tom could have picked up the egg while making snowballs. Stop worrying. It's not serious.'

Yvette thanked God that Victor had drunk himself into a stupor, gone into the spare room from where his snores reverberated through the house. Maybe next year it would be different, she thought, maybe, maybe, maybe.

By the end of March the snow was gone. Though Emily told the young wives it wasn't unknown to have a fall in April.

The twins and Lizzie's girls were settled in school. The medical officer confirmed Emily's diagnosis. Tom had passed a long roundworm.

Until early February Lizzie looked forward to having only one child around the house. She'd have more time for Tom. More time to try out the recipes in *Woman's Weekly*.

She, Sheila and Beth began to find the gilt of living in Germany tarnishing slightly. One morning, while having coffee, Sheila said, 'I was mad about it at first, the extra money, the central heating. I thought I'd learn a bit of German. So far all I can say or understand is *Bitte*, *Danke*, *Wiedersehen*. I feel such a thick trotting out what little I know and the baker, the milkman and shop assistants answer you in almost perfect English.'

Beth, who often quoted Bill's opinions, said, 'Bill was telling me German children learn English in school. He says English people are the worst in the world with foreign languages. Maybe we should enrol in a class.'

'I'm enrolling in nothing. I hate being committed. And as for the Wives Club, that sends me round the bend. The CO's wife is the chairwoman for life. That's really democratic.'

'But the women themselves are nice, Sheila.'

'I never said they weren't, Beth, but they're not exactly exciting. Look at the daft things we do, guessing how many peas or sprouts are in a jar. And the clapping when someone nearly guesses the right number. You'd think we'd won the Irish Sweep. It's all so artificial. It's the class thing. No one gossips, no one tells a dirty joke.'

'It is a bit boring,' Beth admitted.

Lizzie made more coffee and passed round the duty free cigarettes.

'You're very quiet, Liz,' remarked Sheila. 'Are you not well?'

'I'm great, a bit tired. I read for too long last night.' She didn't want to announce that she was pregnant. Not while Beth was still hoping. All her tests were normal. Now Bill had to be tested. Lizzie picked a safe topic to talk about – Yvette. 'I asked her again to come in this morning. But as usual she had an excuse. She was going to Fallingbostel. Last week it was somewhere near Lüneburg.'

Beth said, 'Still, what else has she to do? Run a mop over the kitchen and hall. Not spend hours like us polishing, even my electric scrubber doesn't get rid of the yellowish tinge on the kitchen floor.'

'My Fergus says her trips are to other NAAFIs. If he's making his extra money selling tea, coffee, fags and booze to the Germans they'd have our NAAFI wiped out. Maybe he could be done for it.'

'But everyone knows it goes on.'

'I know that, Lizzie – but for their lifestyle he must be selling tons of stuff. So she drives round to other NAAFIs and shops.'

'I wish I could drive or that I had a job.'

'Not much chance of that – I loved my job in Brecon.'

'You'll probably get pregnant, then you'll have your hands full.'

'I hope you're right, Sheila.'

Sheila said she'd better go. 'I'll see you later. I'll pick Paula and Susan up from school. Have a nice cup of tea ready for me.'

She was hardly out the door before Beth started to cry. When Lizzie asked what ailed her she said, 'Bill has to go to the hospital for tests.'

'What sort of tests?'

'A sperm count.'

'What's a sperm count? What do they do? Is it an operation? It isn't dangerous, is it?'

Beth wiped her eyes and giggled. 'It's embarrassing. I don't know how to tell you—'

'Come off it, we talk about everything.'

'He has to, well, you know, he has to make himself come – into a condom, I think – and then the sperm is tested or counted or something. Bill is dreading it. Promise you won't tell, not even Bob.'

'Well of course I won't – but why?'

'Bill says if it got about they'd nickname him "The Wanker".'

'Bob wouldn't.'

'I'm not saying Bob might, but there's plenty would. Fergus for one. Oh, good-naturedly, but Bill'd hate it.'

Beth went home.

Lizzie peeled the potatoes. She was too tired to cook a proper dinner. She talked to herself: 'I'd love to have a sleep. That's a sure sign I'm pregnant. I'll be carrying all through the summer. And me looking forward to the swimming pool. It's an Olympic-sized one and it's only round the corner. I could have learnt to swim. Still, I suppose it could be worse. At least Bob's not complaining. As he said, "It's only a baby – it could have been cancer." Now he's in charge of contraception. The top shelf in the wardrobe full of them. "A bit late in the day," Bob joked, "but afterwards we'll make short work of them. Though I hate using the bloody things, it's like washing your feet with your socks on."'

Lizzie promised that after the birth she'd have a rethink about the pill, and consoled herself that once the sickness and tiredness passed she'd feel fit as a fiddle, as she had with the others. Then she'd look forward to the new baby. Hanover hospital was eighty kilometres away, so the minute you felt more than a niggle you had to send for the MO. The army didn't want the baby being born on the way. Generally, so she'd been told, you went in a

Volkswagen. Not the best vehicle for an emergency delivery. So the alternative was to stop at a German hospital and they billed the army an exorbitant amount. If it was a false alarm and you were near your date you had to stay in Hanover until the real thing started. But she wouldn't worry about any of those things until nearer the time.

Chapter Seventeen

The women had guessed right. Yvette spread her shopping around many NAAFIs. To Celle, Munster Lager, Falling-bostel, as far as Hanover.

Once she drove to Lüneburg. She remembered it was very close to the East German border and that it was on Lüneburg Heath that the Germans had surrendered to the Allies. One day while exploring the Heath she came upon a statue of Heinrich Heine. She had read little about him but knew he was a poet, a wise, good man, Jewish and revered by the Germans. Of course, he had lived a long time ago. She made a mental note to find out more about him. Get a book from the library. But she knew that like so many of her resolutions it would go by the wall. For her mind was too constantly occupied with thoughts of her predicament to have the peace to improve it. It was permanently filled with hatred for her husband; curiosity as to why he went away whenever it was possible; why he never told her about his trips. There was more to it than selling his Black Market merchandise. That he could have sold ten times over in Hohne and its surrounding villages. And the camera and the locked darkroom.

Sometimes, when Victor was away overnight, she would stay down, drinking endless cups of coffee and accuse herself of having neither courage nor character. Telling herself that no woman with an atom of self-respect would stay with a man like her husband. They'd find a way out. Sell their clothes, jewellery, anything valuable from the house. The car. Even without selling she could raise enough money for a passage to England. She'd find work. Washing dishes, scrubbing floors, cleaning lavatories. Qualifications weren't required for those jobs. She'd even go on the street. Being a prostitute would be less brutalised and demeaning.

Halfway through the night her spirits would rise, strength surge through her. She could do it: she could do anything. If Victor walked in the door now she would have the strength to kill him. But her manic state only lasted a short while. And then, as new-found courage had surged through her like an oncoming tide, it ebbed away and she was sucked down into a morass of depression. Before the light of morning came she would fall asleep.

She never slept for long, and woke in the depths of despair and longed to die, knowing that her thoughts last night had been fantasies. She was shallow, a worthless creature and amoral. She would go on living with Victor. Submit to torture, sodomy, whatever he demanded rather than go into the world unprovided for. For days, some-times weeks, the depression weighed her down. There was no one to notice her mood swings. Often she drove carelessly, not caring if she was killed. Then she came to her senses and realised she might kill someone else.

The other three women had young German girls who helped in their houses. Victor, when Yvette asked for one, had refused. 'No strangers in the house. You've every labour-saving gadget money can buy.'

She didn't argue, avoiding confrontations that finished up with her being used as a punchbag.

One night he brought a case into the living room, opened it and showed her his equipment, whips, hand-cuffs, objects that looked like huge penises. Some made of rubber, some of leather which were studded along their sides, and some thin nylon ropes.

'What are they, what are they for?'

'For me and you. To enhance our lovemaking. You're not the most passionate of women.'

She envisaged herself trussed like a chicken while Victor performed unspeakable things on her body. Using the false penises and photographing her. As he did when he made her wear the lurid, disgusting underwear.

'Well, that was my intention. Pain and ecstasy go together. You'd have revelled in it but Bill doesn't oblige. I don't think he ever sleeps or else spends all night humping. I've checked night after night. Sometimes it's three or four o'clock before their light goes out. I don't want him breaking down the door to know why you're screaming. I could gag you but genuine screams are very exciting.'

'That's pornography, taking pictures of me in those positions and taking pictures of me tied up is sadomaso-chism.'

'Rubbish. It's husband and a willing wife pepping up their sex life. And where did you get your information all of a sudden?'

'I saw a magazine in Hamburg. I glanced through it.' She knew her admission had risked a beating but couldn't resist asking, 'Why do you do such things? Supposing I was to tell Sheila?'

He laughed derisively. 'Sheila, that tramp, she'd be banging the door down pleading to try them out.'

'That's a vile accusation.'

'I think it's spot on. Or have you forgotten the tango demonstration?'

'You were the cause of that. I saw you put something in the punch. What was it?'

'Spanish fly.'

'But that's poison. You read about people dying from it.'

'Not when it's used by an expert and that's me. Not that Sheila needs an aphrodisiac. Just a man to hand.'

Victor's manner was cocksure – always a danger sign. It was time for her to stop the questions. For reasons of his own he had answered them. A display of arrogance. She pretended the beginning of a migraine and he let her go to bed without an assault.

One weekend there was a Schützen Fest in a local village. It was a small affair, a few stalls, one with a rifle range, rubbishy prizes except for one huge pale-blue teddy bear, the star attraction. Fergus and Bill were on duty so Bob was taking the women and children. Lizzie, because of her size, was unable to take Tom on her lap. He stood by the dashboard, which wasn't considered dangerous.

As the women were squeezing into the back seat, Victor came to the car and offered to take Tom in his. Tom eagerly left the dashboard and jumped into Victor's arms.

'Isn't Yvette coming?' Lizzie asked.

'No she's not, she's got a migraine.' He didn't add that as Fergus and Bill had been on the ranges for part of the night he'd submitted her to manacles, ropes and photography.

'A pity, it's such a lovely day.'

'She'll go to bed and stay there until the headache's better.'

The band was very loud. Many of the Germans wore funny hats, drank lots of beer and sang with great gusto. Young girls went round in giggling groups and were sized up by young boys. There were stalls selling varieties of sausage in bread rolls and there was a small roundabout. The atmosphere was joyful. Lizzie remarked on it to Sheila.

Cynical as she was, more and more lately, she replied, 'Change their funny hats for helmets and they'll sing "*Deutschland über alles*" and demonstrate the goose-step.'

'Oh, you,' Lizzie said affectionately, 'you're always moaning about something.'

'I know,' Sheila admitted, 'this place is getting me down. I wish I could drive. It's like being in prison here.'

'Have you asked Fergus about giving you lessons?'

'That fella! Every time I mention driving he has a ready-made excuse. How dangerous it is on the autobahns. His insurance would shoot up. He wouldn't have an easy mind if I was driving. The bloody liar. Men, they don't want their wives to be independent. The Germans have a saying for it. *Kinder, Küche, Kirche*. That's how men want it. Women with lots of children, in aprons, cooking; on Sundays wearing their knees out praying. The rest of the time obliging them in bed. Jesus, sometimes I hate them.'

Lizzie knew that Fergus's drinking was the cause of Sheila's fault-finding with almost everything. He went to the mess every night when he wasn't on duty. He wasn't quarrelsome in drink but, Bob had told her, Fergus could sink ten pints a night. That must make a big hole in their finances. Sheila had a right to object to that and to spending so much time on her own. They had terrible rows, Sheila screaming like a tinker, and smashing cups and plates. But Fergus went to the mess just the same, the only one of the four men who did so regularly. They were still mad about each other. You could see that when they were dancing. How they looked at each other like young lovers.

'Look at your man.'

'Where?' asked Lizzie.

'Over by the shooting gallery. Your Tom's mad about him. Clutching on to the leg of his trousers. He's having a go with the rifle. Bloody show-off. I hope he misses every time.'

But he didn't. He won several celluloid ducks and then the big blue teddy bear, which he handed to Tom. Tom squealed with delight. The teddy was almost as big as him. It needed his two arms to carry it to where Lizzie was sitting.

'Look, Mammy, look. Look what Uncle Vic got me.'

Victor was behind him, a protective hand on his shoulder.

'You're a great marksman,' Sheila said. 'I suppose you've won prizes at Bisley.'

'Dozens of them,' Victor said. And thought, you're a sarcastic bitch. One of these nights I'd like to show you what my marksmanship is really like.

There was a roll of thunder in the distance. Then sheet lightning.

'I could feel it coming. I get a headache. I hate storms. I'm terrified of lightning.'

'That was only sheet lightning. That doesn't strike anyone, Sheila—'

'I know that, Lizzie. But in this kip of a place you know what happens. One minute it's sheet then two or three storms get going and the fork lightning is striking out left right and centre. You never know where it'll strike next.'

'If you count from the clap of thunder to the flash of lightning you can tell how far away the storm is,' Victor said.

'Oh, is that a fact, Victor?'

He grinned and said it was.

She had to admit that, bastard though he was, there was a great attraction about him, an animal sort of thing. She wondered what he'd be like in bed but still got her dig in: 'Then would you mind telling me how you can tell one storm from another when there's maybe three going at the same time?'

'Well—'

'Don't bother, I'm going home. Come on, Lizzie, let's find Bob. I don't like the look of those clouds.'

Bob's coaxing had no effect on Tom who refused to leave Victor's side.

'Let him go with him,' his mother said. She was very tired and uncomfortable. Having carried and given birth to three ten-pound babies, her abdominal muscles were almost non-existent, so that she appeared to be much further in her pregnancy than she was. It was no longer a secret. Every morning Sheila offered to take Paula and Susan to school, and enquired if Lizzie wanted anything from the NAAFI. Sometimes she did.

Sometimes she refused their offers: 'Not today. I'll meet the girls from school. The fresh air and a walk will do me and Tom good.'

They were wonderful neighbours. She was very fond of both. Sheila was like quicksilver, one minute planning how she'd shorten her summer frocks. Saying that according to the magazine Sarah had lent her they were all dressing like hicks. Then, in an instant, she'd have some complaint about living in an army camp miles from anywhere. For Beth, Lizzie had great affection. She was never bad-humoured, a pleasant, gentle person who'd listen to your moans and groans, and was wonderful with children. Endless patience with them. Lizzie prayed every night that Beth would have a baby. Yvette, well she didn't know what to make of Yvette. She had a feeling that she would have liked to be more friendly. But you could only try so much to include her in the free and easy relationship shared with Sheila and Beth. Bob told her when sometimes she puzzled over Yvette's aloofness that Victor was to blame. 'Bastard. He's after a commission and he'll get it. Probably the reason why he isn't as pally as the rest of us and why Yvette isn't allowed to be too chummy with the other wives.'

'But how would that affect his commission?'

'He wouldn't want the hoi polloi dropping into his officer's house.'

'That's us.'

'That's us.'

'I always thought that when someone was commissioned they were posted somewhere else to avoid that sort of thing.'

'They are, but somewhere or other they'll bump into people they knew before they left the ranks. And the last thing they want is to be claimed as bosom pals of other ranks.'

'You're probably right but lately he's improved. Look at the fuss he makes of Tom. And the night of the party he brought us some of the buffet. He didn't have to do that.'

'I suppose not. Even so I don't like him. There's something not right about him. And I'd say that Yvette is terrified of him—'

The young wives didn't read newspapers. A quick glance at the front page of the *Daily Mirror* and that was it. During the day they listened to BFN, the army radio station, to the latest records and request programmes for families and serving soldiers. News bulletins they generally turned off. They were stationed very close to the border with Eastern Europe. From conversations overheard between their husbands they knew that trouble was brewing between Kennedy and Khrushchev. It was connected with Cuba. The finer points of the crisis they didn't grasp. Didn't want to. They could do nothing about it, so they said to each other, and changed the conversation. Gossiping about this and that. Disbelieving the latest warnings about smoking and lung cancer as they passed round their drum of duty free Players, drank coffee and pastries they'd bought from the German baker who delivered their delicious bread.

They had all bought twin-tub washing machines with electric mangles attached; standard lamps set in gimmicky Formica-topped coffee tables; free-standing ashtrays within hand's reach, a boon in houses where husband and wife smoked. The ashtray opened by the touch of a button and swallowed butts into its capacious maw, the tight-fitting cover ensuring no unpleasant smell of used tobacco.

Their labour-saving devices, novelty ashtrays and lamps were bought from Herr Woolfe who had a shop in Bergen, he called once a week to collect the hire purchase payments. He was handsome, pleasant and courteous, as were the shopkeepers and other Germans they came in contact with. Grocers giving the children biscuits and in the delicatessen they were handed slices from the great variety of cooked meats. Life in Germany, they convinced themselves, was good so long as they kept thoughts of how desolate it could be and fears of what could happen repressed. And when that wasn't possible they took consolation that if the worst came to the worst they had their husbands, experienced soldiers who, if the balloon went up, would get them out of the camp and to safety.

If the war was a nuclear one they would all be killed but they'd die together. Everyone would be killed. There was nothing you could do about it, they told themselves.

One day, after a coffee session at Lizzie's, Sheila came running back looking distraught. She was crying, mascara had leaked down her cheek. She held a sheet of paper. 'Take it, take it. Read it. Jesus, Mary and Joseph protect us—'

Lizzie was alarmed. She had never seen Sheila cry. It must be something very serious. The sheet of paper was creased and slightly damp.

'Read it,' Sheila urged, 'go on, read it. I'm in bits. Shaking all over.'

Lizzie smoothed out the paper and Sheila continued sobbing and talking at the same time. 'I always search his pockets before I put his shirts in the machine and that's what I found today.'

Lizzie lit a cigarette, gave one to Sheila and began to read the document. It was an army directive instructing the wives that in the event of an emergency they would go to the barrack square where major Burney, the Q.M., would be in command. Women with babies would bring feeding bottles and tins of formula, as many blankets as they could carry. On no account should unnecessary possessions be taken with them. Further instructions would be issued as they became available.

'Oh, God,' said Lizzie, laying down the paper, 'then it's serious. The Russians must be about to invade.' She began to cry. 'I knew it was always on the cards. But so long as Bob would be with me and the kids I thought we'd stand a chance.'

'Me too,' sobbed Sheila. 'I don't want to be killed but I could face it with Fergus beside me. He'd protect us to the bitter end. And instead we've got Burney, that excuse for a man. All he knows about is cracked cups and saucers, stained mattresses, dishing out bedding and light bulbs. We'll be mown down. I'm going home. I'm going back to Dublin. I'm not staying here to be slaughtered.'

'Where will our husbands be if something happens?' asked Lizzie.

'Heading, I suppose, to where the fighting is.'

'But if it's a bomb and not an invasion, will there be time to fight?'

'God only knows. If it's a bomb it would probably pass over our heads on its way to England. I know no more than yourself – except that out of here I'm getting. Me and the twins back to Ireland—'

'The fare will cost you a fortune. Where will you get the money?'

'Fergus has a few bob in his Posby. It'll take a few days' notice to get it out. But even with the money in my hand it won't be easy getting to a port. We are like prisoners in this camp. Have to walk miles to reach anywhere. Now and again if there's a Volkswagen available and its to the dentist you're going, you might get one. Wouldn't you think the army could run a bus through the garrison? There was no transport available last week when I had that abscess. Nearly three miles I had to walk there and back to the dentist. My face swollen, the pain in my jaw agonising and to top it all there was a freezing wind. It's worse than living in the bogs in Ireland. After you've had the baby, please God, insist that Bob teaches you how to drive. You'll be buried alive otherwise. It's disgraceful, so it is. For most of the time during practice camp our cars are locked up in the garages while the men ride around in champs and we have to walk everywhere.'

They had temporarily forgotten about the bomb and threats of an invasion. They gossiped, drank coffee and smoked.

Then Beth arrived, her eyes swollen from crying. Lizzie and Sheila assumed she had also found the directive. But Beth's grief was for a different reason. Not the threat of what might happen but evidence of something definite. She put her head in her hands and cried as if her heart were broken. 'We will never be able to have a baby. Bill got his results. His sperm count is so low it's almost non-existent.'

Lizzie filled the kettle. Tea or coffee was their panacea even though their sideboards were laden with varieties of duty free spirits. Generally women didn't drink at home.

'When did he find out?' Sheila asked.

'This morning, he came in to tell me and went back to work. It's not as if he is sick.'

Lizzie poured the tea and asked, 'Isn't there any treatment?'

'Nothing. He had mumps when he was fifteen. It makes men sterile.' She had stopped crying and began to laugh hysterically. 'You know Bill, a great believer in saving the pennies so the pounds look after themselves and when we weren't trying for a baby he bought the condoms wholesale. By the score, packets and packets of them by mail order.' She laughed hysterically again. Then she saw the directive and asked if she could read it.

'It's meant for us to read,' replied Sheila, handing the paper to Beth. 'You think there's anything in it, Beth?'

'At the moment I couldn't care less. What's life got for me and Bill? Oh, God, I'm sorry! I shouldn't say such a thing to you who have children.'

'We know you didn't mean it,' Sheila said. 'It's been a dreadful shock. It'll take some getting used to. Jesus, isn't life unfair. When you think of all the unwanted children in the world. You'd ask yourself if there's a God at all.'

'Being infertile doesn't mean, you know, that you won't be able to do it.'

For the first time since arriving Beth laughed loud and naturally. 'No Liz, I know that. After all, what ails him has been there for years. It never interfered before. Six times a week and twice on Sunday.' She paused and looked pensive. 'We had a good love life but maybe the news will upset him. Make him think he's less of a man.'

'I don't think so,' Lizzie and Sheila said simultaneously.

'I hope you're right. I'm going in to wash my face and go to the NAAFI for a fillet steak to cheer him up.'

Sheila put the directive in her pocket, suggested that Lizzie should have a nap when Tom was asleep and went home.

Chapter Eighteen

That night, when Sheila's girls were in bed, she showed Fergus the directive. 'I found it in your shirt pocket when I was doing the washing. Does it mean what I think it does?'

'Well, it does and it doesn't. You know what the army's like – always be prepared.' He took the paper from her and tore it up. 'You weren't supposed to see that,' he said, dropping the directive into the bin. 'We get one of those every month or so.'

'And why shouldn't I be allowed to see it, isn't it me it concerns?'

'For the simple reason that you and the other women would work yourselves into a state.'

'I see, keep the little women barefoot and pregnant. No opinions. No say in anything even if our lives are in danger.'

'For Christ's sake, Sheila, don't start a row.'

'I won't start a row. I haven't got the energy, not after the fright I got from that thing.'

'That's the reason you're not supposed to read it. I was careless to leave it about.'

'I'm glad you did, it's helped me make a decision.'

'About what?'

'It doesn't concern you.'

He looked tired. She felt sorry for him. If only he weren't in the army they'd be as happy as the day is long. She loved him so much. 'Sit down. I've made you beef stew and dumplings, and there's a couple of cans of Carlsberg in the fridge.'

She laid a tray and brought it to him, and when he had eaten the stew with relish asked, 'What did you mean when I asked you if that paper was serious and you said "It does and it doesn't"?'

'Well, just supposing the balloon did go up, you'd have to do what the directive orders.'

'You mean you wouldn't be with us?'

'Yeah, I'd be long gone and don't ask where.'

'You mean that bloody oul shite would be in charge of the women and children? God, oh, Fergus. How could anyone trust him to look after us?'

'Probably because he's one of the few not fit for active service.'

'I'd die, so I would, if we were separated.'

'If a nuclear bomb was dropped we'd all die.'

'I know that. I've thought about it often enough. But with us all together I'd be brave. The four of us would die in each other's arms.'

Sheila's face was wet with tears. Fergus put away his beer and took her on his lap. He wiped her eyes and smoothed back the black curls that had fallen forward on to her face, and talked to her as he did to the twins when they woke from a nightmare. 'It's all right, darling. Hush now. There'll be no bombs.'

'How d'ye know that?'

'Because everyone everywhere would die. There'd be no winners.'

'It's no laughing matter. I'll have nightmares for weeks. I'll never get the thought of nuclear war out of my head.'

'Well, you can stop from now on. Kennedy and Khrushchev have done a deal. No more than us they don't want to be killed.'

'But what about if we're invaded from the East?'

'That's always a possibility. But we have intelligence working for us. We wouldn't be taken unawares. That's where the directive comes in. I'd have to report to wherever I was needed and the women to the square. There'd be transport laid on to take you away from here. In no time you'd be back in England.'

'Is that the truth?'

'As true as God. Only don't tell anyone else. You weren't supposed to see that paper and I'd get a bollocking for letting it fall into your hands. Will we have a bath and go to bed and—'

She smiled for the first time that evening, went to him and, playfully punching him, said, 'I can guess the rest.'

Lizzie and Bob had a similar conversation about the directive and a similar ending to the evening. But long after the two men were asleep their wives lay awake, imagining a nuclear Holocaust.

Beth and Bill lay in bed in each other's arms, he crying bitterly about their childless future.

Unlike Lizzie and Sheila, Beth wasn't thinking about nuclear war, but making plans to adopt a baby. She wouldn't broach the subject until Bill had come to terms with his handicap. He would eventually. They went to sleep not having made love, an unusual occurrence for them.

'I've heard so much about the ranges, isn't it time you took us to see them?' Sheila, after coming back from mass, said to Fergus.

'You wouldn't like them.'

'I'd still like to see them. God knows there's nothing much else to see or do here. I might as well be locked up in Mountjoy—'

'You'd better get used to it – there's years to go yet.'

'Don't I know it. Though in the summer we can do a bit of touring. You want to see the exhibition of camping equipment in the Roundhouse. Tents that don't look like tents as we know them. Brilliant colours, fabulous gadgets to make life easy. Huge tents divided into bedrooms and living rooms. We could maybe drive to France, Holland even Italy or Spain. Imagine that.'

'Imagine the price of the camping gear,' Fergus said.

'No problem, you can buy on hire purchase. Of course, it would cut down on your pocket money.' Your beer money, she thought, but didn't say so. For the time being she wanted to keep him sweet.

'Sheila, practice camp starts next month. I'll be working day and night.'

'I know that but I know you'll still get leave. Anyway, think about it and for the time being a trip to the ranges will have to do.'

Fergus prided himself on knowing every move of Sheila's. Knew she wasn't interested in the ranges. That asking to go there was a ploy to stop his pre-lunch drinking session. 'Love, you'll hate it, there's nothing to see,' he said. He didn't intend giving in without some opposition. 'The ranges are an eyesore. They're barren, disgusting, nothing of interest. You'll be bored out of your mind.'

'Then let's make it interesting. I'll ask Lizzie and Bob to come and on the way back we'll stop at that *gasthaus* you're always on about. You know, the one with all the ties hanging from the ceiling.'

'I'm jaded. We had a late night, remember,' Fergus complained. 'And don't forget the hundreds of miles I drive every day.'

'You do in your eye. All you have to do is sit in the Land Rover. Someone else does the driving.'

'OK, but that doesn't make the work I do when I arrive at a camp any the less demanding.'

'Ah, but how you glory in it. The big cheese. Lording it over everyone. The young gunners probably quaking in their boots. Yes sir, no sir, three bags full sir, and give us a good report on our gun drill. While I'm stuck in this kip, smoking myself sick, drinking gallons of coffee or an exciting trip to the NAAFI. We're going to the ranges. I'll put the meat in to slow roast then slip into Lizzie's.'

He could dig his heels in and refuse. But she'd create a scene, recount how much he drank, the waste of money. The hours she spent alone while he was guzzling lager, then pissing it up against the wall.

And she had a memory like an elephant, recalling sessions he'd long since forgotten. Christmas Days when he helped serve dinner to the other ranks while she slaved over a hot stove and the twins only infants. He didn't know which he hated or feared most, her nagging or when she went berserk, smashed crockery, whatever came to hand. She had a terrible temper. His drinking did nothing to improve it. He hated her tempers. It aroused him.

Maybe she knew that. Knew that in the middle of her screaming rage he wanted to grab hold of her, hit her, not hard, just a slap, and then kiss and caress her and make love wherever the row was taking place. Only he never had the courage to try it. Not because he feared rejection. She never refused him. But during the struggle she fought like a dervish and would lash out with whatever she had in her hand. Many's the bang of a saucepan he had suffered. Occasionally it was a carving knife she brandished.

Usually it was a bang of a wet floorcloth, a cup whizzing by your head, minor injuries and humiliations, joked about later on. But the hilt of a carving knife sticking out of your chest was another thing altogether.

He talked to himself while she was at Lizzie's: it's me

that's to blame. Me and the drink. I'm full of good intentions. Telling myself I'll only have the one pint. Then, before I know it someone's called another round. I could refuse, of course. Other blokes do. Say they don't want to upset the missus. My stupid pride wouldn't allow me to do that. It's the Irish in me. I take after my father. He had the weakness too. I'll have to take the Pledge. I'd die if she left me. She could, too. Her mother'd be only too delighted to have her and the twins in Dublin. And Sheila would have no trouble walking into a job. I do forget that she is years younger than me – only twenty-five – ten years' difference. And this is a bloody awful place for women. I'll take the Pledge. Never let another drink pass my lips. Maybe save enough money for this camping gear she's on about.

Sheila came back all smiles. 'Lizzie'll come, Bob never refuses her anything. What about Bill and Beth? Will I ask them?'

'I saw them go out earlier,' Fergus replied.

'How's he taking his results? I don't like to keep asking Beth.'

'Haven't a clue. He told us the bad news. Hasn't mentioned it since. Men don't.'

'He looks terrible, so does she. Will I make a few sandwiches?'

'It's not a picnic, only a drive over the ranges,' Fergus retorted, a temptation still lingering to refuse the outing.

'Whatever you say, darling,' Sheila replied, humouring him, and changed the conversation. 'I saw your man drive off at eight o'clock. Yvette wasn't with him. Hamburg, I suppose, he goes there a lot. She let it slip the other day. The Reeperbahn probably.'

'With a wife like Yvette he'd have to be mad.'

Yvette had breathed a sigh of relief when Victor left the house. She had cooked him a huge breakfast. She'd have roasted an ox, done anything to be rid of him for a day.

Maybe a night, he had hinted as much. He took pyjamas, shaving kit and, of course, his camera. Occasionally he'd show her scenic views taken on his outings. And since becoming captivated by Tom, snaps of him. He had given copies to Lizzie who was thrilled with them.

He was a great photographer, Yvette had to admit, and yet she felt uneasy about the pictures he took of Tom. More so about his relationship with the child. He showered him with gifts, sweets, chocolates, matchbox cars, kites, always little gifts. Tom, who could now talk, called him Uncle Vic, watched for him coming home and greeted him with as much if not more affection than he did Bob. Vic would hoosh him up in the air, ruffle his hair and do the same to the teddy bear, which Tom was very seldom without. The child was enamoured of him.

For Yvette it was like seeing a replay of Victor and Sean when he began coming regularly to Paddington. Tom was under his spell just as Sean had been.

At that time she had been delighted that Victor made so much of Sean, took so many snaps of him. And as his monthly visits continued he took her and Sean to Regent's Park, to Little Venice and the Zoo, promising that when Sean was older they'd visit the Natural History and Science Museums.

Mags was charmed by Victor. She described him as a gentleman and said he'd make a great husband and father for Sean, adding, 'Anyone can see he's fond of you. More than fond. It wouldn't do any harm to give him a little encouragement.'

She began considering the idea of marrying. Not that Victor, as far as she could see, had ever been more than polite to her. All his attention was for Sean. When she reminded Mags of this she smiled and said, 'Well of course, he's working his way through the child. Oh, what he feels for him is genuine enough, but you're the catch, mark my words.'

One day as they walked along the canal she told him her

parents were coming up for the Easter weekend and that her father had taken early retirement. 'He's a changed man,' her mother had written. 'Forgiven you for leaving home. Mind you, I said nothing about little Sean, though I think he'd have forgiven that as well. And I know when he sees him he'll be mad about him. I'm telling you it's a miracle what's happened to him. Either that or he feels his days are numbered and he's preparing himself to meet his Maker. He's become charitable in the true sense of the word.'

'You're miles away,' Victor had said. And she'd said she was sorry and that she'd been thinking about her mam and dad.

'I'll be here over the Easter weekend. I'd like to meet your parents.'

'You're bound to, then.'

He was carrying Sean on his shoulders like a doting father. She wondered what her mother would think of Victor.

She was never to know. Outside Reading the coach in which they were travelling collided with a lorry. Fifteen of the passengers were killed, her mother and father among the dead.

Mags advised against going to the funeral, she would go instead and collect or have sent to Paddington anything she thought worth keeping. 'You know how nosy they are back there. Can't help it, see. And for the most part it's good-natured nosiness. But they'd be asking you questions. What hospital you're in? When will you be a proper nurse? You know what they're like. I'll say you have a bad dose of flu. And I'll see the Council about giving up the house. If that's all right with you?'

And of course it was. The last thing she wanted to do was go back. 'I'd have lost my mind to see Mam and Dad go down into their graves. If I didn't see their burial I could let on to myself that they were still alive at least for a little while.'

Mags, who had been failing, never recovered from the shock of her sister's death and died within a year. She left Yvette her savings of £200. The guest house had been rented and was quickly sold.

The new owners objected to a young child on the premises. They hadn't yet given her notice but she knew it would arrive soon enough. Her parents had lived in a council house and left no money or valuable possessions. All she had between her and destitution was Mags's £200.

Then Victor proposed to her. She didn't love him nor dislike him. She considered her options. The new owners were making her life a misery. Sean was confined to the bedroom for most of the day. She worked like a slave, wasn't appreciated and from her wages had keep deducted. She would have to find another job. A live-in one where a child wasn't objected to. Again and again she sought alternatives to marrying Victor but couldn't. Eventually desperation drove her to accept his proposal.

Chapter Nineteen

He bought clothes for her and Sean, booked a table in a restaurant for lunch after the wedding. There were no guests, no bridesmaid, no best man. Two witnesses were provided by the register office. They stayed for the weekend in the boarding house. He returned to camp and arranged for her to follow him during the week. He met her and Sean from the train and brought them to the flat he had rented.

The landlady, a pleasant woman, gave them tea when they arrived and made much of Sean. He didn't respond and clung to Victor. Sometimes Yvette felt jealous, but told herself she should be grateful that Victor loved him, would be a good father to him and that despite the doubts she had harboured about marrying, so far he was being a model husband. He was also a skilful lover. She remembered Sean and how she had responded to his foreplay and then the disappointing experience of intercourse. That wasn't how it was with Victor. Yet though she could experience passion with him, she never felt love. Unlike Sean, he lacked tenderness, making love to her, he was having sex. After bringing her to a thrilling climax he left her, turned away and went to sleep.

Sean continued to adore him, watched for his return from work, running to meet him, laughing delightedly and showering Victor with kisses. For his third birthday Victor bought Sean a tricycle. At about the same time he bought a new camera and, once a month, went away for weekends. Pursuing his hobby, he said. His trips took him to English towns, French ones but more often to Amsterdam.

Her life in the village was lonely. She missed the comings and goings in the guest house. Every day she took Sean to the park, pushed him on the swings, helped him climb up the slide and waited at the bottom to receive him. All the while she hoped that one of the many women there with children would talk to her. No one did. Shopkeepers were civil but no more than that. She raised the subject once to the woman who rented her the flat.

'It takes time,' the landlady said. 'They're suspicious of strangers. Take me, I've lived here for six years and still don't feel that I belong. But all that will change once you get your quarters. You'll have lots of friends. Army wives are like that.'

Victor had little to say when he came home in the evenings. After dinner he'd play with Sean before bathing him and putting him to bed, where he'd read to him until he fell asleep. Sean shared their bedroom. The second one Victor used as a darkroom. It was kept locked.

Yvette accepted his explanation that the chemicals used in photography were dangerous.

She didn't approve of Sean sharing their room. 'He's

172

three and a half and I'm always worried that he'll wake up while we're—'

He interrupted, 'We never have a light on and in any case our quarters will soon be allocated.'

She was thrilled. Her loneliness would end. Gushingly she told this to Victor. 'The landlady said army wives are very friendly. Oh, I'm so glad. I can't wait to move from this village.'

Victor quickly disabused her of the idea of friendly neighbours. 'There'll be no living in each other's pockets. I won't have that. You'll keep your distance.'

'But when Sean starts school I'm bound to meet the other mothers.'

'I have taken care of that, he won't go to the garrison school. There's a small private one three miles outside the camp.'

'That's too far for him to walk.'

'We'll get another car, you'll learn to drive.'

She did. The house had three bedrooms, though she thought that whoever designed the kitchen must have had shares in a company selling doors. There were six in the small space. One into the living room, one into the coalhouse which was in the kitchen, another opened into the bathroom, the fourth door exposed the pantry, the fifth the airing cupboard and the sixth led into the porch. She got used to them, only finding them a nuisance when Sean opened all of them at the same time.

But there were many compensations. A Rayburn stove which supplied gallons of hot water and warmed the kitchen. Sometimes the water reached boiling point and she had to run it off, filling the room with clouds of steam. The stove had a slow oven in which she cooked casseroles and delicious rice puddings, and a second one in which bread could be baked and pastry cooked.

Sean now had his own bedroom. She never went to sleep until Victor began snoring, then she got up and locked their bedroom door, fearing always that when it was daylight Sean might come in and see her in some of the positions Victor demanded she should take while they had sex.

It was from the time he demanded what she considered unnatural positions, that she wished for him to die. This period in their life coincided with him buying her expensive clothes. It was to ensure that she wouldn't be overtly welcomed by her new neighbours. As was Victor's ban on her inviting other women in when he wasn't there and Sean going to a private school. He'd be the only child whose father wasn't commissioned attending the school. They were a two-car family when the majority didn't have one. It all added up to the neighbours giving her the cold shoulder. Victor had worked it all out. He knew the army, knew that the mothers collecting their children from school wouldn't be overawed by Yvette's Country Casuals and Jaeger suits. She'd be considered overdressed for the school run, vulgar. From that group she'd get no invitations to coffee mornings. He had her where he wanted her.

Bob and Lizzie led the way to the ranges.

Sheila, having got her way, chatted to Fergus. 'It's a lovely day and the run out will be nice. It'll break the monotony. This feckin' place is desperate. What are you supposed to do in it? The mess on Saturday night, the stupid games and the fellas who think they're comedians telling jokes. D'ye know my face aches from pretending I'm enjoying them. Most of them are filthy without being funny.' She broke a large bar of chocolate and shared it with the twins, then continued. 'The back of beyond. Mass on Sunday and the Wives Club once a month.'

Fergus made no comment. She was now in reasonable humour and he didn't want to say anything that would change it. He kept his thoughts to himself. After four pints he'd have come home in great humour, enjoyed his dinner, read the papers, had a little doze. Sheila would have washed up, the kids probably in Lizzie's, he'd sloother her and she might have a lie-down.

He wasn't going to put a foot wrong. She frequently threatened to go home to Dublin. She might, too. He'd die without her and the twins. He'd have to go and see Father Tom, ask for his help with the drinking problem. It wasn't as if he was an alcoholic. He liked a drink, that was all. Fellas in the mess joked about it. Said he had the biggest swallow. But he never got legless. Never had to leave his car behind. His mother had made allowances for his father. But women were changing. Sheila certainly was. His mother and father had been married for forty years. He couldn't remember one of their neighbours who had split up.

Sheila interrupted his reminiscences. 'I've just noticed the apple trees planted along the verges all the way between one village and the next. Why is that?'

'Thrift,' he said. 'Using all the available land. They share the work and the harvest.'

'Just like in Ireland, I don't think.'

'I forgot to tell you, there's going to be a big do for Father Tom's Silver Jubilee. Everyone's invited. Should be a good night.'

'I heard about it in Mass this morning,' said Sheila, 'but not about everyone being invited. D'ye mean Protestants as well?'

'Everyone. It's in the Roundhouse.'

'I think he's the best priest I've ever come across,' Sheila said and Fergus knew she was now completely off the boil. 'I'll never forget', she continued, 'the night he told us when his billet in Cyprus caught fire. And his first thought was to rescue his golf clubs not his religious things.'

'Sometimes', said Fergus, 'I think he spins yarns, doing the hardchaw, wanting to be popular. And the story about his mother hiding rifles underneath him in his pram, there's hairs on that one.'

'Mind you,' Sheila said, 'that could be true. He's from Donegal, Donegal people were always great Republicans.'

The tiff was now definitely over. In a minute she'd be talking about a new frock for the party.

'For the next six months you wouldn't be able to set foot on here,' Fergus told her as they arrived at the ranges. The barren, blasted area spread in front of them, a scene of desolation: the ground rutted with the tracks of armoured vehicles, lorries, Range Rovers and gun carriers; here and there shell craters filled with stagnant water; trees without tops, one wide trunk with a hole blown through it. Despite the barrenness, grass was attempting to grow and the occasional tree still with branches trying to bud. And over one pool less stagnant than the others two dragonflies hovered.

'Sacred Heart of Jesus!' Sheila exclaimed. 'It's like a battlefield without bodies.'

'That's what it is,' said Fergus. 'Did you bring sandwiches?'

'Whether I did or not, no one's eating here and don't let the twins out of the car. I want to go back, this place is like a glimpse of hell. And you'll be spending most of the summer here.'

'Aye,' said Fergus. 'Out at all hours. Night firing. Sometimes you can get home for an hour or two's kip. Not often, though. It's practice for the real thing.'

'And you'll all glory in it.'

'We're soldiers. It's what we're paid for. A job, that's all.'

'So was Pierpoints. Are there accidents?'

'Very few considering it's live ammunition. Now and then you get a premature. That's when a shell explodes before it leaves the barrel. I've never witnessed one, thank God.'

'Is it only the British army that come here?'

'All the NATO forces, French, Dutch and the Yanks come.'

'I feel as sick as a dog, take us back.'

'No sign of Lizzie and Bob, they must have driven further on,' Fergus said as he started the car.

Niamh and Deirdre were whispering to each other. Maybe they heard me fighting with Fergus, threatening to leave him. I'll have to mind my tongue, Sheila thought.

Fergus was gasping for a pint. 'We'll stop at Range Four.' Sheila said nothing. Range Four was a small *gasthaus*. Fergus had a pint of lager, Sheila a half and the children apple juice.

From the ceiling hung dozens of ties cut off below their knots. The girls were intrigued and asked, 'What did they do that for?'

'An initiation ceremony.' The girls looked blank. 'Just a bit of fun, love, the first time a soldier comes in. One of mine is up there.'

'Filthy looking things. Dust gatherers,' said Sheila contemptuously. 'A dump, like everything else around here.'

Chapter Twenty

Father Tom's Silver Jubilee was a great success. Catholics and non-Catholics, other ranks, non-commissioned and commissioned ranks came to the party. Their wives also attended. Army padres from other garrisons were there too.

The evening began with speeches by clerics and senior officers; some of which were entertaining, some boring. All were eulogies praising Father Tom.

'I can't get over the size of the American military policemen,' Sheila whispered to Lizzie who whispered back, 'I know, and fancy them coming to Mass with revolvers in their holsters.'

'Fergus says you can't get near the bar for Yanks. Still, if it keeps him short of his quota of pints I won't object. What did Bob think of your new outfit?'

'Mad about it. It was very good of you to make it.'

'I enjoyed making it, the stuff was a dream to work with,' Sheila said, fingering the pale coffee-coloured brocade. 'And the colour suits you.'

'I didn't recognise myself when I tried it on. My hair's not as rusty looking, nor my face like a beetroot.' Lizzie smoothed the smock top over her pregnant belly and spoke again: 'Next week the firing camp starts. I'm dreading it. The men coming and going at all hours of the day and night.'

'I hope you're not planning on getting up at the crack of dawn, not with your blood pressure.'

'I couldn't let Bob go out with no breakfast.'

'More fool you. We'd better shut up, we're getting dirty looks.'

They were silent for a few minutes, then Sheila asked, 'Did Bob tell you about the bison?'

'What bison?'

'Of course, you were in hospital for your blood pressure. I thought he might have mentioned it when he went in to see you.'

'All he talked about was the kids and then not much. I wished the army let someone other than your husband visit. God knows most men haven't much to say at the best of times, but in a hospital ward they're tongue-tied. So what about this bison?'

'It's a kind of buffalo and it's the Yanks' mascot. They had it on display in an open-air compound. We took all the kids to see it. Your Tom went frantic trying to climb the railings and get in. It was groomed within an inch of its life. I'd swear to God its hoofs had been polished. That's the Yanks for you. Our fellas can't stand them. They crowd out the mess, push and shove, and talk louder than anyone else. I suppose the bison gave them a chance to get one over the Americans.'

178

'What happened to it?' asked Lizzie, stifling a yawn.

'It was nicked during the night and a tin of bully beef left in its place.' Sheila laughed so much she spluttered a partly masticated sausage roll in a shower of crumbs over Lizzie, who thumped her on the back and warned again about the dirty looks. But Sheila wasn't deterred and went on with the bison story. 'There were ructions over it. We thought it was hilarious but the Yanks didn't. Fergus said it could cause an international incident.'

'A war, you mean?'

'Don't be such an eejit, not a war but questions raised at the highest level.'

'So what happened in the end – where was the bison?'

'Only up in an empty barrack room. No one admitted taking it so the whole thing fizzled out.'

The eulogies finished and there was an interval during which Lizzie and Sheila talked without whispering. 'I hope', said Lizzie, 'the kids don't give Yvette a bad time.'

'I was amazed when she offered to mind them.'

'He's away for the weekend. She's all right, I'm beginning to get fond of her. Mind you, he's not so bad either. He's great with Tom and he adores him. Got him a ride in a tank last week. And he's taken some smashing snaps of him. Remind me to show you,' Lizzie said.

Then she talked about Beth and Bill not coming to the party. 'I don't know what's happened to them except that they've never been the same since he got his results.'

'I've noticed that. Maybe it's the shock of knowing they can never have a child, I suppose.'

The party was now under way, dancing, then individual singers were called to perform. Father Tom was the first volunteer and sang 'The Sash', the Ulster Protestants' marching song.

'Has he lost his mind and him a rabid Republican singing that?' asked Sheila. 'Mind you, apart from its connections, it's a great tune. It makes me want to get up and march.' She stood up and sighed. 'God, I wish Bob or

179

Fergus was here. I hate going to the bar. Another John Collins?'

'Please, I could drink them all night.'

While Sheila was at the bar a sergeant sang 'Kevin Barry', a rebel song which Lizzie's father had taught her. Her grandfather, he told her, had seen Kevin Barry shoot the young English soldier. He was sentenced to death by hanging and the song was supposed to be his plea from the dock, when sentenced to hang: 'Shoot me like a soldier, do not hang me like a dog, for I die to save my country, 'tis a good and noble cause.'

Lizzie sang along with the sergeant and remembered asking her father, 'Are dogs hanged?'

'I wouldn't say they were in England. Though I heard my father, Lord have mercy on him, say that it happened down the country in Ireland now and again,' he had replied.

The sergeant got great applause. The clapping brought Lizzie to her senses and worried her so that when Sheila came back with the drinks she was in a dither. 'I forgot where I was, Sheil, and sang along with the sergeant. In a place full of British soldiers! No one looked crooked at him. And the clapping they gave him. All the same, aren't the English very tolerant?'

Sheila put the drinks on the table before saying, 'Tolerant my eye. Arrogant bastards is more like it.' She sat down, took a mouthful of the cocktail and spoke again: 'The Irish are great characters, don't you know,' she said, imitating an officer's voice. 'I'll be back in a minute. I'm bursting for a pee.'

She left the table and when she came back said, 'Well, that's me finished with cocktails. There was me thinking I looked gorgeous. But my face in the mirror was like a well-slapped arse.'

'You are a bit flushed but what's that got to do with cocktails?'

'Everything,' replied Sheila. 'How many have you had tonight – four, five?'

'That's the fifth,' said Lizzie running her tongue around the frosted rim of the glass.

'And if it was whiskey or gin how many would you have had?'

'Never more than three.'

'Exactly. But these bloody cocktails taste so delicious you forget how much spirits are in them. The pair of us are stocious. From tonight I'm back to seeing what I'm drinking.'

'I never noticed any difference in my face.' And Sheila thought kindly, you wouldn't, Lizzie. I suppose the only time you look in the mirror is when you comb your hair. Not like me. Forever studying my physiog. And your face, red as it is, hasn't a line on it.

There was more dancing and men singing, then the party was over and everyone stood for 'God Save the Queen'.

Sheila changed her stilettos for a comfortable pair of shoes and, linking arms, she and Lizzie walked home. Yvette told them the children hadn't stirred and that the twins had fallen asleep while she was reading them a story.

Lizzie looked round her tidy kitchen. 'You shouldn't have bothered washing the supper things, but thanks all the same.'

'It was nothing and I liked the novelty of being in someone else's house. I wish I could mind the children more often.' She shrugged and said no more.

'But you do get out a lot,' said Sheila, probing.

'I go here and there. Sometimes I sit for ages in the little cemetery near the swimming pool. Have you been to see it?'

'The weather's been too cold. Maybe when it's warmer I'll pay it a visit. Me and you, Liz, and Beth.'

'It's not very far, a little way past the fish farm.'

'Who's buried there?' asked Lizzie.

181

'The ones who survived Belsen but later died from typhus and typhoid. Before dying they were moved into what had been officers' quarters. Those buildings facing the Roundhouse. After they'd died, those still alive were sent to rehabilitation camps. The quarters were probably fumigated, done over, and the first lot of British families moved in. Anne Franks is said to have died in Belsen, but I don't think that has yet been proved.'

'We'll have to visit Belsen as well,' Sheila said. 'I'd feel it was an insult to all who died there if I didn't pay my respects. Tell us more about the little cemetery.'

'It's small and well cared for. Like a small country churchyard. Every grave has a stone and the name of whose buried there. The majority of inscriptions are in Hebrew and the others mostly gypsies by the look of their inscriptions. Hungarians, Czechoslovakians, I'm not sure. But there is one stone on which the inscription is in English. Lily Prinze, London, and her three-year-old daughter. It has me intrigued and I wonder how did Lily Prinze come to be in Germany? Had she married a German Jew? Had she come to live with Jewish relatives before the rounding up started? Left it too late to get out or was too poor, or like so many unfortunate Jews didn't believe the rumours they heard about concentration camps? Maybe one day I'll try to find out more about her and her little girl.

'I met two elderly women there one day and have seen them several times since. One is German and the other Belgian. Their daughters are married to English soldiers. The German woman's only son was reported missing on the Russian front, the other woman's son was killed fighting the Germans. They visit their daughters every year and the cemetery is where they met. At least the Belgian woman knows her son is dead, but the other still lives in hope that hers will one day come home. They console each other, the mothers of enemies. Two nineteen-year-old boys.'

Lizzie shuddered and thanked God that her Tom was safe for many years to come and Sheila also gave thanks that she didn't have sons.

Except when her blood pressure had shot up alarmingly, Lizzie's pregnancy was progressing normally. No more morning sickness, no more bone-wearying tiredness. She borrowed a book from the library on how to have a virtually pain-free birth. Breathing and relaxation was the method required. She read and read it until she knew it by heart. She involved Bob to monitor her breathing and relaxation, and convinced herself that this birth would be a walkover.

Beth did all she knew how to lift Bill out of his depression, telling him she understood what a terrible shock the results of his tests had been. And when he couldn't get an erection, consoling him. 'You know that the doctor said a low sperm count has nothing to do with virility.'

When the erections failed again and again she would offer the same consolation until one night he snapped at her, 'Well it bloody well has.'

'Give it time. You were a great lover and you will be again. I'll do anything for you, just tell me what.'

He turned away from her and said, 'I know what'll happen. You'll get fed up, frustrated and find someone else. And why not? I'm finished as a husband. I'm finished as a man. Find yourself another bloke.'

'Bill, Bill, don't talk like that. I'd never do such a thing. I've never looked at another man. Never even flirted jokingly with one. And if you never got better I'd still love you. You believe me, don't you?'

He made no answer but moved further from her in the bed and thought that if he didn't get back to normal soon he would do himself in. He was no use to Beth any more. She'd be better off without him. Soon forget him. Marry

183

again. And so she should. She was a young woman. She'd have the children he couldn't give her.

Sheila became more discontented with her life. Fergus came from and went to work at all hours of the day and night. Her sleep was disrupted, her housework disrupted. And from the ranges, twenty-four hours a day, the screeching whine of shells, then their thunderous explosions, the repetitive stuttering of machine-guns and the sound of anti-tank armour-piercing shells nearly sent her out of her mind. She found it difficult to sleep and more often than not when she did drop off would be woken by the rumbling of tanks. Sweat pouring from her, her heart racing, she'd sit up in bed and be convinced that the camp was being invaded. The East German army were crashing through the perimeter fence. Then she'd remember what Fergus had told her: tanks she imagined were invading the camps were theirs, NATO tanks arriving for practice camp. Her heart would stop racing and she'd tell herself she was neurotic. She smoked too much, drank too much coffee. But she'd turn over a new leaf.

Maybe see the doctor. Get some iron tablets. She bled a lot when she had her periods, probably anaemic. She had all the symptoms, palpitations, nervy, irritable . . . A good tonic and she'd be as right as rain. The thought of it made her think that everything wasn't as bad as she made it out to be. Fergus wasn't the worst husband in the world. She had beautiful, healthy daughters, a lovely house and two marvellous friends, Lizzie and Beth. Many, many blessings. And the camp, well, it wasn't like Dublin. But neither were any of the other army camps in which she had lived.

She got off the bed where she'd been sitting moping, showered, dressed and woke the girls. 'Breakfast in a few minutes, OK?'

She took the twins to school along with Lizzie's girls. Then went to the bookshop to buy her copies of *Woman* and *Woman's Own*. The shop sold a variety of things: toys, toiletries, greetings cards, paper beakers, napkins, cocktail sticks and cosmetics. She longed to be able to apply eye make-up. She had bought shadow, mascara and an eyeliner, but so far had never succeeded in applying any of it properly. The eyeshadow made her look like a clown, so did the eyeliner. And the mascara came out of its holder either plastered with the paste or its bristles almost bare. She practised and practised. Her eyelashes were dark but sparse and didn't curl. Sometimes she managed to make the lashes of her right eye look as she wanted them. But never could she coat those of her left eye properly.

Frequently she saw a woman who had the expertise in making up her eyes. She looked neither like a panda nor a clown. Her husband was a medical officer and rumour had it that she had been a model. Often at the make-up counter Sheila stood next to her, envying her attractiveness, attractiveness enhanced by her shadowed, pencilled eyes and curling black lashes. She seemed a pleasant person as she chatted and laughed with the assistant. Several times Sheila had been tempted to make a remark that would bring her into the conversation. In Ireland she wouldn't have hesitated. In no time the three of them would be chatting and she'd be complimenting the officer's wife on her eye make-up. Admitting how impossible she found the applying of it even though she had once worked on a cosmetic counter in Dublin. In Ireland the chances were she and the ex-model would strike up an acquaintance. And eventually visit each other for coffee and she'd learn the knack of using eye make-up.

But that couldn't happen here. Not in the army set-up. Officers' wives and those of non-commissioned ranks did not mix. If they knew you, you would be acknowledged, the health of your children enquired after. They were polite, as they were in the Wives Club. Sheila knew that not all of them nor their husbands were top drawer, as the saying went. Not all of their husbands had been at public school. Many were grammar school, their wives ex-secretaries. But once the men were commissioned, working- or lower-middle-class backgrounds were not admitted and the wives followed suit. Probably, Sheila would think, they were kind, decent people but had to toe the army line. And occasionally she admitted to herself that not every stranger in Ireland fell over themselves to become acquainted with someone they didn't know.

Even so, on the whole the Irish were less hidebound. And on this particular day her newly made resolutions were forgotten and other memories of the class-ridden army came to mind. A girl she'd been in school with who'd been commissioned in the Queen Alexandra's Royal Army Nursing Corps married a sergeant. He could invite her to his mess. But she couldn't invite him to the officers mess. In a letter she told Sheila how furious she had been and was thinking of resigning. Sheila had ranted and raved to Fergus about the army and its rules and regulations. His response was to laugh and say, 'Surely to God you've got used to them by now.'

'I'll never get used to them, never.'

She did some shopping for groceries, then made her way back to Lizzie's.

Lizzie poured coffee for Sheila and put out a plate of German biscuits, pale gold and of several different shapes.

'Where did you get these? They're gorgeous,' Sheila asked after eating one.

'I made them. One of the German wives gave me the recipe.'

'But the different shapes?'

'You put the dough in the mincer and change the slide for whichever shape you want. Eat another few.'

'No, thanks. I'm in bad humour.'

'I thought as much, you've a very expressive face. So tell me what put you in bad humour?'

Sheila did, beginning with her nightmare. Her resolution to take hold of herself. All her good intentions. Then seeing the woman with the expertly painted eyes and the thoughts that had followed that. Lizzie poured more coffee and let her talk. Rant about the army and class distinction.

When it seemed that Sheila had got it all off her chest Lizzie spoke: 'Listen, Sheila, it is true about class and rank distinction but we're all guilty of it.'

Bridling, Sheila said, 'Don't include me in that.'

'Keep your hair on. There's rules in the army same as in Civvy Street. OK, they're more rigid perhaps, but that's all. There are several officers' wives I meet when we go to the club that I think are OK. If they seem distant it's because they're following the rules. And don't forget Lady Avonmouth, she's a dote.'

'One of the few,' Sheila admitted grudgingly.

'Remember the night of the Wives Club dinner when Beth dropped her fork. You know how Beth reads all the magazines and books about etiquette. In one of them she'd read that if in a restaurant you dropped cutlery you called the waiter. I suppose to bring you a clean piece. Poor Beth was in a dither. Hadn't the nerve to call the waiter, you know what she's like. Anyway, while she's wondering what to do Lady Avonmouth says, "You dropped your fork," bends down, picks it up and hands it to Beth.'

'That's breeding for you. It's that we admire in Ireland. And it's not only aristocrats that have it.'

'That's right enough, I've known many ladies and gentlemen at home who were lucky to have a roof over their heads. I've meet the other kind too. Some of the worst snobs I've ever met were priests, Irish into the bargain. So it's not just the English or the army.'

Sheila was calmer now. Lizzie always had that effect on her.

Chapter Twenty-one

May came and with it warmer days. The sledges and winter clothing were put away and on afternoons when Victor wasn't on duty Lizzie let him take Tom for a ride in his car. The blue teddy went too. Tom went willingly and waved to his mother. Grateful for the break, she stretched out on the bed, her legs propped on pillows to avoid varicose veins, she hoped. They'd be gone for at least an hour. Tom would come back excitedly telling her of the cows he'd seen and the storks and their nests on the roofs of houses, and showing her another matchbox car or model of a gun Uncle Victor had bought for him.

Always after the rides Tom was reluctant to leave Victor. Clinging to the leg of his trousers when Lizzie tried to bring him into the house. And Lizzie would think that Victor had certainly won Tom over and wondered, as she often did, why Yvette and he had never had children.

'Have you noticed, Sheila, how seldom people die here? We've been here five months and apart from that poor Irishwoman no one has died. But then I suppose it's because we are all so young and the men very fit.'

'Yeah,' said Sheila, 'and don't forget they chuck the men out at forty-five and officers unless they reach the rank of major at fifty-five. Then there's the Y List. Be in hospital for twenty-eight days and you're on the Y List. Get cancer, you're on it and packed off to the Millbank Hospital in London. Remember the woman with the malignant melanoma and the other one with non-Hodgkin's disease. Off they went to the Millbank. And when there was no hope for them their husbands were posted back to the UK. The same thing happens to men who are seriously ill. That's the army all over for you.'

'Could it not be that the Y List keeps the numbers right?' asked Lizzie and continued, 'Like if someone isn't on the strength, a replacement can be got for him? And in London you'd have top-notch specialists.'

Reluctantly Sheila admitted that that was possible, then added, 'But the strength has nothing to do with the women.'

'They may need treatment you can't get here,' said Lizzie.

'Again, maybe you're right, but I think it's because the army pretends we're all supermen and women. It would be bad for morale having too many people dying of natural causes in a garrison. Let them die in London. Only a handful would know about that. The army's business is killing others, not burying their own. That's how I see it,' Sheila said, then asked, 'Anyway what's made you morbid all of a sudden? Don't tell me you're missing funerals. Maybe it's being pregnant.'

'I don't know. Just thoughts that came into my head. The way we live, for instance, is unreal. Our rent stopped at source, same with the electricity. The family allowance, which is supposed to be the mother's, included in the man's pay.'

'I've been telling you that all along. I wouldn't be surprised if they open our mail.'

'Now, Sheila, that's ridiculous.'

'Maybe. All the same we are treated like kids. So are the men. But they're so enthralled learning how to blow people to bits they're not aware of it. I'm telling you we're like tied tenants. It goes back to before there was a standing army when the Lord of the Manor raised his own from among his tenants if war threatened. That attitude still exists today. God forbidding all harm, if Bob or Fergus died tomorrow we'd be out of our homes in no time. You must think like that sometimes.'

'Seldom. So long as I have Bob and the children, class, rank, none of that bothers me. I'm happy with my life whether it's in England, Germany, anywhere. I love my house, having extra money. But I know things aren't the same for you. It'll change. It'll change for the better, you'll see.'

Changes for the better, they both knew, depended on Fergus if not giving up drink, at least curtailing the amount he drank.

'I hope you're right for if there isn't a change I'll do something drastic.'

Things didn't improve. A couple of weeks later Fergus announced that they had been invited to a cocktail party.

'Beth and Lizzie too?'

'Only us.'

'Why is that?'

'It isn't one of our dos. D'ye remember Paddy Macken?'

'Could I ever forget him, the drunken waster. Don't tell me he's out here.'

'Yeah, he's a sergeant major with the REME. He's divorced. Found his wife in bed with a German driver.'

'More luck to her, he deserved a taste of his own medicine. Is he the one who invited us to the party?'

'He is and he'll pick us up and drive us back.'

'I'm not going.'

'Ah, come on, Sheila, it'll be a night out for you.'

'Definitely not and don't try to get round me.'

But before they went to bed he had got round her, promised not to drink between now and the party and told her to buy a new dress. The NAAFI stocked good-quality clothes: Horrocks's cotton shirtwaisters and glamorous cocktail dresses. Sheila bought one with a low-cut back, sleeveless and bubble-skirted. It barely reached her knees. Too short, she thought, looking in the mirror at the black dress, the colour relieved but not overdone with sprays of carnations. The skirt intrigued her. Why it was called bubble she didn't understand as its shape was that of an upside-down tulip with the end of its petals gathered into a band. She fell in love with it but was still doubtful about

190

the length, then remembered that in England dresses were being worn short. Lizzie had the twins.

'I'll be back by eight. D'ye know, Liz, I hate cocktail parties. You're just getting in the mood when it's all over,' Sheila said and kissed the twins.

Despite Paddy Macken being a waster and womaniser, Sheila had always found him attractive and great company until drink overcame him. She flirted with him, he responded, admired her dress. Told her she was as beautiful as ever. Neither he nor Fergus drank a lot. Sheila was relieved. Once Paddy had too much he'd forget that the flirting wasn't a come-on and his hands would wander. She was also pleased that Fergus was sober and thought of how much she loved him. For once in her life she had thoroughly enjoyed a cocktail party.

When they arrived back at the house Fergus said, 'Look, love, while you collect the kids and tell Lizzie about the party, me and Paddy will drive up to the mess and get a few bottles to take out. We'll be back before you and Lizzie finish gossiping,' and off they drove.

She read the girls two stories in bed, heard their prayers, kissed them and put out the light. The band around her knees was digging in. She changed into another dress, combed her hair, renewed her lipstick and went downstairs where she made sandwiches for when the men came back.

At ten o'clock she got annoyed. She hadn't expected them back as soon as they had promised but ten o'clock was a bit over the top. They'd got in with a crowd and were boozing. And there was me, she thought, believing Fergus was turning over a new leaf. He had spoiled everything. She'd planned on them having a few beers in the house and the sandwiches. Then she'd complain of a headache, Paddy would take the hint and go. She and Fergus would make love on the sofa and again when they went to bed.

Another hour passed. Lovemaking was now out of the

question. Fergus would either fall asleep or try one of his fumbling efforts. She hated those. At midnight she went to bed. Until then she had been annoyed, not worried. Cars driving through the garrison seldom exceeded ten miles an hour. An accident was unlikely. But supposing they had gone outside the camp. Driven to Celle or even further afield.

She couldn't sleep. Downstairs she made a pot of coffee and chain smoked, fumed and raged. They had gone out of camp, gone to a *gasthaus*. They stayed open as long as they had customers. They could have gone to a club where there were woman no better than they ought to be, taxi dancers. She cursed Paddy. Fergus was a boozer but never a womaniser. Paddy was both.

Every time she heard a car approach she looked through the window. Anger was now mixed with worry. Out of the camp, Paddy would have driven like a drunken lunatic. He had by now probably killed her Fergus. She forgave him everything praying aloud, 'Please, God, let him be alive. I love him. I'll never fight with him again. Please, Jesus, don't let the military police come to tell me he's been killed.'

Every time she heard a car she went, to the window. At five a.m. on what promised to be a fine May morning she heard another car and again went to the window, and saw Paddy's bouncy Citroën pull up outside her house. Of Fergus there was no sign. Her heart hammered as thoughts of him in a hospital, in a morgue, raced through her mind. Silently praying, she went to the car.

Paddy smiled the drunkard's smile, a mixture of lechery and stupidity. Curled on the back seat, Fergus opened his eyes and struggled to sit up. The bastard! Nothing ails him except drink. I'll split him open. Keeping me up all night. Frightening the life out of me. She took a few deep breaths. I'll say nothing. Keep calm until that other louser's gone. I won't make a show of myself in front of

192

him. I'll ask Paddy in for a cup of coffee – then wait until he goes.

Paddy talked incoherently while she made coffee. Fergus sat to the table swaying in his chair. She poured the coffee and sat down. Fergus pushed the cup away from him, spilling most of it, and Sheila thought, didn't I do right to serve it in the kitchen. Paddy kept talking about everything and nothing. Sheila's eyes focused on Fergus's mouth. It was stained with lipstick. 'I'm imagining it,' she told herself. 'How could it be lipstick?'

Paddy, with the help of the table, rose to his feet. 'I'd better be going, so.'

Sheila didn't discourage him.

Fergus went into the hall and stumbled up the stairs. She followed him into their bedroom. He kicked off his shoes, undid and stepped out of his trousers, took off his shirt and dropped it on the floor, then collapsed on the bed and fell asleep.

She leant over him again, scrutinising his mouth. She hadn't imagined the lipstick but to be absolutely certain she picked up his shirt, wound her fingers in its tail and vigorously rubbed it across his lips. The tail of the shirt was stained red. 'Jesus!' she exclaimed. 'Not my Fergus, he wouldn't do that.' She stared down at him. 'He wouldn't, sure he wouldn't,' she said aloud.

He opened his eyes with their eejity smile of a drunken man and his hand reached for her, lust and lunacy there in his bleary eyes.

'You kissed someone.' Her voice rose to a shriek. 'You kissed another woman.'

The smile remained in his eyes. 'Yeah,' he said, 'and it was bloody gorgeous.'

Rage consumed her. She wanted to hurt him. Tear his face. Smash his head. She looked for a weapon and on the bedside table saw one. The Roman Catholic Bible she had bought on instalments from a door-to-door salesman. She knew she'd never read it but the illustrations were gorgeous. The twins would love them. And at Easter and Christmas – well, Christmas – she'd read the nativity story. Later on, when she had more time, she'd fill in the spaces for Births, Christenings, First Communions, Confirmation and Marriages. Please God she'd never have to fill in the Deaths sections.

Now it was just a weapon, a great heavy weapon. She raised it above her head and crashed it on to the sleeping, drunken, foolish-looking Fergus with his red-stained mouth.

'Jesus Christ!' he bellowed. Blood was streaming from his nose. 'You bloody bitch. I'll kill you.' He started to get out of bed, his expression wild.

He might, too, Sheila thought. He's still drunk. She ran from the room and down the stairs, opened the hall door and went on to the step, thinking that Fergus would fall asleep again. She would wait a few minutes before going into the house. She drew the door over but didn't let it lock. Then she heard him coming down the stairs and saw his face looking like a madman. The blood from his nose had dripped on to his naked chest. She banged the door to. He could open it, of course, come after her. She was frightened. Never in all their rows had anything like this happened. Never, no matter how fierce the rows, had she ever felt fear of him.

He stood, a ludicrous-looking figure, naked to the waist, his underpants slack so that one hand was holding them up. Maybe I've really injured him, she thought. I didn't mean to. Shock him, that was all. Maybe I've broken his nose. I didn't mean that.

Then she heard the twins screaming, 'Mammy, Daddy, Mammy, Mammy.' Pity for Fergus was forgotten. Only the girls mattered now. She banged on the door, screaming for him to open it. He put his face against the amber rippled glass. The glass distorted his features. He looked like a monster, reminding her of the Hunchback of Notre Dame.

He didn't open the door. If it weren't for the terrified twins she'd have woken Lizzie and stayed with her until Fergus sobered up. But Deirdre's and Niamh's voices were wrenching her heart. She asked him again to open the door and he ignored her. Then, with a closed fist, she hammered at the glass panel. The glass broke and her hand went in, tearing her wrist. With blood seeming to spurt from it, making her believe she had severed a vein or artery and would bleed to death in seconds, she opened the door. Fergus had backed towards the stairs. 'Look what you made me do. I'm bleeding to death.'

'Bleed, you bugger, bleed,' he roared and went upstairs. The twins were sobbing loudly. She had to see to them. But first a cloth for her wrist. From the kitchen she took a tea towel and bound the wound. 'Oh, darlings, everything's all right.' She held them to her. 'Daddy drank too much beer and we had a row. I was trying to show him a picture in the Bible and I dropped it, an accident, it fell on his nose. I think I hurt him. He got mad and chased me down the stairs. Then I locked myself out. I had to get in so I smashed a panel in the door and cut my arm on the broken glass.'

They had calmed down in the comfort of their mother's arms and now wanted to see her wound. 'Later on,' she promised, 'if I take the cloth off now the bleeding will start again. Now I want you two to go back to bed and have another little sleep. It's only six o'clock. Creep up the stairs so you don't wake Daddy. Off you go now.'

She found sticking plaster for the cut on her arm, wiped away bloodstains from the hall, kitchen, hall door and front steps. And all the while she could only think of the lipstick-stained shirt and what he'd said when she woke him. She'd never as long as she lived forget it. He must have meant it. There was a saying, in vino veritas. Her Fergus to cheat on her – never in all their time together had she suspected him of touching another woman. Not even when they were separated for a length of time.

She knew that a lot of women did. Not her mother but that wasn't because she trusted her father. As she told Sheila when she was grown up, 'I'm not flattering myself that he's faithful because of me. Few men are. But your poor unfortunate father when he's footless wouldn't know where to find it.'

'And there was me, kidding myself that Fergus was a saint. I'll be the laughing stock of the place. It'll be round the garrison like wildfire,' she told herself aloud. While she made a cup of tea she wondered how she was to handle the situation. One thing was sure and certain: he was into the spare room from tonight.

Her mind was in turmoil as she washed the dishes; she couldn't remember if Fergus was going out at midday or midnight. Dozens of thoughts chased each other through her brain. But one was more insistent than the others. Her Fergus had done that. Her Fergus had kissed someone else, not a peck on the cheek but lips on lips. Kissed her, admitted it and boasted that it had been bloody gorgeous. She'd never forgive him and never, ever forget. She couldn't live with him any more. She'd leave him, take the twins and go home to Dublin. Now. Today. As soon as she packed, dressed and fed the girls.

She drew back the kitchen curtains. It was going to be a fine day. A lovely day for travelling and the crossing to England would be calm. She'd worry about the Irish Sea when she got to Holyhead. In any case it was only three and a half hours. Halfway up the stairs she stopped. The packing – how could she do that without waking him? Maybe she could borrow a frock and coat from Beth, a pair of knickers. Her shoes were in the living room where she'd kicked them off last night. A frock and a raincoat, they would do. It wouldn't be her first time to go without knickers and a bra.

She'd have to tell Beth what had happened, though she had probably heard the commotion.

To think that in a couple of hours she'd be on her way home. Her handbag was also in the living room, a lipstick and her passport. Fergus was always telling her she should keep it somewhere safe. God must have directed her not to.

Then she remembered and a wave of despair engulfed her. She only had fifty marks. She had no savings; even if she had, unless they were under the mattress, money was unobtainable. No banks. A post office that sold stamps and postal orders – no saving facilities. And even if she had her fare, how could she get to the station? She couldn't unless one of Fergus's mates drove her. Emily was the only woman with a car but she wouldn't help her to leave her husband. Emily wasn't the only woman driver. The other was Yvette but she wouldn't give you a lift to the NAAFI, never mind Soltau.

I'm a prisoner, all the women are prisoners. Like in a gaol we are confined within the perimeters of the garrison. Only officers' wives have cars. She knew she was exaggerating. You could go anywhere outside the camp within walking distance and it was lack of money that stopped the buying of a car. The truth didn't console her.

Fergus's snores reverberated through the house. She put her hands over her ears, sat on the stairs and wept. She'd never heard him snore like that before. It reminded her of her grannie when she was dying: Cheyne-Stokes breathing. She remembered a nurse saying that . . . Maybe the blow to his nose had damaged his brain and he was dying.

'Oh, God,' she said, 'I didn't mean it. I wouldn't harm him for the world. I love him. What would I do without him? My lovely Fergus.' She talked to herself as she opened the bedroom door and there he lay, stretched out, naked, snoring, definitely not dying. The bastard, she thought, but thank God you're not dying. I'll never forgive you but I don't want you to die. I hope I didn't break your nose. I didn't really want to hurt you. Well, I did in a way, but not badly. All the same, I shouldn't have hit you with the Bible, it's a ton weight. It wasn't a sin, though, using it as a weapon, it's not holy, I never got it blessed. I should have hit you with something a bit lighter. But the Bible was to hand.

She backed quietly out of the room, not closing the door, and went to the bathroom, where she doused her face with cold water, then scrutinised it in the glass above the washbasin. 'Jesus, look at me,' she said aloud to herself. 'Is it any wonder he fancied someone else. I look like the Hag of Beara. The poem I learnt in school. I never knew if she was a real old woman or supposed to be Ireland lamenting her sorrows. Anyway, she was ancient. Like me now, I suppose, rings under her eyes as black as night and her skin yellow.

'I'll have to do something about myself. Go down and have strong, sweet coffee. I've the girls to think of. I'll lay the table, have a shower, that'll buck me up. But first I'll empty the bin. Walk down to the bunkers, the fresh air will revive me.' She picked up the plastic bucket and in the hall put on a coat over her nightdress, then opened the door. A cool breeze fanned her face reviving her until she saw the rats. Three big, slimy rats squeezing up through the drain grating. Fear paralysed her. Reason told her they were on the way to the waste bunkers for breakfast, but her troubled mind gave a different message. They would run across the road and pounce on her. Go for her throat. She shut the door, ran into the kitchen and vomited into the sink, vomited until there was nothing left in her stomach, then she retched and retched, while sweat broke out all over her body, and on trembling legs she moved to a chair and sat down.

She rested for a while, then rinsed her mouth and sipped iced water. Still feeling weak and wobbly, she showered, washed her hair and tiptoed into the bedroom, took some clothes and went out quietly. She dressed. She felt better and the mirror reflected a more normal face.

'You don't look yourself,' Lizzie said when Sheila came back from the school.

'I don't think I'll ever be the same again.'

'What happened?'

Sheila told her and also what she believed had happened. 'Did you not hear the row?'

'I slept very well last night for a change. What's his nose like?'

'I don't know and don't care. I'm leaving him, definitely.'

'Because of that.'

'Mainly because of that.'

'D'ye want tea or coffee?'

'I'll never touch coffee again. I drank gallons of it through the night.'

'Tea, then, and a piece of toast?'

Sheila broke down and cried as if her heart would break.

'Oh, love,' Lizzie said, putting an arm round Sheila, 'it isn't what you think.'

'How do you know?'

'I know Fergus, he's a decent bloke. Bob's told me about those clubs. The girls throw themselves at you. They get paid for dancing with the blokes and for the drinks bought for them. Some of the blokes do have sex with them. But not everyone.'

'Has Bob been there? Because if he hasn't you don't know what you're talking about.'

'I know you're upset but don't bite my head off. And no, Bob hasn't been there. But all the blokes talk about it. Lots of them do go. I suppose some of them have sex, but not your Fergus.'

'How do you know that?'

'Because I remember what you told me he said to you.

He told you of all the cases of VD in Germany after the war when the fraternisation began. About the young soldier who shot himself when he thought he'd got it. And Fergus promised you that he'd never be unfaithful for fear of bringing home a disease.'

'Yeah, well, that was then and what's to stop him using a condom?'

'It wasn't only because of disease. He adores you. You know that. If you left him he'd be destroyed.'

Sheila stopped crying, lit a cigarette and said, 'Lizzie, I'm sorry for snapping at you. I'm half out of my mind. I want to believe what you're telling me, I really do, but it'll be a while before I can.'

'That's understandable but try not to let it take too long.'

Sheila said she wouldn't, knowing she was telling a lie. For a long time it would be fresh in her mind. Not from choice. She'd give anything to put the clock back, have nothing to accuse Fergus of but his fondness for drink.

'So what are you going to do?'

'What I'd do if I had the money is take the twins and go to Dublin.'

'Just because of a kiss?'

'How do I know that's all it was?'

'I'm so sorry for you and I can't help you. Even if I had money I couldn't lend it to you.'

'Because you'd be helping me to leave my husband?'

'I suppose so. I don't think you should. And then there's Bob, he wouldn't approve.'

'Don't worry about it Liz,' said Sheila. When what she felt like saying was 'fuck you and Bob'. To stick up for Fergus or any other man would be the general reaction. Though she knew that Lizzie was genuinely trying to help. Genuinely believed there had been no more to the incident than kissing. 'I'll pull myself together not for his sake but for the twins'. I won't mention last night. He can do the explaining. I'll let a little time pass and then give him an ultimatum.'

'An ultimatum – about what?'

'Packing in the army. He's done twelve years, could come out on a pension. If he loves me he'll do it. If he refuses I'll leave him. Now I'd better go back and face the music. Say a prayer that his nose isn't broken.'

He was in the living room, sitting in an armchair holding an ice pack over his nose. 'I nipped up to the MO just in case it was broken. It isn't. I'm fit for duty. Just as well as I'm on the ranges tonight. I'm sorry, Sheil. I drank too much. You know how it is. Like an eejit I kept up with Paddy.'

She had intended to say nothing about the previous night. But listening to him talking as if all he'd done was get drunk loosened her tongue. And she berated him. 'Get drunk, was that all? And what about the whore that plastered your mouth with lipstick? And whose kissing you told me was bloody gorgeous, you rotten louser?'

His expression was one of amazement. 'I don't know what you're talking about. What woman? What lipstick? What kissing? I kissed no one as true as I'm sitting here.'

'You bloody liar. There was lipstick all over your face. Don't tell me you nicked one of mine to do yourself up.'

'Honest to God, Sheila, I haven't a clue what you're on about. I drank too much, passed out. I don't remember anything else.'

He probably doesn't, she thought. Now I'll never know the truth. Not that if it had gone beyond kissing he'd have told me. I didn't imagine that lipstick. But maybe I did. I'll soon see. She ran up the stairs, took the shirt out of the linen basket and examined the tail. 'I didn't,' she said out loud. There it is, I haven't lost my mind yet. I'll say no more about it. I wouldn't be able to contain myself. I'd create murder. And I mustn't do that for the sake of the twins. For myself, too. Ordinary rows never took a feather out of me. I enjoyed them. Then they were never about anything as serious as this. Oh, God, if he really doesn't remember last night then the worst could have happened. It probably did. It'll be a long time before I'll lie on a bed beside him. In the long run I'll leave him. How could I live with a man I don't trust?

Chapter Twenty-two

'I wish to God Fergus was on the Y List.'

'That's a terrible thing to say, Sheila.'

'Sometimes you get in on my nerves.'

'Everything gets on your nerves these days.'

'Is it any wonder? And I wasn't wishing for Fergus to be dying. Something chronic, slightly disabling: stomach ulcers, a limp, vertigo. Then he'd get a medical discharge. Otherwise he'll be in the army till he finishes his engagement. And that'll be us finished.'

'Is it that bad?'

'I can't get it out of my mind.'

'D'ye talk about it?'

'He does all the time. Same story. He got drunk. Passed out. Remembers nothing about it. Says I put the lipstick on his shirt. Pretended I wiped it off his mouth. He's full of "plaimas". Always saying how sorry he is for going off with Paddy Macken. And I've had more boxes of chocolates than ever in my life. It's driving me mad. He admits to remembering nothing. Where does that leave me?'

'Maybe if you talked to Father Tom he could put you on the road to forgiveness.'

'It's nothing to do with forgiveness. It's a hypnotist I need to wipe out the memories. I want to forget it ever happened.'

'Is he still in the spare room?'

'I'm ashamed to admit he's not. But nothing's like it was before. The minute he touches me I think about your woman. And though I'm on the pill I make him wear a condom.'

'I wish I knew what to say that might comfort you, but I don't. I believe Fergus is a good, decent bloke. And that like Bob he'd never go with another woman.'

'It's well for you, Lizzie, I used to believe all that, too.'

'To change the subject, because brooding on it isn't doing you any good, did you know that Yvette's not well. Palpitations, dizzy spells and she fainted in the NAAFI during the week.'

'Who told you?'

'She did. I met her in the Medical Inspection room when I took Tom for a jab.'

'So she's human like the rest of us.'

'I never thought she wasn't,' replied Lizzie.

Without telling Victor, Yvette went to the doctor.

He was very young and had a pleasant manner. 'Yvette,' he said as he filled in her record card. 'I haven't come across that name among my patients so far.'

'My mother was reading a French novel before I was born and liked the name. When I grew up she told me it was a nice change from all the Maggies, Nellies and Katies.'

He asked what ailed her. She told him her symptons. 'What's your loss like when you menstruate?'

'Very heavy, Doctor.' She didn't add that bleeding from her anus was often heavier.

He looked at the palms of her hands, pulled down her bottom eyelids and scrutinised them. 'I think you have simple anaemia. I'll take some blood, send it to Hanover for testing. Come back a week today. If it is simple anaemia I'll prescribe iron and in no time you'll feel on top of the world.'

She thanked him and left.

Victor looked alarmed when she told him of her visit to the Medical Inspection room, then his expression changed to one of anger. 'You shouldn't have gone, he'll be nothing but a quack. All the MOs are. You could have gone to one of my German friends. Much better doctors. Did he give you a thorough examination?' (Had he seen the bruises?)

'He only looked at the palms of my hands and pulled down my bottom eyelids, and he took some blood. The result will be back next week. If it's simple anaemia an iron tonic will put it right.'

And if it wasn't anaemia there would be more tests. She could be hospitalised. Army hospitals were never under-staffed. To justify the numbers men, women and children were admitted for conditions which in Civvy Street were treated in the outpatients.

Yvette mustn't have further tests nor go in to hospital. Quacks though MOs might be, they couldn't all be fooled with stories of falls on the stairs, accidental bangs and bumps. If more than an iron tonic was needed she'd see his German friend. He had a private clinic in Hamburg. She could be treated there. He'd have to treat her for the rest of the summer with kid gloves. She'd want to go to the swimming pool. He couldn't forbid it all the time. That bloody Sheila would spot a bruise a mile away. From now until the end of September no more knocking Yvette about. And she could have a German maid. Emily would find one for her.

It was simple anaemia, and Yvette was presented with her iron tonic and a German maid in the same week. She was young, big and very strong, and her name was Else. On her Yvette practised the little German she had: '*Sauber machen die Küche, Wohnzimmer und Schlafzimmer, bitte.*' And when the vegetable man stopped his truck outside the door she would tell Else to buy *Kartoffeln, Blumenkohl, Salat* and whatever else was needed. With the oilcloth-covered floor, powerful vacuum cleaner and other labour-saving devices, Else wasn't overworked. Yvette would have let her go long before her three hours were up but Else found other things to do. She prepared a flowerbed, brought plants from her parents' garden and told Yvette that she intended moving every bit of furniture away from walls to get at the dust.

The swimming pool had been built to train promising swimmers for the 1936 Olympics. Once the weather was warm enough the young wives went every day when the children finished school. On their first visit there Yvette drove past them and felt miserable and guilty, seeing Lizzie and Sheila on their way to the pool. Sheila pushing Lizzie's go-kart laden with Tom, towels, rubber rings and bags with food, spare knickers and toiletries. Lizzie waddled beside Sheila and the girls walked on the sun-scorched grass verge. Through her rear mirror Yvette saw the group stop at the fish farm and guessed it was to rest rather than admire. Apart from a pool of still water there was nothing of interest. Somewhere further up the river which fed the pool the fish farming took place. What must they think of her driving past? she asked herself. But Victor had threatened her: 'No lifts. If you do, no swimming pool.'

Along the verges grew a profusion of bright yellow flowers. She had noticed them before but didn't recognise them. She described in halting German their heads and colour to Else who told her they were camomile flowers. Yvette had read about camomile and its soporific effect. Else said she would show her how to make tea from the flowers. But though she drove past many times she had yet to pick them.

Emily was already at the swimming pool and had spread two rugs to reserve places for when the others arrived. Yvette joined her. They talked about the weather, the disruption practice camp caused in their lives. Emily did most of the talking, it was a strain and she was glad to see the others arrive.

'You're all looking very glamorous,' she said. She meant that Sheila was in her pale grey sundress splashed with daisies, Beth displaying as little flesh as possible and Lizzie's belly straining against a drab maternity dress.

Sheila eyed Emily's nondescript cotton trousers and short-sleeved Aertex T-shirt, thinking how Emily, with a different hairstyle and a bit more attention to what she wore, would be an attractive woman.

The children were undressed, put into swimming costumes and warned not to go into the pool until their mothers were ready to take them in. Sheila and Yvette unbuttoned their sundresses, under which they wore bathing suits. Emily and Beth went to the changing cubicles.

Lizzie sighed. 'I'd love to be floating in there, I'm roasting.'

'I know I'm wasting my breath,' said Sheila, 'but why don't you? You've been to the German pool and seen the sights there. Women twice as big as you, oul fellas like skeletons. They don't care what they look like. They're in the pool to swim not to be admired. And more luck to them.'

'I couldn't do it. If I was just fat, maybe, but not pregnant. I'd feel ashamed.'

'I suppose I'd feel the same myself. And yet why should we? Why should carrying a baby make us ashamed to wear a swimsuit?'

'Our rearing, I suppose. Our mothers, nuns and priests. Modesty. And pregnant bellies tell everyone you've done it. It's all mad. And yet the minute the child is born you're treated like a queen. You've done what God wants women to do. That's so long as you've been churched. You're unclean until that's been done.'

'Don't I know it,' said Sheila. 'Me ma . . . Eh, look at

that.' She pointed to a group of young girls approaching the pool. 'I thought they were all away in school.'

'They'll have left at Easter. Not trying for college or uni. There's no work in the camp for them. Some will go back to England if they've relations willing to have them, the others just hang around.'

Sheila looked admiringly and enviously at their high rounded breasts, slinky costumes without foam-filled cups to uplift breasts. The group of girls made a lot of noise, screeching, giggling, then erupting into roars of laughter. Young off-duty soldiers eyed their long, blemish-free legs, made to appear longer by the high cut of the swimsuit.

Sheila, Yvette, Beth and Emily took the children into the pool where they splashed, screamed, peed in the water and attempted to follow Emily's swimming instructions. Beth stayed in the shallow end, attempting to improve her breaststroke; Sheila and Yvette did an elegant crawl to the deep end, turned and, exhausted, swam slowly back. 'Will you look at them,' Sheila said as she dried her hair. The young boys and girls had clicked. There was a lot of pushing and shoving, and squeals of pretended indignation from the girls. 'They make me feel ancient. I noticed their frocks, almost up to their bums. Tomorrow I'm going to shorten mine.'

'Not up to your bum, I hope.'

'No, I'm not that much of an eejit, but a long way up my thighs, Emily.'

Yvette, although the women included her in their conversations, felt an outsider. They made good-natured fun of their husbands, quoted their advice and criticised them. There was nothing Yvette could contribute to their conversation, for if once she started where would she stop? Sheila would make sarky remarks, Beth stare at her unbelievingly. Sheila's expression would convey that she was either a liar, a fool or mad. Emily might advise her to see the welfare officer. From experience she knew how welfare officers operated. The squash she had brought with her had been drunk. She was still thirsty. 'I'm going to the kiosk, anyone want anything?' They did. She memorised their orders and walked slowly to the kiosk, remembering her one encounter with the army's welfare system.

An appallingly neglected child, often left alone while his mother and father went to the pub. One evening, when Victor was out, a neighbour asked her to witness the state of the child. She did and was horrified. The neighbour called the duty officer. He came, asked their names and told them to go home. During the week, gossip had it that an officer's wife acting as welfare officer was involved with the case. The neglectful family were posted shortly afterwards.

She was served the drinks and began walking back to the group, thinking as she went that perhaps the child was taken from his family and how nowadays such happenings were frequently reported in newspapers. But she had never read of child neglect in army families. As with the incident she had witnessed, they would be buried.

As would hers, were she to complain to Victor's commanding officer. She wished she belonged to a Mafia family who would rub him out. His or her death was the only solution. But she was a coward and a Catholic, even if she no longer practised. Suicide was a mortal sin, a sin of despair for which she would never be forgiven.

Sheila and Lizzie sat on the front step, Lizzie talking about Beth while Sheila shortened her summer dresses. 'I don't know what ails her but something does.'

'I've noticed the changes, she looks like a rake. And there's not a drop of colour in her face.'

'Maybe it's knowing that she'll never have a baby.'

'I suppose it could be. D'ye think she'll adopt?'

'So far,' said Lizzie, 'she's never mentioned it.'

On the sun-scorched patch, where later in the year the cranberries would grow, the twins and Lizzie's children were making a den with cardboard boxes in which the electrical goods had come, calling now and then to their mothers to admire their efforts.

'D'ye know what I'd love,' said Lizzie.

'What?'

'A shower of rain. The heat kills me. If it rained I'd lie down in it.'

'Sure couldn't you do that in the bath?'

'It's all very well for you with your gypsy colouring.'

'Spanish, if you don't mind. Me ma says her great-grandmother was from the West of Ireland where the Armada ships came to a sticky end. Some of the sailors must have made it ashore. You'll see my colouring down in Cork, Galway and Kerry. So a relation far back gave a Spanish sailor the glad eye.'

'Pity my ancestors were Dubliners. I could have done without my red hair and skin to match.'

'Then thank God you didn't finish up posted to the Middle East. The heat's not that bad here, really. Tomorrow it could be lashing,' said Sheila as she finished the hem on a frock. Lizzie gave her a cigarette, they smoked for a while, then Sheila said, 'I can't get that poor fella that was killed by lightning out of my mind.'

'Terrible, wasn't it. There he was, sitting in the champ and the next minute dead. It struck the aerial, so Bob said.'

'Lord have mercy on him. It's all the fault of this bloody place. Last night there was a clap of thunder right over the roof. I thought they'd dropped the atomic bomb. Did you not hear it, Liz?'

'I did, but thunder and lightning doesn't bother me. If my mother comes out I hope it's not in the summer, she'd be terrified. When we'd have lightning at home she'd run around pulling plugs out of everything, putting the cutlery in the drawer and making me take out my curlers in case I was struck dead. There I'd be with a head full of Dinkies so my hair would be nice for a dance and they'd have to come out.'

'I don't blame your ma, I'd do the same. We get more

thunder and lightning here than in Ireland and England. Is it any wonder I'm hating the place? I'm going up now to try on the frocks. Stay where you are, I won't be a minute.'

Lizzie watched the children playing and thought again about rain. A downpour might revive her flowerbed. Until the drought it was gorgeous. The stocks scented the air, wafted in through the open french windows; the petunias and impatience were a riot of colour. And then I forgot to water them and Bob had the cheek to complain, and I told him I had enough to carry without lugging a watering can about. Poor Bob, he'd been out all night and was irritable. He said he was sorry, that it was his fault for not having bought a hose and fixed it to the tap in the cellar. In her womb the baby kicked vigorously. She ran her hands over her belly. 'I'll be glad when you're out of there,' she said to herself. Then remembered she hadn't done her relaxation and breathing exercises, and was debating whether to go in and do them, decided she would when she heard the scream. Sheila! Something's happened to her.

But before she had time to investigate she could hear Sheila running down the stairs and shouting, 'Look, look at me.' Lizzie looked and saw Sheila wearing one of the shortened dresses. 'That's right,' Sheila snapped. 'Have a good laugh, Lizzie. Don't hold it back. I can see the smile in your eyes.'

'Ah, Sheil, I'm sorry, really sorry. It was a lovely dress.'

'It's up to my arse now, so is the other one.'

'Didn't you measure them? I'd have pinned up the hems for you. How did you come to ruin them?'

'You know me. The genius. Full of cleverality. I measured them against a sundress. From the yoke down, forgot about the straps.'

'Can you do nothing with them?'

'If I had a fire I'd back it with them. You can give them to Ulla, she's not much bigger than a midget for all that she's the best of the maids.'

Beth arrived looking anxious. 'I was in the shower when

I heard the scream. What happened?' Sheila told her and modelled the shorn dress. Beth sympathised. Her hair was wet, flat on her head, wispy bits framing her face.

'That hairstyle really suits you,' Sheila said, sitting down again.

'You're kidding me.'

'I'm not. Tell her, Lizzie.'

'Sheila's right. You look like Audrey Hepburn.'

'You've made my day.' Beth blushed and beamed. 'I've iced coffee in the fridge and I made a sponge this morning. I'll fetch them. I won't be a minute.'

While the coffee and sponge were being consumed, part of the cake put aside for the children, Beth asked, 'Did you know this place is haunted?'

'I wouldn't be at all surprised.'

'I'm serious, Sheila.'

'So am I. Amn't I Irish? Ghosts are ten a penny in Ireland. I've seen one myself.'

'You haven't,' said Lizzie, 'or we'd have heard about it.'

'Why would you? I never attached any importance to it. This place is bound to be haunted.'

'How d'ye say that?' Beth asked.

'Because of the thousands in Belsen and the Russian soldiers who died untimely deaths.'

'I'm always aware of that,' said Lizzie.

'Anyway,' Sheila told Beth, 'go on with the story.'

'I heard about it this morning. I was having coffee in the YM and two women I know from the hairdressers joined me. One of them had seen a ghost.'

'Do we know them?' asked Lizzie.

'I don't think so. Out of nowhere he came, made not a sound as he walked across the carpet and out through the locked french windows.'

'What did she do?' Sheila wanted to know.

'Nothing. Once he had disappeared she thought she might have imagined it. But now the more she thinks about it the more she's convinced she did see a ghost.'

'She probably did. We're all living in new houses but who's to say how many might be buried under them? The whole place is littered with the dead. Remember when Fergus was supervising the digging of a gun pit and hundreds of shoes were dug up? Tell us about the other haunting.'

'That was terrifying. A German woman living in one of the blocks where after Belsen was liberated the prisoners went to live for a while. She woke in the middle of the night and a young girl was about to lift the baby out of its cot. The woman screamed and the girl disappeared. But she came back night after night, even when the baby was in the bed between its mother and father. The padre came and blessed the flat but it didn't help. In the long run the German woman and her family were moved to other quarters. No more ghosts.'

Lizzie was trembling and sweating. 'I'd have died on the spot the first time the ghost appeared,' she said.

Sheila told her to take a few deep breaths, went into the kitchen, brought a damp dishcloth and bathed Lizzie's forehead.

'I shouldn't have told you that, not with you being pregnant, I'm sorry, Liz.'

'It's OK now, don't worry, Beth. I wonder why the ghost appeared and tried to take the baby?'

'I'd say the girl or woman had lived in that flat after Belsen. It could have been her baby or sister. Then, like a lot of the Belsen prisoners, she got TB, was shifted and died. She came back to look for the child.'

'That's enough about ghosts,' Lizzie said, handing Tom to Sheila and getting up from the steps. 'I never want to hear about them again.'

'I've more coffee in the fridge. I'll fetch it.'

'No you won't,' said Sheila, 'here's your husband.'

The champ stopped outside Beth's house. She was all of a dither. 'I wasn't expecting him. I've nothing ready for him to eat.'

Bill got out of the champ and it drove away. He came to Sheila's steps. 'It's well for the women,' he said.

'I wasn't expecting you, Bill. But it won't take a minute to cook something.'

'I'm only in for a couple of hours. Don't bother with food. I want a shower and a kip first.'

'Have a nice sleep,' Sheila said as Bill and Beth walked towards their house.

'My bladder's bursting, I'm going for a pee.'

'Go up to my bathroom. I'll put Tom on the sofa and make a few sandwiches and tea for the girls. Have a shower if you want to.'

When the children had been fed and gone to the cellars for another game, Sheila and Lizzie sat in armchairs, drank tea, smoked and talked.

'What d'ye make of the pair of them?' asked Lizzie.

'She's a nervous wreck. But I think he's gorgeous; he's smashing-looking.'

'Sheila!'

'Don't look so shocked.'

'I'm more surprised than shocked. I've heard you say Victor's a bit of all right. But never a word about Bill.'

'No, well, I only noticed him for the first time today. And as for Victor, he is attractive, like an animal, a tiger maybe, dangerous. But I wouldn't touch him no more than I would a tiger.'

'I'm going home. I've missed my lie-down, didn't do my exercises and listened to you go on about ghosts and men you fancy.'

Sheila laughed. 'Don't take everything I say seriously. I make up the half of it. Go on for your lie-down. Leave Tom where he is and I'll see to the girls.'

Chapter Twenty-three

The kitchens in the young wives' houses faced the road. When Sheila first moved in she had welcomed this. So much of her time would be spent in the kitchen. Washing up, peeling and preparing vegetables, filling the washing machine from the hot tap, emptying it into the sink, which was below the window. While she worked she could look out of the window, watch passers-by, know what was going on. It wasn't long before she realised that few passed by and little went on. The baker, milkman and the vegetable man created a diversion, but not for long. And she would brood on what a lonely, desolate place the camp was, even compared to camps in England.

Those were always near a bus stop. Several buses ran during the day at hourly intervals. You could get to Salisbury, Andover, Richmond; to towns and shops, decent cafés, nice buildings, nothing like Dublin but easy on the eye. Not that you often used the buses. But they were there – you had a choice.

She lost interest in window-gazing until the day after she had said she found Bill attractive. Now, whenever she heard a vehicle come down the road she looked out of the window, hoping it would be Bill in for a few hours. It seldom was. But when he did come for the couple of minutes it took him to go into his home she scrutinised him with a hawk's eye and afterwards thought, if anyone had asked me to describe Bill before the other day I'd have said very ordinary looking. Tallish, on the thin side, darkish hair, greeny blue or grey eyes. I'd have shrugged: 'Nothing to write home about.'

That wasn't how she had seen him on the day he came home unexpectedly. He didn't appear as the fuddy-duddy she had once labelled him. His eyes were hazel and his hair black. He wasn't tallish but definitely tall, well-built and no beer belly. He'd come in off the ranges – no brilliant brass buttons, no brass except his cap badge and his cap sat slightly crooked on his head, giving him a rakish look. When he had taken off the cap she had seen the true colour of his hair. And his teeth were dazzlingly white in a golden-tanned face.

How didn't I notice him before? she asked herself and the answer came to her: Fergus and the nightclub. He had spoiled her life. No matter how often Lizzie assured her that Fergus had never been unfaithful to her she couldn't rid her mind of the suspicion. After meeting Fergus she had never looked at another bloke, certainly never fancied one. Admitted that Victor was attractive, yes, but as she had told Lizzie, in a dangerous way.

And then she had began to fancy Bill, fantasising about having an affair with him; getting her own back on Fergus and one day, but not for years, letting him know. Beth never figured in her fantasy.

All through July she continued to imagine how she and Bill would come together. It would happen on a night when Fergus was on the ranges and Bill wasn't, a warm night when the french windows were open. She would be wearing a glamorous nightdress, stretched out on the sofa, a Martini on the coffee table. Bill would step over his garden fence and come to the windows, make an excuse to borrow something, a torch because the battery in his was gone, something like that. Say he hoped he hadn't frightened her. Apologise for coming when Fergus was out but that he had mislaid his car keys, searched the house and his pockets. Thought he might have dropped them in the garden. He'd been down to the compost heap, could have pulled them out of his pocket when he felt a sneeze coming on, pulling out his hankie – this bloody hay fever. She would fetch the torch from the kitchen, displaying a lot of tanned leg as she went, and after giving it to him she'd offer him a drink: whiskey on the rocks. He'd sit beside her. He'd light two cigarettes and he'd place one between her lips.

And then? Then her fantasy would fizzle out. She'd castigate herself. Think of Beth. Think of Fergus. Remember that she was a Catholic. That fornication was a sin and adultery a mortal sin. She didn't believe in hell, but all the same, you couldn't be sure that it didn't exist. Supposing she died suddenly. Didn't have time to make an Act of Contrition. She dare not risk going to hell, roasting for all eternity.

There were other ways of getting her own back on Fergus. Making him leave the army, that's what she'd go for. That wouldn't harm anyone. And in the long run Fergus would thank her. They'd be back in their beloved Dublin. The twins would grow up with an Irish accent. Her mother and father would dance with joy. What a party there'd be when she came home. Her mother would mind the girls while she went to work. Maybe train as a nurse. The sight of blood would no longer turn her stomach. According to her mother's letter things were looking up in Ireland, more jobs than there'd been for years. Fergus would have no trouble finding work.

Beth worked hard at keeping up appearances. What was happening in her life was too humiliating to share with the wives. So she kept the brave face, went with them to the swimming pool, sat on the steps gossiping. Babysat if it was necessary. She loved every one of the children. Tom, especially, was young enough to sit on her lap, put his arms round her neck, kiss her without being asked. She didn't envy the mothers their children. She was deeply religious and envy was one of the seven deadly sins. She accepted that Bill was sterile, hoped that one day they would adopt a baby. Not once had she regretted marrying him. You married for better or worse. She could have been the one who was infertile and had never doubted for a moment that Bill would not have thought less of her.

After his results she believed she had been sympathetic, understood when he couldn't make love. Believing that affection and cuddling and anything that he might suggest, which lovingly she would have done, would get him through his terrible disappointment and shame. She knew him so well, knew he felt he had failed as a man. She had tried to reassure him it was only a temporary thing. It would pass. She loved him, always would. All they needed was for a little more time to pass.

Time passed but their situation didn't get any better and so, one evening when Bill and Bob were night-firing and Sheila was keeping away from Lizzie because she had a sore throat and didn't want to pass the bug on to her, Beth went to ask advice from Lizzie. 'I know,' she said, 'that I shouldn't be bothering you with my troubles and you not far from your time, but I couldn't confide in anyone else.'

'Don't worry about me,' Lizzie said. 'I'm fine and it's at least six weeks before I'm due. I suppose things haven't improved?'

'Oh, Lizzie, if you only knew. It's like living with a stranger. He's moved into the spare room. He's rejected me . . .' She couldn't continue, could only put her head in her hands and cry.

Lizzie thought, you don't know how lucky you are. A double bed to yourself and me the size of a house, the baby doing somersaults and kicking like a frantic colt. The heat of Bob's body and the weight of his arm across me. I'd give anything for a bed to myself. Well, for the time being anyway . . .

Beth was still crying, sobbing heartbrokenly. Lizzie moved closer to her on the sofa and put an arm round her. 'I'm so sorry. You were such a happy couple.'

'Never', sobbed Beth, 'had a serious row in our lives. Never. Never. He was everything you could wish for. Kind and gentle and we had a great married life. What am I going to do, Liz?'

Lizzie sighed and said, 'I don't know, Beth. Maybe he should see the doctor.'

'I suggested that when he first became peculiar and I

thought he was going to hit me. "I'll never see a doctor again unless I'm bleeding to death," he said.'

'What about a separation?'

'A separation, Liz!' Beth dried her eyes, blew her nose and stared unbelievingly at Lizzie. 'I'm trying to get us together. Have us as we were, not leave him.'

'No, that's not what I meant. I was thinking of you going home for a couple of weeks. You and your mother write regularly, don't you?'

'Every other week.'

'Well, what about this for an idea? Ask your mum to write you a letter saying that your father has been taken bad. Nothing serious so you don't fly in the face of God. Done his back in, broke his leg, something, anything that means bed rest. And because your mother has angina she could do with a bit of help. Get her to lay it on. The district nurse comes in every day and the bed's been brought down. But even so she's worn out and you'd be a comfort to her and your father.'

'How would that help me and Bill?'

'I don't know, maybe it wouldn't. But it would certainly be a break for you and perhaps bring him to his senses. You've been so close he'd miss you. Bound to. Realise how badly he's been treating you. It might not work but it's worth a try.'

'I suppose so,' Beth said doubtfully. She wiped her eyes, sighed a few long sighs and then said, 'I'd love to see my mum and dad. And as you said, the change would do me good. But I'll have to think about it. I'll let you know what I decide. You're a great friend, Lizzie. There was no one else I could turn to. Yvette might be sympathetic, I don't know. None of us knows much about her. And Sheila, well, I know Fergus has a problem with drink but apart from that he'd eat out of her hand.'

'Sheila can be flippant, sarcastic, but she's kind hearted. I think she'd have felt for you. Anyway, you think about it. If you do decide to go, me and Sheila will see to it that Bill comes to eat with either one of us when he's off duty, do his washing. He'll be well looked after.' Lizzie made tea and while they were smoking and drinking she suggested the sort of letter Beth's mother should write, how apart from her help the sight of her would be a tonic for both of them. She knew it wasn't the best time of the year for Beth to come with Bill working all hours. And if he wasn't willing she'd understand and manage. 'You write that sort of a letter; your mum can copy it. Appeal in a roundabout way to Bill. You know what men are like. He'd be flattered that the decision was up to him.'

'At the moment I don't think he'd care if I went away for good.'

'You know, Beth, that's not true. God knows how Bob would be if he'd been told he was sterile. Bill will come round, I'm sure of that. You go home. In no time he'll be asking when you're coming back.'

'What would I do without you. You've given me a bit of hope. You've convinced me. I don't need to think of it. I'll write the two letters tomorrow, one for Mum to go by and mine telling her the truth.'

'That was sudden, Beth going home,' Sheila said the day after Beth left for England. 'She told me her father's sick. Something wrong with his back, nothing life-threatening but her mum needs a hand. I wish my father had something wrong with his back. I'd be over like a shot. I wonder how long she'll be gone.'

Lizzie said she wasn't sure and Sheila that she thought there was something fishy about going home to help nurse her father. 'I know her mother has heart trouble but all the same, wouldn't you think the neighbours could have helped? It's not as if he was on his last. It's only a bit of lifting and that.'

'I suppose the neighbours are as old as Beth's parents and in any case it'll be a break for Beth, and her parents will be delighted to have her.'

'D'ye know what I think?'

'What?'

'I think she and him are having a bad time. He's never been himself since he got his results. Haven't you noticed?'

'Not really, but then I'm not as quick as you at weighing people up. He looks the same to me. And only the other day you were saying he was smashing-looking.'

'I'm not talking about how he looks. It's how him and Beth aren't as lovey-dovey as they were. He was forever touching her. Arm round her shoulders, you remember the way they were. And another thing, the spare bedroom is being used.'

'How do you know that?'

'Eh, don't look at me with those accusing eyes. I'm not spying on them. They go to bed hours before I do. And sometimes I forget to bring in the washing or just go out into the garden. I love looking at the sky if it's a starry night. I look up at them and think the same stars are shining down on Dublin. And I noticed a light in the spare bedroom. At first I thought nothing of it. They'd forgotten to switch the light off. That wasn't the reason. It's been on every night for weeks now. I did get nosy then and checked on the front bedroom. That light was on as well. So, d'ye know what I think?'

'What?' asked Lizzie.

'I think they're not sleeping together. His choice, I'd say, not Beth's. Maybe that's the real reason for her going home.'

Beth hadn't sworn her to secrecy, nevertheless Lizzie knew that she did not want anyone else to know how things were with her and Bill. If the separation didn't work out, Beth might look for a more drastic solution. Then would be time enough for Sheila to know that her suspicions had been right. 'It might be because the weather's so hot. If I didn't know that Bob would be hurt I'd be in the spare room too. The comfort of a bed to yourself. I'd be in heaven.'

220

'That's only because you're pregnant.'

'I often wish I was one of the aristocracy. The woman has a huge bed where she and her husband make love. Afterwards he clears off to sleep in his dressing room. Imagine the bliss.'

'Oh, give over, Liz. You've told me many a time how safe you feel sleeping in Bob's arms. Dropping off with your head on his shoulder.'

Lizzie laughed. 'You're right,' she said. 'It's the pregnancy and my belly being bigger than it ever was. Roll on September.'

Fergus complained of not feeling well. Sheila was in bad humour and unsympathetic. 'I'd be complaining of feeling sick if I drank the amount you do. It's probably the beginning of cirrhosis.'

'That's great consolation, thanks very much.'

'What d'ye expect, your belly rubbed and a hot-water bottle?'

'Give over, Sheila, it's not funny. I feel lousy. I'm going up to lie down.'

'Do, then you'll be in good form for the mess tonight.'

'I'm on the ranges tonight.'

'I lose track of where you are. Worse still, I'm losing my mind. It's this place. If I don't get out of it soon I'll do something desperate.'

'The way I feel now I wouldn't care,' said Fergus, leaving the room.

That's not like him, Sheila thought when he had gone. Usually when she went for him he'd fight back, point out that he never had a hangover, that he didn't suffer with stomach trouble. And as for her hating Hohne she had better get to like it. They were there for another four years.

She was sorry she had been so short with him. Maybe he was sick. The twins had had vomiting and diarrhoea, so had Lizzie's three. It was the heat; germs flourished. They never bothered her. She knew the reason. Anyone was tough who was reared in neighbourhoods like hers in Dublin, slaughterhouses where on Thursdays the cattle were killed, where she and friends lay on the cobbles to look under the door while it was happening. Stained their frocks with blood that flowed under the badly fitting gates; went from deadhouse to deadhouse looking at the corpses, touching them, fingering the pennies that closed some of the dead eyes. Walked through Mill Street where Keefe's the knacker's yard was. You had to hold your nose. The smell of rotting animals being boiled for glue turned your stomach. In lanes and alleys there were dead cats, rats and fish, their burst-open bellies writhing with thick white maggots. And the rag stores. If you had an apple kids would say 'give us a bit' and you would. Play on the city's Corporation dump.

My mother never knew where we went in the school holidays when I was in the primary school. If she had I'd have been killed. The day I got the cow's blood all over my frock I covered the stains with tar. The day was that hot the tar was like melted butter on the road. I came in roaring crying. Telling her I'd fallen into a tarry patch. She was full of pity, took off my dress and threw it out. I think all that dirt and filth stood me in good stead. I got used to germs at an early age. I can't remember when I last had diarrhoea.

She went up a few times to look in on Fergus. If he wasn't asleep he was letting on to be. At one o'clock she made weak tea and dry toast. She woke him. 'How are you now?' she asked.

'A bit better, still an ache in my belly.'

'Whereabouts?'

'Round my navel and my right side. I think it's passing, though.'

'Eat the bit of toast, if it's wind the food will shift it.' She arranged the pillows behind him and the tray on his lap. 'Shout if you want anything else. I'm going down now to do the washing.'

She started the water running into the washing machine, at the same time keeping an eye out to see Bill arrive home from his early morning stint on the ranges. Lizzie had heard from Beth who wasn't coming back at the end of her two weeks. She might stay for a month. As soon as she spoke to Bill she'd pretend ignorance of Beth's letter to Lizzie and ask when he expected her home.

But before the machine had filled she heard an ear-piercing scream from Fergus. 'Jesus, Mary and Joseph!' she exclaimed, reaching to turn off the tap and at the same time seeing Bill's Land Rover arrive.

She ran up the stairs where she saw Fergus writhing in agony, his knees drawn up to his belly, screaming, 'Get the MO. Get the fucking MO.'

She saw the sweat on his forehead, the fallen tray, the spilled tea and sodden toast. She opened the bedroom window and shouted, 'Bill, Bill, come quickly,' then went back to the bed. 'You'll be all right. Bill will get the doctor.' She bent and kissed his forehead and remembered that the front door was on the latch, that the twins were in Lizzie's and she hoped they wouldn't suddenly appear and see Fergus as he was. She held Fergus's hand, stroking its back with her thumb. She heard Bill come up the stairs, went to meet him and asked him to get the MO. Back in the bedroom with Fergus, it seemed an eternity until the doctor arrived.

'Appendicitis,' he proclaimed after the examination. 'You'll have to go in. I'll send an ambulance.' Sheila saw him down the stairs and asked if Fergus was in any danger. He told her, 'No. It's a simple operation so long as the appendix doesn't rupture.'

'And could it?' she asked.

'They often do, so the sooner he's in Hanover the better,' he replied, taking his leave.

Lizzie and Yvette were by Sheila's steps. 'Where are the children? I hope they didn't hear Fergus screaming.'

Lizzie assured her they hadn't. Siggie had taken the five of them for a walk. 'What ails Fergus?'

Sheila told her and that an ambulance was on its way. 'I'll have to leave the twins with you. God only knows how long I'll be.'

Yvette said she'd help Lizzie mind the children. Bill joined the two women and asked Sheila if he could do anything. 'I'll have to pack a few things. Go up and sit with Fergus while I do.'

She went in the ambulance as she was. Wearing her old faded house dress, no make-up, her hair a curly tangle and keeping on her slippers. While Fergus was being loaded into the ambulance she filled a flask with iced water, thinking as she did, I know he can't have a drink but I can wet his lips and I'd better take a table napkin as well.

As she was about to get into the ambulance Bill said, 'I'll come with you.'

'You mightn't be let,' she said not even glancing at him. He didn't exist any more. He was just a voice, a neighbour. No one mattered now except her beloved Fergus.

'The hospital will lay on transport but you might have to wait hours for it. I'll take you home,' Bill said. She nodded her assent.

Balancing herself on the edge of the stretcher, she wished that Hanover hospital weren't so far away. Eighty kilometres! Fergus had told her how to convert – divide by eight and multiply by five or maybe it was the other way round. What did it matter? One way or the other it was an awful long distance. And she talked in her head. Shaggin' Germany. In Dublin nowhere is far from a hospital. Here you might as well be in the back of beyond.

Before they'd been travelling for long she noticed a change come over Fergus. At first he had looked almost like himself. Now he resembled a corpse. His face the colour of putty, his eyes sunken in his head. His hands were clenched and his teeth biting his lower lip. She was sitting on the edge of the stretcher. 'Am I squashing you?' she asked. He shook his head. 'Is the pain worse?'

'Oh, Jesus,' he moaned, 'I'm in agony.'

He looked too pale to have a temperature but nevertheless she laid a hand on his forehead. It felt like a furnace. She soaked the napkin and bathed his face, and wondered if she should knock on the window behind the driver, beckon him to stop. Then changed her mind. She wasn't sure if he had any medical training. It would waste time.

In a hoarse whisper Fergus said, 'Put your hand on my belly, it feels like a lump of iron.'

She did and the hardness terrified her. 'It's hard all right, maybe it's wind. Don't forget you were constipated yesterday.' She didn't believe it was but could think of nothing else to say. He closed his eyes. She spoke to him and he didn't answer. The sleep'll do him good, she thought.

Silently she prayed: 'Please, God, let us get there soon. Holy Mary, Mother of God, don't let it be anything serious. Nothing worse than his appendix.' She lifted his hand and held it tightly and talked, but not too loudly. If he was only dozing he'd hear her. 'It won't be long now. We're on the outskirts. They'll whip out that oul appendix and you'll be as right as rain. Sure appendicitis is nothing. Loads of people get it. Even little kids. You'll be home in no time.'

Fergus didn't stir. Again she bathed his lips and burning face, while tears streamed down hers. 'I'm sorry, I didn't believe you were sick and for giving out to you. But sure you know what I'm like. All blather, I don't mean the half of it. We're here now. Don't you dare die on me or I'll kill you. I love you and never again will I say a cross word to you.'

Chapter Twenty-four

Fergus was lifted from the ambulance and transferred from the stretcher to a trolley. Sheila followed it into the reception area and Bill caught up with her. An English nursing sister received them and asked if Sheila was the patient's next of kin. 'Yes,' she replied, 'but don't wake him, he's very sick.' Ignoring her the nurse bent over Fergus and spoke to him. He opened his eyes and she began asking him for his rank, name and number. He attempted answering, then became confused and closed his eyes. 'Come on, now,' she coaxed, shaking him gently. Sheila fumed inwardly, asking herself why didn't she leave him alone. Couldn't she see how sick he was? The nurse tried again, then called two porters, spoke to them and Fergus was wheeled away towards a long corridor. Sheila and Bill began to follow.

The nurse stopped them and said, 'You aren't allowed to go with the patient. There's a waiting room across the hall. Stay there and soon the MO will come and talk to you. But before you go I'll want your husband's particulars.'

'While you're giving them I'll find a machine and get coffee,' Bill said.

After giving Fergus's number, rank, name, age and regiment Sheila walked disconsolately to the waiting room. Despite her fear and sorrow, she noticed the room's decor. Apricot-coloured walls, matching curtains splashed with green flowers, prints of seascapes and an aquarium. She looked out of the window and saw something she had never seen before, a red squirrel scurrying across the grass, then climbing a tree. She looked at it with as little interest as she had the waiting room. Her mouth kept filling with saliva and although it was not obvious, every bit of her was trembling with unease.

'Drink the coffee while it's hot and have a fag,' said Bill, offering his cigarettes.

'I've been dying for one.' Sheila inhaled deeply. They sat for a while in silence, then, for the sake of something to say, she asked Bill when Beth was coming home.

'Supposed to be next week, now she's staying on for a while. Her father's on the mend but her mother's not well.'

'You must miss her.'

'I do.'

You bloody liar, Sheila thought. You miss your meals on the table. Nothing else or you wouldn't be in the spare bedroom. Beth's an eejit. Dancing attendance on you, hanging on your every word.

The doctor arrived, making short work of Sheila's thoughts. 'Mrs Brady?' She nodded. 'Are you together?'

'Yes, sir,' Bill replied, standing to attention, 'I'm a neighbour. I'm driving Mrs Brady home.'

'Sit down, Sergeant Major. I'm Captain Lacey. I have just examined your husband, Mrs Brady.'

'How is he? Can I see him?' she asked.

'Afraid not. He's on his way to the theatre. His appendix ruptured. We have to operate urgently.'

'Oh, God, that's dangerous, isn't it.'

'It was before antibiotics, seldom is nowadays.'

'Will he be all right? I'll wait. I want to see him. I have to see him.'

'Not possible, I'm afraid. It's a more serious operation than removing an appendix. He won't be in good shape when he comes round. Tomorrow he'll be more himself, come then.' He bade them goodbye and left.

'It's not fair. It's the bloody army again. I want to see him.' She buried her head in her hands and sobbed.

'Eh, come on now, Sheila. The MO is right. Fergus will have tubes sticking out of him all over the place and won't be in the mood for talking even to you. Come on, up you get.' He helped her to her feet and for a moment held her close. 'Another coffee and a fag, then we'll go home.'

While he went for the coffee she pulled herself together, smoothed her hair and used the damp napkin to wipe her face.

Nervousness kept her talking for most of the journey back. She wondered why his appendix had burst. Why he had got it in the first place and was the doctor telling her the truth that antibiotics would cure him.

Bill didn't speculate as to how or why Fergus had appendicitis, or why it had ruptured. But he did assure her that antibiotics were miraculous. And said she must believe what the doctor had told her.

The twins wrapped themselves round her and asked numerous questions about Daddy.

Lizzie cooked steak and chips, and Sheila, who had said she couldn't eat a thing, devoured the meal. 'I didn't realise I was so hungry. Thanks, Liz. What would I do without you?'

Lizzie brushed the thanks aside. 'You'd do the same for me. And Yvette was a great help. She looked after the kids so I had my lie-down. Victor has organised a roster for the visiting. And believe it or not he's included. You must be tired – you've been gone for hours.'

'I'm jaded,' admitted Sheila, 'but I know I won't close my eyes tonight. This feckin' place – no phones unless I walk half a mile to one. It'd put my mind at ease to know that the operation had gone all right.'

'You'd know soon enough if it hadn't,' Liz told her.

'Can I give you a hand with the washing up?'

'No, you can't. Go home, have a bath, and you and the girls go to bed.'

Despite her prophecy Sheila fell asleep as soon as she lay down.

On her first and second visits Fergus didn't look well and didn't have much to say. The hour's visiting seemed to drag on for ever. The army again, she thought, only the next of kin allowed to visit. Bob had driven her in on the first two days. He and Fergus got on well, they could have talked about how the firing was going, if only for a little while. It might have roused Fergus more than her questions as to how he felt and anecdotes about the twins. But what else could she talk about? On the second day, to break the monotony of long silences, she made an excuse to go to the lavatory. There was another woman in the toilet, retching over the washbasin, retching and sobbing. Sheila went to her. 'Are you not well? Can I do anything for you?'

The woman raised her head and looked at Sheila. 'No one can do anything for me, I'm destroyed.' Her face was red and puffy, her hair disarranged. She looked, thought Sheila, like a mad woman. Maybe there was a mental section in the hospital and she'd come from there.

But mad or not, she'd have to offer some help. 'There's chairs by the wall, come and sit down. I'll get you a drink of water.' There was a plastic beaker in a metal ring above a washbasin. Sheila filled it and brought it to the woman, held it to her lips while she drank a little of the water.

She had stopped crying but now and then a sob hiccuped through her. She held on to the beaker and then began to talk. 'You must think I'm a lunatic. And you won't believe what I'm going to tell you.'

'Sure I'll listen anyway.'

'My husband's dying.' She began crying again. 'He's in a coma and last week my little boy was killed.'

'Oh, my God! That's terrible.' And, being Irish, Sheila wasn't embarrassed to ask the woman what had happened: 'Was it a car accident?'

The woman, crying as if her heart would break, mumbled, 'No, not a car. It happened in the house. I'd been nagging Frank to fix the stair carpet. On one step it had got rumpled. He wasn't much good at fixing things. I kept on at him, telling him David could trip on it and break his neck. He was six. His birthday was just gone.

229

Our only child. Frank fixed it. I didn't bother to check. And the next thing David fell down the stairs and broke his neck. I still can't believe it and when I do I blame myself. If I'd said nothing maybe it wouldn't have happened. Maybe David had got used to the crease in the carpet. You know how you do and go carefully. He died instantly. He was lying in the hall like a doll whose head had been screwed on the wrong way. I kept screaming and Frank was crying and blaming himself. We came here with him, though we knew he was dead. But I wanted to be with him.

'That night after we'd gone to bed Frank said he was going into the garden. It was a close night. He said it might be cooler outside. I should have gone with him, but I fell asleep. Then I woke up, it was three o'clock. I went to join him in the garden but he wasn't there. I couldn't find him. So I knocked up my neighbours and they found him in the garage, the exhaust pipe plugged in. Frank in the car, the engine running, the doors and window closed. Back here to the hospital where my child was in the mortuary. I can't believe it. It's like I'm telling you something I read in the paper. You know the way you do. A terrible tragedy. You're so sorry. The next day you've forgotten it.

'It's like that with me for a little while. Then I remember and I want to kill Frank. Kill him. Kill him. Kill him. I didn't blame him. I loved him. He was my consolation. Why did he do it? Didn't he think of me? Didn't he know I'd be left alone?'

'I'm so sorry.' Sheila was crying. 'It's hard to know what to say. Such a tragedy! But sure, God help Frank, his mind must have slipped for a minute. He'd have been blaming himself for what happened. What's his chances?'

'If he does survive he'll be brain damaged. Let him, I don't care. I hope he doesn't die. Let him linger for years. Then we'll both be suffering.'

'I'll pray for you,' said Sheila. It was what Catholics said to each other: promised to pray for the afflicted, the dead, the dying, women expecting a baby, barren women, for the conversion of Russia. 'I'll have to go back to the ward now. But I could get you a cup of coffee first.'

The woman thanked her and refused. 'I'll be all right now. It was good of you to listen.'

'My husband's in for a while yet, so I may see you again.'

'Maybe,' replied the woman.

Sheila sensed she didn't want to talk any more. Was probably regretting having said as much as she had. 'Goodbye, then.' There was nothing else to say. God forgive me, she thought, full of pity for myself and that poor woman has gone through hell.

In a complaining voice Fergus said, 'You were gone for ages.'

She restrained herself from giving him a snappy answer and didn't relate the woman's story as an excuse. He mightn't be dying but he wasn't well enough to hear such tragic events. 'I've a bad stomach. I haven't been eating right since you were taken bad,' she lied. 'God how the time flies. The visiting hour is nearly over. D'ye want me to bring anything in tomorrow?'

Like a sulky child he shook his head. 'What, for instance? I'm on slops.'

'Liquids you mean, slops are what's fed to pigs. Poor love.' She bent and kissed his cheek and thanked God he wasn't dying. 'Ten days the nurse told me. Only eight to go. Won't it be grand when you're home again.'

He again shook his head in assent and she panicked, thinking maybe he'd had a relapse. A German nurse opened the door, smiled and indicated that visiting was over. Sheila again kissed Fergus and waved to him as she left. The nurse was in the corridor. 'Excuse me, I was wondering if my husband is all right. He hardly spoke and is very irritable.'

'He's doing fine but he's having antibiotics, massive doses and painkillers. They could make him cranky.'

'Thank God. Are you a nurse or sister? I don't want to be giving you the wrong title.'

'Before I came to the English hospital I was a sister. Germans are not sisters here.'

'Oh, I see. Thanks a million. *Wiedersehen.*'

'You speak German?'

Sheila laughed. 'Wish I did. *Guten Tag* and *Wiedersehen* is about it.'

Once in the car with Bob she relaxed, smoked and told him about the tragic woman. Bob was sympathetic and for a few miles they talked about terrible fates befalling some people. 'How you never know,' Sheila said, 'from one day to the next what might happen to you or someone you love.'

'No use dwelling on it,' Bob said and brought the conversation round to how Fergus was and when he would be out of hospital.

As usual, Lizzie had a meal ready, which Sheila ate ravenously. The twins didn't make too much of her return. As children do, they were getting used to her being away for hours each day. After a few hugs and kisses and enquiring would Daddy bring presents from the hospital they went into the garden to play with Lizzie's children.

'Was your woman in today?'

'Yvette?'

'Who else?'

'She was and took them for a ride in the car. I like her. She'd be a grand neighbour if she had a different husband. I get the feeling she's afraid of him.'

'Come off it, Lizzie, you make excuses for everyone. She's probably got nowhere else to go this week and likes playing the goody-goody. Practice for when he gets a commission and she comes visiting the other ranks' wives. All the same, I'm grateful that she helps you out.'

Bob had told Lizzie he wouldn't eat until later and was

sitting on the patio drinking a bottle of Carlsberg and reading the *Daily Express*.

'Had enough of women for one day. Me gabbing all the way to Hanover and back.' It was on the tip of her tongue to tell Lizzie about the woman she had met in the hospital. Then she decided not to. Lizzie looked the picture of health but all the same she was carrying a child and in Dublin you never told bad news to pregnant women unless it concerned people close to them. So instead she talked about pretending to Bill that she didn't know when Beth was coming back. 'He told me she was staying on and that he really missed her. The bloody liar and him after moving out of their bedroom. I wanted to give him the bang of it.' Sheila then shrugged and said, 'But it wasn't my business so I didn't.'

'Now I know you'll jump down my throat and accuse me again of making excuses, but I think it's very sad.'

'It certainly is for Beth.'

'For both of them.'

'How can you say that?'

'Think about it. Imagine if Fergus had found out he was infertile.'

'As long as he could still perform I don't think he'd have given a damn.'

'And you, how would you have felt?'

'Terrible, I suppose. Brokenhearted that we couldn't have children. But I wouldn't have let on.'

'I don't suppose Beth did either. In fact, I know she didn't. It didn't work, though. He wasn't able to have sex any more. His pride was hurt, he didn't think he was a man. It got to the stage where if she put her arms round him he shrugged them off.'

'How d'ye know all this?'

'Beth told me. She didn't ask me to keep it a secret but all the same she wouldn't want it spread around.'

'I hope you're not suggesting that I'd be the spreader,' Sheila said indignantly.

'Who would you spread it to, Emily or Yvette? You're not mad about either of them. I was thinking more along the lines of Bill.'

'Bill! Well, may God forgive you. Why would I say anything to Bill?'

'Keep your hair on. Have a fag while I make a pot of tea.'

Sheila sat while Lizzie poured the tea, looking offended. 'Don't look so pouty. I'm sure you wouldn't deliberately say anything. But the thought went through my mind when you were telling me Bill had said how much he missed Beth. I'm sure he does. They were mad about each other. And knowing how you can fly off the handle I was afraid you might have a go at him.'

'That's not fair, Liz. OK, so I've got a quick temper but the only one I vent it on is Fergus. You've never seen me have a go at anyone else.'

'That's true and I'm sorry. I'm worried about the pair of them. You see it was me who put the idea into Beth's mind to go home.'

'You! Well, if that wasn't interfering I don't know what is.'

'You're right. I shouldn't have interfered. I thought a couple of weeks away might help things. And to tell you the truth I was worn out trying to comfort Beth. Only now she's in no hurry to come back. For all I know she may be thinking of packing Bill in.'

Seeing Lizzie was distressed drove the suggestion that she might be loose-tongued from her mind. Her only concern was for Lizzie. Good, kind Lizzie. 'Liz, I'm sure you did the right thing. And in any case you couldn't have made Beth go if she hadn't wanted to.'

'Oh, I don't know. I keep cursing myself for suggesting she went.' And lovely Lizzie, who apart from the night she thought Tom's entrails were falling out was the most placid and kindest woman Sheila had ever met, was breaking her heart crying.

'Stop that, Liz. Bob'll hear you. You'll give him an awful fright. And the kids could come in any minute.' Then Sheila thought of something and banished from her mind the Dublin old wives' tales. Lizzie was eight months pregnant. She was carrying a big, healthy baby. The worst that could happen was that the baby could be born prematurely. But she thought that unlikely. Moving to sit beside Lizzie and putting an arm round her she said, 'Listen to this.' And she told her about the woman she had met in the hospital and the appalling tragedies. Then they were both crying. Thanking God for how lucky they had been so far. Tomorrow Lizzie would go to see Father Tom and have Masses said for the woman, her son and husband. And they agreed that compared with those tragedies, Bill's and Beth's predicament wasn't so terrible and certainly nothing to cry about.

Chapter Twenty-five

Bill drove Sheila to the hospital two days before Fergus was being discharged. Victor had taken her the previous day. 'How did it go?' Bill asked as they drove off.

'Better than I'd expected. Never mentioned Yvette. Told me about his hobby, the photography. Said if I wanted him to he'd take snaps of the girls. Talked about the different cameras he had. His latest he said was a super model. Takes photographs without you having to hold it.'

'An automatic. I suppose he uses colour film as well.'

'Oh, yes. He went on about that.'

'Colour film is very expensive, so is the developing. Beats me how he does it. We're all the same rank – same pay. A bit more for longer service – he'd qualify for that but not by much.'

'His legacy and the Black Market, I suppose.'

'Maybe.'

Fergus had made a quick recovery. After his discharge from hospital he would have fourteen days' sick leave. Sheila was irritated by his cockiness. I should be thanking God he spared him, not feeling irritated. But I do. I'm worn out with the going to and from the hospital. Worried sick in the beginning that he might die. And never once has he said how much he appreciated me never missing a day. No consideration for anyone but himself. Counting the days until he's fit for duty and then he'll be back to his old habits. Drinking as much as he ever did.

Here's the summer nearly over and not once when he was off duty did he come with us to the swimming pool. Bob went with Lizzie a couple of times. So did Bill and Beth, even though they weren't getting on. But not Fergus. Oh, no. He was too tired. Wanted a kip. Read the papers. Any excuse. Wouldn't even offer to run us to the pool. But if I'd been willing to go to bed with him he'd have soon recovered from his fatigue.

He has a shock in store, though. For one thing I'm going home for Christmas, me and the twins. It'll be like heaven to be back in Dublin again. It's eighteen months since I saw me ma and da. I'll suss out what the job situation is like in Dublin. How long I'd have to wait for a house. I'll tell me ma everything. She'll understand after living with my father. I know she'll be upset and want to know what I'll do if Fergus digs his heels in, won't take his discharge. She's a great believer in marriage is for ever. Make your bed and you lie on it. My head is like a bucket with all the thinking I'm doing. But make a change I will or die in the attempt.

Fergus was sitting on his bed. 'You're miles away. What ails you? I thought you'd be in great form knowing I'll soon be home.'

'Well, of course I am, only I saw the woman whose husband is in the coma. I didn't let on. I couldn't have

236

faced her. Thinking about her tragedy's made me depressed.'

'Get out of the chair and sit beside me,' Fergus said. She did, he put an arm round her and kissed her. 'That's your kind heart, always feeling for someone else. In another two days I'll be home.' He kissed her again. 'Think of the time we'll have. I've missed you so much.' He slid his hand under her blouse and caressed her breast.

Against her will she responded, then pulled away. 'Give over, will you. Any minute a nurse could walk in the door.'

He pretended to be crestfallen. 'You've gone off me already. I suppose you'll be back in the spare room. We'll be another Bill and Beth.'

'Don't you ever let on I told you about that.'

'As if I would. Any word of when she's coming back?'

'Not as far as I know.' They talked about the twins. She told him they prayed for him every night. That Yvette had helped with the minding of them whenever she could. 'Maybe she's not as bad as I thought she was and he couldn't have been more friendly when he drove me in yesterday. All the same, there's something not right about them. I'm not sure whether it's her or him. It's just a feeling I have.'

'Woman's intuition.'

'You could be right.' Sheila looked at the clock on the wall. 'Another five minutes. Did you ever hear anything about the man in the coma?'

'I never asked. This place is so feckin' big he could be miles away.'

'I wouldn't think so. His wife was using the toilet on this corridor. But you're right about the size of the place. I got lost the first day I came to see you. Wandering up and down corridors like an eejit. And you'll never believe what I saw.'

'What?' asked Fergus.

'On some of the corridor walls there were maps and notices saying "YOU ARE NOW HERE". I didn't know where

here was. In the end I found a nurse who showed me the way. I'll go down now. See you tomorrow.'

They held each other and kissed. Fergus said, 'I love you. I can't wait to get home.' And Sheila said the same while thinking, if you don't change your ways then I'll change mine.

It was great to leave the hospital and breathe in fresh air.

'How was he?' Bill asked.

'Grand. Himself again. Last trip for you. I bet you're not sorry.'

'It was the hour's wait that got me down. Too far from the town. I got sick of canteen coffee.'

They drove for several miles in silence, then Bill asked Sheila did she fancy a meal.

'Lizzie'll have one waiting.'

'I meant going to a restaurant.'

'How could we? There's the kids and Lizzie'll have food ready.'

'It's all arranged. The twins can sleep in Lizzie's. Bob's not out tonight so he'll give a hand.'

'But why?'

'It was Lizzie's suggestion. She thinks you're worn out. The long car journeys. The visiting. Meeting that poor woman. A change will do you good according to Lizzie.'

'I'd love to. But I'm a sight. Look at my hair and this dress I'm wearing.'

'You're never a sight. I should know, I see enough of you.'

Sheila was thrilled. It was like having a date. 'Where will we go?'

'Jaeger's. Have you been there?'

'I've been nowhere. What's it like?'

'Pleasant and the food's delicious. Their Wiener Schnitzel is mouth-watering. A bloke plays a violin. You'll like it. I've taken Beth a few times and she raved about it.'

'She never said.'

'It was when we first came here. Everyone was busy settling in. I expect she forgot. So it's on?'

'Definitely.'

The restaurant was as Bill had said, pleasant. Tables well spaced, pink-shaded lamps, no clattering of pots and pans or other noises from the kitchen. The air was cool and smelled of delicious food. Herr Jaeger welcomed and seated them. He was a small fat man, with rosy cheeks and hair once blond, now the colour of platinum. He spoke very good English. He advised them on wine and recommended the Wiener Schnitzel. When he had left the table Bill said, 'He always makes a fuss of the English. Knows his business. We'll be here for yonks and have money to spend.'

'He's a dote. You'd want to cuddle him.'

'Probably a Nazi.'

'I don't believe it! Not a lovely old man like him.'

'A lot of them were lovely old men.' He lowered his voice and told her, 'When Belsen was liberated, Jaeger, the Bürgermeister, anyone of importance were all marched to the camp, forced to look at the corpses and the starving. This I'm not sure of but the story goes that they were made to bury the dead. And everyone denied knowing anything about the camp's conditions. Of course they knew. From miles away you could smell the putrefying bodies.'

'So why do you eat here?'

'Life goes on. And this is the best grub for miles around.'

'You've put me off my dinner.'

'No, I haven't. If that was the case you wouldn't buy from the milkman, the baker or the greengrocer. Even if they weren't Nazis they all knew what was going on.' He poured her a second glass of the white wine. It tasted gorgeous, sweet and fruity, she thought.

'The fiddler plays requests. Would you like a request?'

'I don't know any German songs, well there's "Lilli Marlene", not mad about that.'

'A little Strauss. "The Blue Danube"?'

'I'd love that. I saw the picture. Everyone in Vienna singing or whistling it.' Bill called the musician, spoke to him and gave him money.

Sheila was on her third glass of wine when the meal was served. Golden bread-crumbed Schnitzel and Bratkartoffeln with a side salad. She seldom drank at home and wasn't used to wine. It was a long time since she'd felt so happy. The food was delicious, the music divine and Bill gorgeous. She hadn't given him a thought since Fergus was sick. Now she did and fantasised again.

Bill ordered more wine and plied her with it. She ate every morsel of the meal. 'How about a dessert?'

She gazed at him before replying. His hair was jet-black and his eyes melting. She could eat him. But not the dessert. 'I'm stocious,' she said. The musician was playing a German song. She lilted the words: '*Ich tanze mit dir in den Himmel hinein, in den siebenten Himmel der Liebe.*'

'Go on, it's lovely.'

She shrugged. 'That's all I know. I want to go to the lavatory but I don't think I can make it.'

'Hang on a second. I'll get the bill and we'll go.' He linked her to the toilet. Holding on to the washbasin she reapplied her lipstick and, talking to herself, said, 'I don't look too bad.'

They didn't say much in the car: agreed the meal was lovely and that there might be a thunderstorm. As they drove into the garrison, Bill said, 'I enjoyed taking you in and out to the hospital.'

'Why?'

'I just did.'

When they arrived at their block of houses only the lamps above the porches were on. 'Everyone in bed. What time is it?' Sheila asked.

'Almost twelve.'

'God Almighty, we must have been in Jaeger's for hours.'

'Over three hours,' said Bill and took her arm as she staggered. 'We should have had black coffee.'

'No bother. We'll have it in my place.'

'You should go straight to bed.'

'I never do if I'm drunk. The ceiling comes down to meet me and I think I'm dying. I drink coffee and gallons of water until I sober up.'

Bill helped her up the steps, unlocked her door and switched on the hall light.

'So, are you coming in or not? Yes or no?'

'OK, I will. First I'll have to garage the car. Ten minutes, all right?'

'Great. I'll put the kettle on.'

Ten, twenty, thirty minutes passed. Changed his mind, Sheila thought. Shag him. I'll wash my face, put on my nightie and drink the coffee myself. Upstairs she put on an old baby doll nightdress, a present from her mother. White lawn with masses of broderie anglaise and matching knickers, long lost. She seldom wore it. Fergus preferred her black or red nylon nighties. He wasn't here so it didn't matter and the baby doll nightie was cool. Just as well he didn't come, she thought, this week my shopping's gone to hell. No filter cups and barely a spoon of Nescafé. She took the weak cup of coffee to the living room and sat on the sofa. I misunderstood his signals, she thought. Then asked herself, what signals? There were none. It was all in my mind. Me fantasising again. May God forgive me and me a married woman who never looked at another fella after I met Fergus.

All the same I wish Bill had come. We could have passed an hour. It's another thing I dislike about the army. Everyone goes to bed early. Not like in Dublin. Two, three o'clock in the morning and there'd be lights on somewhere, people still up gas bagging. She finished the coffee and was about to go to bed when she heard tapping on the french windows. The curtains weren't closed and she saw Bill. Sacred Heart of Jesus, he's here and I'm half naked. I can't let him in. But I want to. What'll I do? She looked round frantically for something to cover her, then saw the scarf. Thank God I'm saved. A corner of it was hanging over the sofa. She pulled it down, a big square scarf, draped it round her hips and tied it carelessly sarong fashion round them. 'So you decided to come after all,' she said, unlocking the windows. 'What kept you?'

'I had a shower and then second thoughts.'

'Why?'

'You might have changed your mind and gone to bed.'

'Another few minutes and I would have. I've sobered up enough.'

'You go to bed. I don't fancy coffee anyway.'

'Just as well, there's none. But now that you're here, stay for a minute. We'll have a fag. Come on,' she said.

He followed her. 'I like the sarong. What's it in aid of?'

To cover my arse she wanted to say but answered, 'For decency's sake.'

They sat together on the sofa. She was at a loss for what to say and very aware of Bill beside her. She could smell the soap he had used showering and his own smell. The whorls of black hair on his arms fascinated her. She knew they'd be silky to touch.

In the distance there was a rumble of thunder. The air was heavy and humid. She was excited by his nearness and felt afraid. She could bear the silence no longer and said, 'I could make tea.'

Bill laughed. 'I seldom drink tea. Now a whiskey I wouldn't refuse.'

'No bother. The sideboard's full of spirits. I think I'll have one myself. Scotch or Irish?'

'Irish.'

She tightened the knot on her scarf before going for the drink. She poured him a generous measure and a smaller one for herself. 'I like Jameson's,' Bill said and Sheila

242

agreed that so did she occasionally. The scarf was silk and the knot kept loosening as she moved. Bill tossed back his drink and Sheila gave him a refill and topped up her drink. She finished it quickly, felt slightly dizzy in a pleasant way.

'Oh, God, I'm banjaxed.' She yawned, then stretched her arms above her head. The knot again loosened and she began fiddling with it. There was tension between them that was tangible.

'What are you trying to do with your sarong?'

'The knot keeps slipping.'

He bent towards her and looked at how she had fastened the scarf. 'Were you ever a Girl Guide?'

She giggled. 'Me a Girl Guide? Never. Why d'ye want to know?'

'Pity, you'd have learnt about slip knots, reef knots, granny knots and sheep shanks.'

'So?'

'You sarong wouldn't keep slipping. Let me fix it.'

She looked at his bent head, the hair still damp, and she kissed it. He abandoned the tying, lifted his head and kissed her. Greedily she returned the kiss and maintained it. Leaning into him she felt the scarf slip to her thighs. Bill, still kissing her, lifted the nightie over her head and placed his head between her breasts. Kissed each in turn, then took a nipple in his mouth and his hand caressed her thighs. It was ecstasy. It was a sin, she knew that, but didn't care. Her hands undid his fly. Returning his lips to hers, he eased her down on the sofa. She spread her legs and he lay between them and entered her. She groaned with pleasure and raised her bottom.

The storm raged, coming closer by the minute. She writhed beneath him. They climaxed as the thunder exploded overhead, lay exhausted for a while. Then Bill gently kissed her eyes and her lips before sitting up. Sheila was already asleep.

She woke very early the next morning with an appalling hangover. I must have been mad to have drunk all that wine, she thought. Then, looking towards the french windows with the undrawn curtains, she remembered and clapped her hands over her face. 'Oh, Holy Mary, Mother of God,' she said out loud. 'I committed adultery. Oh, God, forgive me. Maybe I only dreamt it. I wouldn't do a thing like that. Oh, my head. It had to be a dream.' She sat up and saw the silk scarf on the floor, the glasses and whiskey bottle on the coffee table.

And she remembered. She staggered from the sofa to the french windows and tried them. They were locked but no keys. Don't let him bring them back. I couldn't face him. I'm destroyed,' she said to herself as she went into the hall. The keys lay on the doormat. He had come from his house and posted them through the letter box. No one would have seen him, thank God. She moved the keys with her bare foot, the coconut matting tickled it. She spoke again: 'They can stay where they are. If I bent down I'd faint.' Please, God, don't let anyone have seen him come in the back way. Fergus would kill me. But sure how could anyone? There's no houses at the back. No, I think I'm safe on that score. Lizzie would have been fast asleep so wouldn't have heard anything. I think I let out a kind of scream. I'm sure he put his hand over my mouth. I don't know. I really don't remember much about it. In any case there was thunder, a big clap. So even if anyone was listening they couldn't have heard. Sacred Heart of Jesus take pity on me. If only I could have the time back. I'm losing my mind. Everything's mixed up. I couldn't swear that I screamed, or that he covered my mouth, that there was thunder. I'll have to take something for my head before it bursts.

Chapter Twenty-six

She took two Alka-Seltzer, a spoonful of honey and a glass of fruit juice. She needed coffee. Looking through the kitchen window she watched the day breaking and wished it were this time yesterday. She wanted coffee but made do with tea. After a second cup she removed the glasses and whiskey bottle and, still feeling fragile, sat on the sofa before bending to pick up the scarf. The sofa wasn't stained. She peered closely at the cushions, but not trusting her eyes she turned them over.

As she showered, dressed and made up she recalled last night. How attentive Bill had been in the restaurant; the delicious meal, the music. It was all heavenly. Not since she met and fell in love with Fergus had she felt so enchanted. But she hadn't meant it to end as it had. Never, not in her wildest fantasies. Kisses, compliments, yes, maybe an attempt to caress her breasts but not what happened in reality.

She had committed adultery, been unfaithful to Fergus – a mortal sin. If she died this minute in the next one she'd be in hell for all eternity. And then there was Beth. How could she ever look her in the face again? Have coffee in her house, laugh and gossip as if it had never happened. Bill could talk in his sleep, call her name. Beth might guess. So might Lizzie – read it in her face when she went to collect the girls.

In the dressing-table mirror her face looked as it always did early in the morning: drawn, her eyes a bit baggy and dull. Her face wouldn't give her away to Lizzie. But what about her body? When Fergus made love to her would she react differently? . . . 'Oh my God,' she asked her reflection, 'why did I do it? Why did I let it happen? I didn't mean to. It just, I don't know, it just happened.' If it was intentional wouldn't I have done myself up? Put on something with a bit of glamour instead of the hicky baby

245

doll nightie. Thank God I'm on the pill. Did he know that? Beth could have mentioned it. Some women talk like that to their husbands. Not me and Fergus. Oh, Fergus, little do you know what I'm guilty of and Blessed Virgin Mary don't ever let him. I'll go to confession this morning. I am truly sorry and ashamed. Never, not even if some lunatic had a gun at my head, will I be unfaithful to him again.

The thought of confession paralysed her with fear. Confession always had even when all she had to confess were venial sins. This was a mortal sin and she had to go. And Father Tom would know who she was. She'd die. If only I were in Dublin, she thought, I could go into a dark chapel and tell my sin to a priest who had never before heard my voice. The bloody army. Bloody Hohne with its converted bathhouse for a chapel. And a confession box unlike any she had ever seen. As if that isn't bad enough I'll have to find Father Tom. He could be anywhere, gone to Celle, Hanover, miles away.

She looked at the bedroom clock: half past seven. There was a nine o'clock mass. She could corner him after that, tell him she needed to confess urgently. That's what she'd do. She dressed and waited until eight o'clock before going to Lizzie's.

'Mammy, Mammy, Mammy,' the twins shouted and flung themselves at her. 'What did you bring us?'

'Ah, darling, the shop in the hospital shut early yesterday,' she lied, 'but I'll make it up when we go to the NAAFI. Now let go of me.'

'The night out did you good, you look marvellous,' Lizzie said as she plugged in the kettle. 'Did you enjoy the meal?'

'Never tasted anything like it.' Sheila went on to describe the food and the music. 'When Bill told me how you had organised everything I was bowled over. Thanks a million, Liz.'

'You needed a break. I didn't go to bed until late in case you might have dropped in.'

Sheila felt faint, her heart galloped, jumped into her throat and was choking her. She complained of thirst and Lizzie poured her a glass of water. She sipped it slowly and calmed a little. Then asked, 'What time did you go up?'

'About eleven.'

I'm done for. Lizzie takes ages to go to sleep. She probably tossed and turned for hours, heard everything. I'm destroyed. She's too good and kind to upbraid me. Too decent to spread it around. But I'll know she knows and it'll spoil our friendship. 'You must be jaded, so,' Sheila said as Lizzie poured the coffee.

'I'm not. I went out like a light and didn't open my eyes until seven o'clock.'

Relief surged through Sheila and the hot strong coffee revived her as she prepared to tell Lizzie a lie. 'This feeling came over me when I woke up this morning. All of a sudden I wanted to go to Mass. To give thanks, you know. Fergus was seriously ill. Peritonitis is a terrible thing. Even nowadays people die from it. Could you put up with the girls for the hour I'm gone? I know I've got a nerve asking after you had them most of yesterday and through the night.'

'They're no trouble. If anything, they're a great help. Keep my three occupied. You go to mass and say a prayer for that poor woman and her husband. Did you hear any more about him?'

'No. I asked a nurse, she knew nothing. She wasn't on his ward.'

Lizzie made toast and put out bowls of cereal for the children. Then, until it was time to go to Mass, she and Sheila gossiped, ate toast and drank coffee.

She went the long way round to avoid hearing Mass: convinced that she couldn't endure half an hour in the

247

chapel. She'd faint or go hysterical. From a vantage point she saw the congregation leave and went to the sacristy.

Father Tom greeted her like a long-lost relation. Not someone he had seen at Sunday's Mass and again during the week as he left Fergus's ward. 'Come in, come,' he said. 'Didn't that man of yours make a grand recovery?'

'He did, Father, thanks be to God. I don't want to delay you but I have to make my confession. Could you hear me now, please?'

'Of course I could. You're lucky you caught me in the nick of time. Another few minutes and I'd have been on my way to a conference in Hanover, a visiting bishop. You go round to the chapel and I'll be there in no time.'

Walking back to the church she thought that Father Tom was the nicest priest she had ever known. As a soldier's wife she had met several RC padres. Not one could hold a candlelight to Father Tom but all were kinder and more approachable than priests she had had contact with in Dublin.

Her mother's voice came back to her. 'Holy Joes, every one of them. Thinking themselves already canonised. Always laying down the law. I wouldn't mind if it was to do with religion, the commandments and that. That's their business. But not at all. Everything under the sun they think they're an . . . authority on. How young girls should dress. Make up. How they dance. And telling poor unfortunate women in confession to go home and have another child when they've already got housefuls. I wouldn't be at all surprised when they meet their Maker if they aren't hauled over the coals.'

Her mother had mentioned the commandments – the sixth commandment: 'Thou shalt not commit adultery.' Shivers ran up and down Sheila's back and at the same time she felt roasting. Talking to herself, she said, 'Adultery, that's the sin I have to confess.' Nearing the chapel's doors she was tempted to run away. 'I'm not able to do it. I couldn't face the priest and tell him what I did.'

She raised an argument: 'If you don't and die suddenly with no one to whisper an Act of Contrition in your ear you'll be in hell for all eternity.'

'D'ye think I don't know that? Even so I can't talk to the priest.'

'It's God you'll be talking to. It's God who'll grant you forgiveness. The priest's only a stand-in for God.'

'I learnt all that in school, but I'd forget about God and be afraid of the priest. It was his voice I heard. He asked the questions. Father Tom might ask terrible, dirty questions. A priest from Saint Kevin's did that to a girl from the Buildings. She was going with a fella and they did it and she confessed. Shocking, she said it was. A sin for a priest to ask her what he did. And she wasn't married. Her sin wasn't as grievous as mine. She never went to confession again.'

She reached the doors and saw Father Tom come from the sacristy, walk across the altar and genuflect before the Tabernacle. Then he turned and walked towards the confessional. As he stepped off the altar he may have spotted me, she thought. I'll have to go in now. I can't make a fool of him. She saw him enter the confessional. Silently she prayed, Holy Mary, Mother of God, have pity on me, as she walked on shaky legs and with a racing heart, ready to collapse. She entered the semi-darkness of the cubicle next to the one in which Father Tom waited for her and knelt down.

The mesh grill was level with her eyes. Above it was a crucifix and she smelled a smell she was familiar with since she made her First Communion: stale air, sweat and polish. The mesh grill was drawn back and she saw a hazy image of Father Tom's face, saw him making the sign of the cross. The signal for her to begin. 'Bless me, Father, for I have sinned. It's a month since my last confession. Father, I did a terrible thing. Oh, Father, I slept with . . .' She couldn't continue and began sobbing.

'Stop that immediately and go on with your confession.'

She was shocked by the priest's voice. Never in the time she had known him, except when preaching a sermon, had she heard it raised and never in anger. She felt as if she had been slapped across the face or had icy cold water thrown into it. She stopped crying.

'Well . . .' she searched for words. 'I . . . well, what happened was that I slept with a man.'

She waited for another savage roar. It didn't come and in his usual voice the priest asked, 'Where did you sleep with this man?'

'In my house.'

'And how did this event come about?'

'I don't know, honest to God I don't.'

'Are you telling me you were unconscious, drugged or drunk?'

'I wasn't, well, maybe a little bit drunk.' Her mouth was dry, she kept licking her lips trying to swallow. There was nothing to swallow.

'Something like that doesn't just happen. There has to be a lead-up to it. Was it drink? Had you both been drinking? And did you tempt this man?'

'No, no, it wasn't like that. We went to this restaurant. We both drank.'

'And then?'

'And then he drove me home.'

'Did you invite him into your home?'

'Sort of. To have a coffee. He said he would later on. I waited, then gave up on him and got ready for bed. Then he knocked on the window. I let him in and we drank whiskey. Then it just happened.'

'So you were drunk and in a state of undress?'

And Sheila thought, now he's going to ask the questions the girl in the Buildings told me about. Oh, Sweet Jesus, help me. I want to make a good confession. But I won't be able to.

'Where was your husband?'

'In hospital, Father.'

'And the man – do you know him well?'

'He's a neighbour.'

'So he's a married man. Where was his wife last night? Did you hear what I said?'

'I didn't, Father. I feel a bit faint.'

He repeated it.

'Away in England, Father. I didn't mean for it to happen, honest to God. I've never in my life known any man except my husband.' She desperately wanted to keep talking so the priest couldn't ask the questions. If he did she would run out of the confessional, risk not getting absolution, risk going to hell.

'You have committed a grievous sin. Sinned against God, your husband and your family, sinned against the man's wife. Are you aware of what you have done?'

'Yes. That's why I came to confession as soon as I could.' She was crying silently, tears spilling down her face. 'I know I committed a mortal sin.'

'Were you aware that you were sinning last night when you lay with this man?'

'No. I don't think so. But I don't really remember to tell you the truth. I don't know what was going on in my mind, Father, but I wouldn't have thought I'm going to commit a mortal sin.'

'This man being a neighbour you'll see more of him.'

'I'm bound to.'

'How will you react in future?'

'I'll avoid him.'

'So that you won't sin again?'

'No, not that. I never would. It's because I'm so ashamed I couldn't look him in the face, utter a word to him.'

'Were you friendly as couples?'

'In a way. We'd sit together in the mess. Sometimes have drinks in each other's houses. And I see a lot of his wife.'

'Won't your husband, the man's wife, other neighbours think it strange if all of a sudden you ignore him?'

'I suppose they would.'

'No suppose about it. They'd notice and suspect. Your husband in particular. You committed a dreadful sin. Endangered your marriage and another woman's. Your guilt and shame you'll have to cope with. You must not behave in any way that will arouse suspicion. Do you understand what I am telling you to do?'

'I do and I won't.'

'The pair of you should be thrashed. There was a time when an adulterous woman was stoned, run out of wherever she lived. There are places in the world where women who commit adultery are put to death.'

Sheila's tears fell down her face, dripped off her chin and soaked her blouse.

Father Tom cleared his throat and continued, 'From now on you must never be alone with this man. You must never tell anyone else what took place between you and him. Not to avoid shaming you but for the sake of your family, his family and so that you don't give scandal. Is that clear?'

'It is, Father.'

'And do you promise God that you will never commit such a sin again?'

'Oh, yes, Father, I do. Never, never again as long as I live.'

'For your penance say the Rosary. Now make a good Act of Contrition.'

'Oh, my God, I am heartily sorry for having offended You.'

While she prayed aloud the priest spoke in Latin. The words of absolution finished, he blessed her with the sign of the Cross, then said, 'God bless you, my child' and slid the hatch shut.

She left the confessional and went to the back seat to kneel and say her penance. The beads slipped through her fingers, her head was bent and her eyes closed. She heard the priest leave the confessional, peeped and saw him return to the sacristy. Her relief at no longer being in the state of mortal sin was overwhelming. So much so that she considered saying three Rosaries instead of one. Then her religious ecstasy began to ebb as she thought of Lizzie minding the twins.

Lizzie knew that the nine o'clock mass only lasted half an hour and would be wondering what had kept her for so long. Poor Lizzie, jaded with the tiredness. She speeded up her praying and then went to the doors. There was a small damp patch on her blouse, she dabbed it with her handkerchief. I've never cried so much in all my life. Then she remembered her eyes. They'd be red and puffed. Lizzie'd want to know why. She found a solution – the holy water font and her hanky. The water was soft and tepid, as was holy water in every font she remembered. It soothed her eyes. She imagined she could feel the puffiness shrinking.

Walking back to Lizzie's, she thought about her confession and her now state of grace. And the seal of confession. No one, only God and Father Tom, heard or ever would hear it. Father Tom knew who she was, knew Fergus was in hospital. Yet he'd treated her as if she were a complete stranger.

She passed the play park where sometimes she had a go on the swings, so relieved and happy that if Lizzie weren't waiting she would have had a swing.

Chapter Twenty-seven

'I'm awful sorry, Liz. That oul blather from Kerry kept me talking for hours. I wouldn't mind only her accent is so strong I couldn't understand a word she said. How were they?'

'Not a bit of trouble. Yvette's taken them for a ride.'

'She's getting very pally all of a sudden,' Sheila said, sitting down and lighting a cigarette.

'She's been a great help lately.'

'I know. I must thank her. I wonder if we'll ever know what she's really like.'

'Given time I'd say so.'

'Say what you like, there's something queer about the pair of them.'

Lizzie changed the conversation. 'What time will Fergus be home tomorrow?'

'After the consultant's made his morning round. The hospital's seeing to transport. Tomorrow afternoon some time, I suppose.'

'You'll be over the moon having him home.'

'I'll be over the moon not having the visiting. Poor oul Fergus, I'll have to mind him. He's got fourteen days' sick leave. He won't like that – no trips to the mess. I'll have him all to myself. But knowing him he'll have me bringing Carlsberg from the NAAFI. I'd better go home. Send the girls in when Yvette brings them back.'

'I will,' said Lizzie, then asked, 'What happened to your eyes?'

'Nothing, why?'

'They're a bit red.'

'Grit or something. While the Kerry woman was gabbing to me there was a bit of a breeze, anything could have blown into them,' Sheila lied.

At home she inspected the living room again. Turned the cushions right side up and examined them. There were no stains. She sat on the sofa and cried bitterly. Her soul was immaculate, she wouldn't go to hell. But tomorrow she had to face Fergus. Go to bed with him. Look at the innocent faces of her children, and sooner or later there'd be Bill and Beth to cope with. She would never, as she had promised the priest, breathe a word to anyone of what had happened. No one could offer her comfort, disapprove but console her, point out that she wouldn't be the first who in the heat of the moment gave in to temptation, tell her to put the incident out of her mind, that in time she would forget it. And if it were to a Catholic she had opened her heart they'd advise her to pray to Our Lady.

She heard a car. Yvette, she thought, bringing home the children. They mustn't see her like this. She ran upstairs, undressed and went into the shower. Yvette would take them to Lizzie's she hoped as she held her face up to the water. And if she dropped them off here the twins would find her in the shower. Where she'd stay, telling them she'd be out in a minute.

She lowered the water's temperature and concentrated the cold water on her face, stinging it, hoping it would restore her eyes to normal. Wrapped in a towel, she scrutinised her face in the mirror. It was fine.

'When is Daddy coming?' the twins asked over and over again later.

Sheila wanted to scream, 'Will you two shut up,' but restrained herself. How could they know or understand the turmoil that was in her mind? Wanting him home, longing for him and at the same time terrified a sixth sense would reveal to him that she had been unfaithful. She put sausages under the grill and opened a tin of spaghetti while still thinking about Fergus. Maybe there was such a thing as a sixth sense but Fergus didn't have it. Fergus was uncomplicated. Fairies, ghosts, premonitions, he dismissed them.

In her mind's eye she saw her mother. Saw her mother who had found out that she had committed adultery. Her mother for once in her life struck dumb, disbelief and disgust fighting for a place in her eyes. Sacred Heart of Jesus, I'll go mad if I carry on like this. No sooner will Fergus be in the door than I'll be confessing to him. Holy

Mary, Mother of God assist me. She said three Hail Marys and calmed down.

'Will Daddy bring us a present?' Niamh asked and Deirdre repeated the question.

'Maybe. Probably sweets and chocolate.'

'What's for dinner?' Deirdre enquired.

'Sausages.'

'I hate them,' the twins said in unison.

'These are lovely ones,' she said, her voice placating, her hands itching to clatter them.

'And for pudding?' enquired Niamh.

'Ice cream and bananas, and now the pair of you go upstairs and wash your faces and hands.'

When Fergus arrived Sheila fell into his outstretched arms and cried as if her heart would break.

'Eh, come on, Sheila, I'm home, I'm OK. You've seen me every day. Cut it out.' He kissed her, his familiar lips on hers, his strong hard body close to hers, his body scent enveloping her. She clung to him, sobbing and telling him how much she loved him, and asking herself how could she have betrayed him. Round each of his legs a twin was entwined, clamouring for his attention. He let go of Sheila, she moved back and gave the twins their turn.

In bed he told her he had to take it easy for a couple of days.

'Why's that?' she asked. 'Did the doctor say so?'

'No, but haven't I had an operation? Maybe the stitches would burst.'

She didn't think that was likely. Nevertheless she felt relieved, convincing herself that a few days without sex mightn't be such a bad thing. By the time Fergus felt ready she would have pulled herself together.

They lay in each other's arms, kissed and caressed. She slept with her head on his breast and woke with an easier mind than she had on the previous days.

As she had foretold, Fergus had his beer brought from

the NAAFI. During the following days Bob, Victor and Bill came to see him. Remembering Father Tom's words, she welcomed Bill as she did the others and he reciprocated in the same way. She wondered if she had imagined that they had made love, but didn't dwell on it, although from time to time during the following week, when she was least expecting it, the memory came back to haunt her.

As soon as Fergus was fit for duty he resumed his old habits. On nights when he wasn't on the ranges after supper he went to the mess, often not coming home until midnight. Sheila sank further into discontent, hating army life, hating Germany and hardening her resolve to leave Fergus if he didn't apply for a discharge.

Lizzie's parents were coming to Hohne for Christmas, and Sheila had thought of asking her mother and father to visit also. Now she changed her mind. She would go to Dublin for Christmas. Hopefully Fergus would go with her. If not, she and the twins would go without him. While in Ireland she'd suss out the job prospects and enquire about housing.

Lizzie no longer went to the swimming pool. The weather was still very warm and she tired easily. Sheila, Emily and sometimes Yvette took the children to the pool while Lizzie rested. One afternoon when Sheila brought the children home, Lizzie was all smiles. 'Guess what,' she said.

'Go on, tell me,' said Sheila.

'Bob brought the mail at lunchtime – Beth's coming home.'

'About time too. She's been gone for a month.'

'I thought you'd be pleased.'

'I am of course,' lied Sheila, who was terrified at the prospect of meeting Beth again. So far she had managed to be sociable with Bill and neither by word nor deed had he put a foot wrong.

She no longer indulged in fantasies. She had learnt her

257

lesson and still paid the price from time to time by being overcome with a sense of guilt and shame.

From upstairs Yvette heard furniture being moved about the bedroom and thought, hard-working, tireless Else. I've told her every week isn't necessary. But still she pulls the rooms asunder, dusts, polishes, hoovers and replaces everything.

Yvette was washing parsley and listening to British Forces Network playing a request programme. An Irish tenor was singing 'Danny Boy'.

> O, Danny Boy, the pipes the pipes are calling
> From glen to glen and down the mountain side.
> The summer's gone and all the roses falling.
> 'Tis you, 'tis you must go and I must bide.

Looking out the window at the silver birch and rowan trees, their leaves changing colour, the bramble bushes heavy with ripe blackberries, the cranberry bushes soon to fruit, she was saddened by the waning summer. No more swimming. Victor wouldn't have to worry about bruised flesh. Soon practice camp would be finished. No more peaceful nights when he was on the ranges, her only respite his trips to Hamburg or Amsterdam to take photographs and sell his Black Market haul.

She dried the parsley, put it on the chopping board, went back to the window and thought how much she had enjoyed the summer. More than the relief of not being beaten and sexually abused was her acceptance by the women. She believed that Emily, Beth and Lizzie were her friends. But not Sheila and Sheila was the one she yearned to have a friendship with. One day at the pool she had overheard her tell Lizzie that if Fergus didn't curtail his drinking she would leave him. Yvette believed Sheila meant what she said. It didn't sound like a spur-of-the-moment threat. More like something that had been thought out.

And if Sheila, who loved Fergus, was being driven by his drinking to consider leaving him she would understand why she wanted to get away from Victor. At Emily's coffee morning Yvette had felt drawn to Sheila. She had had more to say than Lizzie or Beth. Chopsy was how she would have been described in Wales, chopsy and fit. Her own woman. Later Yvette had discovered that unlike the other women, though loving Fergus she wasn't a man worshipper. Beth seldom started a sentence that wasn't prefixed with 'Bill says', 'Bill thinks', 'Bill wouldn't agree with that'. She considered Lizzie a friend. But there was an innocence about her. Yvette knew that were she ever to confide in Lizzie the appalling way Victor treated her, Lizzie wouldn't believe her, think she was deranged. Emily was out of the question. She was an army wife, her husband a senior warrant officer. She would want no part in anything that could bring the army into disgrace. And in any case Emily's husband didn't belong to Victor's regiment.

Yvette believed Sheila would listen, be shocked and ask what Yvette intended to do about it. She imagined how the interrogation would go: 'Don't tell me you're in love with a bastard like that.'

'Oh, no, I'm not. I loathe him.'

'Then why haven't you left him?'

'I'm afraid.'

'Of what, for God's sake?'

'I'd be destitute.'

'I don't believe it! Destitute my arse. You're a young, healthy woman with neither chick nor child. You could work.'

'At what? I've no training, no qualifications. I'd have nowhere to live.'

'Listen to me. More than half the women in England and Ireland have no qualifications. But they work. In factories, shops, laundries, pubs. Maybe you think you're above that sort of thing. And if that's so you deserve all you get.'

'I know you're right, but where could I live?'

'In a hostel, rent a room, anywhere. Years ago women, especially if they had children, had to put up with shocking lives. It was that or starve. Nowadays it's different. You'd get Assistance until you found work. And I'd help in any way I could. I'm telling you you're no better than a prostitute, living with that man.'

Yvette began chopping the parsley viciously, wishing it were Victor's neck she had beneath the knife. Wishing that the dialogue between herself and Sheila hadn't been imaginary. With Sheila's encouragement she could find the courage to leave. But she knew it was wishful thinking, she and Sheila were unlikely to become friends. For whatever reason, Sheila was never more than barely polite to her. Perhaps it was coincidence but never once had she and Sheila been alone. Sometimes in the early evening, when both of their husbands were on the ranges, she had been tempted to knock on Sheila's door, bring a couple of magazines, ask if Sheila had read them, proffer them. But at the last minute she'd lose her nerve.

Sean died and in her heart she knew that Victor was in some way responsible for his death.

An accident perhaps, as the inquest had found. A childish game that had gone wrong. And maybe so. But where was Victor? Sean was a little boy. Why wasn't Victor keeping an eye on him? Were he and the other man so drunk as to not supervise the children? She sighed, remembering how many times she had pondered the same questions. How many times after Sean's death she had pleaded with Victor for an explanation. In the beginning he had refused to talk about it. And when, from time to time, she would again raise the subject he beat her.

She finished chopping the parsley and put it aside. Else,

having finished the bedrooms, came down. Yvette made her coffee and while she drank it they chatted. Else's English was good, as was the English of so many Germans working in the camp. Yvette would use her few German phrases when telling Else what she wanted done. And Else would congratulate her. But when Yvette asked her to translate English words or phrases into German Else wasn't interested. It happened also when Yvette went to shops in Bergen, Celle or Hanover, where she nervously used the little German she knew. Almost always she was answered in English. She supposed you couldn't blame the assistants. German children had been taught English in school and wanted to perfect it. It gave them the prospect of better jobs, more money. The probability of emigrating to America.

After Else had gone home Yvette sat for a long time brooding about her life. Asking herself why, when Victor was posted to Germany, she agreed to go with him. That was the time to leave him. He had left her £100 in case of emergency. The money, he told her, was from the selling of the second car. Why, once he was gone, didn't I leave? All I had to do was walk out. I had clothes and jewellery to sell, several weeks' worth of my army allowance. It would have been at least two weeks before Victor became suspicious when my letters didn't arrive. Two weeks at least before the army discovered I'd abandoned our quarters and stopped the marriage allowance. I could have gone anywhere. I could have paid for a room or lodgings. I couldn't because I was afraid. For most of my life I was looked after, by Mam and Dad, then Aunt Mags and before she died, Victor was on the scene to rescue me.

We'll be together until one of us dies. I'll grow into an old woman living with a man I loathe. If by some miracle Sheila became my friend she couldn't give me the strength. No one could. And no more than I have the courage to leave him, neither have I the courage to take my own life, though God knows I think of suicide often enough. Ways of doing it. Wash down a bottle of aspirins with whiskey. At high speed on a lonely road, drive the car into a tree or telegraph pole. Hang myself. Cut my wrists in the bath on a day when Victor would be out for hours. A day when I had told Else not to come. That would be the surest way. The least painful once the blood began to flow. I might not die in a car crash, might not die from the tablets. I'm not sure what a lethal dose is. The whiskey could make me vomit and hanging – I wouldn't know how to go about that. But I'll never take my life because suicide is a mortal sin. I'm a Catholic whether anyone else knows it or not.

A coroner might bring in a verdict of accidental death, but God would know the truth. I would go to hell and never see my child for all eternity. May God take pity on me, dim my brain, let me enter my second childhood, become senile, helpless and be put in a home until I die.

Sheila wrote to tell her mother that she and the twins were coming to Dublin for Christmas, that Fergus was on duty over the holiday but was trying to get a single bloke to swap duties. This was a lie. Fergus was adamant – he was not going to Ireland. She hoped he would change his mind. She'd give him until the middle of November to decide. He thought he had her cornered. What savings they had were in POSB. She couldn't touch them. But she'd have the last laugh. If by November he still refused to spend Christmas in Dublin she would borrow the fares from her mother.

But if he came she would stop demanding that he apply for his discharge. She felt that after her transgression she owed him that. She would endure another year in Germany. She loved him. She loved Dublin, yearned to be there, but knew that if she left him she'd exchange one yearning for another. Deprive the children of a father they adored. She didn't expect miracles. Fergus would always drink. But if they were living in Ireland she could, she believed, cope with it better than she did as an army wife.

When he went to the pub at home she'd have company: her mother, young women whose husbands were also fond of the gargle. They'd give out yards about their men. But so long as they weren't whore masters, violent, didn't spend the housekeeping money on drink they accepted it. The majority of men they knew – fathers, brothers, uncles – drank on a regular basis.

There were compensations. The city was on their doorstep. Cinemas, theatres, cafés and streets you could ramble through at night where the shop windows were ablaze with light. Always, day and night, there were things to see and do, talk and laughter everywhere. You weren't stuck in a place miles from anywhere. Alone in a house that wasn't yours. Filled with furniture identical to every other house in the garrison. In Dublin your husband might go to the pub, but he wasn't bound to go to the mess to celebrate the Queen's official birthday.

But another year in Hohne wouldn't kill her. She'd have twelve months to work on Fergus. Put up with his regular bingeing. Never mention buying camping equipment. Never refuse to make love. She seldom did, only if he was stocious, fumbling and foostering, telling her it would be all right in a minute. It was never a blank refusal and by the time she came back from the bathroom he was out for the count.

Chapter Twenty-eight

Beth came back in the second week of September. Sheila dreaded meeting her.

Beth invited the three women to tea the day after her arrival. Only Sheila and Lizzie could accept the invitation; Yvette had to go on one of her Black Market buying trips. The women embraced and kissed each other, and complimented Beth on how well she looked, admired her new clothes, becoming hairstyle. Sheila, not supposed to know the real reason for her trip, enquired about her parents.

Beth said they were well and then unpacked a bag of presents for the women and children: toiletries for Sheila, Yvette and Lizzie, and Marks and Spencer sweaters for the children. 'I missed you all so much,' she said as she distributed the gifts. 'It was great seeing Mam and Dad, but there was no one of my own age about. Everyone married and moved out to new estates. So all there was to talk about was the past, the good old days, as Dad calls them. And the television was on all day. They're both a bit deaf so it was blaring. I went to bed every night with a splitting headache. I'm dying to hear all the news. Fill me in, girls.'

'Fergus was rushed into hospital with appendicitis.'

'Oh, Sheila, I am sorry. Is he all right?'

Sheila, inhaling a cigarette, took a fit of coughing, couldn't control it until Beth brought her a glass of water. 'It wasn't a simple appendicitis. You tell her the rest, Lizzie. Something's gone against my breath.' To Sheila her voice had sounded quavering. She feared she might break down, start crying, apologising to Beth and make another confession.

'You must have got an awful fright,' Beth said sympathetically after Lizzie had told her of the peritonitis.

'I was petrified,' Sheila replied and thought, I still am. She was sweating, her heart racing, her face felt flushed and she imagined it to be as red as a crimson rose.

'How did you manage to get in to Hanover?'

'The men took me. Worked out a rota.'

'All of them, even Victor? What was he like?'

'Very pleasant, I was surprised. Usually he's a sarcastic sod.'

'My Bill's not the best of driving companions. I sometimes feel like screaming just to break the silence. How was he with you?'

The blood rushed again to Sheila's face. 'I'm roasting,'

she said and drank some more water before saying, 'Bill was great, they all were.'

Then, to her relief, tea and home-made cakes were served and Beth's questions were directed to Lizzie. 'When is the baby due?'

'Yesterday,' Lizzie replied. 'Little sod. The others were always early.'

'How long will they let you go over your date?'

'Not long because of my blood pressure. It's under control but they won't take chances.' *Poor Beth, your knowledge will always be at second hand. Though given the chance at this minute I'd swap places with you, Lizzie* thought. *Then immediately thought again, God forgive me, I don't really mean that.*

The women drank, ate and smoked until Sheila, looking at her watch, exclaimed, 'The kids! It's nearly time to pick them up. By the way, where's Tom? I forgot all about him.'

'Out with his Uncle Victor, I thought I told you. Don't kill yourself rushing to the school. They take ages to come out.'

'I'll see you later. Thanks again for the presents and the tea.'

All the way to the school Sheila was consumed with guilt and shame. *Poor Beth, looking so happy and contented. If only she knew. It would kill her.*

She arrived at Lizzie's and after the children had presented their drawings to their mothers, been fed and gone out to play, Lizzie said, 'Guess what?'

'I'm not in the mood for guessing, tell me.'

'You're in some sort of mood. You were like a hen on a hot gridle in Beth's.'

'That's an Irish saying. Where did you pick it up?'

'From you, probably. Anyway, listen to this. Last night I couldn't close my eyes. This child played football all night.

About three o'clock I went downstairs and made a cup of tea. The house was stifling so I went into the garden, walked to the bottom and coming back what d'ye think I saw?'

'I don't know,' said Sheila.

'No light in Beth's spare bedroom. I was delighted and thought, well, thank God my advice worked.'

'You mean . . .?'

'Of course. What else?'

'I suppose you're right,' Sheila said and a thought flashed through her mind. Maybe the separation helped but I made a man of him again. The thought gave her great consolation and diminished her sense of guilt.

Early in the morning of the following day Lizzie woke from a dream in which she had been sitting on the lavatory peeing. The bed was soaking wet. Immediately she nudged Bob awake.

'What's wrong? Have you started?'

'My waters have gone.'

He was as panic-stricken as he had always been when Lizzie went into labour. While dressing he kept asking her how she was, telling her he'd make her a cup of tea, then go for the doctor.

She laughed. 'Keep your hair on. I'm all right. And leave calling the doctor for a while, it's only six o'clock.'

'I'm sorry, love. It's my fault. We shouldn't have done it last night. You're not supposed to.'

'I didn't have to let you. Now calm down. Make the tea. Then about half-seven go to the MI Room. They'll phone the doctor. On the way back tell Sheila.'

She got up, changed her nightdress, put on two maternity sanitary towels in case she might dribble, then stripped the bed. Bob brought the tea. They sat on the mattress and while drinking it he asked if she was having pains. 'Sort of little niggles that's all. Stop worrying. I'm fine and this one will pop out with no trouble. They say the fourth baby falls out. But in any case I'll have no trouble. I know the exercises inside out and how to breathe.'

The doctor came with the clinic nurse who was a midwife. Lizzie knew both of them. They were young and pleasant people. She lay on the bed to be examined. Smiling at her, the doctor said, 'You'll know more about this than I do.' He laid his hands on her belly and waited until he felt a contraction. 'Hurting?' he asked.

'Not much,' replied Lizzie.

He, and then the nurse, gave her an internal and confirmed that her waters had gone. They wished her well and told her the ambulance would arrive within the next ten minutes.

Sheila came as they were leaving. 'What did he say, Liz?'

'Not much. He's not long been a doctor. You know where everything is. I hope Tom won't be a handful.'

'Give over, Lizzie, sure he knows me as well as he does you. What d'ye want me to do?'

'There's a few more things to go in my case. Put my good dressing gown in as well. I'll wear the old one for the time being in case of accidents.'

Bob made breakfast for the children, offered some to Sheila and Lizzie. Both refused but asked for more tea. The children came and sat on the bed, gambolling like lambs, asking if the baby would be a brother or sister. Lizzie told them she didn't know and that soon she'd be going to the hospital to collect the new baby. They were to be good girls, do what Daddy and Sheila told them, and give Tom lots and lots of cuddles.

Lizzie arrived at the hospital, was admitted and taken to an antenatal ward where she was put to bed. A nursing sister came to examine her, confirmed that she was having contractions but not to bank on delivery for at least six to eight hours. The nurse, like all the others she had met in military hospitals, was friendly. Even so, she didn't ask the question that bothered her. Why was she in bed? Walking about was advisable in the early stages of labour. Her book – her bible – stressed that. She didn't ask because she was in awe of doctors and nurses – priests, too. So she lay, reading a novel she had brought with her, from time to time putting it down to do her relaxation and breathing exercises.

Before lunch a gynaecologist came to see her. Neither he nor the sister gave her an internal examination. She knew, unlike when she was in labour with her first baby and every nurse and doctor who came into the ward did, that nowadays internal examinations were only performed when it was absolutely necessary. It was a great relief. Not that they had embarrassed her. It was the discomfort, especially when they were rectal ones. She had read about the curtailing of internals in a magazine. The reason they had been curtailed was that they could cause infection. The gynaecologist laid hands on her belly and confirmed what the sister had told her. She was hungry but knew that she wouldn't be served food in case there was an emergency and she had to have a Caesarean section.

She read a little, dozed a little and thought of Tom and the girls. This would be the first night of his life without her. The ward was four-bedded but she was the only occupant. Another woman to talk to would have been pleasant. Her well-spaced contractions, almost pain-free, continued. In mid-afternoon she was woken by the sister who told her that Major Rowland had rung to ask how she was progressing. Once again hands rested on her belly. Then the sister said, 'I'm going to do an internal' and did. She was smiling when she told Lizzie that her waters hadn't broken.

'But they did, I was soaking.'

'You wet the bed. It often happens. You're carrying a

big baby and he was pressing on your bladder. You can get up now and go for a shampoo and shave.'

The relief of leaving the bed overcame Lizzie's awe of authority and she asked, 'Why did I have to stay in bed?'

'Because we only do internals when necessary. You'd had one before you came in so another wasn't advisable. And so we assumed your waters had broken and as the baby's head isn't engaged you had to stay in bed.'

'Why?' asked Lizzie, already in her dressing gown.

'If the waters have gone and the head isn't engaged there can be a prolapsed cord. That's a medical emergency. The cord would be trapped between the head and the pelvic bone, the baby suffocated.'

'I never knew that.'

'As they say, we live and learn. Now off you go.' The Sister took her into the corridor and pointed to where she'd find the barber nurse. Her pubic hair was shaved and afterwards she was given an enema and sat on the lavatory for what seemed for ever. Then she went into real labour. She walked about for a while before lying on the bed to practise her breathing exercises, convinced that she would give birth with only a modicum of discomfort. The sister, who was going off duty, came to wish her well. She was replaced by a short, fussy, unattractive Irish nurse. According to the gynaecologist and the other sister, the baby should be born at about eight o'clock. Another two hours, Lizzie thought, I can manage that. The relaxation is working and when the pain gets worse the breathing technique will help.

By ten o'clock she was in agony. She would have liked someone with her. She wanted to scream but didn't, telling herself this was her fourth child, she couldn't make a fuss. 'Oh, God, oh, God, oh, Mam, Mam, help me. Don't let me lose control of myself or I'll go mad,' she said almost silently again and again. The hands of the clock on the wall seemed scarcely to move. By eleven o'clock she was being wrenched asunder and no longer cared that she might be thought an hysteric – she put a finger on the bell and kept it there until the fussy little nurse came. She was unsympathetic, told Lizzie she 'would go until morning' and left the ward.

Not long afterwards Lizzie knew she was now in the second stage of labour and pushed the bell hard once more. 'You again,' was the nurse's comment. She lifted Lizzie's nightie, parted her legs, told her to get up and go to the pre-delivery room. Taking her to the door, she pointed the way down what appeared a long, endless corridor, then bustled off in the opposite direction.

With one hand against the wall she moved slowly, resting now and then against a radiator, desperately resisting the urge to push. Her body told her she should be pushing, but she remembered other labours, nurse's voices: 'Don't push, don't push until you're told to.' When pain and exhaustion became unbearable and she was about to collapse on the floor, what in the following days she thought of as an angel of mercy appeared by her side: a German nurse who put an arm round her, gave her words of comfort and escorted her to the pre-delivery room and helped her into the bed.

Leaving the room, she said she would send the sister. There was little interval between the engulfing pains and the want to push was insistent. She rang the bell after what seemed an eternity and the Irish sister bustled into the ward, annoyance written on her face, not a word of comfort uttered. 'That nightie should have been off by now. Put this on,' she said, stripping the nightgown off and replacing it with a fastening-down-the-back short labour gown. 'The labour ward is opposite. Go over there now. I'll be back in a minute.'

Lizzie staggered across to the delivery room. Soon it would be over. The delivery couch was high and the step not there. She stood, holding her belly, terrified that the baby would fall out on to the floor. The flustered, fussy sister returned and became more agitated, blaming someone for the removal of the steps and rushing away to find another pair.

For many months after her delivery she believed that as soon as she lay on the couch the baby was born. He shot out like a bullet. No urging from the sister to push now, to stop pushing, push again. As time passed she wasn't sure if that was how the birth had been, but was in no doubt that he didn't cry, that oxygen was puffed into his mouth and that for the short while it took to revive him she didn't care if he was dead or alive. Her indifference lasted only for seconds and when she heard his cry she thanked God. He weighed ten pounds one and a quarter ounces and she fell in love with him.

She knew she had been neglected by the Irish sister and intended to complain about her. But as the days passed she relented, making excuses that perhaps on the night Jack was born she had been very busy. And in any case no harm had been done. One day, during her stay, she met two other women who had recently given birth. In the course of their conversation they discovered that each of them had read the book of breathing and relaxation exercises, had implicit faith in it, recommended it to all their pregnant friends. But they agreed that now, if they came face to face with the author they would strangle him.

Bob visited every evening. He brought flowers, sweets, letters and coloured drawings from the girls, gifts from Sheila, Beth, Yvette and Emily. He hadn't taken leave, the women were looking after the children, and Tom went for drives with Vic. He'd take a week off when Lizzie came home.

She felt guilty occasionally. Apart from feeding Jack she had nothing to do all day. Time to read, manicure her nails, soak in the bath for as long as she liked, help herself to milk or cold drinks from the fridge. And the food was good. Jack was a lamb, took to the breast as if he'd been sucking for ever, gave up his wind easily and slept from one feed to the next. It was like being on a holiday. Before he was taken back to the nursery she would stroke his face, nuzzle his neck and whisper to him, 'You're my last baby. You're so gorgeous I could eat you. But you're still the last. When I go for my post-natal I'll ask for the pill. I'm not supposed to but I will.'

Chapter Twenty-nine

October: red and gold leaves, clusters of orange berries on the rowans, the bracken rusting, the cranberries picked and frozen for the turkey sauce. The air was crisp, with little risk of thunderstorms. It was a pleasure to go walking.

On 1 October the central heating in all the quarters was switched on. The occupants could control it from their cellars, but from the beginning of November must leave it turned up. Freezing weather often occurred early in December. With the heating at the right temperature, a high one, the plumbing wasn't affected. Tenants knew that should the ruling be disobeyed and pipes burst they were responsible for the damage. It was the army and the rule wasn't broken. Sheila complained, as she did about the majority of rules and regulations. 'I'm suffocated,' she'd say to Lizzie, Beth and Fergus. Lizzie would advise not wearing sweaters indoors. Fergus ignored her moans and Beth quoted Bill's opinion on coping with a house that was stifling: 'You'll get used to it, by next year you won't notice the heat.' Sheila would think, please God, by next December I won't be here. I'll be back in Dublin. I'll have coaxed Fergus into getting his discharge.

Fergus was still adamant about not spending Christmas in Ireland. Sheila had now accepted that he wouldn't change his mind. She would say no more about it. Borrow from her mother. Announce her departure in time for him to arrange time off so he could drive her and the twins to the railway station. He wasn't spiteful, he would take her and pick her up when she returned.

She didn't welcome the prospect of four sea crossings in December. The Hook to Harwich, train to Liverpool Street, tube to Waterloo where she'd stay the night in the Union Jack Club. The following evening she'd catch the boat train from Euston to Holyhead. It would be just her luck to have rough crossings. At least the Holyhead to Dublin was only three and a half hours. The Hook to Harwich was an all-night one. If there was a gale she'd be terrified and have no one to comfort her. With Fergus she would have felt safe. When she was fifteen a boat sailing between Larne and Stranraer had sunk. The Irish papers reported the tragedy in detail. One report had it that not a woman or child survived. Sheila had never forgotten the incident. With Fergus beside her she knew that if it was humanly possible he would save them. They wouldn't be knocked down, trampled on by drunken men as was the case on the Irish ferry. And if, God forbid, they were to die they would drown in each other's arms.

She would pray for calm seas. But one way or the other she was going home for Christmas. Only for ten days, but time enough for Fergus to regret not going with them.

For six weeks after coming from the hospital Lizzie, to avoid Tom feeling jealous of the new baby, left Jack with Sheila or Beth and took Tom to the NAAFI. Jack wouldn't miss her and after all the weeks when Tom was landed on Sheila he would be better having his mother's undivided attention. Tom appeared to love the baby. One day, in the nick of time, she had prevented him feeding Jack jelly babies. He kissed him, stroked his hair, hadn't wet his bed or trousers, not thrown any more than his usual tantrums and left as happy as a lark for rides with Vic. But you never could tell what thoughts he might think were she to take Jack out and leave him behind. There were dangers she couldn't always protect him from. But from those she could, she would.

Stationed in the garrison were the Eighth Hussars, a regiment that had taken part in the Battle of Balaclava, and in October they celebrated it with the Balaclava Ball. Members of other regiments were invited including the gunnery staff. Emily, in whose house Sheila, Beth, Lizzie and Yvette were having coffee, told what a fabulous affair the Ball was: 'All very posh. Evening dress and it goes on all night. Breakfast is served in the morning.'

'It's a wonder they'd invite the hoi polloi,' Sheila said deliberately to annoy Emily.

Emily, as far as the army hierarchy went, wouldn't consider herself the hoi polloi. She rose to Sheila's bait: 'You don't understand. There were gunners at the Battle of Balaclava and in any case our husbands are high-ranking warrant officers. Now privates and the likes, you could call them the hoi polloi, but Hussars, whatever their rank, will be invited to the ball.'

'Big deal,' Sheila said sarcastically.

Emily lectured her, 'It's all about the regiment, Sheila. The regiment's like a family. So if you're having a do they're all invited. But then, of course, you don't know about regiments, or very little. After all, you hadn't been married all that long when Fergus went to the gunnery staff – that's not the same as a regiment. Do you know that in many regiments it's a father-to-son thing, even grandfathers and great-grandfathers, they may all have served in the same regiment.'

Sheila retorted, 'What I did see of regiments, the wives in particular, I didn't like. The CO's wife head of one committee, the regimental sergeant major's wife head of another. Other ranks' wives allowed to help at fêtes and bazaars, sell the things on the stalls but not hang on to the cash for any length of time. And honest to God, the RSMs' wives were worse than the officers' wives. They at least had good manners. Some of the others made me sick. Fergus says it's because they came up through the ranks with their husbands. Had to kowtow to each rank above them and so when they reached the top they treated those below them as they had been treated. We have a saying in Ireland for their sort: "Put a beggar on horseback and he'll ride to hell."'

Lizzie tactfully changed the subject by asking Emily where she would advise buying a ball gown. She suggested Celle. Yvette, who seldom pushed herself forward, politely contradicted: 'There is a new shop opened in Bergen-Belsen. I've been there. They have gorgeous clothes. Nicer than anything I've seen in Celle.' And Sheila, Lizzie and Beth, aware that Emily wasn't exactly a fashion plate, said tactfully they'd look in both places.

Later in the day, when Lizzie and Sheila were alone, Lizzie took Sheila to task. 'Maybe you weren't aware of it, but you were very rude to Emily.'

'I only spoke the truth.'

'The truth in your opinion. I think you did it deliberately to annoy Emily.'

'You get in on my nerves sometimes, Lizzie.'

'And sometimes you get on mine.'

'You should have told me before then, I'd have behaved myself. You know what I said was true. How many times have we talked about such things? How many times have you told me how your father hated the very things I was talking about?'

'It wasn't the same at all. For the most part my dad was talking about hundreds of years ago and my dad, although of Irish descent, is English. You're not. Many a one would say if you don't like how things are in the British army clear off back to Ireland.'

'Oh, Liz, how could you say such a thing?'

'It's time someone did. I know you miss Dublin and don't like the way many things are run in the army. It's

OK letting your hair down to me. We're friends. I understand you, know that your bark's worse than your bite. Not everyone does. And another thing, it wasn't fair to attack Emily. Her father was in the army, she was reared in quarters. The army's her life. Besides that, she is a very kind woman, always ready to do a good turn. You should also think of Fergus.'

'What's he got to do with any of this?' Sheila asked belligerently.

'He's a regular soldier. He'll be hoping for promotion, maybe a commission.'

'What you're telling me is that I might stand in his way.'

'Possibly.'

'Because Emily will spread the word that I'm discontented, not the stuff army wives are made of. That I'm anti-English, anti-establishment.'

'I never said that. And Emily's not the sort to spread gossip.'

'That's you all over, excuses for everyone. Emily now, always Yvette. Honest to God, you're too good to be true.'

Lizzie moved Jack from one breast to the other. Sheila stood up, collected her lighter and drum of cigarettes. 'I'm going home now and it'll be a long time before I darken your door again.'

'You're supposed to be bringing home the girls.'

'And so I will. I may be anti-everything but one thing I do is keep my word.'

She hurried from Lizzie's kitchen and was no sooner in her home than she cried as if her heart would break. She'd had a row with Lizzie, her friend Lizzie! What would she do without her? Lizzie was like the sister she had never had. She cried until she almost made herself sick, sat in silence and thought for a while. Then washed her face and went back to Lizzie's.

'Oh, Liz, I'm so sorry. God, I'd die if we fell out.'

Lizzie smiled and said, 'Sheila, you missed your vocation. You should have been an actress.'

'I should have been committed years ago. I think a relation died in an asylum. There's a mad streak in my family, on my mother's side anyway.'

'Here,' said Lizzie, 'see if you can get his wind up and I'll put the kettle on.'

When she came back with the coffee Jack was asleep. Lizzie put him in his carrycot and said to Sheila, 'You're cut down off my father. I suppose that's why I love you. We'll be friends for the rest of our lives. You know when you leave a place where you've been stationed and you promise to write to the neighbours you're leaving? You do for a while, they reply and then the letters fizzle out.'

'Don't tell me. Many a time I'm overcome with guilt especially when some of the women carry on writing and I never answer.'

'It won't matter where we go in the future, we'll keep in touch.'

Sheila realised it was time to tell Lizzie that her parents weren't coming for Christmas, instead she and the twins were going to Dublin. Lizzie looked crestfallen. 'I was planning all we'd do. Looking forward to meeting your mam and dad, and you mine. I was going to throw such a party. Couldn't you change your mind? Christmas won't be the same without you.'

'I'll be back in the New Year, back for *Silvester*. But I'll not be here for the following one, if God spares me. I'm not happy here. Only for you I'd go mad. The time at home should bring Fergus to his senses. And I'll work on him to apply for his discharge all through next year.'

'Supposing he doesn't agree, what then?'

'I'll leave him.'

'You couldn't. You're mad about him and he about you.'

'I know all that. I think about it every minute of the day.

But I don't want to spend the rest of my life rowing about his drinking. Rowing about the money he's squandering. My father's a drunkard. My mother's worked all her life. Me and her are alike, both fiery but she's not as bad as me. Maybe because she's older, more religious. I don't know. It's very seldom Catholics split up. And God knows some of the husbands are bastards, guilty of every sin under the sun. Fergus and my father are not like that. The drink is their only failing. But I create more than my mother ever did. And I don't want my girls growing up in a house where there's always rows.'

'I don't know what to say. It's so sad for all of you.'

'All he has to do is something to please me. And if he doesn't then that's it.'

'For all our sakes I hope he does.'

Practice camp was nearing its end. But Fergus and Bob were on the ranges when the women wanted to go to the boutique in Bergen-Belsen. Yvette solved the problem. The German maids worked a half-day on Saturday so if Else and Lizzie's maid, who were friends, would mind the children for a few hours in the afternoon the women could go shopping. They agreed delightedly, they liked the children and welcomed earning extra money.

The variety of dresses, ball gowns and glamorous skiing apparel mesmerised Sheila. Fingering a beautiful lemon sweater and matching anorak, she thought, if only Fergus were a different man we could go on a skiing holiday. Knowing that he was what he was, she didn't linger long on the thought. The German owner of the boutique was very attentive, displayed gown after gown and explained that she sold on credit. Lizzie's figure, which had never recovered from her pregnancies, was worse than ever six weeks after Jack's birth. She wasn't hopeful of finding a gown that would fit or become her, but had decided on trying some on. In case her milk should leak she had padded her bra with layers of cotton wool. One look at the attractive gowns and she knew they wouldn't fit.

The shop owner brought from another rack a selection: old women's dresses, outsize and dowdy. 'Try this one on,' she suggested, holding out a large dress of cerise taffeta, long-sleeved with silver embroidery. My mother, though Lizzie, wouldn't be seen dead in it. More gowns were brought, sludge-coloured and ornamented like Christmas trees. Eventually the assistant and Lizzie admitted defeat.

In between looking for 'the dress' Sheila had kept her eyes and ears open, and when Lizzie lost hope she said, 'I'll make you something stunning. We'll buy the stuff next week and you'll be the belle of the ball.'

Sheila bought on credit a scarlet strapless dress. She knew it was her the minute she looked in the mirror. She came out of the cubicle and modelled it for her friends who congratulated her on her choice. It was Yvette's praise she valued the most.

Beth bought a demure pale-blue gown with puff sleeves, ribbons hanging from its yoke and a modest neckline. 'Yes,' the other women said. 'It suits you. It's your colour.' Sheila agreed. It did suit Beth, it would also have suited a nine-year-old as a party dress. Then she thought, as the man said when he kissed his donkey, 'it's every man to his taste.'

'And you, madame, haven't you found anything you like?' Yvette thanked the assistant and said she had only recently bought a ball gown.

'How much was it?' Fergus asked, after first having admired the dress.

'Fifty quid.' Sheila had thought of lying about the price, but as the extra money would have to be given by Fergus he had to know the truth.

'Jesus Christ! Have you lost your mind?'

'Keep your hair on, it's on the never-never, two quid a

week, that's all. Two nights away from the mess each week that's all it'll take.'

'Bloody bastard,' she said to herself when he stormed out of the room. 'Feck him anyway, I've got the dress and that's that.'

On Sheila's advice Lizzie chose peppermint green georgette for her caftan. 'It's light and floaty, hanging from the shoulders. It'll hide the lumps and bumps.'

'You can see through it,' said Lizzie, holding a piece of the material up to the light.

'Not when it's finished. You bought double the length so you'll have two caftans, the under one without sleeves, OK?'

'I wondered why it cost so much.'

'Now you know. I did the buying, remember? And the caftan cost half what I paid for the dress.'

'Is Fergus still going on about it?'

'No, it's one of the things I love about him, he never goes on. I'm the one who does that.'

'It's a gorgeous dress.'

'I'm mad about it. I look at it every day. I'm tempted to try it on every day. Only I'm afraid of soiling it. But d'ye know what I was thinking?'

'I don't.'

'That if I leave Fergus I'll never get the chance to wear it again.'

'Another reason for staying with him.'

'From time to time I'm tempted, but not for long.'

'Come back after Christmas and see how it goes. And don't forget there'll be another Balaclava Ball next year.'

'You're right, but knowing me I probably wouldn't want to wear the same dress twice.'

'D'ye remember telling me someone belonging to you died in an asylum?'

'Of course I do.'

'It runs in families, you want to watch yourself.'

'Thanks very much. I'm going now. I want to start cutting out the caftan before the twins come home.'

'Before you go I have to tell you this. I won't wear it unless you let me pay you.'

Grinning, Sheila said, 'Suit yourself.' She shrugged. 'Why should I care if you don't wear it?'

Chapter Thirty

Lizzie looked lovely in her caftan. Before dressing for the ball she fed Jack until he was sated and bluey white milk dribbled down his chin. Her maid was babysitting and knew that if Jack woke crying, and cuddling, singing to him, walking the floor with him, changing his napkin failed to pacify him, he was hungry or thirsty. Then she'd feed him from the bottles Lizzie had left, one with expressed breast milk, the other with boiled water. When Lizzie brought him home from hospital she had started him on boiled water, because she believed it was good for him and to get him used to sucking on a rubber teat. For days he had rejected the teat, but eventually he accepted it. Tonight she could leave him with an easy mind. He'd suck the expressed milk with as much relish and satisfaction as he would from her breast. She padded her brassiere with cotton wool, applied the little amount of make-up she used, took out her rollers, put on the caftan and did her hair. She was delighted with herself. So was Bob. He kissed her and began to grope. 'Lay off,' she said, pushing him away reluctantly. 'You should be ashamed of yourself and the babysitter downstairs.'

'I am. I am,' he said. 'But there's always tonight.'

The ball, as Emily had said, was fabulous; the music, the colours, the men's mess dress, the fantastic gowns, sequined bodices, dazzling colours, many of them bought in London costing hundreds of pounds – dresses of very wealthy women. It was rumoured that some of the Hussars' wives flew to London to have their hair done for a special occasion. There were other dresses run up at home from imitation silks, their skirts draped with yards of net. And others nondescript, ankle-length and so complying with the conditions of the invitation.

The latest music was played. Couples jived. Couples tangoed, quickstepped, slow-foxtrotted. Clasped each other's waists to conga, the snaking ring circling the ballroom, dancers bending from side to side, shooting out alternate feet and singing, 'I came, I saw, I congaed, aye-aye-aye.' Military two-steps, Strip the Willow and Scottish set dances.

Perspiration spilled from the dancers. They collapsed on chairs, the women drank iced drinks, the men beer, recovered and joined the dancers again.

The young wives and their husbands sat at a table for eight. As the evening progressed they danced with each other. Sheila watched Fergus ask Yvette to dance and marvelled at her dress of silver lamé fitting like a snakeskin. Victor danced with Sheila, Bob with Beth, Bill with Lizzie. And when the dance finished Bill asked Sheila up. All night she had dreaded this, dreaded being in his arms again, being held close to his body. To her great relief it seemed as though she might as well have been dancing with Bob or Victor. They made small talk about the band, the enormous crowd and admitted that the delicous smell of food was making their mouths water. As he escorted her back to their table she wondered, as she often did, if she had imagined or dreamt of what happened on the night they came back from the restaurant. It suited her to do so. But now and then she acknowledged the reality, and guilt and shame engulfed her.

They queued for the buffet set out on several long tables. There were roasted geese and turkeys, carved and reassembled. Chickens boned and reshaped with stuffing, hams and salmons. Salads of many descriptions. And Indian and Malaysian curries. On other long tables varieties of desserts were laid. Sheila was contemptuous of many people's greed, their plates piled with samples of every food. 'You'd think they hadn't eaten for a month,' she said to Lizzie.

'They probably have never seen, never mind eaten, anything that's on that table.'

'I suppose so. I often look in their shopping trolleys. The things they buy! Tinned everything, sausages, pies, rubbish, mince. The only mince my mother would serve was what she minced herself. The scrapings of the slaughterhouse she said bought mince was. And I'm not commenting on the buying of those on lower incomes than ours. You see all sorts buying the rubbish.'

'It depends on how you were reared, Sheila. Will you stay for breakfast?'

'I will if Fergus doesn't collapse from the drink.'

'I'll have to go soon. I can feel my milk coming in.'

'Didn't you leave a bottle?'

'That'll be gone this long time. Jack's a gannet. Have you enjoyed yourself?'

'More than I have for a long, long time.'

The money lent by Sheila's mother arrived on 1 December. On the following Friday, after taking the children to school, she caught the bus to Celle and booked her passsage on Monday, 17 December. For the sake of the children she had bought and hung an Advent Wreath, even though the last two candles wouldn't be lit.

When Fergus saw the wreath he said, 'You've changed your mind, then, about going home?'

'I haven't. I'm still hoping you'll change yours.'

'You can forget that. I won't pay your fare. It's not right what you're doing. Christmas is for the family. You're depriving the kids of that.'

'And what about the family Christmas when the twins

were only a twelvemonth and you were serving the men Christmas dinner? Oh, I know it was a duty. Though I'm bloody sure the men could have done without you lot and the officers there. And there was me basting the turkey, reheating the pudding, keeping an eye on the kids who had started walking. I was like a lunatic. Run off my feet getting everything ready for three o'clock. Remember, that's the time you said you'd be home. And what happened? I'll tell you. Five o'clock you arrived footless drunk. The dinner was ruined. The twins were cranky because I was cranky. That's what you call a family Christmas?'

'I'm not with a regiment now. I won't be serving the troops.'

'And I won't be serving you.'

She knew he didn't believe that she would go away for Christmas. It was just another of the threats she made from time to time. She'd come round. And so when she showed him the train and boat tickets he lost his colour and looked so shocked, so vulnerable that she wanted to change her mind, put her arms round him, say, 'I was having you on. You know I wouldn't desert you, not even for a few weeks.'

Watching his face, she saw his colour return, his eyes regard her coldly. He had pulled himself together. He's a proud, arrogant sod. It would kill him to give in to me, she thought. 'Your dinner's in the oven.'

'I don't want any dinner. I'm going out.' And out he went. To the mess, where else, she thought. She didn't care. There was no give in him. He had no one belonging to him. No one to miss. She hadn't seen her parents for eighteen months. He'd say, as he had, 'You'd see them if they came here for Christmas.'

'That'd be great for them in the weather we'll have.'

On the Friday before she was due to travel Fergus made an

announcement at lunchtime. 'I won't be able to take you to the station on Monday.'

'You're joking,' she said, hand poised over his plate holding a soup ladle.

'I'm not. I have to go to Dortmund.'

'What's to stop you running us in before you go?'

'Nothing if you don't mind a four-hour wait on the platform. I'm being picked up at half-five in the morning.'

He had done it on purpose. To stop her going. She wanted to pour the hot, home-made chicken soup over his head. Watch it dribble down his face on to his immaculate khaki shirt. 'You did it deliberately. You lousy, sneaky bastard. Left it till the last minute before telling me.' To resist the temptation of scalding him she emptied the soup back into the tureen. 'Get your own shaggin' lunch. I'm going out. Going to tell Lizzie what sort of man you are.'

He let her get to the door before saying, 'I didn't do it on purpose. I might have if you were going alone. But I know how the girls are looking forward to Dublin. I wouldn't do anything to disappoint them.'

'Except not come with us.'

'Leave it now. The Dortmund thing couldn't be helped. The bloke who was supposed to go broke his arm, I was next in line. And whether you approve or not I couldn't have the order changed for my wife to go on holiday.'

'The army, of course. Anywhere else you could get a taxi, a bus. But I'll find a way. You won't best me.'

'I wasn't trying to. I've arranged transport. You'll be picked up at nine o'clock.' He left the table, made tea, drank it, then went back to work.

Sheila waited until Bob had left and went to Lizzie's. She related what had happened.

Lizzie said, 'You're like a pair of kids. You want him down on his knees pleading with you not to go. And he wants you collapsing, crying and sobbing, telling him you're sorry, that you never really intended going home. Kiss and make up then.'

'Not any more. We've both dug our heels in. I can't believe that he won't come with us. And if tonight he came in and went down on his bended knees, to Dublin I'm going.'

'You'll eat with us on Sunday and have breakfast before you leave on Monday morning?'

'Ah, Lizzie, you're so kind but I won't. Thanks a million all the same.'

'You said you would.'

'I know I did. Then I thought about it. On Monday morning you'll be getting the kids ready for school. Running round like a mad thing looking for what they can't find. Coaxing one or the other to eat breakfast. And as for Sunday lunch, that's not on with the humour me and Fergus are in. God, we might even start a row in your house. I'll be fine. Toast and cereal for breakfast. And lunch's no bother. Cold ham and chips.'

'If that's what you want I won't try coaxing. But if you change your mind that's OK. I forget to tell you that Beth and Yvette were here on Monday when you went to Celle. And we decided not to give the girls Christmas presents until you come back for New Year. Save you dragging them to Ireland and it'll be a nice surprise afterwards. Yvette bought crayons, pencils and colouring books for the journey. Me and Beth'll make up a bag of chocolate and sweets, nothing heavy.'

'That's great. As it is I'll have a job fitting everything in. Don't make coffee, I haven't a minute. Piles of ironing and odds and ends to wash. I'll pop in some time on Sunday to see you and Beth and say our goodbyes.'

Chapter Thirty-one

During the next few days Sheila experienced moments of regret, asking herself what had made her decide to go home for Christmas. Last year had been such a wonderful Christmas. The snow, the German decorations, lighting the candles on the Advent wreath. How excited the twins were every morning opening the windows on their Advent calendars, finding a sweet and, as the days passed, reminders of the birth of Baby Jesus. Neither she nor they had ever seen Advent calendars and wreaths before. And the fabulous parties. How she had enjoyed them. How she and Fergus had danced, showing off as they did years ago in Dublin ballrooms. Their lovemaking. How she believed he would have died for her.

Then she'd remember that lately they seldom made love and recalled how, despite the magical first Christmas in Germany, she had became more and more dissatisfied with her life. Hohne, she hated Hohne, a place in the vicinity of Bergen-Belsen, the statue of weeping Mother Russia, the little cemetery Yvette had introduced her to. Graveyards all, where thousands of people who hadn't died natural deaths were buried. They were enough to put years on you. Then there was Fergus and his drink. Her pleading, rowing, threatening to leave him. Grovellingly asking him to apply for early discharge. Her pleas, tantrums and threats. And then the night he stayed out all night, the lipstick on his mouth . . . The broken door, his almost broken nose. And finally the night she had slept with Bill. That was the beginning of the end, for though she had confessed and been forgiven, what she had done came back now and then to haunt her. Sometimes she tormented herself, wondering if Fergus knew about it. Was that the reason he seldom wanted her? Bill could have told him. Men sometimes did on occasion, even when they hadn't slept with the woman they were boasting of. In rational moments she knew her suspicion was unfounded. Fergus, drunk or sober, would have attempted to kill Bill, kill her.

Being honest, she would admit that a lot of the fault was hers. Like her mother had her father's, she should have accepted Fergus's drinking. She married him for better for worse. Her tongue, she knew, was like a knife and again and again she'd use it to wound and humiliate him. Drunkard or not, he didn't deserve that. She was convinced that if they moved back to Ireland there would be a great improvement in their lives. Her going there for Christmas was the beginning of her campaign to achieve that.

Fergus came in late on Saturday afternoon with the signs of drink on him. He picked at the dinner she put before him. Niamh and Deirdre made a fuss of him, tried coaxing him to go to Dublin with them. 'You'll be terrible lonely, Daddy, all on your own,' Niamh told him. And Deirdre reminded him of all the things there were to do. 'Member the zoo, Daddy. And the elephants. We had rides on them. And the big monkeys, the black ones. We laughed and laughed. Please come with us. You'll love it.'

He fobbed them off with excuses and promised that they'd go to Ireland next summer. 'I'll drive us all the way.' Then he went to lie down. Got up at six o'clock and off he went to the mess again. After the girls had gone to bed she ironed and folded, and packed more clothes and presents for her parents. Some white Christmas tree ornaments for her mother and a musical stein for her father. She was very tired and went to bed early, hoping she would be asleep when Fergus came in, that he'd wake her with a kiss and they'd make love. It was his snoring that woke her. After turning him on his side she moved as far away from him as the double bed allowed and dozed fitfully until morning.

On Sunday morning she suggested he should take the

twins for a drive. 'They're under my feet and I still have more packing to do.'

'Don't look to me for sympathy about packing. It's your choice. And I won't take the girls out. It's lashing freezing rain. It could snow. I'm going to the mess. I'll see you when I see you.'

Shag him, Sheila thought. I don't care when I'll see him. At this minute I wouldn't care if I never saw him again. She relented, said a silent prayer for forgiveness and for God to protect him.

He came home at half past eight, fairly sober. He wanted nothing to eat. He had packing to do and he was going to bed early. He put the girls to bed. Sheila could hear the three of them laughing, then Fergus reading them a story. Then silence. Leaving enough time for all three to be asleep, she had a shower, put a few clipped pincurls in the bottom of her hair, removed the chipped nail polish and repainted her nails.

The packing was finished, the cases labelled. She checked her tickets, passport and money, and put them in her handbag. In a small holdall she put a facecloth and hand towel, the colouring books and crayons, the chocolates and sweets, an extra tin of cigarettes. In the morning she would pack toothbrushes and paste, brushes and combs and her make-up bag. By half past eleven she was relaxing with a cup of hot chocolate and a cigarette when there was a knock at the door. Lizzie, she thought going to answer it.

On the doorstep stood a dishevelled, distracted-looking Yvette, holding out a small coloured snapshot. Sheila was so amazed to see Yvette and how she looked that she hesitated before asking her in.

'I'm sorry for coming so late. I couldn't go to Lizzie. I didn't want to go to Beth. You'll be the best to advise me.'

'Come in, come in and tell me what ails you.' Taking hold of Yvette's arm, she brought her into the living room and sat beside her on the sofa. 'Tell me now whatever it is.'

Yvette gave her the snap and Sheila studied it. 'I don't understand. What is it about the photo that's upsetting you?'

'It's Victor with Lizzie's Tom.'

Sheila looked again at the snap. She saw a man and a little boy sitting on his lap. The boy was naked. 'What makes you think it's Tom and Victor?'

'I recognise Victor and the child has red hair.'

'It doesn't look like Victor to me and lots of kids have red hair. Anyway, where did you get it?'

'Else found it behind a chest of drawers she had pulled out from the wall.'

Sheila looked again at the picture. 'I suppose it could be Tom, but wouldn't swear to it. You can't see his face.'

'And why not?'

'He's bending down. The man has his hand on the child's neck. His face is almost in the man's lap.'

'I know it's Victor. And why is Tom naked?'

'I wouldn't mind that. It could have been a hot day. Kids take their clothes off at the drop of a hat. What were you thinking?'

'Not thinking. I know. I know it is Tom and Victor. And I know what was going on.'

'God bless us and save us, that's a terrible thing to suggest about your husband. And especially without any proof.'

'Sheila, you know nothing about my husband. No one in the garrison does. Look at the teddy bear, the blue teddy bear by the chair that Tom takes everywhere with him.'

'It certainly looks like Tom's, but there's probably dozens of them in the camp. What about the deckchair they're sitting on. Recognise it?'

'Yes, it is the same as ours. They sold them in the NAAFI by the dozen during the summer. Listen, Sheila, I want you to come to my house and then you'll believe me.'

'Well, all right, but you know I'm going to Ireland in the morning and I'm terrible tired. I'll tell you what, we'll have coffee, you'll calm down and maybe we can sort something out.'

After bringing the coffee Sheila said, 'Drink some first and then tell me again from the beginning.'

'Well, as I said, Else brought me the photograph. I didn't pay much attention to it until she had left. When I did I was in no doubt as to what it was about. You see, Victor's hobby is photography. He has a dark room, always had wherever we lived. I was never allowed to see any of them. Victor said there were dangerous chemicals in the rooms. There's more to the story than photography and darkrooms. Victor is a devil incarnate.'

'A what?' Sheila asked.

Yvette began to explain the literate meaning.

'Not all that. I'm a Catholic, learnt about it in school. Tell me what it means as far as you and Victor are concerned.'

'He buggers me, chains me to the bed, photographs me in obscene positions.'

'And you let him?'

'I'm terrified of him. He beats me if I refuse. Batters me.'

'I've never noticed you looking battered.'

'In places that don't show. I'm sorry, Sheila, I shouldn't have come. It's not fair to burden you with the story of my life.' Yvette stood up and began to cry.

Sheila took hold of her hands. 'I'm a bitch. I'm sorry. I'm tired and not the best of friends with Fergus. Sit down. You can sit there all night and pour out your heart to me. I'll help however I can.'

'You have to come to the house. Help me search the darkroom. After Else went home and I studied the snap and recognised Tom and Victor, I had to get into that room. I thought about Dieter, you know, the German carpenter. And I drove to his place in the village. He was out. Wouldn't be back until ten o'clock. But his wife said she'd send him straight down. I told her a lot of lies. That Victor had gone to Hamburg, was lecturing on Sunday and Monday. That he'd left the slides he needed for Monday behind. He'd sent a message to the duty sergeant who brought it to me. He wanted Dieter to pick the lock of the darkroom. Someone from the unit would pick up the slides from my house and take them to Victor. Dieter came as soon as he could.'

Sheila interrupted Yvette. 'Hang on a minute, where is Victor and when's he due back?'

'In Hamburg. Private business and he'll be back tomorrow in the morning.'

'OK, go on with what you were saying.'

Yvette continued from where she had left off. 'It was just after ten when Dieter came. I made up another story, telling him I had forgotten where Victor had said the slides were so all the drawers and cupboards would have to be opened. And they were. I gave Dieter a carton of cigarettes and said Victor would fix up with him next week. Oh, my God, the things, the pictures I saw. I thought I'd go mad. That's when I ran to you. You have to help me search the whole place. There's something I must find. Please, Sheila. Please help me.'

'Of course I will. But tell me this, what time are you expecting him in the morning?'

'Between seven and half past. In time to go to work. He's never late.'

'That gives us a few hours' grace. I'll nip up and check that the twins are all right and then come with you.'

As they walked up Yvette's stairs, Sheila asked, 'Is it the truth that you've never been in the dark room, not even when it was being fitted out?'

'Never, not in this one nor any of the others. As for the fitting out of it, once the quarters had been allocated and I was waiting for my passage, that's when he would have had it done it.'

Sheila stood at the door looking into the darkroom. 'Well, will you take a look at that! The gear! It's like a posh photographer's shop. Stainless-steel sinks, filing cabinets, shelves stacked with God knows what. Where's the furniture that would have been in this room?'

'The tallboy and chest of drawers are still here.'

'I didn't recognise them piled with boxes and papers. What about the bed?'

'I don't know. It could be in the attic. The fitted wardrobe as you can see is stacked with all sorts of stationery,' Yvette said, sliding open the wardrobe doors.

'This lot must have cost him a fortune.'

'He's never short of money.'

Looking at a sheet of black hardboard that covered the window, Sheila said, 'I often wondered why you never drew back your curtains in here.'

'So did I the first time I noticed from the garden that they were closed. I asked Victor. "It's a darkroom," he said.' Yvette shrugged. 'That was all.'

'What'll happen when he sees this lot?' she asked Yvette.

'I won't be here. He'd kill me if I were.'

'That's a bit of an exaggeration.'

'He would. He's hidden all this from me since we married. I suspected something was going on, but wasn't sure what. His Black Market dealing I knew about. I was the one who did the buying. But I knew it was more sinister than that. Drugs, maybe, he spends a lot of time in Amsterdam, Hamburg, other places too. Says he's photographing landscapes. Now and then he'd show me a few. And when he began taking the pictures of me, the ones I told you about, I knew it wasn't drugs.'

'So now where d'ye want me to start?'

'I don't know. I think I'm in the middle of a nightmare.'

'He seems such a good husband. Very generous. Look at the clothes and jewellery you have, never mind the car.

It's hard to believe there's another side to him,' Sheila said.

'When we've finished in here you'll believe it. And as for what he buys me, that's all part of covering up. He buys expensive clothes to alienate me from my neighbours. I know that apart from a few officers' wives I'm the best-dressed woman in the garrison. In every army camp where we've been stationed. And it worked with the majority. I was thought of as being stuck-up, stand-offish. You know how seldom I can invite you in for coffee. He's afraid I'd get too pally and voice my suspicions, draw attention to him.'

'You certainly drew attention to yourself.' Sheila said and thought how she had misjudged Yvette. 'Attention and dislike. I know that only too well. So before we start on the room, tell me, where will you go tomorrow?'

'I don't know. I'll take the car, take whatever I find that'll go against him. And just keep driving.'

'What about the photograph of Tom, you'll show that to Lizzie.'

'*No*, oh, no! I couldn't do that. It would break her heart.'

'Yvette, you have to. Tom's crazy about Victor, will go anywhere with him. That has to be stopped.'

'And I'm afraid of what Bob might do. Kill Victor. Rightly so but Bob could then be charged with his murder.'

'If you don't tell Lizzie I will. Tom has to be kept from Victor, that's the important thing. Anyway, I suppose we'd better make a start. I'll have a fag first,' Sheila said, about to light a cigarette. 'I don't suppose I should. We might be blown up.'

'According to Victor you would. That was another of his reasons for never letting us go in, though we didn't smoke.'

Sheila wondered who the 'us' was but didn't ask. Instead she said, 'So show me where to start.'

'I've had a quick glance at the photographs, I wouldn't want you to see them. Go through the filing cabinets by the chest of drawers.'

They worked non-stop until three in the morning. Yvette opening large envelopes in which were photographs of young children, boys and girls, some naked, bound, gagged, manacled, the girls' legs in stirrups. There were men in the pictures with erect penises, pictures of men inserting their penises into the children's orifices. And photographs of large dogs investigating the naked boys and girls.

From the other side of the room Sheila called, 'Dozens of addressed envelopes. To all sorts of places. Jesus, Mary and Joseph to a priest in Dublin. There's a ledger with hundreds of names and addresses.'

One drawer clanged shut and another opened. Again Sheila called out, 'No wonder he could afford two cars. This lot's about money received. Hundreds and thousands.' While Sheila perused the ledgers, Yvette looked at more photographs. She was revolted by them. She felt faint. Afraid of what she still had to find. Finding it would crucify her. But still she must.

'I'm banjaxed,' Sheila said. 'It's time for a break and to talk.' She left the drawers and came to Yvette, who held up a hand and said, 'Don't look. You make coffee and I'll finish this drawer.'

While drinking their coffee Sheila quizzed Yvette. 'What are you going to do with all the stuff we've found?'

'I don't know. The army would bury it. Maybe discharge Victor. I'm not sure if the German police could do anything. It is a civil crime and police have precedence over the military when it is. But maybe not the Germans yet. I don't know.'

'For a start you want to get the evidence out of the house. Yourself and the car as well, away from here. It's not safe banking on Victor coming back when he said, he could be back sooner than you think, so here's what we'll do, right? I've got a huge carton that one of the gadgets came in. I'll get it in a minute. Bung all the papers and photographs into it and we'll drag it to my place. You grab whatever you're taking with you and hide in my house. After Victor's gone to work you can clear off. I somehow can't see him starting an enquiry about his missing wife once he's seen the darkroom.'

'Of course not. He'll go to work and do his investigating on the sly. Plans to track me down. Kill me. I'll do as you say. When will you tell Lizzie?'

'I've had a rethink about that. Once Victor knows the gaff is blown he'll leave Tom alone. But just in case he doesn't I have a story concocted. Victor has VD. He confided in Fergus. Victor hasn't been to see an army doctor. A German medical friend is treating him. He has an unusual strain of the disease. It can be passed on without sexual contact. By kissing on cheeks, holding someone close.'

'Is there such a disease?'

'There could be for all I know.'

'Will Bob and Lizzie swallow the story?'

'At one go. What else can they do, confront Victor? It'll work. They wouldn't risk harm coming to Tom.'

'You're fantastic. What an imagination.'

'What a liar. I'll fetch the carton and the spare keys, then look at some more stuff. I'll have to go home again at four thirty, wake Fergus with a cup of tea, wave him off. You stick by the window and watch for him leaving. Then put your car in our garage.'

Yvette went quickly through the last but one drawer of photographs. She no longer lingered over the pictures, sorry though she felt for the victims. So far she had found no more snaps of Tom. She hoped there had been only the one incident. And she was grateful that there were none of her. Her back, shoulders and arms ached. She stretched and walked about. The pain didn't ease and she considered a hot shower, then decided there wasn't time. She had the last drawer to search and her clothes to pack.

Sheila returned with carton and key, sitting down to begin sifting again.

'What time are you leaving?' Yvette asked.

'Nine. No more talking or we'll never finish,' Sheila said and delved into the drawer, striking gold, as she afterwards described it. Bundles and bundles of notes in several currencies. 'Yvette, Yvette, come 'ere, wait'll you see what I've found.' She turned to look.

Yvette was bent double on her chair and, as Sheila approached, cried out in what Sheila would ever afterwards describe as a keen she had heard at a funeral of a great-aunt she and her parents were attending in Kerry. She had never forgotten the keener's cry, wailing cries of loss and desolation.

Sheila put an arm round Yvette. 'Let me help you, love. Sit up, there's a good girl.'

In her hand Yvette held a photograph and sobbed. 'I didn't want to but I had to. I knew once I'd seen the other pictures there would be one of him. Oh, God, oh, God, my little love. My little Sean. My beautiful baby.'

Sheila knelt and took Yvette in her arms and rocked and rocked her until her sobbing grew fainter, with longer pauses.

'Look how they killed my baby.'

Sheila let go of Yvette, stood and looked at the picture. 'Sacred Heart of Jesus! I don't believe it. It can't be real. It's a fake. A bit of play-acting. It has to be for who in the name of God would do such a thing.'

'My husband's friends. Look, you see that man, his penis is on Sean's lips. Victor is holding his head. That's how they killed him. That man pushed his penis into Sean's mouth, pushed it to the back of his throat and he suffocated.'

'Get up, Yvette,' Sheila ordered. 'We've got to get out of here. There's evil in it. I can feel it. We'll go downstairs and have a brandy. And when we come up again I'll bring the holy water.'

While they drank their brandies Yvette told Sheila about Amsterdam and that Sean was not Victor's son. 'If there's time before we leave in the morning I'll explain it all.'

'I'll run in now for the holy water. While I'm gone, pack your things. And once Fergus has left we'll throw all the rest in the carton and you'll have time in my place to pack properly.'

Chapter Thirty-two

Back with the holy water and carton, Sheila shook the water in front of her as she and Yvette entered the darkroom. They scurried round emptying remaining drawers, not looking at the contents, tipping them into the carton. Just before half-four Sheila went to call Fergus. Looking at his sleeping face she longed to put time back, back before they had come to Germany. And she asked herself, 'How have we reached such a state of misery? We love each other. Why can't we live as we used to?' Fergus stirred. 'I brought you a cup of tea and a bit of toast.' He thanked her, coolly, she thought, as one might thank a waitress.

He sat up. 'Are you still going to Dublin?'

'I am.'

'So that's that,' said Fergus, going into the bathroom.

Sheila went down to the kitchen and put on the kettle for coffee. Fergus, when he came down, refused it. 'Tell the girls I said goodbye.' He put on his tunic and cap, collected his holdall and left.

Sheila was flabbergasted. She watched the car emerge from the garage, knew he knew that she would be watching from the window. He drove away. 'Had I known how he'd be I'd have doused him with the tea. He'll live to regret it. I'll be in no hurry to come back,' Sheila declared to the empty kitchen.

She saw Yvette drive the Citroën into their garage and lock the doors afterwards. It was quarter past five. She and Yvette could clear the darkroom and be out of the house by six clock. Yvette could do most of the sorting while she kept 'nix' from the bedroom window in case Victor arrived early. They'd have time to get out the back way, through the gardens and into her place. Yvette would be safe there.

The carton was packed and its lid sealed with Scotch tape. Between them they carried it to Sheila's house, then went back for the cases. Sheila heard a car turn the corner and went to the bedroom window. It's not Victor's, thank God, she thought. When it was nearer the house she recognised it as a staff car. She relaxed. Then she heard the car slow down and stop. Her heart jumped into her mouth as she saw two figures emerge. The light above Yvette's door illuminated them. She saw pips on their shoulders and one of the men wore a clerical collar. The padre and duty officer! Fergus had been killed and they were knocking at the wrong door. Yvette was down the stairs before her.

'Mrs Smithers?' the young officer asked.

'Yes,' Yvette replied.

'May we come in?'

'Of course. Come in. Come into the living room.' The men followed her in and Sheila went in after them, no longer fearing for Fergus's life.

'Shall we sit down?' the padre suggested. The young officer told Yvette that Victor had been killed on the autobahn outside Hamburg. The padre then took over, consoling Yvette in what he said were tragic circumstances. 'He died instantly and no one else was involved in the accident.'

The young lieutenant offered his sympathy. The padre asked if Sheila could stay on with Yvette. She assured him she could. 'Later in the morning the CO and his wife will come to see you,' the young officer told Yvette and the padre asked was there anything they could do, anyone she wanted notified.

'No,' she replied. 'We are – were – both orphans, no relations at all.'

After again expressing their sympathy the men left. Yvette looked stunned. Sheila waited for her to speak first. 'D'you think he's really dead?' she asked.

'The German police are very efficient. Unless the car was burnt out they'd have had plenty with which to identify him.'

'Are you sure?'

'Yes, I am.' And Sheila said a silent prayer that she was right.

'I always suspected he was in some way responsible for Sean's death. Not in the way he did die. I couldn't have envisaged such an act. I didn't know anything about such things. But you learn as you go along, discover that these vile men do exist. They could live next door to you and you wouldn't know. Like Lizzie, you would trust them with your child. I've seen the photograph. I know now. I'm sorry Victor died. Died instantaneously. He didn't deserve such a death. He should have been arrested, shamed, gaoled and lived to be ninety. A mewling bag of bones incarcerated for life.'

'Will you wait here for the CO and his wife?'

'No, I want nothing more to do with the army. I'm walking out of this house. I'll leave the keys in the door. I don't care what becomes of it. I'll go to your place.'

'I'll just take a look upstairs to make sure you haven't forgotten anything.' Sheila was back in no time. 'You left most of your clothes. Why?'

'They were bought with the devil's money.'

'The beautiful ocelot coat, you're not taking that?'

'The ocelot coat especially. I hate furs.'

Sheila wished there were some way she could ask for it.

But there wasn't. 'Come on then,' she said, 'the twins will soon be waking.'

As yet there were no lights in either Beth's or Lizzie's house. 'I'm relieved,' Yvette said. 'I don't want to talk to anyone. I'll have some coffee and then be off.'

'Where will you go?'

'England, maybe back to Wales. I don't know anyone there. I don't know anyone anywhere.'

'I was thinking', said Sheila, pouring coffee and coaxing Yvette to eat something, 'that we could travel together. I suppose you'll go from the Hook same as me. You could give us a lift. It'd be company for both of us.'

'I'd be delighted. Keep my mind occupied. Not that I'll be grieving for that man. But I'll be racking my brains for what to do with the papers and photographs. Someone has to be told about that ring. Break it up. Those other men must be punished. If I've you and the twins with me I'll be less of a hazard on the road.'

'That's great. I've everything ready. Now that Victor's dead I don't have to see Liz. There's no urgency to protect Tom. But hang on a minute. Whose name is the car in?'

'Mine, I found that out recently, why I don't know. It must have suited him. Perhaps if you own two cars bought duty free you wouldn't be allowed to sell both in England. Something like that. It wasn't for my benefit.'

'The accident couldn't have happened at a better time – you've owned the car for over a year and can sell it. I'll get the girls up, fed and dressed and we'll be on our way.' Then she remembered the driver coming to pick her up. 'Maybe I'd better wait for him. When they find you gone and me having cancelled the driver they'll put two and two together. I don't suppose it would matter but the less they know about you the less you can be involved. So here's what we'll do. You go off and wait for us in Soltau. You'll have a few hours to put in. Drive around, find a café. Take one of my cases and the hand luggage. I'll take the other

301

case. It'd seem peculiar me travelling to Ireland with no baggage.'

Sheila, while the twins ate, packed the remainder of her things, rinsed the cups and cereal bowls, and waited for the driver.

'How are you off for money?' Sheila asked as they set off for Holland.

'I have enough. Victor left me cash to buy goods from the NAAFI. I was supposed to get them today. Marks, so I can fill up on the way, pay for lunch. I'll change them for sterling on the boat.'

'Don't mind me asking, but how much did he leave you?'

'The usual, about a hundred pounds.'

'That'll last no time after you've paid your fare and got digs in London.'

'I'll manage. Sell the car.'

'You haven't forgotten that there's thousands of pounds in the carton. All the transactions must have been in cash.'

'Bound to be for what was being bought and sold. I wouldn't touch a penny of that money.'

'That's understandable. But some of it must be for the Black Market trading. I know that's illegal but not like the other business. How much would you say was made on the Black Market in the last year?'

'At least a thousand.'

'There'd be nothing wrong in taking that amount.'

'I want none of it.'

'Ah, well, it's your decision. I won't mention it again.'

Nor did she for the time being. The twins chattered to each other; asked how soon would Daddy come to Ireland. How soon would they go home again? Was the boat near? Would Santa know they had moved to Dublin? On and on the questions went until Sheila forbade them to ask another until after lunch. 'You can sing instead.' She began with 'Nellie the Elephant', followed by 'Tom Dooley'. Then the four of them sang carols.

Before crossing into Holland they stopped for lunch. As had been every café and restaraunt she had eaten in in Germany, the place was spotless, crisp tablecloths, vases of greenery and coloured berries, and a welcoming staff.

Yvette ordered roast pork with red cabbage. The twins wanted the same. Sheila dissuaded them. 'You hate red cabbage and only eat the crackling on pork. Have sausage and I'll ask the waitress to mash your potatoes and for pudding you can have chocolate gateau. You love that.'

She chose Wiener Schnitzel, Bratkartoffeln and a side salad. Not to remind her of the meal with Bill, though fleetingly it did. Her mind was too occupied with thoughts of Yvette and how she could persuade her to go with her to Dublin. Alone in London, and especially at Christmas time, she'd lose her mind, maybe do something desperate. She decided she'd wait until they were aboard the ship and the twins asleep before broaching the subject.

There weren't many travelling and they had no trouble getting a cabin for four. They ate again, Sheila and Yvette drank wine and the girls Coca-Cola.

Niamh and Deirdre went to bed, said their prayers for Grannie, Grand-dad and, making her an honorary aunt, Yvette. When they were fast asleep Sheila suggested that Yvette should come to Dublin with her. 'Stay for over the Christmas. You'll be with friends and have time to work out what you want to do.'

'You're so kind. But I couldn't just arrive unannounced in Dublin.'

''Deed you could. Me ma and da would welcome you with open arms. You're my friend, of course you'd be welcome.'

'I couldn't think of anything I'd like better. I'm terrified at the thought of being alone in London. All the same, I couldn't come.'

'Why couldn't you?'

'Put yourself in my position. Would you?'

'It'd depend on who was asking me. I'm your friend. I know it's only recently. But I feel as if I'd known you all my life. And it's nothing to do with the life you've led. That's not true. What you put up with from that bastard was terrible but wouldn't influence me. Millions of women are battered and abused. But what happened to your little child brings me closer to you.'

Yvette cried. Sheila sat beside her on the bunk. There was a swell and they were thrown together now and then. 'Come with us. My Christmas will be spoiled thinking of you in a Lyons Corner House eating your Christmas dinner. Say you will for the few days anyway.'

'If you're sure, I'd love to.'

'Great,' said Sheila. 'Now I'll go up to the bar and buy two brandies. We'll go out like a light and be in Harwich before you know it.'

The next morning they drove from the port to London and booked into a service club near Waterloo Station where they showered, had breakfast and then went for a walk. 'I lived here for years before I married, with an aunt and this is the first time I've ever stood on Waterloo Bridge,' Yvette said. She and Sheila leant on the parapet and looked up the river. The twins looked through the pillars.

'Did you see the picture, *Waterloo Bridge*?'

Yvette hadn't and as they walked on and turned into the Strand, Sheila told her about the film. About Robert Taylor and Vivien Leigh. 'After Clark Gable he was my favourite. I cried my eyes out at that picture. If it's ever on anywhere, don't miss it.'

They had lunch in a Lyons Corner House and went into Woolworths where they bought rings, bracelets and little purses for the girls. On the way back, lingering again on the bridge, Yvette asked Sheila, 'D'you think the army will be looking for me?'

'For what, the funeral expenses?'

'I don't know. Leaving the door open, not taking all my clothes.'

'I doubt it. The car's gone so they'll assume you went in it. If you had barrack damages, like stained mattresses, smashed crockery maybe they'll chase you. Like hell they will.'

'Why, then, were you concerned about not waiting for the driver?'

'I suppose because the army would have wanted you to identify Victor. Attend his funeral. And they'd have been concerned about your welfare. He didn't die on active service so no pension in that regard. But if he had served long enough, twelve years at the least, you might be entitled to a third of what pension he would have got had he decided on a discharge after twelve years. Those are the things the army would want to sort out for you. But not to worry. You can look into it at any time.'

'Whether I was there or not, I wouldn't have identified him nor gone to his funeral. Imagine listening to the padre praising him, praying for him. I'd have gone mad, stood up and shouted out the truth.'

'If you change your mind about the pension you can always contact them. But not the other way about. So forget about the army.'

Chapter Thirty-three

Yvette drove leisurely to Holyhead. The sea was moderate and with company Sheila had no fears. It was only a three and a half hour sea crossing. 'We don't need bunks,' Sheila said. 'The kids can stretch out beside us and we'll be there before we know it.' They bought sandwiches, drank many cups of tea and talked.

'And to think I thought you were a stuck-up nothing.

May God forgive me. But I'll make up for it. You'll never be in need of a friend again.' And while she was talking, at the same time she wondered if it would be possible to coax Yvette to stay longer than the Christmas holiday in Ireland. Even after I've gone back to Germany she'd be better off at my mother's than on her own in London or Wales. A couple of months would make all the difference. The raw edge of her grief would be smoothed.

Yvette took Sheila's hand and held it. 'I don't know what I'd have done without you. I was very fond of Lizzie, Beth and Emily, but all the time it was you I wanted for a friend.'

'Well, you're stuck with me now.'

'I was wondering how much I should tell your parents.'

'For the time being just that you're a widow. Your husband died in a car accident a couple of months ago. You've had to give up your quarters. That'll be enough information for the present.'

As the boat approached Dun Laoghaire Sheila gave Yvette instructions where to meet once she had collected the car. Then she woke the twins, took them for a pee, wiped their faces with a damp flannel and tidied their hair. 'Will Daddy be meeting us?' Niamh asked and Deirdre repeated the question.

'Ah, darlin', sure isn't Daddy minding our house in Germany until we go back. But he'll write us letters and send gorgeous presents. You'll see Grannie and Grand-dad in a few minutes, won't that be grand, and tomorrow I'll take you to see Santa.'

'In all the snow and the deers?'

'No, in Dublin. Santa will fly there tomorrow. He's very kind. He loves children and knows they couldn't all go to where he lives. So he flies to other countries where they are. He stays in a big, big shop where there's a grotto made with snow blocks exactly like his real home. He sits in the doorway and the boys and girls tell him what they want on Christmas morning. Because he's magic he doesn't have to write it down. He'll remember. And then he gives the children lovely presents.'

Niamh and Deirdre clapped their hands and shouted, 'I want a doll with a blue dress and silver shoes. And mine will have a pink dress and golden shoes.'

'That's not what you'll get tomorrow. That'll be what Santa brings on Christmas Day. So don't forget to tell him.'

'What'll we get tomorrow?' Niamh wanted to know.

'A surprise,' Sheila told them.

'I hate surprises,' whinged Niamh and Deirdre agreed with her.

Sheila was tired and irritable. She lost her patience. 'Not another word out of the pair of you or you won't go to see Santa. In a minute we'll be getting off the boat. Grannie and Grand-dad will meet us, and I want no bawling like jackasses. All right?'

With sullen faces they regarded her for a few seconds, then promised to be good.

They disembarked and went to the meeting place. Ginny spotted them, called out, pushed her way through others waiting and embraced Sheila and the twins. There were kisses and hugs, tears and laughter. Sheila was in her seventh heaven. She was home. The air smelled different, there was salt on it. She could see Howth Head. The voices around her were Irish voices. Then she remembered her father and asked, 'Where's me da?'

'Back there. You didn't think he'd push his way through. Gentleman Jim. Though it'll be more to do with his hangover than manners.' Sheila knew she was truly home.

'Come on,' said her mother. 'It's freezing cold and there's a taxi waiting.'

On the way to greet her father Sheila said, 'Ma, I've brought a friend. Her husband died a few months ago. She was coming to England to look for a place. I felt sorry for her and asked her over. I hope you don't mind.'

'I'd have welcomed a bit of notice. But as she's here I'll see her all right.'

She embraced and kissed her father. 'Da, it's great to see you, great to be home.'

The twins pushed their way between Sheila and her father, demanding his attention.

'Well, will you look at the size of my girls. What are they feeding you over there, eh? God bless the pair of you. Living beauties, that's what you are. And the spitten image of your mammy and granny.'

'That taxi man's meter will be ticking over so we'd better make a move,' said Ginny.

'Ma, in the excitement I forgot. Yvette has a car.'

Ginny ordered her husband to get to the rank as quick as possible. 'Tell him we didn't know about the car. He'll charge you for the wait, but that can't be helped.'

'Stay by the rank, Da, and we'll pick you up.'

Yvette was waiting for them.

'Never mind the introductions till we're in the car. That wind will cut through the children like a knife,' Ginny said. On the way to pick up her father Sheila introduced her mother and Yvette, and her father when he got in.

She savoured every minute of the drive, telling the names of seaside resorts they passed and promising the children that next summer, when they came again to Dublin, she and Daddy would take them to Blackrock, Sandymount and Merrion to pick cockles.

Sitting beside Yvette, Mr Brophy congratulated her on being a grand driver. 'Not that I can drive myself but all the same I know when I feel comfortable with a driver.'

From the back seat Ginny apologised to Yvette for her brusque manner when they first met. 'I was afraid of the twins catching a chill. I'm very sorry for your trouble. What happened to your husband, the Lord have mercy on him?'

'A car accident. It was a terrible shock. But at least no

one else was killed or injured. He must have lost control of the car and hit the central reservation. He died instantly.'

'Thanks be to God he didn't suffer.'

As they neared the city Yvette admired the variety of lovely houses.

'Spoiled for choice if you'd the money to buy them. There's Georgian, Regency, early Victorian that's hard to tell from the Georgian, all sorts of beautiful houses. Not for the likes of us, though. I wouldn't live in one of them if I got it for nothing. Oul relics. The Buildings are grand. Built in nineteen hundred and four or six. You'll see for yourself the right date when we arrive. We have all the conveniences. But my ambition is to have a brand-new house. I'm savin' up for one. And if I live long enough I'll have my wish.'

'It's the likes of you,' said her husband, 'that'll be the cause of destroying Dublin. People without an eye for beauty, with their taste in their mouth.'

'The bloody cheek of you,' Ginny said, then asked what hand could she have in destroying Dublin.

'There's plans afoot already for it. Progress, they call it. Philistines, that's what they are, wanting everything modern. The next thing you know we'll have skyscrapers.'

'You swallyed the dictionary this morning. But you're right about one thing.'

'And what's that, may I ask?'

'Me lacking an eye for beauty. Lacked it I did, otherwise how would I have finished up with a fella like you?'

I'm home. I'm home, Sheila thought. It's grand to hear the two of them at it.

Ginny fried rashers, eggs, black and white pudding and sausages. Yvette and the twins said the sausages were gorgeous. Yvette added that she had never tasted such delicious ones.

'Hafner's,' Ginny told her. 'A German pork butcher.

There's nothing to hold candlelight to them. I'll fry another couple for you.'

'No, please don't, I'm bursting with food. I haven't enjoyed a meal so much for a long time.'

Pot after pot of tea was made, questions asked about Fergus. Why hadn't he come? Was Hohne as desolate as other army camps, Ginny wanted to know. And Mr Brophy talked about Belsen-Bergen. How, though he didn't doubt the truth of it, many a one found it hard to credit. Ginny asked Yvette had she liked living in Germany. She said she had. Ginny said she'd have a Mass said for her husband and Yvette thanked her.

Then the twins in unison said, 'We want to see Santa. We want to see Santa.'

Sheila tried fobbing them off. 'It's freezing cold and I'm terrible tired. I'll tell you what, maybe tomorrow might be a nice day, we could go . . .'

'No, no, no,' they shouted and their grannie backed them up.

'Well,' said Mr Brophy, getting up from the table, 'I'd better go and earn my few bob.' Then, putting his hand in his pocket, he withdrew a handful of coins. 'Here y'are my little dotes,' and gave each twin two half-crowns.

'What d'ye say?' Ginny prompted.

'Thanks very much, Grand-dad,' they said one after the other.

'Have you nothing else for me?' Mr Brophy asked. Deirdre and Niamh giggled and looked shy. 'Ah, come on,' he coaxed, holding out his arms into which they ran and kissed him.

'About the sleeping arrangements,' Ginny said as she cleared the table. 'Your father'll sleep on the sofa bed in the parlour. The twins in the double bed with me and you and Yvette have the other room.'

'It's very kind of you to have me, Mrs Brophy. All the disturbance I'm causing.'

'Not at all and sure isn't it only for the few days.'

Walking down Grafton Street with Yvette and the children, Sheila felt on top of the world. All the shops displayed Christmas decorations, tableaux of reindeers, their hides flecked with snow, sledges laden with brightly wrapped boxes, trees draped in tinsel and small furry animals peeping from cotton wool holes.

The flower sellers were in their usual places, so were the beggars, whistle players, fiddlers and singers. 'No wonder you miss Dublin,' Yvette said as they neared Bewleys. 'There's a magic about it. I haven't been to many cities. When I lived in London I seldom went far from Paddington. My trips to Hanover were to NAAFIs on the outskirts of army camps. In Wales there was Cardiff, I went there a few times and to Swansea, but they were nothing like this.'

'It's us. The people. We're Irish. Put enough of us in them cities and we'd liven them up.'

'Everyone I look at is talking, smiling or laughing. And your mother and father made me so welcome.'

'Hospitality is said to be one of our virtues.'

'Are all Irish people like that?'

'Don't you believe it. Some are begrudgers, liars, some have the gift of the gab, same as everyone everywhere. Only we have the charm. They say we're easygoing. But wait'll you see two oul ones having a go at each other. Scalping one another. I'm exaggerating, another habit we have. But I love Dublin and here I'll end my days.'

In Bewleys, with its smell of pastries, newly baked bread, chocolate and coffee being ground, Sheila said to Yvette, 'An improvement on the YMCA in the Roundhouse, eh?'

'Don't remind me.'

Eating and drinking, reassuring the girls that in a minute they'd go to see Santa, Sheila recalled the day she had met Fergus in Bewleys. They had sat not far from where she was now sitting. She wished for a miracle to see him walk in the door. Creep up on her. Put his hands over her eyes and say, 'I couldn't exist without you.' And in front of everyone in the café kiss her passionately.

311

'You're not listening Mammy,' Niamh's raised voice proclaimed. 'We want to see Santa. You promised. We want to go now.'

Sheila, dragged back to reality, wanted to lean over the table and give Niamh a clatter across the face. Restraining herself, instead she caught hold of her arm, squeezed it and said, 'One more word out of you and you can forget Santa. Straight home we'll go. Now finish that cake.'

On the way to Santa's grotto in Clerys Sheila pointed to Brown Thomas. 'That's where I worked. You'll find your sort of clothes there, Yvette.'

'I won't be buying those sort of clothes again. Can't afford them and don't need them any more. Such a relief. Sometimes I think I'm dreaming and that I'll wake up and Victor will be there, and I thank God that it's not a dream. I hope your mother isn't spending too much on the Masses she's having said. I want to say don't spend your money on him. I want to shout out the truth.'

'Then she'd be having them said every day.'

Sheila pointed out the Bank of Ireland and told Yvette it had once been where the Irish Parliament sat, and that her grannie and many other old people long after it became a bank still referred to it as the old Houses of Parliament.

They walked on down Westmoreland Street and crossed to O'Connell Bridge. The tide was out and seagulls foraged in the muddy sides of the river. Niamh and Deirdre had to be lifted up to lean over the parapet. Further down the street Sheila showed Yvette the General Post Office, told her it was there the 1916 Rebellion started and of all the Sundays her father had dragged her around Dublin showing her the sights. As they crossed to Clerys she said, 'Me da fought in the Rebellion but whatever you do don't bring up the subject. Once he starts on it there's no stopping him.'

Niamh and Deirdre had a turn sitting on Santa's knee and whispering in his ear what they wanted for Christmas. He told them he wouldn't forget: a doll in a blue dress, a doll in a pink dress, but they had to be good girls otherwise Santa might forget what they wanted, bring them cars and trains instead of dolls. They promised they'd be very, very good.

'D'ye fancy another cup of coffee, Yvette?' She did and they made their way to the Gresham Hotel. O'Connell Street was flooded with children and a sea of brightly coloured balloons. When seated in the hotel the children opened their presents from Santa. Deirdre's was a kaleidoscope and Niamh's a cardboard sweet shop. Sheila slotted the pieces into place, a backdrop, counter and two shelves on which to stand miniature bottles filled with coloured sweets the size of seeds. 'Daylight robbers,' she said, 'catchpenny things, gone in no time.'

'It's a lovely hotel,' Yvette remarked, looking around.

'Second-best to the Shelbourne. It's where the majority of Dubliners come, or used to, for their first dress dance. The fellas hire their dress suits and bring flowers for the girls. It goes on till three o'clock in the morning. God be with the days. D'ye want a cake?' she asked Yvette.

Yvette didn't. But the girls demanded ice cream.

Sheila told Yvette that one day through the week she'd leave the twins with her mother. 'Then me and you can saunter through town. I'll show you more of the sights. We'll have our lunch in Brown Thomas. Maybe some of the girls I worked with are still there. Hurry up you two with that ice cream. Your granny will have the dinner ready and go mad if it's ruined.' And then, speaking to Yvette, she said, 'Prepare yourself to meet the neighbours and friends tomorrow.'

'A party?' asked Yvette.

'No, just them dropping in to see me and the kids, and have a gawk at you. It'll be all over the Buildings that there's a posh car outside our place. You'll like them, grand people.' They took a taxi, which the porter in the Gresham called for them.

Ginny cooked steak, fried onions and boiled floury

potatoes for dinner, with stewed apple and custard for pudding. 'The pair of you look jaded. You should go to bed early,' she said after dinner.

The carton filled with pornographic photographs, negatives, ledgers, lists of names and addresses, and money was in the bedroom. Sheila, while undressing, asked Yvette what she intended doing about it.

'I don't really know. I thought of destroying everything. But I mustn't do that. Those men must be punished, gaoled so that they can't harm other children. Only I don't know where to start. Who to send the evidence to.'

'There's no hurry to make a decision. What about the money?'

'That I was going to tear up, burn, throw in the sea, but I've changed my mind.'

'I hope you'll keep enough to support you till you get on your feet.'

'The thousand from the Black Market only. The rest I'll send anonymously to children's charities. I don't know of any but I'll enquire when I go back to England.'

'That's a great idea. When were you thinking of going back?'

'If your mother doesn't object to me staying, I thought I'd travel as far as England with you.'

'That'd be smashing.'

'I'll drive you to Harwich.'

'You'll do no such thing. I'll get a train from Liverpool Street.'

'In that case I'll go back tomorrow. I mean that.'

'OK, then, I'd be delighted.'

From their beds they talked for ages, Yvette still worrying that the army would pursue her.

'Why? For what?' Sheila asked.

'I don't know. But you always felt they had power over you.'

'They had to a certain extent but only while you were

married to a soldier. Now he's dead you are nothing to them. If you were still in Germany in another six weeks you'd be out of your quarters on your ear. If you had nowhere to go they'd fix you up in a hostel and help you get a council house. After that, if you were in bad straits, the British Legion, more likely SSAFA, would give you a handout.'

'I hope you're right.'

'I'm always right. Seriously, I am telling you the truth. D'ye want a cup of tea?'

'No thanks, you have one.'

Sheila came back with a cup of tea and a plate of buttered bread, and sat on the side of the bed. 'I don't suppose I'll hear from Fergus until next week.'

'Probably not, especially with all the Christmas mail. Are you missing him?'

'Not yet. I'm too happy and excited being home. Seeing me ma and da and Dublin. I will next week. My first Christmas for years without him. His fault. He could have come with me. He should have come with me. His pride wouldn't let him. D'ye know he never even kissed me goodbye. He's like a mule. I'm hoping he'll learn his lesson while I'm away.'

'You still love him, though.'

'I'm mad about him. I'd die without him.'

'You're so lucky, Sheila. You've a family and a lovely man. God spare him and them.'

'God help you, you were unfortunate, but please God there might be some happiness yet. I'll pray for you. I'm getting into bed now. Is it OK if I turn off the light?'

'Of course.'

For a long time after the light was out Sheila heard Yvette crying.

Chapter Thirty-four

Dozens of people called the next day, old and young, the majority women. The woman from the rag store, the woman from the bakery, young married women who had grown up with Sheila and were still living with mothers or mothers-in-law while they waited for Corporation houses. There was no one from Brown Thomas. For a while Sheila had kept in touch with Rosaleen but only for a while. She probably had a family by now. One of these days, Sheila promised herself she'd get in touch. When she was back in Germany.

The twins were petted and showered with sweets and chocolate. Regrets were expressed that Fergus wasn't home. Sheila was assured that she hadn't changed a bit. Yvette was introduced and welcomed warmly. Older women told Sheila it was a pity she had gone far away to live and daughters and daughters-in-law desperate to leave Ireland rolled their eyes heavenwards behind their parents' backs. When word got around that Yvette's husband had died recently she was sympathised with. Prayers for her husband's soul were promised and an old woman said, 'Husbands can be contrary and many is the time you'd wish them from under your feet. But it's only when they're gone for good you miss them.' Sheila and Yvette exchanged glances.

The evening finished with several of the men and women singing old Irish songs: 'If I Were a Blackbird', 'She Moved Through the Fair', 'The Irish Emigrant' and 'Danny Boy'. Sheila's father, in keeping with his Republican past, sang 'Kevin Barry', reminding Sheila of Father Tom's Silver Jubilee when Lizzie was amazed that a British army sergeant sang it. Poor Lizzie, Sheila thought. I don't know what to do about Tom. Now that Victor's dead the need for her to know isn't so urgent. But Tom is a friendly child, a beautiful little boy. And who's to say that there aren't other men like Victor in the garrison. After all, no one suspected him. And another thing, God only knows how whatever Victor might have done to Tom could affect him. He seemed OK, happy, but you never could tell. She decided to do nothing until she was back in Germany. Then she'd tell Lizzie about the photographs. Not Tom's, she wouldn't mention that there was one. Lizzie and Bob she felt sure would be concerned, remembering the affection Victor lavished on Tom, the numerous car rides. They might consult a doctor. They would certainly discourage Tom from forming relationships with men, sad though that might be.

After the guests had left and the twins were asleep Yvette, Sheila and her parents sat round the turf fire talking. Ginny asked Sheila if Fergus had thought any more about applying for a discharge. 'Ma,' Sheila replied, 'that thought's as far out of his head as the wind that blew his first shirt.'

'I can understand that,' said Mr Brophy.

Ginny pounced on him. 'Of course you can. When did you ever know a man who couldn't understand another when his wife was trying to alter something about him.'

'Don't always jump to conclusions, Ginny. What I was considering was Fergus's worry about giving up a secure position and a good pension. And his worrying would be for the sake of Sheila and his family.' He took a long drink from his pint of stout, wiped the froth from his lips with the back of his hand, lit a cigarette, inhaled deeply and after exhaling said, 'On the other hand things are picking up in Ireland. Sean Lemass is a grand man. We were in the GPO in Sixteen. Lemass is going to put this country on its feet. I'd say that in the not too distant future there'll be jobs galore.'

'D'ye think so, Da?'

'I do. And it's not guesswork either. I read the papers and in between the lines. And many of my pals are in the know. Many in the government. Men that fought beside me in the GPO. Things won't change overnight. But change they will. There'll be men and women who took the boat in the Fifties taking it home. Work will be plentiful. The education and health schemes improved.'

'God, wouldn't that be marvellous. Would you ever drop a line to Fergus telling him all that?'

'If he wasn't my son-in-law I'd write with a heart and a half. But he is and he'd think I was interfering and resent it. But what I will do is, when you go back, send newspapers, moryah for you. But they'll be papers referring to what I've been saying.'

'Do, promise you won't forget.'

'I won't forget,' her father promised.

On Christmas Eve morning Ginny, the twins and Yvette went across town for last-minute shopping. Sheila had gone the previous day and bought the dolls the girls wanted for Christmas. While they were out she would wrap and hide them. And hopefully a parcel, but more importantly a letter, would come from Fergus. Though it might not. She had only been gone a week and whatever the postal service was like in Germany in Ireland it wasn't great and at Christmas a shambles.

Surrounded by wrapping paper, decorative labels, ribbon bows and sellotape that kept vanishing, she wrapped the presents for the children, Yvette and her mother and father. She was in the parlour where her father had slept since their arrival. In such a short time he had put his mark on Ginny's sewing room. The reek of tobacco marked it as his territory. And she thought how her arrival and Yvette's had knocked her mother and father out of their own way. But neither had complained or made Yvette feel unwelcome. Thank God their stay wouldn't be too long. Another week and she'd be on her way back to Fergus. The break would have been good for both of them. It would be a happy reunion. A celebration.

And then she asked herself what about Yvette? Where

would she go? How long would the money she had agreed to keep last if she couldn't find work? She pictured her in a bedsit somewhere, bereft, grieving for her son with no one to turn to. Fiddling with the Christmas paper, which tore easily, she put the parcel aside, lit a cigarette and looked through the window watching for the postman, and there he was, heading for their door. She hurried into the hall as envelopes cascaded through the letter box. No knock on the door, no parcel. But please God a letter. And among the many Christmas cards, there it was. A letter from Fergus. A long letter she knew by the thickness of the envelope. Leaving the cards on the hall table, she went back to the parlour, tearing open the envelope as she went. There were five sheets of paper. The top one addressed to her. It read:

Sheila,

Despite having the tickets and everything packed, I didn't believe you would go to Dublin. On the way to and from Dortmund I kept thinking she'll change her mind. Cancel the driver and be waiting when I come home. You weren't. You were gone, taking my family from me. At any time that would have been a blow but to do it at Christmas! What more can I say?

Kiss my girls for me and remember me to your mother and father.

Fergus

'You bastard,' she said aloud. 'You lousy bastard. I didn't leave you. I pleaded, ranted and raved for you to come with us. You had plenty of leave to come. Nothing to stop you except pride and stubbornness. What was wrong about me wanting to see my mother and father? Only you. The bloody cheek of you to put me in the wrong. I must have been mad to marry you. And there I was, like an eejit planning my campaign when I went back to Germany. A gentle one. Not nagging. Pleasing at every hand's turn. Making you understand that I couldn't take another fifteen years as an army wife. Moving from here to there. The children going from school to school. And believing my campaign would work and you'd capitulate. Deluding myself. Making a bloody fool of myself. You're a heartless louser. Only someone like you could write that letter to his wife. You deliberately never mentioned Victor's death and Yvette's disappearance. You weren't to know that I was in on it all. But you did know that I'd have been intrigued by such a happening. And not a word did you mention. Well, stick your married quarters up your arse, Hohne and the army with it. And don't cod yourself that I'll shed a tear for you.'

But she did. Cried heartbrokenly. Smoked cigarette after cigarette until her stomach turned and she rushed to the lavatory and vomited bile. She rinsed her mouth with cold water and sponged her face. And told herself that Fergus wouldn't spoil Christmas. Hers, yes, but not the children's, not her mother's and father's nor Yvette's.

She returned to the parlour, and finished wrapping and then hiding the presents, while her mind considered what were her options.

'Well,' asked Ginny when they came back from town, 'did the letter you were waiting for come?'

'It did on the last post.'

'And how is Fergus?'

'Missing us. Sorry he didn't come,' she lied.

'You never know, he could fly in at the last minute.'

For a second Sheila believed he might. But the hope went as quickly as it had come. 'What was it like in town?'

'Heaving. I was glad Yvette was with us. You'd be afraid of your life, of losing the children in the crush.'

'Did you buy me something nice, Yvette?'

'You'll have to wait and see, Sheila. Will I fry bacon and eggs for us?'

'Bacon on Christmas Eve! I thought you were a Catholic.'

'I am. I was. I forgot all about it being a day of abstinence.'

'I've got fillets of plaice, Ma. I'll fry them and make chips. Take off your coats and have a cup of tea while you're waiting. And you two, have you lost your tongues?' Sheila asked her daughters who were assembling a doll's house from Lego bricks bought while they were in town. 'I've got something for you.'

The bricks were left and they ran to her. 'Show us. Let's see. Is it from Daddy? Is it a present?'

'No, it's a letter for each of you.'

They were written in block capitals and they read what they could of them. Sheila filled in the gaps. Twice they had to be read. First one twin and then the other began to cry. 'Poor Daddy. All on his own for Christmas. Who'll make his dinner? And maybe he'll forget to leave mince pies for Santa and Santa won't give him presents. And he'll have no one to make dinner for him. I want to go home. So do I.' One after the other they lamented for their poor father. Sheila held them close and kissed them, and said that Beth or Lizzie would invite Daddy for Christmas dinner. At the same time she silently reviled Fergus. The bastard. Looking for sympathy from the children. Turning them against me.

Ginny stayed with the twins while Sheila and Yvette went to Midnight Mass. The church was packed. There were many drunks, the majority men. And the smell of porter mingled with that of the wax candles. After Mass the drunks were singing, staggering and wishing everyone they passed 'Happy Christmas'.

Ginny made tea and cut slices from the boiled ham. They relished the meat after the day of abstinence. The presents were taken from their hiding place and put underneath the tree, and the children's stockings filled. They talked for a long time before going to bed. Ginny told Yvette that Christmas was a sad time for the bereaved and Yvette agreed that it was. Sheila listened and contributed to the coversation while with her mind in turmoil she thought of Fergus and wondered what she should do about the situation. She fell asleep remembering other happier Christmases.

Gifts were exchanged the next morning. Mr Brophy had cigarettes, socks and slippers.

Yvette gave Sheila a black satin slip and knickers. Ginny gave the two young women perfume and chocolates. Sheila presented Yvette with a pure silk blouse she had got Ginny to make. Ginny's lap was loaded with chocolates, scarves, nylon stockings and an antique pearl Rosary that Sheila had bought in one of the shops on the quays, into whose windows she had looked often and longingly on her way to dancing competitions.

During the morning neighbours called to sample the pudding and have a glass of port wine. The plum pudding was served cold and sliced like cake. Everyone was in joyous mood. It was the birthday of their Saviour. They had celebrated it at Mass and received the Blessed Sacrament. And for the remainder of the holiday they would make merry. Sheila acted her part, outwardly as merry as anyone, inwardly broken-hearted.

For dinner there was roast goose stuffed with apples, breadcrumbs and thyme. The crackers were pulled and paper hats put on. The whistles, tin rings, key chains, bead bracelets given to the twins. They had taken their dolls to the table, more interested in combing their hair, dressing and undressing them than in the food their mother and Ginny coaxed them to eat.

St Stephen's Day was when visitors called bringing gifts and stayed to tea. More dolls for Niamh and Deirdre, toy teasets, crayons and pencils, and coarse white net Christmas stockings bulging with money boxes, sweets, chocolate gold-wrapped coins, boxes of chalks. On principle

Ginny never bought such stockings for any child, dismissing them as catchpenny rubbish.

A man had brought a melodeon. The company danced and sang to his tunes. Sandwiches were passed round and glasses refilled. Not until two o'clock in the morning did the guests begin to leave. Mr Brophy was already asleep in his armchair. Ginny said, 'I'm going to bed. I was up at half-five for six Mass. I'm falling out of my standing.' Sheila and Yvette washed the delft, tidied up and they too went to bed, Yvette saying what a wonderful Christmas it had been. How grateful she was to Sheila and her parents for making it so. She looked more beautiful, more relaxed than Sheila had ever seen her. She had meant, when they were in bed, to tell her about the letter from Fergus and that she didn't intend going back to Germany. But seeing Yvette's lovely, happy face she couldn't. It would be cruel. It must wait yet awhile before she burdened her.

She told her mother the following day.

'You're coddin' me, Sheila.'

'No I'm not. It's over, finished. I'm staying here.'

'Why, in the name of God Almighty?'

'Here, read this,' Sheila said, handing Ginny the letter.

'The man's written no more than the truth.'

'You're taking his side.'

'I'm taking no one's side. But you did deprive him of his family over Christmas. He's a good man. He doesn't beat you. He's not a womaniser.'

'How do you or I know that?'

'I'm only going on what I know of him. What I've heard from you. And you've never uttered a word about other women.'

'Maybe I don't tell you everything.'

'Maybe you don't. But in any case if you're serious about leaving your husband, where were you thinking of staying?'

'Here, of course.'

'I wouldn't refuse you shelter, but I'm not encouraging you either. When were you going back?'

'If I was to get there in time for New Year's Eve it should have been today. But I changed my mind about that when the letter came.'

'And her?' Ginny nodded her head towards the bedroom where Yvette was reading to the twins. 'When and where will she go?'

'We were supposed to travel together. She has nowhere and no one to go to.'

'The poor unfortunate. For the week you're thinking things over she can stay here. I wouldn't throw a dog out in the street.'

'You're very kind, Ma, but don't bank on me changing my mind.'

'Let me know your decision and in the meantime we won't talk about it.'

The following day Sheila told Yvette she was leaving Fergus. She was flabbergasted. 'But why? I thought you loved him.'

'I do. Or I thought I did. Read that,' she said, handing the letter to Yvette.

'Oh, Sheila that's his way of saying how disappointed he was finding you gone.'

'A funny way of going about it.' She was about to itemise Fergus's faults. Prove that she was justified in leaving him. Elicit sympathy and approval from Yvette but checked herself in time. To Yvette, Fergus was a saint compared with the evil, barbarous man she had married. And so she made herself partly to blame. 'My problem is not with Fergus. It's the army life I hate. And where we are stationed in particular. You have to admit it's a kip of a place.'

'Compared with Dublin, yes, I agree. But with a man like Fergus couldn't you stick it out for four years?'

'No. I want him to apply for early discharge. If I don't go back now maybe he'll think seriously about it.'

'And have you thought what the outcome will be if he doesn't?'

'Not thoroughly. Not yet. I'm hoping the threat of not going back will bring him to his senses.'

'We've only been friends for a short while, but already I love you and the children. I'd hate to see your marriage break up. Promise me you'll think carefully before doing anything rash.'

'I will, of course I will. Now, tell me, when are you thinking of going back to wherever?'

'Tomorrow, I suppose.'

'Listen to this. To please me ma I'm sending Fergus a telegram that I'm sick and can't travel for another week. And she, thinking I'm not serious about leaving him for more than that long, suggested you also stay for the extra week.'

'I couldn't do that. Not that I wouldn't like to. But I've imposed enough on their hospitality.'

'Another week won't kill them.'

'Well, if you're sure. I could stay here for ever.'

'Then that's settled.'

Chapter Thirty-five

During the week Sheila persuaded Yvette to stay for a while longer. 'I'm not going back for at least another week so you might as well stay on. For one thing I'm worried about where you'll go and for another I'll be glad of the ride to London.'

Yvette, desperate as to where she would go, agreed.

When Sheila told Ginny of her intentions she said. 'Well, I hope you weren't thinking of planking your arse here. I'll play no part in the leaving of your husband.'

'You'll have to, I've no money.'

'May God forgive you for bringing trouble into my home. But you always were a self-willed little bitch. That's what ails you now, wanting your own way.'

'It's not, Ma. Some of it maybe. But you've no idea how I hate army life. Fergus drinks. You pointed that out to me. That's really his only fault. And that I could put up with if I was here at home. Honest to God, that's what ails me.'

Ginny relented. 'Ah, love, I'm sorry to see you unhappy. I know he's a good man except for the weakness. I know you love him. I'm broken-hearted to think of you parting. And I can't lift a finger to help you.'

'Letting me stay until something's sorted out would be a help.'

'Sure you know I only said that in the heat of the moment.'

'Now don't jump down my throat, but I've asked Yvette to stay for a bit longer just in case I change my mind and go back to Germany.'

'So long as it's only for a while. Your poor father's crippled on that sofa. He can't put up with that much longer. Even after Yvette's gone it won't be fair on the twins sleeping head to tail. So for all our sakes I pray to God that you and Fergus come to your senses.'

No more letters came from Fergus. And Sheila was determined that she would not be the first to write. She slept badly, lying awake wondering what the outcome would be. Fergus was a Catholic but not much of a one. He could divorce her. Knowing little about divorce, she wasn't sure what reason he could use. In the dark, anxious and fearful, she would remember the night with Bill, wondering as before had Fergus found out that she had committed adultery. She was positive that was a right to divorce. Towards morning she'd ask herself was demanding Fergus leave the army justified. It was his job. He loved it. And then justify her actions telling herself that she also was entitled to a degree of happiness. Everything shouldn't be in favour of the man. Not a man who spent a lot of money on drink. A man who wouldn't take his family on a holiday. A man when knowing how much she loved and missed Ireland, refused to go there with his family for Christmas. Sleep would claim her for a few hours. Awake, she'd go first to the hall, looking for a letter. And finding none would strengthen her resolve to remain in Ireland until . . . until, she hoped, Fergus would give in.

Three weeks after Sheila sent the telegram another letter arrived from Fergus. She was overjoyed. This time it woud be a long one just for her. But as before it was a single sheet. It read:

Sheila,

It appears that you are not coming back so I have made you a marriage allowance of £8 a week. The allowance book will arrive shortly after this letter and payments will be backdated to when I initiated the allowance. Regards to your parents. Kiss the girls for me.

Fergus

She ran to the kitchen and threw the letter on the table at which Ginny was sitting. 'Read it,' she screamed, 'read it and then tell me what you think of your son-in-law.'

'Stop screaming like a lunatic, you'll have the neighbours in on top of us wantin' to know who's being murdered.' Ginny read the letter twice before asking, 'What's there to complain about? Isn't he still keeping you and generously at that?'

'Generously! A quarter of what he's earning and you call that generous.' Then Sheila sat down, laid her head on the table and cried, asking between sobs, 'Ma, oh, Ma, what am I going to do?'

'Get your hair out of the butter dish for a start, then go back to your husband.'

'God,' said Sheila, raising her head and glaring at her mother, 'there's times when I hate you. You're all for him. You treat me like a child and you're taking over the children.'

'Pity about you,' said Ginny, unperturbed. 'You brought the trouble on yourself. You act like a child so that's how you'll be treated. And as for taking over the children, what else can I do when you're out morning, noon and night wth your "eddy cong" showing her the sights, going to the pictures and for all I know to them afternoon tea dances. If you don't like it here you know what to do.'

'And what's that supposed to mean?'

'Now that you're in the money, find a place for you and your pal.'

'So I will and the sooner the better,' Sheila retorted, leaving the room and slamming the kitchen door after her. Anger surged through her, making her more determined than ever not to go back to Germany. And she'd find a place to live. Her mother wouldn't browbeat her any more.

Yvette had taken the girls out in the snow to feed the birds in Patrick's Park. She watched through the parlour window for their return. The weather was freezing, snow settling everywhere. She heard the twins' chattering voices before they came in view. Almost every time she saw them after an absence, even a short one, she marvelled that they were hers. Ginny had made them two matching duffel coats in bright red woollen cloth, lined the coats with teddy bear material and had knitted red and white mittens and matching hats to wear under the hoods. Their cheeks were glowing, the picture of health and happiness, God bless and spare them. And I don't think they're grieving for their father, the louser, she said to herself.

She heard the joyous way they greeted their grannie.

Heard Ginny say in a voice meant for her to hear, 'I've lovely milky hot cocoa ready and currant bread.' She knows what she can do with her cocoa and currant bread, Sheila said to herself, at the same time longing for a cup.

Yvette came to the parlour carrying a tray with cocoa and white bread. 'Your mother said I was to bring it. She has the girls up close to the fire and is telling them what a good little girl you were.'

'Sit down, I've something to tell you.' First she drank some of the cocoa, then told Yvette about the allowance.

'How d'you feel about that?'

'Leppin'. It's his way of saying, "Stay where you are."'

'Not concern that you might be short of money?'

'Him! Concern for me! If he had any I wouldn't be in this predicament. And to add to it me ma's told me to find somewere else to live. My own mother. Imagine that.'

'I don't suppose it's easy for her. And me being here doesn't help.'

'If things were right between me and Fergus she wouldn't care how long we stayed. And in any case you pay your way.'

'Three pounds. Who'd keep and lodge me for that? Feed me the way she does, make me one of the family.'

'You offered her more and she refused. No, it's all to do with her wanting me to patch things up with Fergus. Well, she's got another think coming. I'll find somewhere else to live. Will you come with me?'

'I don't think that would be right. You don't know how you'll be feeling in another few weeks. You might regret leaving Fergus. Want to go back and find me a hindrance.'

'Is that what you think? That if I find a place and you come with me, supposing Fergus walked in the next day out on your ear you'd be?'

Yvette laughed. 'I'm sure you'd give me a week's notice. OK, I'll think about it. I'd be delighted to live in Dublin for ever. I'd be more than delighted if you and Fergus were living here. I think we'd have a good life.'

'I'll start looking in the papers for places to let somewhere in the neighbourhood. The girls will have to start school and me ma take and collect them.'

'Why can't you or I take them at least some of the time?'

'We'll be working, won't we.'

'I'd never get work. I've never had a job.'

'In that case you'd better drop some of your principles about how much of Victor's money you'll keep. You won't go far on what you've got. You can sell the car, don't really need it here. Talking about the car reminds me. Did Victor have life insurance?'

'For the car of course. I couldn't claim on that. The accident was his fault. Only if it could be proved that the car was faulty; that the car company or manufacturers were to blame.'

'You weren't listening. Life insurance, I mean. He probably had a policy on both your lives. If he did you could claim it.'

'I doubt he'd have been insured. No benefit to him. And he wasn't concerned about my welfare.'

'But you don't know for sure, search the carton, there could be a policy. Anyway, before we move you'd need to sort it out. Maybe get rid of some things. That carton's enormous, it mightn't fit in if the flat's small.'

'I couldn't bear to touch it.'

'You'll have to if you intend sending the money to charities. You did say that, didn't you?'

'I did and I will, but not yet. Sometimes I dream about the carton, see the vile photographs. Victor comes into the darkroom while I'm searching. He tries to strangle me, I'm gasping for breath, know I'm going to die. Then I wake from the nightmare. My throat is aching as if his hands had been round it and my neck feels sore. I expect to see bruises on it.'

'I've never heard you during the night,' Sheila said.

'You're a heavy sleeper.'

'It's sleeping in the room with the evidence causes the nightmares. The sooner you get rid of it the better. By the way, what did you do with Sean's photograph?'

'Destroyed it. Burnt it in the sink before I left. No one should ever again see my child die such a dreadful death.'

'But the snap was proof positive. Victor's face recognisable.'

'I know. If he hadn't been killed I'd have borne the pain and used it. How or where I don't know. But I'd have spent my life trying. Found courage, suffered anything to see him and the others found guilty. But Victor escaped. No guilt, no shame, no punishment, unless hell exists.'

Sheila saw Yvette's blanched, pain-racked face, the eyes dead in her head, and remonstrated with herself: what a mouthy cow I am to bring up that subject and apologising will only make it worse. She suggested they go and get early editions of the evening papers.

'Start our flat hunting, eh?' Calling to Ginny to keep an eye on the girls, they left the house.

The snow had frozen. The paths were slippery. Linking arms, they walked cautiously. Stand pipes were set up at the corner of the street. The cold wind whipped their faces and knifed through their clothes. A queue of shivering people carrying buckets, jugs and basins waited their turn for water.

'It's very seldom we get this sort of weather here so, unlike Germany, we're always caught on the hop. Look at that poor oul wan across the road, eighty if she's a day, dragging the sack of turf.'

There were people of all ages, including small children, dragging and pushing battered prams, go-karts, box cars, anything on wheels in which coal, turf and logs could be hauled.

'Hohne will be looking beautiful now,' Yvette said as they neared the newsagent's.

'Don't tell me you're missing it.'

331

'I wouldn't want to go back. But I liked Hohne and what I saw of Germany and the Germans. At least I . . .'

I've done it again, Sheila thought, I won't say another word till we're back in the house. To carry her intention through she coughed several times, wrapped her scarf round her face and mouth.

Chapter Thirty-six

'You've hardly broken your fast today. Take off your coat, you as well, Yvette, and sit to the table,' Ginny said from where she stood by the cooker. A turf fire blazed in the grate and although it wasn't yet dark, the curtains were drawn and the room warm and cosy.

Ginny brought to the table a home-made golden-crusted steak and kidney pie. 'That'll warm the cockles of your heart,' she said, setting it down. Sheila's heart lurched as she remembered her first attempt at making a steak and kidney pie. The pains she had taken. How proud she felt placing it in the oven. How she had anticipated Fergus's praise. Her shock when the pie was opened. The melted eggcup, the bluish gravy. Her anger when Fergus laughed uproariously, anger that dissolved into tears. She recalled how he had kissed and comforted her, dried her tears. And later they made love and later still had fish and chips for supper.

What have I done? she asked herself as Ginny served the meal. Walked out on my husband. Left a lovely home. For what? For why? To spend this evening and others poring over 'Apartments To Let' in the *Herald* and the *Mail*. To look for work, leave the girls to rely more on my mother. I have to be deranged.

Then she considered the why, first looking at the clock. In two hours from now Fergus would arrive home. Between six and seven he would eat, then wash, change and go to the mess. That was what he did almost every night.

She'd read the girls stories, hear their prayers, kiss them good night and come down to the living room, where she'd sit thinking of Beth and Bill together doing whatever they did after supper. Envisage Lizzie, Bob and their family, Tom and the girls in bed, Lizzie nursing Jack. She and Bob sitting companionably in front of their imitation fireplace. And she alone, passing the time switching on and off the radio, knitting a few lines, discarding the knitting, leafing through magazine articles offering advice on how to keep your husband, watching the clock. That's why I left. That's why I'm never going back, and to hell with him and Hohne.

The pie was delicious, so were the floury white potatoes and marrowfat peas, soaked overnight and simmered to perfection. Sheila savoured every mouthful. Then in her mind, where a pool of memories, thoughts and questions constantly competed for individual attention, one succeeded in claiming it: Lizzie! I didn't write. Oh, my God, what must she think of me. I never sent a Christmas card.

'You're not eating your dinner,' Ginny accused.

'You gave me too much. It was gorgeous but I can't eat any more,' Sheila replied, then returned to her dilemma. What excuse can I make? Let on me ma and da had the flu. I was run off my feet minding them. But I'll tell the truth about me and Fergus. His letter like one written to a stranger. I always confided in Lizzie, told her everything except the night with Bill. I haven't had an hour's luck since that night.

She drank tea, ate cake and took part in the conversation while she planned the letter to Lizzie. She wouldn't let on she knew about Victor's death. But as she and Yvette were planning on remaining in Dublin she would have to mention her. Tell more lies. They had met on board the boat to Harwich. Yvette was going to Ireland. To see a seriously ill relation. Never knew she had relations in

Ireland. Surprised. Shouldn't have been. After all, we never knew anything about her. Victor was planning a skiing trip over Christmas so he didn't object to her going. All lies and the more I tell the more complicated it gets. I won't mention Yvette. Later on, maybe. I'll write about the girls, me ma and da. Ask her to give me the lowdown on Fergus. How does he look? Any mention of me? Say nothing about looking for a flat. That'll do for the time being.

The twins settled themselves in an armchair by the fire. But not for long. Mr Brophy came home, snow melting on his soft hat. Ginny said, 'You look perished, take off them clothes and you two get out of that chair and let your grandfather sit there.' She took his dinner from the oven, served it on a tray, which she laid on his lap. After kissing their grandfather the twins settled down to read comics and the grown-ups chatted about the weather.

'Never remember anything like it in all my years,'

'Every winter's like this in Germany,' Sheila told him.

'But they're prepared for it, the Germans.'

'Oh, they are indeed. Prepared for everything. And talk about being tidy. As an Irishwoman I know there said, when someone was praising their tidiness, sure didn't they keep the bones tidy in Belsen.'

In the midst of this lovely family that Yvette had come to love, she grieved for Sean who had never known anything like it. The twins were near in age to his when he died. How happy they would have been had Victor never come into their lives.

'I heard on the wireless that 1962 is the coldest winter we've had for years.'

'Is that a fact, Ginny?' Mr Brophy asked as she handed him a mug of tea.

'According to the wireless. And they say there's more to come tonight. A man about your age broke his hip in Kevin Street after dinner.'

'God forbidding all harm, but I think I'll venture out.

After being cooped up all day in the office I need a breath of fresh air.'

Fergus all over, Sheila thought and her resolve to leave him strengthened.

After the twins were in bed and Ginny in the parlour making a dress, Sheila and Yvette spread out the papers and Sheila said, 'Clanbrassil Street, Camden Street, Richmond Street and the South Circular Road. Mark any of those, but only if there are at least two rooms going.'

They found nothing suitable. Yvette went to bed and Sheila wrote to Lizzie.

Their letters crossed in the post and in less than a week Lizzie's arrived. She wrote that she was sorry for what was taking place between Sheila and Fergus, and advised her to have a rethink. Fergus, she said, looked lost. He refused all invitations to eat with her or Beth.

She told about Victor's death and how the garrison was buzzing with rumours about Yvette's disappearance, hers and the Citroën's. Some thought she had been abducted, murdered and dumped somewhere. Others concluded she had a lover and had cleared off. Lizzie said there was something strange about the whole business. Yvette's spare bedroom had been converted into a posh darkroom full of expensive equipment, but the funny thing was although the darkroom had been broken into and drawers of cabinets ransacked, the expensive cameras weren't taken. And another thing, Yvette's gorgeous fur coat, lots of her clothes and jewellery were left behind. She wrote that she didn't know what to make of it. All she hoped was that Yvette was safe.

Up to this point in the letter Sheila intended letting Yvette read it. But then the last line changed her mind. It read, 'Another strong rumour is that the SIB have been brought in.' It would be no good trying to convince Yvette that rumour was probably all it was. She'd panic about the army coming to get her. Slowly she was showing signs of recovery from the heart-breaking discovery of

335

Sean's photograph. Daily loving Dublin more and more, losing her haunted look. She would mention Lizzie's letter but pick and choose what she told her of its contents.

The search for a flat continued for several evenings until Ginny asked if they'd had any luck. They admitted that they hadn't.

'I could have told you that.'

'Why didn't you, then?'

'You wouldn't have believed me in the beginning.'

'Tell me now, then.'

'In this neighbourhood you don't get rooms from the paper.'

'How d'ye get them?'

'By word of mouth. Leave it to me, I'll get the pair of you fixed up.'

Resentfully Sheila agreed. She knew Ginny was forcing her hand. *Finding a flat will bring me to my senses. Make me realise I'm about to burn my boats if I move in. She thinks I'm play-acting about leaving Fergus. In a way I am, for if he walked in the door this minute I'd fall into his arms. Only in no time I'd regret it. We'd kiss and make up, and before I knew it we'd be back in Germany, buried alive in Hohne and him out drinking every night.*

I don't want that. That life is destroying me, turning me into a shrew. I'm not asking for miracles. I know that if he left the army and came back to Dublin he wouldn't become a teetotaller overnight. But he'd come home when the pubs shut. Pubs stuck to the closing time, unlike the mess, or the German clubs and gasthäuser where, as long as there was a customer, they remained open. Like that terrible night which finished up with lipstick on his shirt when I attacked him with the family Bible.

And who except Lizzie have I to turn to in Hohne? Here I know everyone. So far I haven't contacted many but they are here and I can. It's very sad, although at the same time I'm relieved that the girls aren't grieving for him. Now and then they ask about him, but seem to be as happy as Larry. It'd be the same if I dropped dead. So long as they are loved, kids seem to get by.

I'll take a flat. Let him make the next move. It's his fault. He didn't have to write such a bloody awful letter. He's a stubborn bastard. Lived too long doing what he wanted to do. Maybe soldiers shouldn't marry. It might work if a soldier and his wife were the same age. But Fergus is years older than me, not used to anyone but the army having a say in what he does, how he spends his time and money. Kisses and making love isn't enough for a happy marriage.

Ginny found the flat. It was over a shop in Camden Street. There was a boxroom and three other good-sized ones, and a lavatory on the landing. 'No bathroom!' Sheila said when she went with Ginny and Yvette to see it.

'What did you expect for twelve and six a week? Think yourself lucky the lavatory's not in the yard.'

There were fireplaces in three of the rooms. The flat was clean, light and airy. The wallpaper was pale-green, patterned with creeping trellis supporting red roses. Not Sheila's taste but it was in good condition and the previous tenant had left two of the floors oilclothed.

'What d'ye think of it?' Ginny asked Yvette and Sheila. 'A bit of a let-down after your lovely German places. Your letters were never done praising your house.'

Another reminder of what I'm sacrificing, thought Sheila. 'I'll take it if Yvette agrees.'

'I like it. I think living on this level would be lovely. There'll be plenty to see.'

'Unlike our wonderful German places.'

'I hope you know what you're doing. You haven't a stick of furniture, curtains, not a sheet, cup or saucer, nor a bed to lie your arse on.'

'We'll get them,' Sheila said.

'With what?'

'On Provident cheques.'

'Not on my recommendation, you won't.'

'Ma, I know you mean well. I know you think I'm mad for leaving Fergus and maybe I am. All the same, I'm going through with it. Fergus isn't concerned about me. Fergus is concerned about no one but himself.'

'I'll say no more. Are you two staying here?'

'No,' the twins replied. 'We want to go with you, Grannie.'

Left alone, Yvette and Sheila talked about the furniture they would need for the flat. 'We could get it on the weekly. Me da would sign the agreement.'

'I've seen lots of second-hand furniture shops, except for beds it might be better to buy from one of them,' Yvette suggested.

'You're right. We don't want to get into debt.'

'I've got enough money to buy what we need, Sheila.'

'You have for the time being. But if you stick to your principles it won't last that long. I hate mentioning this in case it upsets you. But I think you should do something about the photographs, the papers and that.'

'I thought of taking them out in bags, a few at a time, and throwing them in the Liffey. But if I do that those men will never be stopped.'

'They probably won't anyway. Definitely won't if you get rid of the evidence. I was thinking about it the other night and had an idea.'

'What was the idea.'

'Me da has lots of contacts. You've heard him talk about being out in Sixteen well, so were a lot of the fellas now in government and the Big Bugs in the police. You'd have to tell him about Victor, of course. Let him see some of the stuff. I know you'd hate even touching it. But it's that or throw the lot in the Liffey. At least you'll have tried.'

'How can I talk to your father about such things?'

'You wouldn't have to have a conversation, for God's sake. The pictures, the names and addresses, especially the Dublin priest's, would convince him. He'd know who might be able to do something. Not in Ireland, except for the priest. But fellas in the Castle, they'd know all about Interpol.'

'Sheila, I couldn't get involved with the police or men in the government.'

'Don't flatter yourself, Yvette, you won't. You talk to my father. Show him some of the stuff. And if he can he'll do the rest. Your name won't be mentioned. That crowd he knows are masters of secrecy. Think about it, anyway. Come on and we'll have a dekko round the second-hand shops.'

Yvette was fascinated with some of the curios they came across. Two snowy owls perched on a branch in a glass case in particular. She priced them. 'Twelve quid, ma'am. A pair of beauties,' the man said. 'From a gentleman's residence in the country.'

Sheila reminded her that they were looking for necessities: 'A kitchen table, four chairs, a cooker, those sort of things.'

'I've fallen in love with the owls.'

'Put a deposit on them and decide later in the week.'

'Them things are all the rage again. I'll keep them for you till the end of the week, not a day longer.'

Yvette put five pounds on them. Sheila found a suitable table and four chairs. 'I'll have these, but you'll have to keep them for a few days.'

'Missus, it's selling I am, not storing.'

'I'm buying, OK. But we're not moving for a few days.'

'I'll oblige you, then.'

She paid the money and said, 'I was looking for a gas stove.'

'There's a couple out the back. But take my advice and buy a reconditioned one from the gas shop. I didn't have to tell you that.'

'Of course you did. Aren't you an honest man?'

She and the man indulged in good-natured banter for a while as they moved round the shop. She bought a coal scuttle, a fire guard and a set of fire irons, paid for them and said she'd be back later in the week to arrange the delivery.

'So what did you buy?' asked Ginny. And when hearing from where they'd bought said, 'That fella's a daylight robber. I could have got them for you at half the price in Jemmy Breen's. Oh, and by the way, there's a letter from Fergus. It came in the second post.'

As she opened the letter Sheila wondered what the tone would be this time, half hoping he would be asking to patch things up. He wasn't. He wrote:

Any minute now I'll be questioned as to when you are coming back. Married quarters are for husbands and wives with or without children; for widowers with children. And so in a short while I will have to vacate these. This is the third time I have written to you and have had no reply. When your allowance book arrives acknowledge it.
Fergus.

'Not good news by the look on your face.'

'Read it,' said Sheila, passing the letter to her mother.

Ginny did. 'Well, I have to admit he's not doing much in the way of coaxing you back.'

'He's doing nothing. That's like a letter from an official in the Corporation. The bloody cheek of him. No matter what, I'm still his wife. He's a bastard. I'm glad it came today. It's put paid to any lingering doubts. If he wanted to keep on the quarters he could have lied. Said I was very sick. You were very sick and I had to look after you. Dozens of ways round it. Shag him. No more doubts. I've my own place now. I'll get a job. That's if you'll take and bring the girls to and from school.'

'I was going to mention that to you. It's all arranged.'

'What d'ye mean, it's all arranged?'

'Well, seeing the way the wind was blowing with you and him, I decided the girls had to start school. So I saw

340

Mother Agnes yesterday and she'll be delighted to have them.'

'You'd no right to do that without letting me know. I might not have wanted them going to Warrenmount.'

'And why not? Didn't you go there before the Loretto? Didn't I go there and me mother before me? Them Presentation nuns are ladies.'

'I've nothing against them or the school, but the children are mine and I should have decided where they went.'

'You can't have it both ways. On the one hand you land me with them when it suits you. I can take and bring them from school, but putting their name down is interference. The trouble with you is you've lived away from here too long. Here grannies have rights, especially when the mother is living on their floor.'

'Thank God that won't be for much longer.'

'You're very cantankerous sometimes. You were from a child. But I'll say no more except this. You have to get rid of that wallpaper on the chimney breast.'

Sheila sighed exasparatedly. 'What wallpaper?'

'The one with the big grey stones pattern on the chimney breast, it looks like one of them walls in Connemara.'

'I'd already noticed it.'

'That's great, then. The other thing is, don't go buying hangings. I've three pairs down to the floor and piles of bedding. A lot of delft I never use and a couple of saucepans. One of them was your grannie's, solid iron, you'll never be bloodless if you cook in that.'

Sheila thanked her mother and helped to make the dinner.

Later that evening when she and Yvette were alone Sheila asked if she had decided to show her father the contents of the carton.

'I will. But you do the explaining first, I couldn't.'

'Tell him about Victor and Sean?'

341

'I suppose so.'

'We'd have to let me Ma in on this. There's a lot of talking to do. We couldn't keep her out of it.'

'I wouldn't want to. I like your mother. She's been so kind to me.'

'She's all right except for being too bloody interfering.'

'You're lucky to have someone who cares enough about you to interfere.'

'I suppose you're right. You take your mother for granted. Mine will do the same with me.'

Chapter Thirty-seven

Sheila told her mother and father that Yvette needed advice on a serious matter. 'It's a long, sad story. She's not up to telling it herself. She wants me to do it and ask if you can help.'

Ginny looked interested. Mr Brophy looked at the clock, cleared his throat and said, 'Go on, child, tell us about it.'

'Not tonight, Da. Tomorrow if you'll give the pub a miss for an hour or two.'

'No bother,' her father said, looking relieved. 'I'll be only too glad to help if I can. But for the time being I have to leave you. I promised to meet a fella, he wants advice as well.'

'Oul shite,' said Ginny when he left. Then asked, 'What sort of trouble is Yvette in?'

Sheila told of the life she had led, her suspicion that Victor was involved in something dubious. How her son had died in mysterious circumstances. How she had had the darkroom broken into and what she had found. 'She has all these photographs, names, addresses, piles of money, which she won't touch. You'll see for yourself tomorrow.'

'May that husband of hers roast in hell for all eternity. Things like that set you thinking, questioning your faith, thinking God has quare ways letting that monster die instantly after all the suffering he caused. It's a sin, I know, saying this but sure you can't help the thoughts that come into your mind. The poor unfortunate child. I hope she's found a bit of comfort here. And if the time should come and you see sense and go back to your decent husband, let her know she always has a home here. I'm not the better of hearing all this. Would you like a drop of whiskey to steady your nerves?'

Sheila said she would and when the whiskey was served said, 'Ma, I know how you'd love to sympathise and comfort Yvette but don't, not yet.'

'Not a word. I'll pray for her instead. When the time is right she'll let me know.'

On Saturday afternoon Yvette took the twins to see a Walt Disney film, *The Parent Trap*. She hadn't known it was about twins trying to reunite their separated parents and halfway through made an excuse that she had a headache. 'I'm sorry,' she told the twins. 'We'll go and have ice cream instead in the Palm Grove.' They said they were glad, that the picture was stupid, only the twins were any good.

Ginny bought her husband two bottles of stout so that he wouldn't die of thirst, deprived as he was of his afternoon session. He listened to what Sheila had to tell. The colour left his face when he heard how Sean had died, tears filled his eyes, which he wiped away with nicotine-stained fingers. He looked at only a few of the porno-graphic photographs, made the sign of the cross, then pushed the remainder away.

Ginny opened a bottle of stout and gave him also a whiskey chaser. When he seemed somewhat recovered from the shock, Sheila said, 'You should know, Da, that Yvette doesn't want to have her name mentioned.'

343

'I don't blame her. To acknowledge she was married to such a man would crucify any decent woman. Tell her from me to change her name by deed poll. Though the pity of it is that if she could have produced the picture of her son, the husband and the other men there'd be more chance of a conviction.'

'She couldn't, Da.'

'Indeed she could not and no one would blame her.'

'So what will you do with the stuff?'

'Sure don't I know everyone. Fellas in all branches of the State. One of them will have the answer. No guarantee that there'll be a satisfactory outcome or if there is that we'll ever know. A lot will depend on who the culprits are. The Irish priest, for instance, I doubt if we'll see his name in headlines. And it's a pound to a penny the rest of that corrupt bunch will have friends in high places.'

'What about the money she wants to give to charity?'

'No problem there. Every day you read about anonymous donations, big ones.'

'I'll put the stuff in order and you'll do the rest.'

'With a heart and a half.'

Sheila hugged and kissed him. 'You're a great man and I love you.'

They scoured the flat, bought mimosa-coloured emulsion paint and painted the rooms. From the gas showrooms they bought a reconditioned cooker. The floor covering they decided would do for a while longer. Ginny hung the curtains and admitted, though not approving of Sheila leaving a grand husband and home in Germany, the flat would look great when it was finished. Yvette insisted that she should buy the beds. 'I've plenty of money left from the thousand pounds I took. It's little enough after all you and your family have done for me. You've no idea of the relief I felt when your father took away all the papers and photographs.'

'The neighbours must have wondered what was going

on. Every morning of the week him off to work with a big brown paper parcel. They probably thought we were pawning every stitch in the house. Talking about the photographs reminded me, did you never have another snap of Sean?'

'I have. It's in the house. I'll show it to you when we get back.'

'OK and I won't say no to the beds. We'd better get on with the painting.'

That night in their bedroom, Yvette undid the bottom covering of her toilet box and showed Sheila the snap.

'The little lamb. The Lord have mercy on him,' Sheila said, then embraced Yvette and they cried in each other's arms.

Ginny tapped on the door and said there was a fresh pot of tea ready.

'Come in, Ma,' Sheila called.

'What ails the pair of you?' Ginny asked when she entered and saw the tear-stained faces.

'This,' replied Sheila, handing her mother Sean's photograph.

'Your little child, Yvette. May God look down on you. He's in heaven interceding for you.'

Ginny's crying caused the other two women to weep again.

'Now then, dry your eyes. None of us will ever forget him but we mustn't drag our dead after us. We'll have the tea and a glass of whiskey, and decide on what else you need for the flat and what the sleeping arrangements will be.'

And Sheila thought, that woman wouldn't get her rest if she wasn't organising. She means well, I know, but she gets in on my nerves. Ginny suggested that the twins should have the boxroom. She had seen bunk beds in a sale. They'd be her treat. Sheila and Yvette would have the two smaller of the remaining rooms. The third was big enough to take the table and chairs, a sideboard, a couple of presses for delft and utensils, and the alcove was the place for the cooker. 'You'll need two wardrobes and I'll keep my eye out for a sofa and armchairs.'

Sheila could find no fault with her mother's suggestions, although she resented the interference.

'And another thing,' said Ginny. 'I'll give you the money for the suite and no saying no. When you've got the place to your liking, to look for a bit of work wouldn't be a bad idea. I'll keep my ears open.'

The twins loved school. They'd been made pets. There were still nuns in the convent who had taught Sheila and her mother, and a very old one no longer teaching who had taught their great-grandmother. They had been brought to the convent parlour to have tea with her. She made a great fuss of them. They were fascinated with the number of moles on her cheeks and what they later on reported to their grannie as her beard. 'Ladies don't have beards, do they, Gran?' they asked Ginny after their first visit to Mother Mary Agnes.

'Sometimes they do if they're nearly a hundred. But don't you pass remarks. Passing remarks is not kind.' Days went by without them ever mentioning their father. Ginny was relieved that they weren't grieving for him but sad that gradually his memory was slipping from them. One evening, when Sheila and Yvette returned from working on the flat, she raised the subject. 'Have you told Fergus about the move?'

'We don't write to each other, so how could I?'

'You could get the girls to write.'

'Why should I?'

'He's their father, that's why. You wouldn't want them to forget him.'

'That's up to him. We've been here three months, twice he wrote to them. Sent nothing for Christmas. And I've only had notifications that could have been written by anyone. "Here's your allowance." "I'm handing over the quarters." Where was the encouragement to go back? And

Ma, don't keep bringing up the subject. I'm grand, the girls are grand. Don't be putting doubts in my head.'

'It's your business but I worry that you've made the wrong move. I'm your mother, I can't help it.'

'Try.'

Before moving into the flat Yvette packed money into envelopes and addressed them from the list Mr Brophy had provided. The majority of the donations were sent to charities for children, to African missions, Save the Children and others. Sheila helped and assured Yvette when she doubted the moral principle of what she was doing, 'What else would you do with the money other than burn it? OK, so it was earned by abusing children. Maybe now some of it will bring comfort into the lives of those same children.' She convinced Yvette and the envelopes were dispatched.

With the furniture in place, a few cushions given by Ginny, a folder of Gauguin prints bought from the National Gallery and framed by Mr Brophy and from morning to night a turf fire blazing in the capacious grate, the flat was reasonably attractive, comfortable and warm. The children appeared to be content, spending their days between school, Ginny's and their mother's. They seldom mentioned Fergus. But their grandmother frequently did, talking to the girls about him, telling them what a good, kind daddy he was, how much he loved them and Mammy. Occasionally they would ask when was he was coming to see them. Ginny would feel a lump in her throat and when the girls were out of earshot and Sheila wasn't, would tell her she should be ashamed of herself. 'What sort of a mother are you, depriving the children of their father?'

Depending on her humour, Sheila might let the criticism go. In different mood she would castigate Fergus for his neglect. 'There's nothing to stop him writing to them. If he cared about them he would. If he had cared about me I wouldn't be here to day. He's fine. Hale and hearty. Now that the quarters are handed over he's living in the mess. Won't have far to go for his beer.'

Lizzie wrote reguarly and sent all the news. Her family were well. Tom was going to kindergarten. He loved it. For her it was a bind. She had to take him at ten o'clock and collect him at half past twelve. She was coming to the conclusion it wasn't worth the bother. Unfortunately Tom loved kindergarten.

She had cried on the day Sheila's quarters were handed over. Soon there would be a new family on the block. So far Yvette's were still being redecorated. All the posh wallpaper replaced by cream emulsion and the darkroom renovated. She wondered what had happened to Yvette. She and Beth spent hours speculating about her. Probably the only ones who did. Like so much, it had been only a nine-days' wonder. After reading a letter from Lizzie, Sheila as she went about her day wrote letter after letter in her head. Telling the truth of what had happened. What she and Yvette had discovered in the darkroom, but not the finding of Tom's picture. She warned her to discourage Tom from being friendly with strangers. Then, realising that Victor wasn't a stranger, erased that line from her letter. She'd hint that Lizzie let drop the news to Fergus that she had moved from her mother's. It might galvanise him into writing. The letter that was written was innocuous. No mention of the flat or Yvette. News of the twins in their new school. Maybe soon going to Irish dancing classes. How she and her mother were constantly rowing but made up in the next breath. Praise of Dublin. All there was to do. How much she missed her. Love to Beth. And a promise that if Lizzie came to Bristol she'd never forgive her if she didn't come and see her.

The novelty of having her own home quickly wore off. Her mother took the children to school, had them for lunch and brought them to her house in the afternoon. The day stretched endlessly in front of her. Unlike Yvette, who hadn't yet tired of exploring Dublin. Twice a week the children slept at her mother's. On those nights she and Yvette went to a cinema, to a show in the Gaiety or the Olympia. Once she took Yvette to the cocktail bar where she and Fergus had gone. There she reminisced about that night until sadness overwhelmed her and they left.

At home, she and Yvette sat up until the early hours of the morning. Yvette told her about her life in Wales. Falling in love with Sean's father. Getting pregnant. Hearing the news that he had been killed in Korea. How she had to leave home. For a Catholic girl to have an illegitimate child was worse than murdering someone.

And Sheila related every minute of her love affair with Fergus, breaking down, sobbing and cursing herself for leaving him. Yvette comforted her. Pointed out that there was nothing stopping her from going back to Fergus except stubborn pride.

'You're wrong. There's more to it than that. It's a battle between us. If I go back he has won. Nothing will have changed. Maybe during the first week he'll stay home at night. Not for longer. Then I'm buried alive in a place I hate. And I'm rowing, pleading, screaming and all to no avail. There has to be some concessions from him.'

'And if there isn't?'

'Then I'm here for good. I've thought it all out. Tomorrow I'm going to start looking for work. And so are you. You're too flawhool. The thousand pounds won't last for ever.'

'Flawhool, what does that mean?'

'You're too generous. Throw your money away.' She yawned. 'I'm going to bed. Tomorrow we'll start combing the papers again. Remind me to buy them.'

They spent an hour reading the 'Situations Vacant' in the morning papers and again after buying the evening papers. Made lists of situations that didn't ask for previous

349

experience. These tended to be for petrol pump attendants. One vacancy appealed to Yvette. It asked for a supervisor, age mid to late twenties to supervise young girls packing toiletries.

Sheila found no advertisements for shop assistants in the major stores.

The following day there was one from a shop in Thomas Street. She knew it well, having gone there often with her mother to buy curtain material. It also sold clothes, bedding, underwear and children's clothes. Cheap articles, badly made, common, was how her mother described the merchandise. 'I wouldn't be seen dead in them. Curtains is all Butler's is good for.'

'I think I'll apply,' Sheila told Yvette, after describing the sort of shop it was. 'After all, it's years since I saw it. Maybe they sell a better line nowadays.'

Encouraged by this, Yvette applied for the supervisor's job. They were both invited for interviews.

Before reporting to the office Sheila walked round the crowded shop. The styles had changed but not the quality. Clothes hung from shelves behind the counter; shoes and runners like hanks of onions from hooks outside the door. There were wire baskets piled high with thin, garish-coloured tea towels. Bales of dress material, which she rubbed between her fingers testing for dressing. And sure enough, where her fingers rubbed the cloth went limp as the dressing fell out. She wouldn't buy a handkerchief in the shop. And she wouldn't attend the interview.

Yvette caught a bus to the outskirts of Dublin where the factory was. It was in an industrial estate. A warren of prefabricated buildings. The one to which she was going was smaller than those surrounding it. She knocked on a door and a voice called, 'Come in.' The door opened into a workshop. A young girl approached and asked what she wanted. Yvette explained about the interview. 'Oh, it's him up there, Mr Farrell, the manager.' She pointed to the top of the room. 'There, d'ye see him? There, at that table next to the fire bucket on the wall, bloody oul shite.' Yvette thanked her and proceeded up an aisle between two long tables with girls sitting each side of them. Tittering and guffaws followed her, and she heard a voice say, 'Look at the get-up of her. Farrell'll think he's in heaven.'

Yvette had never seen the inside of a factory, never had an interview. Nevertheless she thought it odd that the manager should be sitting in the workshop and odder still that this was where the interview would take place.

Mr Farrell watched the tall, beautiful woman approach. 'Jaysus!' he said under his breath, 'what's she doing here? Not after the supervisor's job. That lot'd ate her. She's gorgeous. I hope she's not desperate for a job. I was looking for someone the same as that crowd but older.' He stood up as she neared the table and held out a hand. 'You're Mrs Smithers? We're in a bit of a fix. Only opened last week. I'm getting an office built on. Here,' he said, bringing his chair round for her to sit on.

From the workshop there were wolf whistles. He went behind the table, leant on it and said, 'Tell me about yourself.'

'I'm a widow and need a job. I've never worked before. Your ad said experience not needed, so I applied. What sort of work is done here?'

'Work is right. That lot couldn't work in a fit. Wouldn't is more like it. We pack toiletries. Sent in and we box them.' He ran a finger round the inside of his collar, then took a packet of Player's Weights from the table and offered the cigarettes to Yvette. She thanked him but refused his offer.

'D'ye see the wages aren't great and there's no piece work so the girls don't kill themselves. That's why I wanted a supervisor.' He took a long drag on his cigarette and after exhaling said, 'That's why I'm out here, supervising, y'know. You've got a great appearance and all that but I don't think you're the right one for this job. They're good kids, really, but tough. Real Dubs. And the language, honest to God I'm a Dubliner myself, but it sometimes makes me blush. Like what I was wanting was one of their own only a good few years older.'

Yvette knew he was embarrassed, perhaps he hadn't done much interviewing. She told him not to worry. That she didn't think she could control so many girls.

He sighed as if relieved that she had made it easy for him. 'Lookit,' he said, 'we're going to expand, proper offices, a switchboard, all the gear. I've got your name and address. I'll be in touch. How are you getting back to town? I could run you in.'

'Thanks very much, but someone is picking me up,' she lied.

'I'll walk you to the door anyway,' and he escorted her through the aisle as first one voice and then many sang, 'So long, it's been good to know you.'

Chapter Thirty-eight

Back in the flat she and Sheila laughed about their first venture to find work. 'Mind you, that fella was right. The girls would have given you a terrible time. I know. I grew up with kids like that in the Buildings. You can't blame them. Out of school at fourteen and working in dumps for next to nothing. They're never on the side of the staff. It's early days yet and there's still this evening's *Herald* and *Mail*.'

During the following week they considered applying for jobs as receptionists. Except there was a catch. Typing skills were required. Domestic work they didn't consider. There were jobs for those willing to post leaflets through people's letter boxes. But they agreed that though the snow was long gone they didn't fancy traipsing round housing estates delivering leaflets. 'We'll keep looking and in the meantime not be too extravagant.'

'We're not Sheila.'

'You are, buying things for the kids, grabbing the bill for coffee and cakes. Your thousand pounds works out at twenty quid a week over a year. So no more gifts for Niamh and Deirdre, and coffee, cakes, Knickerbocker Glories and being top of the queue at the cinema is out. From now on everything's split down the middle. Don't look like that. I'm serious, Yvette. I only get eight pounds a week, but that's eight pounds weekly for as long as Fergus is in the army. Sod though he is in many ways, deprive me and the kids of the allowance he never would.'

Another week of poring over 'Situations Vacant' passed without results. Ginny had dropped in to the flat, bringing on this occasion cream buns. Sometimes her offering was a pig's kidney, pork sausages and shoulder rashers for a coddle. On other visits it might be a head of cabbage, a piece of pickled pork, two fresh herrings or mackerel with shining scales and bright eyes.

Yvette made tea and they sat to the table eating, drinking and talking. 'No luck so far with the work?' Ginny asked.

Immediately Sheila's hackles rose. 'Don't you know bloody well there isn't.'

'Keep your hair on, I'm only asking. But I must say I'm not surprised. Since you left Dublin you lost your cop on.'

'And what's that supposed to mean?' Sheila asked, her manner and voice still belligerent.

'That nine times out of ten in Dublin you have to be landed into a job. Did you keep in touch with Rosaleen?'

'Off and on, then it fizzled out.'

'D'ye know her address?'

'I have one; whether she's still there or not I don't know.'

'Drop her a line. You've nothing to lose, only the price of a stamp. For all you know she may be working somewhere that she could put a word in for you.'

353

'I never thought of that, Ma. Thanks. I'll take your advice.'

'I only wish you'd take it when it's important.'

'Don't start. I'm sorry I took you short. Have another cup of tea.'

With paper and a pen in front of her before beginning her letter Sheila explained to Yvette that she had worked with Rosaleen in Brown Thomas. 'We got on great. I used to go dancing with her when her fella went down the country to see his mother and father. She was a scream, not in a funny way, very religious. Worried sick when I started going out with Fergus. Afraid he'd take advantage of me. Those were the days. In the long run she liked him and was my bridesmaid. The last time I heard from her she was living in Walkinstown. Well, I suppose I'd better get on with the letter. I won't mention anything about a job or having left Fergus. I'll ask her to come and see me. Tell her all then.' She wrote the letter and went out to post it.

Rosaleen answered immediately, thrilled that Sheila was back in Dublin. If Sunday was all right she'd drop over. She was working in Clerys, half-day during the week, all day Saturday. 'So as usual me ma hit the nail on the head. Rosaleen may be able to put in a word for me. You know Clerys, that big shop in O'Connell Street, has a clock over it. Not in the same league as Brown Thomas, not far behind, though. And you never know, she might be able to fix you up as well.'

'Don't put too much on her. It's a different matter with you. You worked in a store. They'll probably give you a reference. I'm going to do a typing course. That should get me a receptionist job. I've studied the ads. The majority of jobs for receptionists ask for some typing skills. I think with a little bit of training I could manage that.'

'Didn't I tell you,' Ginny said triumphantly when she heard the news.

'You did, you're seldom wrong. She's coming next

Sunday. I want you to do me a favour. Have the twins and Yvette for dinner on Sunday.'

'Don't I always?'

'Yeah, only this week I won't come. I want to be on my own with Rosaleen for a while. I've a lot to tell her.'

'Indeed you have,' said Ginny in a tone Sheila recognised as accusatory. 'I thought you'd have all come to my place.'

'We will. We'll come over for our tea.'

'Suit yourself. By the way, have you decided if the girls are joining the dancing class?'

'I'm still thinking about it. Look at the time, you'll be late for Mass.'

Ginny took the hint and left.

Mr Brophy told Yvette and Sheila that he had passed on the evidence.

'What happens now?' Sheila asked.

'Not much for the time being. God knows how many more times it'll be passed on. In the long run it'll have to go abroad. Whether or not we'll ever hear the outcome I don't know.'

'I'm very grateful for what you've done. I'm sure someone somewhere will look into it. The men I met in Amsterdam were professional people, lawyers, doctors. Their names would have been on the lists, addresses too. They shouldn't be hard to trace.'

'Don't bank on it, Yvette. Scoundrels like that would be fly. The names phoney and the addresses not their homes, practices or places of business. But there's always hope. You've set the ball rolling. What more could you have done.'

'What about the Dublin priest, Da?'

'I'd say his particulars will be erased before the papers leave the country. In Ireland the Catholic Church is all powerful. Although I'm doubtful if he is a priest. Unless he's not the full shilling why would he give his title?'

'We'll live in hope. More than that, I'll do a novena to St Jude. He's the one you pray to for impossible causes. And one Sunday there it all might be in the *News of the World*. I'll bring Rosaleen down during the Holy Hour tomorrow.'

'Do that, Sheila, she's a grand girl, I'd love to see her again.'

Sheila and Rosaleen were genuinely delighted to see each other again. They embraced and kissed each other's cheeks, parted, then looked each other up and down, and declared that neither had changed a bit.

When they were seated each side of the fire Rosaleen said, 'The last letter I had from you was in October 1961. I dug it out to be sure of the date. You wrote that you hoped to be in Germany before Christmas. I never heard from you again. Did the Germany thing fall through?'

'No, we went.'

'So is Fergus finished in the army?'

'No, he's still a soldier.'

'Then what are you doing here?'

'Ah, Rosaleen, I've made a hash of my life. I've left Fergus. Nearly four months now. I never liked army life. I told you that many times in letters. But if anyone had told me this time last year that we'd be separated I'd have thought them mad. Most of it is my fault, but Fergus . . .'

'Sheila, it breaks my heart to see you like this. You and Fergus were my ideal couple. You were gorgeous and him so handsome and the pair of you so much in love. I used to envy you, wish my fella was a bit more romantic. I still do sometimes. Finish your cry. Then I'll make you a cup of tea. I brought a cake from Bewleys. Remember the day you met him in Bewleys? We'll have the tea and then you tell me all about it.'

Sheila told everything about it: Fergus's drinking; spending so much that they couldn't afford a holiday; how he had once stayed out all night. She told what a desolate

356

place Hohne was, miles from the nearest town, miles from the nearest hospital. That she had tried coaxing him to take an early discharge. He wouldn't even consider it. He wouldn't come with her to Dublin for Christmas. She came home and from then on everything had gone wrong. They didn't write to each other any more. He had given up the quarters before he had to.

Rosaleen sympathised but decided it was too soon for her to offer advice. They'd make contact again and for however long Sheila stayed in Dublin they would be in touch. Time enough to start advising. Money, she wondered how Sheila was managing and asked.

'He made me an allowance. Plenty while I was living with me ma. But I had to have a place of my own. You know my mother, she means well but we get in on each other's nerves. And of course there was Yvette.'

'Who's Yvette?'

Sheila told her she had buried her husband shortly before she was leaving for Dublin. Not a soul belonging to her. Not much money either. No insurance. Only a few pounds she'd saved from the housekeeping. If she didn't find work soon she'd be penniless. That, Sheila thought, was enough information about Yvette for the time being. Later on, if she and Rosaleen hit it off, it would be up to Yvette to give confidences.

'The poor unfortunate girl. She gets a widow's pension, though.'

'She doesn't. He died in accident. His fault so no compensation. I'd say she was in such shock that she didn't notify the pensions people.'

'It's a wonder the army didn't.'

'Come to think of it, you're right, they should have.' And Sheila thought that, whether or not it was the army's responsibility to notify the pensions people, no one knew where Yvette was so she couldn't be contacted.

'Don't forget to tell her.'

'You'll be meeting her in a few hours. She's with the

357

twins at my mother's. We're going there for tea. Rosaleen, I've moidered you with my troubles and never asked a word about you. How's himself and have you any children?'

'He's grand and we've two little boys. Not in school yet. A baby minder in the mornings and me ma has them until I finish work. Have you given any thought to working while you wait to sort things out?'

'Me and Yvette have spent a small fortune buying newspapers to read the "Situations Vacant". We got an interview each.' She described what had happened.

Rosaleen said she didn't blame her not wanting to work in Butler's and laughed uproariously at the description of Yvette in the factory. 'Are you still looking for a job?'

'Of course I am.'

'I could put in a word for you in Clerys. I'm managing a department now, haberdashery. I'm in the know, as they say.'

'Would you, Rosaleen? That'd be grand. If I'm independent I'll be able to see things more clearly. You know, like if I go back to Fergus, supposing he'd have me, it won't be for the money.'

'That's very wise. Tell me about the twins. They were only a twelvemonth when I last saw them.'

Sheila talked about the girls and reminded Rosaleen that she'd soon be seeing them. Rosaleen told her she'd start enquiries about a job first thing on Monday and let her know the outcome as soon as possible.

Then they reminisced about Brown Thomas, who else had married from there, who was still on the shelf, the dances they had gone to, their children's births and how the years had flown. Until Sheila, looking at the clock, said, 'Talking about time flying, it has; we'd better make a move to me mother's.'

In the middle of the following week a letter came from Rosaleen saying that she had arranged an interview a week next Monday. She should call in to Brown Thomas and ask for a reference. She also wrote that she had mentioned Yvette regarding employment, but as she had thought, there wasn't a hope. Yvette had never worked and was too old to be taken on as a trainee.

Sheila dressed in her best to go to Brown Thomas. She pushed open the plate-glass doors and was a child again, a schoolgirl, an older girl starting work there. The smell of scent, of luxury, the broad staircase, the well-dressed, assured women – nothing had changed. But as she wandered round the store she realised there were differences. Listening, she heard more ordinary Dublin voices, well-spoken but Dublin nevertheless. In her day the majority of customers who had used the store were what she, Rosaleen and some other members of staff refered to as 'Balls from Dalkey'. She wondered if the new clientele reported assistants whom they considered rude or inefficient as frequently as the ones who spoke as if their mouths were full of marbles.

She had been fortunate, was never reported, never had to climb the stairs to the manager's office. She supposed some staff were sacked for offending customers but didn't remember it taking place. Now she was on her way up the stairs to the manager's office. A reference she believed was her right and when something was hers by right she never felt nervous.

It was the same manager from years ago. She recognised him straight away – he hadn't changed much. But only after she had told him why she had come and given her maiden name did he remember her.

'Sheila, Sheila Brophy, it's good to see you again. So you're back home. Didn't you marry a soldier?'

'I'm still married to him.' Then, as she had so often lately, she lied, 'He's been posted to a part of Africa not recommended for wives and children. So I'm living with my mother for at least a year.'

'Have you children?'

'Twin girls.'

'Isn't that grand. I must say you're looking very well. Is it a job you're enquiring about?'

'Ah, no, I want a reference.'

'We'd have sent one if you'd rung or dropped a line. But I'm glad you didn't or I'd have missed the pleasure of seeing you again. I won't pry and ask where you intend using the reference. Not my business, eh. Leave your address and married name, and you'll have it in tomorrow's first post.' He stood up, proffered his hand. Sheila did likewise, then thanked him. 'A pleasure,' he said and escorted her to the door.

Outside the main entrance she recalled the night Fergus had met her there and taken her to Davy Byrnes, Bewleys was across the road. She needed coffee but knew that in her melancholy mood it wasn't the place to go. She walked on down Grafton Street, thinking about him. Wondering if he missed her. Surely he missed the children but he had only written to them twice. They rarely mentioned him any more. Did that mean they had forgotten him? She didn't want them grieving for him, but maybe in their own way without showing it they were.

Remembering how she had and still loved her father, she was overcome by guilt for having deprived Niamh and Deirdre of Fergus. But what could she do? He had made the major moves. If in his first letter he had shown the slightest affection she would have gone back after Christmas. Now he'd have to go down on his bended knees. She stopped by the Liffey Bridge, leant on the parapet and looked down at the brown, cloudy water, the swans and a Guinness barge on its way to the port. Crowds passed by. People were gathered in groups, talking and laughing. She made a bet with herself that on the way back after looking into Clerys window one or more of the groups would be still on the bridge.

She crossed the wide road to the other side of the

bridge. An organ grinder was playing 'After the Ball Was Over'. She dropped a penny into the cardboard box on the pavement and made her way to Clerys. A big store, bigger than Brown Thomas. Not quite in the same league but renowned for good-quality clothes and other merchandise.

This time next week I may be employed by Clerys, she mused. A big step I've taken. And I'm anything but sure it's the right one. I should be by my husband's side, my husband and my family. She felt lost. Then, turning to go back up the street, she saw the crowds, the shops, double-decker buses, heard voices and the organ music faint in the distance. Saw the seagulls swooping and the people she had passed were still gossiping on the bridge. She sighed and thought, Fergus would make it paradise; I should be by his side. That's where I want to be. But not in Germany.

Chapter Thirty-nine

Sheila went back to her mother's. Yvette had collected the girls from school. They were sitting round the kitchen table eating sugared, lemon-drenched pancakes that Ginny had made. Sheila related how she had spent her time. The twins finished their tea and pancakes, then went into the spare bedroom where a supply of their toys were kept and Sheila took the opportunity to tell Yvette about the widow's pension. 'Rosaleen mentioned it on Sunday and I forgot to tell you. You're entitled to one.'

'But that means getting in touch with the army.'

'It's nothing to do with the army. The pension is on the stamps Victor will have paid for.'

'Don't tell me you haven't been drawing it. I assumed you were. You'll get it and back pay too.' Ginny shook her head and continued, 'I don't understand how you could have overlooked it and you a sensible young woman. First thing tomorrow make enquiries.'

'Give over, Mother. Her husband died in Germany not Dublin.'

Ignoring Sheila, Ginny said, 'The first thing to get is the death certificate.'

'Where?' asked Sheila.

'Where you always get them, the register office.'

'You're a right know-all. I told you the man was killed in Germany.'

'He was a soldier, wasn't he, so she'll have to send to the English register office.'

'Maybe you're right. I'll ask me da when he comes in.'

Mr Brophy wasn't sure. 'If Britain was still occupying Germany what your mother said might be right. They're not any more, so the Germans may have a say in it. Leave it to me. I'll ask in work tomorrow.'

Later that night, in the flat with the children in bed, Sheila said, 'Me da's the best in the world, but sometimes, as they say in Ireland, he puts things on the long finger. Either forgets about them or isn't in a hurry sorting them out. So I thought the best thing is to write to Lizzie. Bob will know the procedure. Only . . .'

'Only what?' asked Yvette.

'I'd have to tell Lizzie you are here with me.'

'I wouldn't mind that,' Yvette said.

'I'd have to say how you came to be here. Lizzie knows you and I weren't boon companions.'

'Yes, I see what you mean. Tell her the truth, all of it except about Tom. She should know, though. Apart from all else, she'll remember how Tom attached himself to Victor. She'll make sure that sort of situation will never arise again.'

'That's a load off my mind. I wanted to warn Lizzie but without telling all I couldn't and wouldn't without you agreeing. I'll write first thing tomorrow. Maybe the army will become involved. If they do it will be to send you back pay of Victor's.'

Yvette visibly shuddered. 'I really don't want anything belonging to him, not even the pension.'

'Being high-principled is one thing, being a bloody eejit is another. The pension has nothing to do with the other money, nor has the back pay. All that money came from his wages. Are you with me?'

'I suppose so. Of course, I'll be glad of the extra. It's being reminded of him I hate. Do you realize how happy I am here? I haven't felt like this since before Sean was conceived. I feel like a young girl. I love Ireland. I love your parents. I'm sure nowhere in the world do people laugh as much as they do here.'

'All right, all right, don't go over the top.' Then Sheila put her arms round Yvette and said, 'I'm so glad for you and myself. And to think I lived next door to you for a year and we seldom exchanged a word.'

'Now, as you say, we never stop gasbagging.'

In the days before being interviewed at Clerys Sheila had periods of anxiety, worrying about the interview and if she got the job would she be able for it. She hadn't worked for seven years. The interview wasn't as nerve-racking as she had anticipated, the questions few. The remainder of the time was spent talking about Brown Thomas, the woman interviewing her having worked there long before Sheila had. It was all very informal, no waiting to be notified by post. There and then, she was told the job was hers, the salary and that she would work in the haberdashery department.

It was a fix, Rosaleen's doing. Sheila restrained herself from being too effusive with her thanks. But on her way home she felt like a schoolgirl, thrilled that she had succeeded, relieved that it was to sell needles and thread, ribbons and wool, zips and patent fasteners, buttons and embroidery silks, and that Rosaleen would be to hand for advice.

To celebrate she went into Bewleys in Westmoreland Street and bought one of their most expensive chocolate cakes.

Yvette and her mother looked expectantly at her as she came into the kitchen. 'I got it, I got it. From next week I'll be bringing home the pay. I can't believe it. I'm over the moon.'

Yvette congratulated her and Ginny said, 'And why wouldn't you have got it? Aren't you well-educated and have experience.'

'You're right, Ma,' Sheila said. Though she knew that her mother would have prayed, lit candles and implored her favourite saints to put in a good word. She also knew that Ginny didn't want her working, getting a taste of independence. She wanted her back with her husband. Me poor ma, she thought, she'll have been working on two saints. Asking one to get me the job and explaining to the other not to let her daughter become enraptured with the work. So the job wasn't to be a cushy one. Keep her on the go. And then she'll come to her senses and realise marriage is a cushier number.

'You two stay where you are,' Sheila said after their tea and cakes. 'I'll collect the twins.'

Walking towards Warrenmount Convent, the euphoria of the last hours left her and she thought of Yvette who needed a job more than she did and had little chance of finding one. The widow's pension, when it came through, would be a help financially. Lizzie had answered the letter by return post. Bob was making enquiries. He'd sort things out. Lizzie also wrote that she and Beth were relieved to know that Yvette was safe and sound in Dublin. They would both write to her. And although he deserved even in death to be shamed, neither would tell the terrible news to anyone other than her husband.

She wrote almost a whole page about Tom and Victor.

When I think of the danger he was in I go cold. I
hope he's in hell, burning. Bob says it's just as well
we never knew or he'd have been up for murder. I
had a vague knowledge that there were men like
that, but I'd never have suspected anyone I knew.
You think of them as strangers, evil-looking people
with what they are written on their faces. Whoever
would have thought Victor was one of them.

I'm going to take Tom to the MO. Not that he's
ill, thank God, the same as ever, has his tantrums,
gets a bit rough with the girls sometimes. That's
boys for you. All the same, I want him checked over.
I'll pretend he's forever scratching and fiddling round
his bum. Without even looking, the doctor may say
he's probably got thread worms. If he does I'll go
back again and again until Tom's examined. If there
is anything wrong I'll then tell him about Victor,
just in case Tom might have ill effects later on. I
read somewhere that children who have been abused
often do.

We went to a curry lunch in the mess last Sunday.
I spoke to Fergus. It's no good telling lies, neither
of us mentioned your name. He doesn't look sick or
anything, but he's not the same man. Keep writing. I
love your letters. And drop a line to Beth some time.

Sheila crossed the road at Patrick's Street, walked along
Dean's Street remembering, as she sometimes did, that it
was named after Dean Swift who had lived a stone's throw
away beside St Patrick's Cathedral. It was one of the many
things her father had told her. She turned left into New
Row, though a plaque on the wall named it Lauderdale
Terrace. No Dubliner she knew ever used that name. Once
round the corner, she smelled Keefe's the Knackers and

wondered, as she always did, how the people living in the Tenters put up with the vile, rancid smell of bones, decomposing flesh burning and glue being made from the residue. She arrived at the school gate, the wrought-iron, narrow gate where her mother used to wait for her.

Now you could go in, walk up the slope and wait outside the classrooms. She'd heard tell that Warrenmount was planning extensions, having a secondary school. She hoped they would. She had liked the Presentation nuns better than the ones in the Loretto. So would the twins. They'd study there for the Inter, maybe the Leaving. She'd be so proud of them. She could be a manageress in Clerys by then, not short of money. They'd have great holidays.

A wave of sadness engulfed her as she realised she was envisaging a time years ahead and Fergus wasn't in the picture. The twins would never know him, never have anyone to call 'Daddy'. She heard the bell ring, a big brass bell wielded by a nun announcing that it was 'home time'. A trickle of children emerged, some carrying drawings to take home, others pushing and shoving their friends, and the very young with anxious eyes, searching the group of mothers for theirs.

Nothing anxious about the twins: talking, laughing, tossing their long curly hair, spotting her, running to her. Sheila embraced them and asked had they been good, all the while thinking, I'm depriving them of their father. I'm a bad mother. God knows how it'll affect them. She castigated herself until Niamh asked, 'Mammy, did you get the job?'

'I did. Isn't that grand? It's a lovely shop. Sells everything. Lovely clothes and all sorts of toys. I don't work on Wednesday afternoon. We'll go in then and you can see for yourself.' Her melancholy mood lifted. She wasn't such a bad mother and the girls would be fine. They'd lack for nothing except Fergus. But that was as much his fault as hers. By the time she reached the

Buildings she had convinced herself she had done nothing terrible.

She settled quickly into the haberdashery department. The customers were Dubliners or up for the day from the country, buying the makings of a jumper or cardigan, buttons, needles or thread. The wool was on display, easy to choose. The majority of customers knew exactly what they wanted and for those unsure she'd make suggestions. It was all very friendly. You were treated as an equal, your advice considered, usually taken. Completely opposite to serving in Brown Thomas.

There were two other assistants, Moira who'd been in Clerys for thirty years, not married, no make-up, a sweet face and pleasing manner. She had to be well over forty, an old maid. The other girl, Brenda was a vivacious eighteen-year-old. She reminded Sheila of herself at that age. Lots of fellas fancied her, but she hadn't met the right one yet and was in no hurry, she told Sheila and Moira daily.

They took turns at manning the counter while two of them went to lunch. Brenda loved to hear about Germany. Sheila told her about the Balaclava Ball: 'Dancing all night and still there at breakfast time!'

'It's like something you'd see on the pictures. Bet you'd love to be back.'

'When Fergus comes back from Africa we might.'

'You must have been raging when you couldn't go with him.'

'Not really, it wasn't a healthy place, especially if you had children.'

'I wish I could get out of this kip.'

'D'ye not like Clerys?'

'Clerys isn't bad, it's Ireland that's the kip. We're miles behind the times.'

'You'll fall in love and get married.'

'I will in my eye. A baby every year. There's ten of us. Ten in a two-bedroom house. That's not for me. As soon

367

as I've saved enough I'm off to America. What d'ye think of this mascara?'

Sheila told her it was gorgeous and Brenda said, 'It's great having you in the department. Moira's a real stick in the mud. She lives in the chapel.'

'Not much else to do if you haven't got a fella.'

Brenda laughed. 'He'd want to be blind.'

When Sheila lunched with Moira she told her about Belsen, all the graves there were surrounding the camp. Moira would listen attentively, promise to remember the dead in her prayers. And Sheila, studying her face, would think, I could do wonders with you. First thing get that mousy hair cut and a tint. You're not bad-looking, really. You've just let yourself go.

During their lunchtime chats Sheila learnt that she was an only child and her parents were dead. Life could be very lonely but she made the best of things. She liked travelling. Last year she had gone to Paris and this year she'd go to Rome. But the rest of the year still had to be got through. Without the chapel she'd be lost. She did the Miraculous Medal every Monday. Then there was the Legion of Mary and the sodality.

Sheila was very moved. The poor, unfortunate woman. As soon as she was used to the job and not so tired she'd ask her up one Sunday for tea to meet Yvette and the twins. See how it would go. See if she would come, you never knew. If it worked then she'd make her known to her mother and father. In no time Moira would have if not a family, then plenty of friends.

Having been on her feet for so long, at the end of the day she was jaded. Nevertheless she walked home each evening. She had her reasons. After the warm and what she considered airless store, she needed a breeze on her face. Also, there were the buses. Crowds waiting for them. No queues. A crush of people who fought their way on to a bus. And most of all the walk was time when she could think, wonder if Fergus would make a move, whether this evening when she went to her mother's Ginny's face would give away the news before she produced the letter. Ginny's face would be lit up. My poor ma, all she does for me, every bit of it against the grain. Her help enables me to stay away from my husband, which me ma considers a sin. When you marry in the sight of God you are married for life. And even if there was a letter it might not be one asking for a reconciliation. More like notifying her of an increase in her allowance, another brusque note. Well, he could stick the extra money up his arse. She was an independent woman. In September she'd go to night classes, sit the Leaving Cert. Maybe work for an external degree. She was a young woman with a life in front of her. She'd make it a good one for herself and her children.

It worried her that Yvette had no such prospects. Bob had got Victor's death certificate; her application for a widow's pension was being processed. God only knew how long that would take. It would be back-dated but even so, unless she got a job when her bit of capital was gone she'd be badly off.

It wasn't for the want of trying that she hadn't found work. She answered all applications for situations where she might stand a chance: solicitors, builders, businesses, all sorts of firms. Small outfits, she suspected, offices over shop, or cabins in builders' yards. She could imagine an employer's reaction when Yvette walked in: a beautiful woman, elegantly dressed. Her appearance and demeanour off-putting. They might fancy her but she wasn't what they were looking for: an ordinary girl who would clerk for them, laugh at their jokes, not object to a slap on the bum – not a fashion model nor an ice maiden.

Poor Yvette, I wish I could help her. But how? Suggest she cut her beautiful hair and get a cheap perm? Buy a costume for thirty-nine and eleven in Butler's? Slouch into the office? It was hopeless. She needed a miracle or qualifications. In a few weeks I'll refuse her share of the rent. There'll be ructions. But I'll insist, point out that I'm not as green as I'm cabbage-looking. The money will help to pay for night classes, the typing and doing business studies or something. And that when she landed a good job I'd be waiting with my hand stretched out.

Chapter Forty

Occasionally on her afternoon off Sheila and Rosaleen would have lunch in a café instead of the staff canteen. On this particular Wednesday, after talking about Fergus and Sheila's dilemma as to whether or not she should make the first move towards a reconciliation, Sheila was coming to the conclusion that really she was happy with her independent life. 'I have the best of both worlds: no man to worry about, answer to, be a wife, mother and mistress rolled into one. And a close family so that I never know loneliness. When I think of Moira and her existence I count my blessings. I'm going to ask her up next Sunday.'

'She won't be able to come on Sunday.'

'Oh,' said Sheila, looking surprised. 'I know she spends a lot of her time in the chapel. Benediction, I suppose, on Sunday afternoon.'

'A rub of the relic on Sunday afternoons. On Monday, Tuesdays, the rest of the week as well.'

'You're codding me.'

'I am not. The saintly Moira has a fella. Has had for twenty years, so I'm told. Married, of course. Rolling in money and mad about Moira.'

'God Almighty! And there was me feeling sorry for her, thinking that if she did this to her hair and that to her face she might click. What's he like?'

'I've never seen him but Miss Hegarty in china bumped

into them in Paris. She told me he's a picture. Fiftyish but a fine-looking man. There's no accounting for taste.'

'The bloody oul hypocrite. Butter wouldn't melt in her mouth, moryah. Does his wife know about it?'

'Probably. Not much goes on in Dublin that everyone doesn't know about.'

'How has she never had a child for him? Y'know, like with no contraception in Ireland.'

'Don't kid yourself about that. Belfast's only a couple of hours away. French letters by the dozen, if you've the nerve, the money and sling a deaf ear to the Church's teaching. And if you've a sympathetic doctor, private mind you, he'll prescribe the pill for period problems. And if the worst comes to the worst, and you've money and are in the know, plenty of private nursing homes in which you can have a D and C. Apart from all that, Moira's not a bad oul skin. I like her. She's a great worker and very kind.'

'So do I. I'm glad you told me. Save her telling lies about Sunday afternoon visiting.'

'Don't let slip what I told you to Brenda. She'd have it all over Clerys.'

'Of course I won't. I suppose I'd better be going home.' She looked out of the window. 'It's lashing. I'll be soaked. April showers. See you in the morning.'

She had promised to take the girls to the zoo, meet them from school and go straight there. They'd be so disappointed, she thought on the way home. Yvette had a lovely fire burning and offered to pick the girls up. 'You don't want to get drenched a second time.'

'Thanks all the same, it's bad enough that they can't go to the zoo, but if I don't turn up as well I'll never hear the end of it. They've become very clingy lately.'

'Probably because you're working.'

'It could be. I hope so. I wonder, though, if they're missing Fergus. Delayed reaction, as they say.'

'I don't know, Sheila. I hope they aren't. I wish it wasn't

so. Sometimes I feel that I'm to blame. That if I hadn't come to Dublin you'd have gone back to Germany at the end of your holiday.'

'You're a right eejit. Leaving Fergus had nothing to do with you. You knew nothing about us. Lizzie did. Me and Fergus were at loggerheads for months. What has happened would have happened sooner or later, so don't ever blame yourself.'

She brought with her to the school the twins' umbrellas. Impervious of the weather, they greeted her by saying, 'We're going to the zoo, aren't we, Mammy?'

'Look at the rain, we'd be soaked. We'd have to get two buses.' They pouted and sulked but she talked them round, promising that if tomorrow was fine Yvette would take them – and for a treat she'd buy fish and chips for tea.

There was no direct bus to the Buildings, no direct bus to where she lived. The Buildings were nearer, so she decided to stop at Ginny's. There were spare clothes there belonging to her and the twins. She'd strip off their saturated coats, shoes and socks, and put them in dry things. Stay for a while. The rain might clear up. As they were passing the turn to the chip shop the girls complained. 'You said you were going to buy fish and chips. You promised.'

'Don't start whingeing,' Sheila, damp and irritable, said. 'We'll go to your grannie's first, then I'll run out for the chips.'

'It's not fair,' Deirdre complained, lagging behind.

'It's not, so it's not,' said Niamh, dropping back to walk beside her sister.

Sheila's umbrella was leaking, water trickling down the back of her collar, then down her neck. Her suede stilettos were waterlogged and at every step her heels threw muddy water on to her calves. She was in terrible humour for on the way from the school she remembered saying to Rosaleen at lunch, 'April showers.' Now it sank in that it was April. Going on four months since she had left

Germany. Practice camp would be starting or already started and Fergus, wearing his white-topped cap, swagger stick under his arm, swanning around, glorying in his authority. And here was she, soaked to the skin, dragging the twins behind her. She turned round, pointed a finger and vented her spleen on them. 'Another word out of either of you and there'll be no zoo tomorrow nor the next day. And no fish and chips either. D'ye hear me?'

Their eyes glared at her. She mustn't smile, though they reminded her so much of her face in the mirror when she was in bad humour, it was difficult not to. Still using a stern tone, she repeated her question, 'Did you hear what I said?'

Not aware that they had almost made her laugh, hearing a voice that they believed meant what it said, they mumbled together, 'We'll be good.'

'Now walk in front of me like good little girls.' They held hands and did. They were talking to each other but she couldn't hear what they said. Giving out about me, I suppose, she thought. The same as I'd have done about my mother, only I didn't have a sister.

Ginny stripped them, dried their hair, dressed them and sat them by the fire. By the time Sheila came back with the fish and chips the bread was cut and buttered, the tea about to be wetted. 'I love a bit of long ray,' Ginny said and told the girls they could eat the bones. 'Chew them well, the bones are good for you.'

When the meal was finished Ginny looked out of the window. 'That's down for the night. Let the girls sleep here, they'll get drenched again if you don't.'

The twins whooped with delight. 'Can we, Mammy?' they asked, one after the other.

'I suppose you might as well,' Sheila replied.

'Go and play in your bedroom now, I want to talk to your mammy.

'Hold on a minute, Ma, I have to take off these

stockings and wash the backs of my legs. Look at them, I'm the dirtiest walker in creation.'

She came back bare-legged, wearing a dressing gown and a pair of her mother's slippers. 'The rain soaked every stitch. Wasn't it a good job you treated us to all the clothes. I brought next to nothing with me. Of course, I thought I'd only be here for ten days. That umbrella's useless.'

'Take a lend of mine for going home. Now sit down till you hear this. You'll never guess who I met today.'

'Who?' asked Sheila, having first lit one of the ten cigarettes that were her ration for the day.

'Zac Goldberg.'

'Never heard of him.'

''Deed you did. His father used to come to the house. He was a moneylender. A decent oul skin. I used to borry from him.'

'I remember him, wasn't he baldy? He used to give me sweets. I never knew his name was Zac.'

'It wasn't. Zac's his son. He's baldy as well. And if you'd seen the head of hair he had, thick red curls. The only red-haired Jew I'd ever seen. D'ye remember him now?'

'No,' said Sheila.

'You've a terrible memory. No, come to think of it you're right. It was in the shop I used to see Zac. Mr Goldberg had a shop in New Street. If I was passing through the week I'd drop in. You'd be in school then and Zac had left. He'd be helping in the shop. Fancy goods, they sold, all sorts. China dogs and sleeping dolls, holy pictures, statues, brush and comb sets, vases, bevelled mirrors.'

Sheila pretended to listen as Ginny went on to describe what must have been Mr Goldberg's entire stock. 'Now and again,' Ginny said when the inventory was finished, 'I'd fancy something or be looking for a wedding present. It was very handy because you could pay on the weekly. Zac would be in the shop and as I was telling you it was him I bumped into today. I heard this voice; "Mrs Brophy." There I was in D'Olier Street and this stranger calling my name. I needn't tell you I was taken aback. And then I recognised him.'

'And him gone thirty and baldy!'

'It was the eyes. Out of his father's head. Big brown eyes with a lovely expression. Gentle and kind-looking. So there we were, like a pair of drowned rats, remembering old times. Him asking about your da and me about his mother and father.'

Sheila was wishing she had gone back to the flat. Exceeding her ration, she lit another cigarette.

'Anyway, to cut a long story short, he took me into the Pearl Bar and bought me a hot whiskey.' Before saying any more Ginny drank the remains of her tea gone cold.

'So was that all?'

'Don't you be hurrying me, you've an awful habit of doing that. I'm just coming to the important bit. Zac's opening a travel agency. He says travelling abroad is going to be all the rage and he wants to get in on the ground floor.'

Sheila refilled the kettle and sighed exasperatedly, knowing the running water would muffle the sound.

'His father sent Zac to college. Are you listening to me, Sheila Brophy?'

'I'm all ears, go on,' Sheila said as she lit the gas under the kettle.

'Well, as I was saying, his father sent him to a college, one of them places where they grind the pupils. His father thought he might catch up. He wanted him to be a doctor. He got into the College of Surgeons. But as he said to me, once he got on the wards he didn't have it in him. Anyway, he left, went to Manchester. He had relations there. They got him into a big travel agency. He loved it. Learnt a lot about the business. Then his mother and father took sick and he came home. And now he's opening up his own place.'

'I hope he suceeds.' Sheila made fresh tea. After the cup of tea, she said, 'I think I'll make a move.'

'I haven't finished telling you the rest.'

'The rest of what?'

'He's got a place in Wicklow Street. It's being done up. Then he'll be looking for staff. He wants a clerk and a typist. When he mentioned a clerk, I thought of Yvette. Nicely spoken, her handwriting's like copperplate. I've seen it when she's been playing with the girls. And where d'ye leave her appearance?'

Sheila's first thought was, my bloody mother, finding the flat, reminding me of Rosaleen and now about to fix up Yvette. She poured the tea and went on thinking. I'm like a child here. She organises everything. Then her good nature overcame her pettiness. Everything her mother had done was for the best. And what could be better than landing Yvette into a job? 'Oh, Ma, that'd be smashing. But for God's sake don't raise her hopes too soon. He might have made it all up, boasting, doing the big blow. And if it's genuine he could have someone already lined up for the job.'

'You're very aggravating. There's times, married and all as you are, I'd love to clatter you. I've the sense I was born with. There's no fear of me raising that poor unfortunate's hopes. Zac gave me his card, made me promise to keep in touch. Take it outa my bag and have a look.'

Sheila read the address, 'Rathgar. Not short of a bob or two unless he's in a flat there.'

'He was born and reared in that house.'

'He's on the phone. You could ring him.'

'Go to a phone box! I'll do no such thing. Nine times out of ten they're broken and always reeking of piss.'

'God, you're great, Ma. I'm always taking the nose off you. I don't mean it. Nowadays I'm not in the best of spirits.'

'Now don't start bawlin'. You brought it on yourself and for the price of a stamp could remedy it.' But Sheila did cry and Ginny wanted to comfort her lovely daughter who'd make such a bags of her life. To deprive the twins of their father. Sometimes she wondered if Sheila was right in the head, there was insanity in the family, a long way back. But you never could tell when it might raise its head again. Then she upbraided herself for such foolishness. All she was doing was making excuses for her stubborn daughter who'd been that way since she was born. Mind you, that Fergus was just as bad, she thought. Three weeks since I wrote and himself sent the newspapers with articles about the economy picking up. She'd kill me if she knew. If there was another woman involved I'd encourage her in what's she's doing. But to leave him because she doesn't like where she's living and he's fond of the drink – you don't break up a marriage for those reasons.

I wouldn't relish army life. Stuck out in the middle of nowhere, that's hard for a girl reared in the city. But she should have given it a bit more time, stayed by his side and tried persuasion. No one is more delighted than me to have her and the girls here, but not at the price of a broken marriage. So I took it on myself to write. But not a word from him. I didn't say she was breaking her heart but let him know she wasn't happy. And I told him the twins miss him. So they do. Sheila says they're grand, but when they sleep here I know different. Not that they cry, but it's 'Daddy used to do this' and 'Daddy used to do that'. It's worse since they've started school and hear the other children talking about their fathers. So I wrote. I interfered, some would think and others say. Not that I care. I'm doing what I think is best. But if he doesn't answer the letter there's no more I can do.

Sheila stopped crying and asked Ginny if she was sure she wanted the children to stay the night.

'Them being here is the greatest pleasure in my life. I think I'm back in my twenties. It's like rearing you all over again.'

'I suppose I'd better be getting back to the flat. I'd love

to be able to tell Yvette about Zac. If he's on the level she'll have a good chance. He's been around, he won't be intimidated by her appearance. Lots of the Jewesses I remember were very stylish.'

'So was his mother, a beauty and always dressed to the nines.'

'You won't forget to write to him.'

'The minute you're gone. I'll start it and catch the last post.'

Sheila dressed in dry clothes, had a chat with the girls, kissed them and went back to the flat.

Chapter Forty-one

Ginny wrote to Zac telling him she knew a girl – an educated, smart girl – who was looking for a position. She explained that she was a widow and a friend of Sheila's. Zac replied, said he'd be interested in seeing the young woman, asked Ginny to forward her address and let Yvette know that he would write asking her for an interview.

After receiving Zac's letter Ginny went round to the flat, hoping that she'd be in.

Yvette was, as usual, pleased to see Ginny. 'You're early. Come in and sit down. Look at me, not dressed yet. I felt lazy this morning. To tell you the truth, since Sheila started working I haven't much heart for anything. It can be lonely. And you can only do so much walking round art galleries and museums. When the weather improves it won't be so bad. I'll go further afield. I've been reading about a castle in Howth that's worth a visit, there are other Big Houses open to the public. Listen to me talking non-stop and not offering you a cup of tea.'

'I don't want one, thanks all the same. Now you sit down and listen to what I have to tell you. Your lonely days may be nearing their end.' Ginny told her about Zac, the travel agency, that he was looking for staff. 'I put a word in for you. I heard from him this morning. He wants your address so that he can make an appointment to interview you.'

'Me! I can't believe it. What sort of work?'

'He wants a typist and a clerk. I'm sure you'd be great at the clerking.'

'Oh, Ginny, wouldn't it be marvellous if I got it.'

'I'd say you've a good chance. Anyway, you won't be surprised when the letter comes. I'll have to run to get to ten-o'clock Mass. I'll offer it up for you.'

The interview was at eleven thirty on the following Tuesday. Yvette arrived in Wicklow Street an hour early. She attracted many glances from passers-by. Her suit, one of the few she had brought from Germany, was exquisitely tailored. Donkey-brown, made from fine gaberdine, the skirt was pencil-slim and calf-length, and her high-heeled shoes matched the suit. Her glorious titian hair she wore in a French pleat. She no longer wore her wedding ring, her only jewellery was small gold earrings. She was elegent, beautiful and gave the impression of a sophisticated, self-confidant woman. Little did those who looked at her know how apprehensive she was. From the other side of the street she looked at the travel agency. If she had read the address correctly that was what she was looking at. There was no name over it. The windows were bare. It appeared to be empty. To check on the address she went to a nearby café, ordered coffee and reread the letter. She had gone to the right address. She killed time reading the *Irish Times*, which she had bought on the way to her appointment. Ordered a second cup of coffee and looked at the Simplex crossword.

At twenty past eleven she went again to the travel agency. She walked slowly by the window, glancing in as she passed. This time she noticed a desk and a man sitting behind it. Turning, she walked back. The door was ajar.

The man looked up, saw her and beckoned her in. He appeared to be tall, but as she entered he stood up and she saw that he was low-sized, a long body and short legs.

'You must be Yvette,' he said, coming forward to greet her, thinking, as he did so, this girl has class. 'Mrs Brophy has given you a great recommendation. Hang on, I'll get another chair.' He placed it next to his, moving them so that they sat facing each other. He had the most beautiful eyes she had ever seen, big, brown, dreamy eyes and perfect very white teeth, so that his smile was enchanting. It wasn't until later that she noticed his baldness. 'It's not a bit like a travel agency, eh? It will be next week. The posters and brochures are in the stockroom and tomorrow the floors, walls, a few counters, a lot of chairs and all the paraphernalia will be installed. If not tomorrow then the next day. That's how it is in Ireland. Would you fancy working here?'

'I would but I know nothing about the travel business.'

'I know it all. Only I've slipped up not opening sooner. Should have in January, that's when people start booking their holidays. Travel, you know, is going to be big business. I'll show you the ropes. That is, if you'll take the job.'

'I'd be delighted. Are you sure I could manage it?'

'Walk it. How about a week today?'

'That would be fine. What time?'

'Half-nine finish at half-four. Salary . . . you never asked about that.'

'I'm so excited, so grateful it didn't cross my mind. In any case I've never worked before so I know nothing about salaries.' She couldn't believe that she felt so at ease with this stranger.

'How about five pounds a week to start and discounts if you want a holiday?'

'That would be wonderful, but I can't type. I was going to take a course in it.'

'You can forget the course if you want to.'

They both stood up. He was inches shorter than her. They shook hands. He saw her to the door and said, 'Look forward to seeing you next week.'

'Me too,' replied Yvette and walked sedately up Wicklow Street, when what she wanted to do was skip along singing out, 'I've got a job, I've got a job and I don't have to do the typing course.'

The first of May next week, Sheila thought one evening on the way home from work, going into the fifth month since she had left Germany. It was hard to believe that she and Fergus had been separated for such a long time. Several times a week she dreamt about him, dreams in which they were rowing, making love, walking in the Dublin mountains. For an instant after waking up she would forget they were apart and, when she realised the truth, wanted to sink into oblivion and never waken again. Only for another instant did that thought prevail. One or both twins were by her bed, squeezing in either side of her, complaining of being hungry, urging her to get up.

Then she envied Yvette whose alarm wouldn't go off for another half-hour, Yvette who before she went to work for Zac often saw to the twins, letting Sheila sleep a little longer. Now, although happy in her new job, Yvette found working almost non-stop for a full day exhausted her. 'I'll get used to it. It's all so different. You'd be surprised how many people come in during the day. Some booking holidays, others thinking it over, asking so many questions. Zac says I'm doing fine, that in another few weeks it won't take a feather out of me.'

'I felt exactly the same when I started in Clerys. Zac is right, you'll get used to it in no time,' Sheila had consoled.

In the mornings when she woke headachy and cranky, she knew her bad humour was caused by lack of love not sleep. There were days when she told herself that she should write, admit she was wrong – asking him to leave a job that he loved wasn't fair. Tell him she exaggerated his drinking problem. He was a good husband and she loved him. Without him her life was worthless. But at some time during the day she would have a rethink, ask herself why in this day and age should she have to spend years of her life living in places she loathed. It wasn't as if Fergus was an Englishman who might find settling in Ireland difficult. And what right had he to spend so much money on drink, to leave her night after night to sit alone while he went to the mess? So he didn't knock about with other women, but that wasn't the only sin in the book.

She was not going to write to him. To make it up without him making amends would solve nothing. For the first few weeks when they were together again he might not go out so often. But gradually his old habits would take over. So would the rows and bitterness be driven deeper into her soul. And yet she knew that if suddenly he were to appear in the street she would run to him, here in the middle of town, run to him, throw her arms round him and never let him go.

Passing a shop in O'Connell Street, she stopped to look in the window. The First Communion season was approaching and the window was decked with miniature bridal dresses: satin, silk, lace and broderie anglaise dresses, handbags to match the materials, white buckskin shoes, wreaths and veils. Next year, when the twins were seven, they would make their First Communion. But this year they would walk in the May procession in honour of Our Lady and would need veils, wreaths and white dresses. She loitered by the window studying the dress styles. Not that she'd have much say in what they wore. Ginny would make the dresses and have the final say in the style and material. Ginny was a fixer all right. She'd never heard the word used in such a context until one evening when she, Yvette and Zac had met for a drink after work. She was giving out the pay about Ginny, complaining half jokingly how her mother was always a step in front of her, how she had found the flat, made her get in touch with Rosaleen, fixed up the job for Yvette.

Zac had smiled and said, 'Sheila, you're a lucky girl. Everything your mother has done was from the goodness of her heart, for the benefit of you, for Yvette, people she loves. Every family needs that sort of fixer.' If you looked at it like that he spoke sense. All the same, Ginny's fixing annoyed her. She was a grown woman, a married woman, the mother of two children and Ginny made her feel as if she was still a child.

She left the window and walked on towards Ginny's from where she would pick up the twins. And as she passed Trinity, still resentful of her mother, she suddenly thought, God, I'm an ungrateful bitch. I leave my husband, land at my mother's with two children and a woman she's never heard of. My father's put out of his bed. I'm almost penniless and we're received with open arms. She'll have food ready for me, have collected the twins from school, fed and amused them and if I was to walk in the door and say, 'Ma, I'm going out this evening,' she might hem and haw, but mind the girls she would. In this frame of mind she went into a confectionery shop in Grafton Street and bought for her mother a big box of chocolates and sweets for the girls.

'Throwing your money away on boxes of chocolates,' was Ginny's initial response to the gift. Then she opened the box and handed them round. 'Mind you, they're gorgeous, have another one. No, don't, I've a lovely bit of plaice. You'll spoil your appetite.'

While they were eating the fish and home-made chips Ginny said, 'I was in O'Connell Street today, looking at the Communion dresses. I saw the dotiest little wreaths. Simple ones, tiny flowers, no glitter. Nowadays some of the rig-outs are more like fancy dress fairy costumes.'

'What took you across town apart from the Communion outfits?'

'I was looking for new beds.'

'For who?'

'Me and your father, twin beds. I was wondering if you could use the double one.'

'What would I do with a double bed?'

'Well, you're always complaining that the twins land on top of you first thing in the morning. A double bed would be grand and there's plenty of room in your place.'

'And what about when they sleep here and want to go in your bed?'

'They seldom do nowadays. They don't like the smell of the porter.'

'They should be well used to it. Their father drank enough to sweat lager.'

'They were younger then and wouldn't have noticed. What about the bed? There's not a brack on it and the best O'Dearest mattress.'

'I suppose so. I love a double bed.'

'That's grand. I'll give you all the double bedding and your single bed can go in Yvette's room. She's getting on like a house on fire with Zac. I bumped into him again the other day. He's thinking of making her the manageress.'

'You're always bumping into someone,' said Sheila, souring a little.

'Sure it wouldn't be Dublin if you didn't. Anyway, it's settled about the bed. I know a fella in the Buildings with a handcart. He'll take it round for a few bob.'

Chapter Forty-two

Zac employed a typist and two clerks, and appointed Yvette as manageress. 'The kids are good workers, but some customers can be difficult. So I want you in charge. You've a soothing manner, sometimes that's needed. We don't want to ruffle any feathers, not at this stage of the business. I've got a hunch we are going places.' He pooh-poohed Yvette's doubts that she couldn't do the job, told her she lent tone to the place. He was the boss and she wasn't to doubt his judgement. He took her out to lunch a few times. He knew where to eat.

After several lunches he told her he had three tickets for a variety show at the Gaiety. 'Maureen Potter.' Yvette looked blank. 'You haven't heard of Maureen Potter! Ah, I forget you're not a Dubliner. She's a great comedienne. You'll laugh till your sides are bad. Ask Sheila if she'd like to come. Don't tell me if you don't want to, but what's she doing living in a flat in Camden Street and her husband in Germany?'

'Hasn't Ginny mentioned anything about it?'

'Would I be asking you if she had?'

'No, I suppose not. As far as I can make out it's a battle of wills. She's crazy about him and as far as I know he's mad about her. But they're stuck in this battle and neither will give an inch. I feel to blame sometimes. Think that if my husband hadn't died when he did and I'd no one belonging to me and nowhere to go Sheila would have gone back after the Christmas holiday.'

'I don't follow you.'

'Sheila was leaving for Ireland on the day I was also leaving, not knowing for where. She persuaded me to come with her and I did. Maybe I gave her Dutch courage to stay on. Not intentionally but it's possible that I did.' That, she believed, was enough information for the present. She liked him very much. He was kind and gentle, and made her laugh more than she ever had in the whole of her life. She wondered if her height embarrassed him. Her five foot seven without heels to his five foot five. So on several occasions when they went out of an evening she wore flat shoes until one night he asked, 'Are you having trouble with your feet?'

'Not really.'

'Why are you wearing those hicky shoes, then?'

She didn't know how to answer him.

'I know, I know.' And he grinned. 'You think I'm

385

bothered about the difference in our heights. That's it, isn't it?'

Yvette blushed and admitted he was right.

'You're a very considerate woman and I appreciate it. But let me tell you this, if you come on another date and wear flat shoes it's the last you'll ever see of me except in work. High heels, OK? If we ever reach the stage of kissing you can slip them off.'

On the first Sunday in May Sheila took the twins, wearing the dresses Ginny had made for them, to walk in the May procession in honour of Our Blessed Lady. Through the beautiful convent grounds they walked, singing the hymns Sheila had sung as a little girl. Her favourite: 'Oh Mary we crown thee with blossoms today. Queen of the angels and Queen of the May.' It was unusually hot. The air was still and laden with the scent of lilac. The line of innocent, beautiful children, their voices singing praises to their Holy Queen, moved Sheila to tears of happiness and sadness; happiness 'for the day that was in it', her lovely daughters walking with her, the sunshine, the sweet voices singing, the smiling nuns. But her heart ached for the loss of Fergus. He no longer loved her, of that she was convinced. Why else had he never written one line to say he missed her or asked her to come back?

She had believed that he loved her enough to die for her, as she would have for him. All she had asked was that he come to Dublin for Christmas. He wouldn't and she went alone, hoping it would bring him to his senses, that he would ask for compassionate leave, a few days over Christmas, and arrive in Dublin. And if not that, a letter telling her that he loved her, that he wanted her to come home.

Instead, the few letters he had written were terse, insulting from a man to his wife. And then he gave up the quarters. He didn't have to do that. The army would have

386

put no pressure on him, not for a long time. That was his way of telling her their life together was finished.

The procession went round the convent grounds. On the way back to where it would finish Sheila felt faint. In the excitement of dressing the girls in their miniature bridal gowns and veils she hadn't eaten, kept going on cups of tea and cigarettes. She felt the same sensations she had had often when as a little girl she had fasted before going to Communion. Then she would be taken from the chapel into the fresh air, sat on a chair and given a glass of water.

She breathed deeply and bent her head. Bent heads, she believed, relieved symptoms of fainting. She walked a little way like that. When she raised her head she thought she was hallucinating for she saw Fergus standing a few yards away. Then she heard the twins screaming, 'Daddy, Daddy, Daddy,' and saw them racing, their veils streaming behind them, to where Fergus stood at the steps to the convent door. It wasn't a vision. It was him standing with open arms to receive his daughters.

She left the line and followed them.

Fergus, with a twin in each arm, walked to meet her. 'How are'ye?' he said.

'Great, and yourself?'

'Game ball.' He put the twins down, took Sheila's hands in his and said, 'Shall we go home?'

And they set off, Sheila holding one of his hands and one of Deirdre's, and Fergus holding Niamh's.

They didn't speak, they couldn't for the girls never stopped talking. 'Are you staying for always, Daddy? What did you bring us, Daddy? Look at my dress.' Fergus caressed Sheila's hand and she his. She walked as if in a dream. Nothing seemed substantial. Her head ached from the heat. Fergus was holding her hand but he couldn't be. Fergus had deserted her. Fergus was in Germany, on the ranges. The guns were firing. She could hear them. The whining, whistling shell flying towards its target. And then the explosion. It reverberated in her head, ending the dream.

She was in Kevin Street. She was holding a hand, Fergus's hand. He was squeezing it. A shiver ran up her back. It wasn't a dream. Fergus was here. He had come back. The twins were saying, 'Daddy, Daddy, sure you won't go away ever again. We missed you, Daddy.' Deirdre, swinging out of Sheila's hand across her body, tripped Sheila. She would have fallen except for the hold Fergus had on her.

'Are you all right, love?' he asked. They had stopped walking. He let go Niamh's hand and turned to Sheila looking into her face, smiling and in that instant hate and anger surged through her. She wanted to tear the smile from his face. Scream, 'You arrogant bastard! You came when it suited you. For going on five months you left me and your children. Not caring if we were alive or dead. If only we weren't in the street. If only we were alone I'd let you know what I think of your arrival. I can't make a show of myself in the middle of Kevin Street. Nor when we get to my mother's. I'll have to bide my time.'

'You've gone very pale. Are you OK?' Fergus's voice was concerned.

'I'm fine. It was the heat and then the surprise of seeing you, that's all. I can't believe it. Come on, we'd better be going or me ma'll think I'm lost. Let me walk on my own for a bit to cool down.'

'Link me, the girls can walk in front.'

'No, the heat of you would overwhelm me and I'd feel queer again.'

While they walked slowly towards the Buildings he told her how marvellous it was to be together again and in a low voice that he loved her.

Inside Ginny's porch the twins left them and they kissed. Despite the fury in her mind Sheila responded, almost forgave him for his neglect of her during the last months. The letters she had waited for that never came.

She should put all that behind her. Rejoice that he was here. That she was in his arms. She might have done if the twins hadn't barged back into the porch demanding that Daddy come into the kitchen.

But once in the kitchen Sheila's resentment returned. Now she was determined that their reunion wasn't going to be a walkover: a walkover for Fergus. The cheek of him suddenly to appear and behave as if nothing had happened between them. Fergus was being welcomed like a long-lost hero, Ginny kissing and hugging him, her father bringing out the whiskey, Yvette telling him how well he looked and the twins wrapped round his legs. The white-haired boy! But she'd soon settle his hash, though not in her mother's home.

'How long are you over for?' her father asked as he poured generous measures of Jameson's.

'A flying visit. I'm going back tomorrow.'

Then Ginny took command. 'Sit over to the table the lot of you. When we've had our tea your mammy and daddy are going back to the flat. They have a lot to talk about. Yvette's staying here tonight.'

The twins protested. 'It's not fair. He's our daddy. We don't want to stay here.'

Sheila was still fuming inwardly while pretending surprise and delight that Fergus had come. She joined in the banter and laughter, smiling, flirting with Fergus, desperately desiring him and at the same time waiting to get him alone and give him a piece of her mind.

The twins were still protesting that they wanted to go with Mammy and Daddy. Ginny told them they would do what they were told. And Fergus, to comfort them, promised that before they went to bed he and Mammy would come back to see them.

On the way to the flat she played him along, stopping now and then when no one was passing to kiss. Her body yearned for him but she was determined to have her say once they were in the flat. As soon as they were he took hold of her, kissed her passionately, one hand round her waist the other on her breast. She wanted it to stay there. Wanted the kissing never to stop, wanted to make love where they stood with her back to the door. She made an excuse – 'I'm bursting to have a pee' – and moved out of his arms. In the lavatory she prepared what she would say. No shouting. She would be calm, cool and collected. Get her message over. Make him understand the callous way he had treated her. Point out that it would take more than a flying visit before she forgave him.

When she went back he was sitting on the bed, his shoes off, smoking. 'Oh, love,' he said, standing up, coming towards her.

Her cool campaign deserted her and she shouted, 'Don't you dare touch me, you lousy bastard. I'm not someone to pick up and then, when the notion takes you, throw away.'

'Sheila, love, what ails you? I came, didn't I? I'm here.'

'So you are after five months. You didn't know or care whether I was alive or dead. Why would you? You were free to get pissed every night of the week. Not that you weren't always. God, when I think of the fool I was to marry you, to believe you loved me, to let myself adore you for years. You're a lousy, rotten bastard. I hate you. I want you to go now, this minute.' She was shouting at the top of her voice.

'Don't you care about the neighbours?' Fergus asked.

'For your information, there are no neighbours and even if there were I wouldn't care. Now get yourself out of here this minute. Go back to me ma and then to the pub. You know where it is. You went there with my father, remember. And like an eejit I let you soft-soap me the next day.'

And then, as on that day, she began to cry. Fergus took her in his arms to comfort her as he had then. She struggled but he held her tightly. Her head lay on his breast. He waited until the crying subsided, then put his hand beneath her chin, raised it and kissed her gently. 'Don't cry any more and don't talk. I love you.'

'Oh, God,' she whispered, 'I love you too.'

He kissed her again and again and, without letting go, inched her to the bed.

After their second lovemaking they lay naked. Fergus lit two cigarettes and placed one between Sheila's swollen lips. They lay in silence, their heart rate slowing, their breathing returning to normal. Languorously they lay, their free hands caressing each other. The cigarettes were stubbed out. Fergus fell asleep as he usually did after sex. Sheila seldom did. She either wanted to wipe herself, have a pee or in this instant a cup of tea. Putting on a housecoat, she went to the kitchen and made tea, brought two cups to the bedroom, deciding that if Fergus was asleep she wouldn't wake him.

She put the cups on the bedside table and, looking down on him, she wanted to kneel and kiss every inch of his body. She asked herself how had she existed for the last five months without him. It wasn't like the waiting to join him in Germany. She was lonely then but it was a different loneliness. He wrote regularly, letters full of love and longing for her, for their being united soon. He opened his eyes and smiled. She was about to get into the bed, make love again, when a thought she hadn't invited slipped into her mind. Jesus, Mary and Joseph! My mother's at the back of all this. The double bed. Yvette showing no surprise when he arrived nor Fergus. There had been some hanky-panky and she'd bet a pound to a penny her mother was at the back of it.

It wouldn't be wise to start quizzing him now, but she had to know the truth. She didn't want to lose him, neither did she want him having come because her mother had arranged it. God only knew what a tale she would have spun.

'What ails you now? You've got that fighting look in your eye,' said Fergus, sitting up in the bed.

'I want you to tell me the truth, Fergus, did my . . .?'

He reached and pulled her into the bed, laid her on her back and put a hand over her mouth. Bending to her, he said, 'I want you to listen. Don't say one word, not one. Promise.' She nodded her agreement. He released her mouth, put an arm under her head and brought it to lie on his breast, his other hand rested on her belly.

'I came because I can't live without you. When you went away I nearly lost my mind. When you didn't come back I did lose it. I gave the quarters up because I couldn't bear being there when you weren't. Everywhere there were reminders of you. I saw you, I heard your voice, I looked and couldn't find you.' He was crying quietly. 'Oh, Jesus, it was terrible. For those first months I drank more than I ever had in my life. Bob kept at me, it made no difference. Then my work began to suffer. I was hauled up in front of the CO and given a bollocking. Hang on, I have to have a fag.' He reached to the table for one, lit it and talked again. 'The CO knew about us, mentioned it but didn't probe. Neither did he leave me in any doubt that if I didn't pull myself together I would be demoted and posted out.

'During the first few weeks as I struggled, not to become a teetotaller, I'll never be that, but to drink a hell of a lot less, I blamed you. If you hadn't left, OK, so I'd still have gone to the mess but not got pissed out of my skull every night. Not been like a zombie the next day.

'And then I had a rethink. I remembered our rows and how almost every one of them was about my drinking. I began to think you had a case. But as for applying for an early discharge, that was out of the question. I love the army. I love my job. And what were my prospects if I did leave? Fuck all. I'm a gunnery instructor. Great job, the cat's whiskers in the Artillery. Thousands spent training me. Had I been a warrant officer in the Army Catering Corp I'd have walked into a good job. In Civvy Street chefs are wanted; who wants an expert gunnery bloke?

'I'd have had no trouble being employed as a commis-sionaire. Me! Opening and closing taxi doors outside a posh hotel. Bowing to all sorts. Debt collecting, perhaps, repossessing people's furniture. There was always the Civil Service. Sit the exam, pass the interview and push a pen for the rest of your life. Not for me.'

Sheila motioned that she wanted another cigarette. He gave her one and lit one for himself. The sun was no longer shining. The room was chilly. Sheila sat up, reached for the bedcovers and pulled them up.

'Are you worn out listening to me?' Fergus asked.

She shook her head.

'You can talk but no questions, you'd confuse me.'

'I don't want to talk until you've finished.'

'Right then. Let's sit up.' He fixed the pillows behind her. 'You know the bloke I said was offered a bailiff's job? He got stuck in my mind, until I remembered that he had done his full whack. Nothing to do with an early discharge. And I remembered you pointing out that I'd stand a better chance of a decent job the younger I was. That unless I got a commission I'd be out on my ear at forty-five, not the best age to go looking for work. And so I've applied for an early discharge.'

Sheila threw her arms round him. 'Oh, Fergus. I love you. God you're marvellous. I would have died without you.'

'There's one other thing I can't promise.'

'What's that?'

'To give up the drink.'

'I don't care. So long as we're together I don't care if you swim in porter.'

'You will, though, so I'll put my cards on the table. The habit is a long time there. Being single for so long doesn't help. But I'll never drink the way I used to. A few pints, and now and again I'll go on a bender. Will that suit you?'

'Oh, darling, of course it will. If you slip up now and

393

then I'll forgive you. I'm at home now. I'll never be as miserable and discontented as I was.'

'Talking about home, it's time we went back to see the kids. We promised.'

'I forgot all about them. But before we go, tell me this and I want the truth. Has me ma been writing letters to you?'

'Not letters. A note now and then tucked into the newspapers your father sends. The papers helped as well with making my decision.'

'How was that?'

'The reports of all Lemass's plans for the Irish economy. They're expecting a boom.'

'I don't understand any of that. But to come back to me ma. What did she say in her notes?'

'That you were working. Looked well enough but she knew you were unhappy. What the twins were doing and saying. And she told me about Yvette being in Dublin.'

'I knew it. When you weren't surprised seeing her. I smelled a rat. And then the double bed. She nearly forced that down my throat. She's a conniving oul witch.'

'She's a great woman. A wise woman. I'll be grateful to her for the rest of my life. She gave me you. And when I thought I'd lost you, helped me to see sense and find you again. Oh, God, I love you.' He took her in his arms and again they made love before going to see the children.

There were tearful scenes when he told them he was flying back to Germany early the next morning. He comforted them by promising he would come back soon and stay for ever and ever.

Mr Brophy asked, 'D'ye fancy a pint, Fergus?' Sheila was in such an ecstatic state she woudn't have objected. But Ginny gave her husband daggers looks. He backed down. 'It's a bit early for you, I suppose. But sure you know where I am if you change your mind.' Fergus said, 'Indeed I do,' thanked him for the papers and told him to keep sending them.

Fergus, who knew nothing about Victor's paedophilia, sympathised with Yvette for her loss. He told her that someone had broken into her house and ransacked it. 'Most peculiar. No one was ever caught. It had to be someone in the garrison.'

'Must have been,' Yvette agreed.

Then Zac arrived, was introduced to Fergus and when he heard he was flying out tomorrow, said, 'That's a pity. If I'd know sooner I could have got you a discounter. I'm in the travel business.'

'I'll keep you to that. This time the army paid for me.'

The twins went to bed. Ginny made tea and Yvette sandwiches. Fergus asked Yvette what she thought of Dublin.

'I never want to live anywhere else. Everyone's been so kind to me. Sheila's mother and father treat me like another daughter. Zac has given me a great job. Sometimes I want to pinch myself in case it's all a wonderful dream. But I wouldn't chance it. If it is a dream then I never want to wake up.'

'I must say you are looking very well. Not that you looked sick when you were living in Hohne. You're different now, more outgoing, relaxed. I don't know. Anyway, I'm glad you're happy here.'

To everyone's surprise Mr Brophy came home early and brought in two brown paper bags with half a dozen of stout in each. 'A little something to celebrate my son-in-law's homecoming. The grandest son-in-law a man could wish for. I knew it the minute I first clapped eyes on him. D'ye know, I fought shoulder to shoulder with his uncle in the GPO. Poor Peader Brady, the Lord have mercy on him.'

Zac was interested in talking about the Rebellion and Mr Brophy delighted to have an intelligent, interested listener. Fergus told Sheila that Lizzie called her all sorts for seldom writing, that Beth and Bill were beginning enquiries about adopting a baby. Sheila felt shivers run up her spine at the mention of Bill's name and made a resolution to go to confession during the week. She would confess her past sin. She had seldom done so. From now on she would as often as she went to confess. And with the help of God the memory of the terrible sin would grow smaller and smaller and smaller, until it vanished altogether.

The men drank the stout and the women had small glasses of port. Mr Brophy asked if anyone was ready to give a song. Ginny came down on him like a ton of bricks. 'D'ye realise what hour of the night it is or that Fergus has an early start in the morning.'

He apologised. 'You're right, Ginny, my love. Sure aren't you always right. What we'd do without you I don't know. I think I'll make my way to bed. Goodnight and God bless you all. And a safe journey, Fergus.'

Shortly after her father went to bed Sheila and Fergus had another look at their sleeping daughters and set out for the flat. They took a short cut through Camden Row, stopping outside a little cemetery where as children they had often played. Although there were gravestones in it, it was more like a leafy glade than a graveyard. Trees and flowers grew there and birds nested. Nowadays, because of vandalism, the gates were locked night and day. But flowers still bloomed and the heady smell of lilac wafted on a light, warm breeze around the heads of Sheila and Fergus as they stood kissing each other. Reluctantly they moved apart and continued walking towards their flat.

'Zac's a nice bloke. I think he fancies Yvette.'

'He does,' said Sheila.

'What about her?'

'I think she's taken a shine to him as well, but she hasn't been lucky with her men, so I don't suppose she wants to rush into things.'

'I know Victor was an arrogant sod, but I thought they got on OK. He showered her with everything.'

'He did indeed.'

'What d'ye mean?'

'My love,' she said, squeezing his arm, 'it's a long story and I'm not going to waste our few precious hours telling you now. What I want to do is give out the pay about me mother.'

'Won't that be wasting our time?'

'It'll only take a minute. D'ye know why Zac was invited tonight. Well, I'll tell you. My mother and her fixing. Zac's in business. He knows everyone. He could land you into a job. That's why she asked him.'

'I wouldn't say no if he did.'

'Oh, you,' she said, pretending to be annoyed.

'Listen,' he said, 'when the twins grow up, please God, you'll be another Ginny. You'll stand on your head for them. Wait and see.'

'I will not. I'll never interfere in their lives.'

He stopped walking before they went into the lighted street and took Sheila in his arms. 'Your mother hasn't interfered in your life. You didn't have to take the flat. You didn't have to get in touch with Rosaleen. There was nothing stopping you doing those things on you're own. Are you telling me she shouldn't have sent the notes, that you didn't want me to come for you?'

'No, no, of course I did.'

'Ah, so it's the double bed you object to?'

'Don't,' she said. 'You're right. I'm an ungrateful bitch.'

'So you are, but I wouldn't have you any other way. Now come on, Mrs Brady, there's a grand bed waiting to be aired.'

He wouldn't let her go to see him off. 'I booked a taxi to pick me up at six. It's three o'clock in the morning. I'll doze on the Aer Lingus flight and again on the way to Hanover. You wouldn't get back from the airport till nearly nine and have to go straight to work. It's not on. Go to sleep now. I love you. I'll be back soon.'

He was gone when she woke up, but his smell still lingered in the bed. She lay savouring it, reliving the night and day they had spent together until half-eight, giving herself just enough time to get ready for work. Any time there was a lull in customers she regaled Moira and Brenda with the news of him arriving unexpectedly, lying about the circumstances of him coming. He'd been in London at a conference about his station in West Africa, had a day to spare and flew to Dublin.

Brenda said it was the most romantic thing she had ever heard. She didn't think the fellas of today would do it. More likely get pissed in a London pub. 'Was it gorgeous for you, Sheila?'

'Fantastic. I'm still on cloud nine.'

'It's like something you'd see in a film.' Brenda sighed. 'I hope I'll get a fella like that.'

Before Rosaleen had told her of Moira's romance Sheila, while relating her reunion with Fergus, would have felt sorry for the lonely old maid. Now she thought a wink would be more appropriate, but resisted the temptation. She and Rosaleen had lunch together. After hearing the news, Rosaleen reached across the table, took one of Sheila's hands, squeezed it and said, 'I'm so happy for you. For both of you. I was in at the start of the affair and it would have broken my heart to see it end.'

During the first week after Fergus left she wrote to him every night, telling him how much she loved him, how happy she was that soon he would be home for good. She enclosed letters from the girls and drawings they did for him. In one letter she told him the truth about Victor, the life he had led Yvette, the death of her son, how Yvette had taken the evidence of his crimes to Dublin and her father. He had passed them on to some big bug in the police. They had watched for mention of the case in the English and Irish newspapers. So far not a word. Her father said he wouldn't be surprised if there never was. The evidence was probably lying in a dusty drawer somewhere in Amsterdam, Hamburg, where ever it had eventually landed up. At the rate she wrote and posted the letters, she reckoned Fergus would receive one a day. So should she. She didn't and was upset, until she remembered now was the height of the practice camp. Fergus would be working all hours.

When letters came from him they were full of plans for when he finished in the army. He'd have a pension and a lump sum. Less than if he had done his twenty-two years, but if she didn't mind working for another couple of years they could manage. He had been reading house prices in Dublin. They weren't too steep as yet. But if the economy thrived then they'd shoot up. So as soon as he was discharged the first thing was to buy a house. He'd have enough for a deposit, take any sort of constant job to qualify for a mortgage. What he had in mind was setting up in a painting and decorating business. He had always been handy with a paintbrush. 'Don't scoff at this and say it's the first you knew about it. Remember we weren't allowed to decorate army quarters. Except Vic, the bastard.'

Another good reason for considering painting and decorating was the low outlay. A few ladders, brushes and a second hand van. You were away so long as you got customers. But if there was going to be a housing boom, people would be crying out for honest painters and decorators. He had no idea when the discharge would come through. Soon, he hoped. For now he couldn't wait to be home, spend every night with her and his girls. He began and ended his letters with paragraphs telling her how much he loved her, how he desired her, she was seldom from his mind. And always there was a promise of how in future he would be a better husband.

Chapter Forty-three

The summer progressed. Some weekends Zac took Yvette, Sheila and the twins to beauty spots around the coast. Ginny was also invited to the outings but always refused, explaining how she welcomed a Sunday afternoon alone. 'With himself asleep, the twins out for the day, I don't know myself. Sometimes I don't lift a finger. Another time I might read the papers or sew. Summer is a busy time for the wedding dresses.' And she always insisted that they come to her for tea after the outing.

One Sunday evening, when Zac had dropped them at the flat and the twins were in bed, Sheila asked Yvette how were things with her and Zac. 'Anyone can tell he's light about you. How are your feelings regarding him?'

'I'm very fond of him.'

'Fond, is that all?'

'I love him. He's the kindest, gentlest man I've ever met. He makes me laugh. I'd forgotten how to. But there are obstacles.'

'Don't tell me he's married?'

'Nothing like that.'

'Because he's a Jew?'

'The obstacles are mine. He has asked me to marry him. Not in so many words, but he made his meaning clear.'

'And what did you say?'

'That I'd think about it.'

'Don't take too long. Zac's any woman's fancy.'

'I know. But there's so much he doesn't know about me. About my first love Sean and my baby. About my life with Victor. I think he'd understand about the baby. But how could he love or marry me once he knew the things I did with Victor?'

'None of it was from choice. I've never know anyone as honest as you. You wouldn't marry Zac under false pretences. Tell him everything. What have you got to lose?

If he's not the bloke I think he is he'll back out. So you'll lose a prospective husband and maybe a job. If he couldn't take your past on board you're not losing much. And listen. You suffered a dreadful loss. The loss of a child. Something I think is the worst loss of all. It broke your heart. I don't think it'll ever heal. But if you survived that, you'll survive being jilted. You'll go on living. When is he taking you to this new restaurant in the mountains?'

'Tomorrow night. I don't want to go. I've an idea he'll try to pin me down. He's been wanting us to get engaged. One of the typists told me she saw him in Weir's. He could have been buying a ring. He's very serious about me.'

'You've got to go. It's a posh restaurant, privacy, no one sitting on top of you. A place that's right for confessions – no confessing is for sins. You've never sinned. Just tell him. Tell him all you've told me. Tell him all you and I have seen. The truth, that's all. You've a night and a day to think it over.'

Zac picked Yvette up from the flat. She looked gorgeous, but Sheila knew she was a bag of nerves.

'Back about midnight,' Zac said as they left.

The restaraunt had once been a small country mansion. Zac was warmly greeted by the head waiter who had previously worked in Jammet's. They chatted while Yvette went to leave her coat in the cloakroom. Zac introduced her to the waiter who then showed them to their table. The dining room had once been the drawing room. It was spacious, nicely decorated. The brass fire irons and club fender, Zac told Yvette, had probably belonged to the original house, as had some of the ornaments on wall shelves around the room. 'On the other hand they could all have been bought in auction rooms. So, what d'ye think of it?'

'It's lovely.'

'Are you all right?'

'I'm fine. No, I'm not, really. I feel a little bit sick.' She did but knew it was nerves that had her stomach in an eruption. From hints that Zac had dropped she believed that tonight he would offer her an engagement ring. And knew that unless she could tell him of her past she must refuse the ring.

'Then we'll order something light.'

The wine waiter came to the table. Zac read the list, suggesting different wines to Yvette.

'I'm sorry to be such a misery but I couldn't drink anything.'

'Not to worry. Have lemonade or water. Then something to eat. And then champagne. That'll settle your stomach.'

Champagne. She knew that was for celebrations. The ring and champagne. How could she refuse him here in a public place? And how could she become engaged under false pretences? 'Zac, I want to go home, I feel terrible, terrible in myself and terrible for spoiling the night.'

'You're not spoiling anything. You're so agitated. I've watched you fiddling with the cutlery, the napkin. That's not like you. Stay there. I'll go and have a word with the waiter and I'll fetch your coat.'

What a man, she thought. How kind and considerate. And I'm going to lose him. Either because I'm too ashamed to tell him of my past or he, if I do, can't cope with it. He helped her into her coat and took her arm. The head waiter escorted them out, bade them goodnight and hoped they would come again.

'What you need is warm milk and a good night's sleep. I'll have you back at the flat in no time.'

She was crying quietly. When Zac heard her he slowed the car and pulled over to the side of the narrow road, driving on to the grass verge. 'What's the matter, Yvla. Can't you tell me?'

She didn't notice the change in her name. 'So much ails me. So much I want to tell you and am afraid to,' she said in between sobbing.

He gave her a handkerchief. 'Blow your nose and take a deep breath and listen. I'm not taking you back to Sheila's. That's not the place to tell terrible things. We have to be alone for that. I'll take you to my place, OK?'

'All right,' she said and they drove to Rathgar. She was too upset to notice the house or its furnishings, only aware of the comfortable sofa he sat her on while he made weak tea and produced plain biscuits. He sat beside her and waited for her to speak, which she did after drinking some of the tea. She began by telling him about Sean and the baby she had for him.

'Where is he?' Zac asked, putting an arm round her.

'He's dead.'

'Oh, Yvla, my love, I'm so sorry. Your little child to have died. What happened to him?'

'The most horrible thing you could imagine.' Before her eyes she saw the photograph of Sean taken in Amsterdam and anger raged through her. She shrugged off Zac's arm, moved slightly away from him and told him the whole story. Not at the moment caring how he accepted it.

'Oh, my God. My poor, poor girl. None of it was your fault. You were trapped in a hell on earth. But it's over, finished. Not the loss of your little child, that'll be with you for ever. You must go on living. It's a sin to give way to despair. You'll have a new life. With me if you'll have me. I love you. I want to marry you. You don't have to decide now. Take all the time in the world to think about it. And now I'm going to leave you while I make scrambled eggs. You look half starved. Scrambled eggs, tea and toast, a glass of brandy and then bed. OK?'

She agreed. She was exhausted from the telling of the story. Astounded and delighted by Zac's proposal. She desperately needed sleep. 'Yes,' she said, 'I will. I need to sleep. I love you Zac. I will marry you.'

They kissed and then he said, 'Now you go to bed. Pity Sheila isn't on the phone, she'll worry. I'll get you up early and take you in. And our engagement on New Year's Eve.

A big party.' He took her upstairs to the bedroom and pointed out the door to the bathroom. 'There's towels, everything you need except a nightie. You'll have to sleep in your pelt. Goodnight, God bless you.' He kissed her gently, showed her how the bedside lamp worked and left the room.

At half past six he woke her, bringing a tray of tea things and wafer-thin slices of bread and butter. She had slept in her camisole and knickers.

'Will I get you something for your shoulders?' Zac asked.

'No, I'm not cold.'

He laid the tray on the bed and poured tea. Yvette noticed that on the tray was a black velvet jeweller's box. She knew it held an engagement ring and was eager to see it. But would wait until Zac was ready to offer it.

Which he did when they had finished their tea. 'You do remember last night that you said you'd have me?'

'I do,' she replied, 'and I meant it.'

'Right, so now with this ring I am manacling you.'

It was a diamond solitaire. She gasped. 'Zac, it's beautiful,' she said.

'So are you, Yvla,' he said, putting it on her finger.

'Why are you calling me Yvla?'

'It's a sign of affection with Jews.'

'I love you so much. I never thought I could love a man again.'

He put the tea tray on the floor and lay on the bed, where patiently and skilfully he caressed her and made love to her in a way she never dreamt possible.

Midnight came and went. Sheila wasn't unduly worried and went to bed. She slept and woke at three in the morning, went to Yvette's room. She wasn't there. They might have gone to a club. By five in the morning she was frightened. The mountain roads could be treacherous, the weather change in seconds. Mist come down. Not able to see a hand in front of you. Not able to see another car approaching.

They were dead. A head on collision. The car had lost the narrow road and gone over the side. In places the drop was steep. An evening bag, handkerchief, lipstick and powder compact. Nothing that could identify her. Zac would have papers but none that referred to Yvette. They were in the morgue. Bound to be. But please God, maybe they weren't. Let them be in bed making love, sleeping, waking, making love again. Please God, let it be so.

If the twins had been sleeping at Ginny's she'd have gone round there. Ginny would have known how to comfort her. Ginny would have given her hot whiskey and put her to bed, telling her she could do nothing until morning. She wouldn't mention the other possibility that might be delaying Yvette. Ginny would have a fit. She sat in an armchair, drank coffee, smoked and smoked, and eventually she fell asleep.

The knocking at the door woke her. 'Sacred Heart of Jesus!' she exclaimed, raising her stiff neck from the arm of the chair. 'They're dead. It's the police, I knew it. Yvette and Zac are dead.'

She went to the window, raised it and looked down. It was raining, soft summer rain falling on the smiling face of Yvette, on Zac's car by the kerb. Yvette was shouting, 'I forgot my keys.'

'The curse of hell on her anyway. Keeping me awake thinking she was dead. Thanks be to God she's not,' Sheila said as she found the keys and threw them down to Yvette. Who when she came into the room wrapped her arms round Sheila and said, 'You were right, so right. Look at the ring' and she flashed her solitaire. 'The engagement party's on New Year's Eve. And Zac has told me not to sell the Citroën. I'm to keep it for running around in.'

In August Fergus came on a long weekend leave. He brought the car laden with clothes, toys, their wedding

405

presents and Sheila's knick-knacks, all that had been left behind when she went away for a supposed ten days. 'When I'm discharged I'll bring the gadgets,' he told her.

It was a rapturous time for Sheila, a foretaste of the life to come, though in flashes of common sense she knew that it wouldn't always be the seventh heaven of brief weekends. But it would be a good life. Before he left she asked, 'When d'ye think the discharge will come through?' Sometimes she worried, fearing that Fergus might change his mind about leaving the army and needed his reassurance frequently.

'I don't think they'll begin the process until October when practice camp finishes. After that a month or two, maybe.'

'Before Christmas?'

'Honest to God, love, I haven't a clue.'

In the first week of December a telegram came to Ginny's striking terror into her heart. It was addressed to Sheila. Seldom did a telegram bring anything other than bad news. Oh, please God, let it be my mind gone astray. Sure it might be nothing. But it's nobody's birthday and there's no one to send us telegrams except bad news from Germany. She put on a brave face for the sake of the girls. Collected them, bought, as was usual, penn' orths of taffee. Nodded to passing acquaintances and walked the long way home, stopping at a playground for the twins to go on the see-saw, the slide and the swings. Anything to delay her return to the kitchen and that thing staring her in the face from the mantelpiece. It was nearly five o'clock, an hour still before Sheila came home. She cut bread and butter for the children and made tea. 'God forgive me for flying in your face. Only you know the future. It's a sin for me to be second-guessing it.' The minutes passed like hours. Despite her prayers her heart was heavy with foreboding. She drank two cups of tea. Answered the girls' questions about Christmas. Advised them on what they should ask Santa for and then she heard Sheila in the hall.

So did the twins who ran to greet her and came back with arms entwined around her. 'You don't look well, Ma. What ails you?' Sheila asked.

'I think I've got a chill. That came for you this morning. There on the mantelpiece.'

Sheila opened and read the telegram, dropped it on the floor, caught the twins' hands and danced round and round the floor until they got dizzy and fell down. Leaving them on the floor, she picked up the telegram. 'Ma,' she said, 'listen to this,' and read aloud,

The discharge came through today. I'll be home for Christmas and for always.

Fergus.